JUST KILL ME

BY WENDY HERMAN

JUST KILL ME

Managing editor - Amanda Meuwissen
Associate editor - Meagan Hedin

Book layout/Cover design - Mario Hernandez

A **BigWorldNetwork.com** Book
Published by BigWorldNetwork.com, LLC
202 North Rock Road | 1303 | Wichita | KS | 67206
www.bigworldnetwork.com

ISBN-13: 978-0615839929
ISBN-10: 0615839924

First U.S. Edition: July 2013
Printed in the United States of America

Dedicated to my favorite author and muse,
Kathleen McGowan, who introduced me to **Mary** and **Matilda**.
You, and they, inspire me on a daily basis.

Acknowledgement

Thanks to my parents for making me part of the generation that never watched TV, that played outside every waking moment, and used our imaginations. Thank you, Dad, for making college a natural progression from high school, rather than a choice, and Mom, for reading everything I write with enthusiasm and unwavering support. Thanks to my older brother for being a bigger nerd than me, thus making me feel less of an outcast in the world. My younger brother, for being the voice of reason, my common sense, and my best friend at times during our childhood. My sister, T, whose selflessness and generous heart give us all something to aspire to.

I would like to thank Grandma D for introducing me to a typewriter when I was seven years old, and for letting me write my first story using only red correction ribbon, and Grandma E for teaching me to crochet at the same age. Like writing, it is pure creation, and ignites my imagination like nothing else.

Thanks to Mr. Mills, my fourth grade teacher for recognizing my passion for writing and giving me the opportunity to learn the art of journalism. Give me a call when you reincarnate. (wink)

To my husband, who never made me feel like writing was just a silly hobby, and who gets up at 6:30 (or earlier) in the morning with our little ones when I've had to stay up past midnight to meet a deadline, and for asking, "When are you gonna start getting paid for this?" only one million times instead of two (which is how many times I thought it). To my four boys, who reluctantly played outside for an hour (torture) so mommy could write in peace.

Thanks so much, Jim, for your vision that is now BigWorldNetwork.com, and for making me feel worthy of your cyberspace. Without you, I would still be writing screenplays, only to hide them from the world on my shelf. Meg, who has been my "sister" for as long as I can remember, and your keen eye, but most of all, for your kick-ass editing comments. They motivate me. Mario, whose talent knows no bounds, and finds time to tweak the cover art to please my picky brain.

I thank my baby sister, from the bottom of my heart, for pulling me into the twenty-first century and encouraging me to not just edit and narrate other people's stories, but to write one of my own. You will always be the boss of me, and I wouldn't have it any other way.

JUST KILL ME

BY WENDY HERMAN

 Fifteen, teenage themes suitable only for readers of fifteen years and older.

BigWorldNetwork.com
Kansas

CONTENTS

EPISODE 1
My Awakening

If I've learned anything from my life thus far, it is this. No matter how much you plan, you can't prepare yourself for everything. I was a planner...no, I was a control freak, bordering on obsessive compulsive disorder. My life was perfectly ordered, and perfectly unfulfilling. I can trace the unraveling of my immaculately knitted existence to one day, and one specific, and potentially devastating, event.

The day was a repeat, a regurgitation of the previous five thousand or so days, since I had had my first child almost fifteen years before... until it wasn't.

I sat at the computer, which was located on a small built-in desk just off my spacious, gourmet kitchen, with my back to the rest of the house. My oldest son, Levi, and his younger brother, Blaise, were in the family room attempting to assassinate each other in the latest as-real-as-it-gets video game on our 62-inch HD plasma screen. I was focusing on my task at hand, but also keeping my ears perked for any inappropriate language. I knew it would only be a matter of time before I would have to abruptly stop what I was doing to break up the latest physical altercation between the two boys.

My youngest, Rowan, who was just three-and-a-half years old, sauntered into the kitchen just then and strode to my side. He held up a quarter and my ears heard him say, "Mommy, I'm pretending this is gum," but my brain only half-registered the meaning.

I murmured, "No, Sweetie, that's a quarter," having no clue what my complacence would give birth to in the next few moments.

As he walked away, I again focused on the gorgeous pair of knee-high black leather boots I was purchasing online, cursing my giant Yeti feet and praying I wouldn't have to return them. Then, it all happened so fast, yet in painfully slow motion, that I had no idea how much real time actually clicked away on the clock. First, I heard a word float from the family room that wouldn't be allowed out of a ten-year-old's mouth in any universe, and, sighing, rose to head off the fourteen-year-old's inevitable response. As I turned, not wanting to disengage my eyes from those awesome boots, I noticed Rowan returning, but this time with both hands clutched around his throat.

His lips were already turning blue.

To say I panicked would be an understatement. I think I screamed, because the other two were in the room in a microsecond, running to me with frightened looks on their faces. When he realized Rowan was choking, Blaise immediately began to sob hysterically, yet froze in place. I had enough presence to know that my brain was not accessing any emergency training I may have had in my past, unlike so many people on the news who claimed "…it all came back" to them in a flash when it was needed, even years after their training. All I could think to do was walk to the kitchen door that led outside, and quickly slip on my bedazzled flip flops. As I turned back around, I grabbed my Odyssey keys from the hook where they lived on the wall next to the door. I opened my mouth to say something—I've no idea what—to the other two boys. That's when I witnessed a miracle, right there in my kitchen.

Levi calmly walked up behind Rowan and, almost casually, administered the Heimlich maneuver as if he was Dr. Heimlich himself. Immediately, Rowan coughed and out popped the diabolical quarter, along with about a tablespoon of bright red blood.

So, the whole thing took about twenty seconds. Then it was over. Rowan was fine, no thanks to me, but fine he was. I should have taken a deep breath of relief and gotten on with my day. I mean, there were dishes to be done, supper to be started, laundry to be sorted. Life goes on, right?

So very wrong.

Grateful as I was that Rowan was okay, and amazed beyond belief at the quick action of my oldest son, I suddenly felt like a completely different person. In an instant, I went from grounded Soccer Mom to detached soul suspended somewhere between the earth and Heaven…I guess I was in psychological Purgatory.

Dishes? Who gave a rat's ass about dirty dishes when, at any moment, my precious baby could choke on a quarter and leave this world…leave me?

Supper? The only thought of food I may have had was that I wouldn't be able to stomach anything for quite some time, maybe forever.

Laundry? Why did we have so many Goddamn clothes anyway? None of it mattered. Suddenly, as I looked around my state-of-the-art kitchen, it was all so…meaningless. I stood there, unsure of what to do next. Levi was sitting at the kitchen table now, Rowan on his lap looking up at his now hero for life with glossy eyes. I realized I was actually hugging Blaise and we were both crying. Thank God. At least I hadn't checked out completely, I thought.

Mustering my courage, and remembering my motherly duty, I gave Blaise a reassuring final squeeze and released him as he began to calm down. Then, I went to Rowan. I squatted in front of the chair he and Levi were sitting in. He smiled and asked me why spaghetti sauce had come out with the quarter. I closed my eyes for a second and grinned. He was so wonderful. How could I have ever gone on without him? His voice was a little hoarse for the next few hours, but within minutes of the incident, he was back playing, having been given the stern briefing that money was to *never* go in his mouth again.

Life seemed to return to normal for the boys almost immediately. But not for me. Even my husband, Trevor, who had been given four versions of the choking before he had even set both feet in the door that evening, was just thrilled it all turned out okay, commended Levi for his instinctual reaction, then asked what was for supper. I told myself to just give it some time. It was a traumatic event, and it was understandable that I would feel out of sorts for a while. But it didn't get better. In fact, it seemed to get worse over the next few days. The feeling that I had been living in a naïve fog up until the quarter, that blasted quarter, had shocked me out of my hazy world. That world where the most important thing was a pair of stupid black leather boots. Boots that had never been ordered. Boots that would forever remind me of the less than half a minute when I almost lost my son.

In this new, sharp world I now lived, every emotion was like an overwhelming wave that made me dizzy and blurred my vision. I was functioning, but I was different. Only my closest friend noticed.

It had been six days since the evil quarter had almost taken my son, and Trevor and I were in the car headed for our favorite restaurant. We were meeting our oldest and dearest friend, Tyler Ripley, and his latest version of Ms. Right Now, for our standard weekly catch-up session. "Rip", as we had always called him, was an FBI field agent so, naturally, his stories since our last get together would be much more riveting than our humdrum family life, though he couldn't even tell us the real exciting parts because they were classified. I had no intention of mentioning the quarter, as I was harboring a lot of shame for my lack of action and apparent instinctual void, and I had told my husband as much. He was fine with it, especially since he had completely forgotten about it until I asked him in the car not to bring it up.

We arrived at the restaurant, and Rip and his companion were there, an already-open bottle of wine next to the table. As we approached them, Rip stood to shake Trevor's hand— these two men were not the hugging type, even after twenty years of close friendship—and gave me the usual enthusiastic bear hug. He introduced us to his current sex partner, Alisa, and it didn't take us long to realize her English was minimal, and entirely insufficient to carry on any kind of conversation. Of course, Rip translated for her every so often, as he was fluent in several languages, her native Russian being one of them, but eventually, she became a fourth wheel and found companionship in her glass of wine, which she refilled several times throughout the evening. Any other night, I would have felt sorry for her, and made a concerted effort to include her in this close-knit circle of friends, but I was on a mission tonight, and it didn't involve charity work.

I had hoped this night would restore my once simple, happy outlook. After all, it was a staple of my old life. This weekly event represented the wooden posts, buried deep in the ground, of the ever-growing fence of my well-ordered and predictable existence. Slat after slat after identical slat. Sitting there, listening to Rip talk about his latest case, using "Jane Doe" and other generic terms so as not to violate any FBI regulations, was the key. I was determined to go back into the Matrix. This new reality was too raw, and frankly, very distracting. For example, I had forgotten to put on the new earrings that I'd bought to go with the specific outfit I was wearing, and didn't notice until I checked my face in the entryway mirror of the restaurant. How could I have forgotten? I never forgot to accessorize. Never.

As I sat there with exaggerated interest in my eyes at every word that left Rip's mouth, he suddenly stopped talking and stared at me for a moment. I glanced at Trevor, then at Alisa, who was managing enough English to order another bottle of wine from the incredibly attentive waiter, but Rip continued to stare into my soul.

"What?" I finally asked innocently.

"What's wrong with you, Freya?" he accused. How the hell did he do that?

"Nothing," I responded, afraid that if I said more, I would explode, and all these new, piercing emotions would shoot out of me, killing everyone in the restaurant...or worse, making me sound like a crazy person.

"Okay," he said, not buying it for a minute. "Are you pregnant?"

"What!?" I exclaimed. Pregnant? Really? What are we now, best girlfriends?

He cocked his head and continued to read my eyes, which I was sure were revealing everything. "What's going on? Something is different about you." We were all silent for a moment, when Trevor, apparently forgetting my instruction in the car earlier, piped in.

"Well, we did almost go from zone defense to man-on-man a few days ago."

"Really? What happened?" Rip had immediately gotten the joke, as he had strongly advised us against having a third child years before by using the same analogy. Apparently, the two kids we already had were severely hindering his social life.

I decided to try to feign indifference. "It was nothing. Rowan was choking on a quarter, and Levi did the Heimlich and saved him." My voice cracked on the word "saved". So much for indifference.

Rip's eyes grew wide. He was a self-proclaimed eternal bachelor, but as much as he joked about our kids being a burden, he wouldn't hesitate to jump into a raging river, or an active volcano, to save each one of them. He was better than an uncle. He was a fierce protector. An FBI-trained one, at that.

"Okay, that is definitely not nothing. Tell me what happened. Why the hell did he put a quarter in his mouth? He's never done that before, has he?"

So, I began to tell the story, and try as I might, I could not keep my obvious disdain toward my own reaction to the choking from showing…a lot. I had known Rip too long, and he knew me almost as well as my husband did…or maybe better.

When I finished, all was quiet for a moment. Then Rip said, "You know, no one can control how they will react in a situation like that. You need to stop beating yourself up about it, Freya. Everything turned out fine, and in the grand scheme of things, that's what's important, right?"

"I keep telling her that," Trevor said, then gulped down the rest of his wine. He most certainly had *not* been telling me that, but I didn't say anything. I barely managed to give him a microscopic glare that I knew he could sense when Rip demanded my attention again.

"So, what's the deal, then?" he asked.

"Um…what do you mean?" I inquired. I had told him everything. Hadn't I?

"I get that Rowan almost died…" Rip began, to which Trevor responded by snorting into his wine glass. We both shot a quick laser beam through his head before we returned our attentions to each other.

"…and you feel your initial response was inadequate, right?" he asked.

"It *was* inadequate. If Levi hadn't been there, Rowan would have—" I started, but he cut me off.

"But, Levi *was* there, and if you hadn't insisted he take that Red Cross Babysitter's course last summer, he would have been just as useless as you were."

I gave him a look of disapproval at his choice of words, and he shrugged an apology. But he was right. I had been useless, and I knew it. Suddenly, I couldn't maintain the mental brick wall I'd been building since the incident, and my heart raced, my breath quickened and, worst of all, my eyes started to water. Trevor decided this was a good time to engage in the conversation and actually showed some compassion, after spending the past six days making me feel like I was drastically overreacting to the whole thing. As he put his arm around me, the tears started to flow, and I was powerless to stop it. Rip stood up and came around to sit on my other side, also putting an arm around me. My two favorite men—adult men, anyway—were giving me their undivided attention at the same time, and I couldn't even allow myself to bask in it. I was in such a selfish place, all I could think of was how that damn quarter had ruined everything. I didn't blame Rowan, that wasn't it at all. I had always loved my children unconditionally, but now...now, the love *hurt*. What the hell was wrong with me?

Fortunately, the restaurant was nearly empty, so my little breakdown hadn't garnered much outside attention. The waiter brought me a clean napkin to wipe my eyes, and I smiled at him reassuringly. That was about the time we all noticed Alisa had moved to a small corner table where two young businessmen were dining, and they seemed to be enjoying her rather inebriated company. She was a looker, but how they were communicating, I had no idea. Then I watched her move to sit on one of the men's laps, and the two men laughed. I guess it had been a while since I had "communicated" with *my* body parts. I really needed to get out more.

Rip proved his undying friendship by barely noticing Alisa's defection, and took the napkin from me after I wiped my tears. He was a good friend. Trevor wrapped both his arms around me and gave me a squeeze.

"I don't know why you've been stressing about this so much. You're a great mother."

I know he was trying to help, but it just made me feel worse. If that was even possible. Yes, apparently it was, I realized. I looked into his eyes, and smiled as convincingly as I could. Not concerning myself with whether or not he bought my false happiness, I wiggled out of his embrace and stood. "I'm fine, really. I just needed to release all that, I guess. I'm going to the restroom to check my face. Be right back, okay?"

Both men nodded, but Rip watched me until I turned the corner, while my husband finished his steak. Rip was on to me, I was sure of it, although I didn't even know what there was to be on to…yet.

Standing in the restroom, I stared at myself in the mirror. My waterproof mascara had proved worth the money, but my eyes were still rather puffy. I wasn't sure what to do, so I stood there, trying to read the reflection of my own eyes, demanding they tell me what was going on. Why was this happening to me? Was I having a nervous breakdown? If so, why? I was a very stable person, normally. Well, I was…wasn't I?

Just then, an older woman entered the restroom, and snapped me out of my self-interrogation. I leaned down and turned on the sink, pretending I had been doing what one usually goes to the restroom to do. I washed my hands. Soap and everything. The woman quickly used the facilities, although I heard no telltale sounds, and reemerged, claiming the sink next to mine. She caught my puffy eyes in the mirror and smiled sadly.

"Having a bit of a rough patch?" she asked, genuine concern in her inquiry.

"Just life, I guess. Normal family drama, you know?" Where had I pulled that lame response out of? Well, we were in the bathroom, so I guess it was appropriate that I was now talking out of my ass.

"Those two good-looking men out there sure seem to adore you, so it can't be too bad," she observed.

"They are great." I replied. Why in the hell was I still standing there, talking to a complete stranger?

I told myself to dry my hands, smile at the nice, although a bit nosy, woman and leave. I retrieved a scratchy brown towel from the dispenser on the wall and began drying my hands, but my feet wouldn't move. Something was keeping me there, goading me to confide in this sweet old lady. She was taking her time washing her hands. She wanted to talk too. I could feel it.

"I have three kids…all boys…lots of drama…always someone sick or…getting hurt…" I trailed off, not sure how to keep this odd encounter going, but I desperately wanted to.

"Did one of your boys get hurt?" she asked, picking up where I had left off. She was good. "Oh, no, not really," I responded. "My little one had a slight choking incident earlier this week...but he's just fine."

"Young children are always putting things in their mouths, aren't they?" she mused. "Why, my son used to fill his mouth with small rocks...scared me to death every time, but he kept doing it, and he never choked, praise God. He grew out of it pretty quick. Yours will too."

I felt the need to elaborate. "Actually, he's never done anything like this before...none of my boys have. It was the first time, and I..." I chickened out right there. I couldn't do it. I couldn't tell someone I had just met in a public restroom that I felt as if my old life was right in front of me, in the mirror, but I couldn't touch it, not really, and I could never, ever go back to it. It was like I was feeling, really feeling, for the first time, and I didn't think I liked it.

That was when she finished drying her hands—I hadn't remembered her turning off the water, but it was off—and turned to me. "Invigorating, wasn't it?" she asked.

"What?" Had she been listening to anything I said?

"You thought he was going to die right there in front of you. But he didn't. You'd never felt more alive, and now you can't get rid of that feeling." She was inches from my face now, her eyes intense as she spoke, as if it was imperative I didn't miss a word.

"What feeling?" I whispered, wondering what Pandora's Box I had just opened, and my apprehension steadily on its way to outright fear.

She gave a quick sigh and smiled at me.

"That you can finally start living."

EPISODE 2
Tearing the Cheesecloth

The surreal encounter with the old woman in the restroom had left me feeling very confused. I returned to our table and, after finally convincing Rip and Trevor that I was fine, I attempted to enjoy the rest of the evening, but the woman's words echoed in my ears, repeating over and over and over...

"You can finally start living."

What the hell was she insinuating? That I hadn't been living? Who the hell did she think she was?

Rip was talking about a fellow agent's wife finding out about his *other* wife in Czechoslovakia, and laughing so hard he was having trouble finishing the story, but I couldn't concentrate on what he was saying. I was a million miles away.

I'd seen hundreds of movies on Lifetime about people finding themselves, discovering their true callings, and suddenly attaining this unbelievable happiness, and I'd always thought that I was already there, at the end of the journey with them. I mean, I had everything. A good husband, healthy kids, a beautiful home, and a bank account that allowed me to indulge when I saw something pretty I couldn't live without...like those god-forsaken boots.

The boots.

Before the incident, those boots were the most important thing in the world to me, at least at that moment in time. Now, they represented my paralyzing naivety—nay, stupidity—which I was beginning to realize was as big as an aircraft carrier. Those were some big boots. So big, I felt like I was being crushed by the mere thought of them. How did I go from an innocent pair of boots to an aircraft carrier? And now I was imagining an aircraft carrier wearing a pair of black leather boots. I was heading for crazy town on the express train.

Releasing a sigh of frustration, which no one else at the table noticed, I realized I was angry. Who was this mysterious stranger who could utter five simple words and throw my life into such turmoil? Wait, the quarter had done that, days before I even met the woman. So, what was the purpose of us meeting? Why did everything have to have a purpose? At this rate, I would be certifiably insane by the time Rip finished his story.

I managed a small smile at Rip, who was now dabbing his eyes with a napkin, to make him think I had been listening…was listening…and took a deep breath. I needed to reason this all out. What did I *know*? I knew that, up until a week ago, I had been perfectly happy with my life. I had had no complaints. Then, Rowan decides to try to chew a quarter like a piece of Juicy Fruit and…BAM! I am catapulted into a world that is so crystal clear and vivid, it literally hurts my eyes. I get through the week, hoping and waiting for my daymare to end, but it doesn't. Then, there is this peculiar rendezvous with a nice old lady…an old lady who, as I now recalled, must have been stunning in her youth. She had resembled Elizabeth Taylor, so put together and classy.

My thoughts drifted to the famous beauty and I remembered the old commercials with her seen through thin, flowing white sheets, like cheesecloth. I grinned at that memory, and the idea that the makers of the commercials thought they were fooling anyone. They used the cloth to hide things they didn't want the audience to see, like the natural signs of aging that might have been evident on the beautiful iconic actress.

Is that what I'd been doing the past forty years? Hiding behind a wall of cheesecloth to avoid seeing the world the way it really is?

I was deep inside my mind, trying to untangle my thoughts and make some sense of them. I honed in on the memory of the Liz look-a-like in the restroom. I hadn't noticed her in the restaurant, neither before nor after our short, but profound conversation. Who was she? Had she been sent from a higher power to help me understand what was happening to me? Her brief message had affected me, I was sure, irrevocably.

I can finally start living.

Through the fog occupying my brain, I deliberately reached for that thought. The boots tried to block my path, but I shoved them away with my determination. I knew if I could grab hold of her words, I would be able to focus again…or for the first time. It was like swimming through canola oil, but I slowly inched forward. My husband's face appeared, telling me everything was fine the way it was, but I ignored him. Then, Ellen DeGeneres was there, urging me on. What the hell was she doing in my head? She raised her hand as I passed and we high-fived. I could do this. When I was close enough, I reached out as far as I could, noticing my virtual arm could extend a lot longer than my actual arm, and grasped at the words floating in front of me. They instantly evaporated except for the word "living". I tightened my fist and refused to let go of this one vital word. I brought it to my chest and embraced it. Suddenly, I realized it had transformed into a newborn baby, soft and smelling of cookies. I hugged the baby as it cooed at me. Then, Rip was there. Wait, he was sitting in front of me at the table in the restaurant, wasn't he? Yes, yes he was. I had returned to my body, and Rip was looking at me with an unusual intensity in his steel gray eyes. His mouth was moving, but at first I couldn't hear what he was saying. Then, the sound returned.

"You did it, Freya. Now don't waste any more time."

What? Was he talking to me? I turned to Trevor, who was taking a sip of his wine, trying not to snort it out his nose as he stifled a laugh. What was so funny? I realized Rip was laughing too, still trying to complete the story of the man with two wives. I gazed at him, confused. He caught my gaze and cocked his head, more confused than I was, it seemed. I noticed him glance down at my arms, so I did the same. The baby was gone, but my arms still held the cradle shape. I let them fall onto my lap, and looked back up at Rip, but he was talking to Trevor now, like nothing had happened. In fact, they both seemed completely oblivious to the internal journey I had just taken. Thank God.

It was like a light switch that had been in the off position since I was born, suddenly being flipped on. I scanned the large dining room, noticing every detail, completely unable to extinguish my newfound smile.

Then Rip said something that caught my attention. "I swear, the guy's great in the field, but what kind of moron tries to juggle two wives? Of course, just about anyone can be an FBI agent. It really isn't that hard, *clearly*." He gestured to himself as he said the last part. His self-deprecating humor was one of the things I loved about him...but wait...

It isn't that hard? To become an FBI agent? Did he really just say that?

"You know, I've always thought I would make a great government agent," I stated, my first real contribution to the conversation since my mini-breakdown during the main course.

Both men turned to me, silently processing what they had just heard. Then my husband gave a low chuckle and reached for his wine.

Rip was taking me a little more seriously, however, and decided to explore this new tangent I had taken them on. "I remember you actually talking about doing it. Back in college, remember?"

"That's right. When we were dating. You thought I could do it then. I remember you dragged me to that government jobs workshop with you," I reminisced, noticing Trevor stiffen beside me.

"You actually tried to pursue a career in the FBI?" Trevor accused.

"I'm sure I told you about that. But we hadn't even met yet, honey. It was no big deal. I filled out some paperwork and never heard from them. Rip, however..." I tossed the ball back in Rip's court, to avoid any more sharp looks from my beloved husband. He wasn't crazy about my history with Rip, and sometimes he let his jealousy get the best of him, especially after half a bottle of wine.

"Yeah," Rip took over, "I filled out the application for shits and giggles. Two months before graduation, I got a call. I didn't have any other plans, except to not open a book for a very long time, so I thought, 'what the hell?'"

"I can't believe I've never heard this story before," Trevor said, seemingly very interested in what I would say next. Rip came to my rescue.

"Well, I do believe you *forbade* us from discussing our relationship from before you became the third wheel, so I think it would *behoove* you to lighten up a little," Rip joked. It was hilarious when he used words like "forbade" and "behoove". Who came up with these crazy words, anyway?

"Fine," Trevor quipped, "would you two like to be alone?"

I immediately put my hand on his thigh, and squeezed seductively. "Oh, honey, you know he's kidding. Besides, the minute I saw you, every other man on the planet paled in comparison…no offense, Rip." I didn't even look at Rip when I said this, wanting Trevor to know I was enamored by him and only him.

"A ton taken," Rip remarked, but smiled at me. My ancient, romantic relationship with him seemed a world away, and a lifetime ago. We were much better for each other as friends, and nothing more, and we both knew it.

Trevor resisted making eye contact with me, but finally I prevailed and he couldn't maintain his scowl. He knew he was the only man for me, and as his eyes softened, I was reminded of how he consistently made me feel like the most beautiful woman in the universe. He was fluent in my love language.

Then it hit me: the reason for his behavior the past week. His lax reaction to the near-death experience of our youngest child was a defense mechanism, built to shield him from the real emotions he would normally have felt…the emotions I *had* felt that day. Confusion. Horror. Helplessness. How could I forget his tendency to downplay very intense situations when it was too much for him to handle? I suddenly felt a pang of remorse for the way I'd treated him since the incident. He just wanted to forget about it and move on, and I wouldn't let him.

He was talking to Rip again, seemingly back to normal, but I reached up and gently touched his cheek. He turned to me, closing his eyes briefly while he leaned into my hand. I raised my chin until our lips met, and gave him a long-overdue kiss. Rip cleared his throat after a few seconds, clearly feeling awkward.

"Alright, you two, give it a rest. This is a family show, you know," he commented, actually sounding a little irritated. I pulled away reluctantly from my sweet hubby to give Rip an exaggerated look of daggers, but immediately regretted it. Although it had faded quickly, I could have sworn I detected something unexpected in his eyes—jealousy. I quickly dismissed it.

Then, remembering what I had set out to do a minute before, I questioned Rip. "So, what would it take for me to become an FBI agent now?"

Trevor, who had been finishing up yet another glass of wine, nearly choked at my words.

Rip, however, gave me a triumphant smile. "Are you serious? 'Cause I don't want to find out I'm being played here," he asked.

"Dead serious," I replied. I was.

Rip's smile was bigger than ever.

▬ ▬ ▬

I don't remember much of the drive home from the restaurant, except that my husband was sure my considerably enhanced mood throughout the evening was all his doing. I didn't argue. Normally, I would have been embarrassed at my teary performance, but I was feeling so renewed, nothing could get me down. My husband reaped the rewards of my improved spirits later that night by a not-common-enough visit from my alter ego, Sexy Wife. After the last six days of Stressed Mommy, she was a welcome sight…and had not lost any of her mojo, if I do say so myself—um, herself.

I woke up the next morning ready to take on my new brightly-colored, ultra fulfilling life, foolishly believing it would just…happen. I knew the normal daily routine couldn't be avoided. I was still a wife and mother first and foremost. I made breakfast, sent Trevor off to work with a passionate kiss, emptied the dishwasher, gathered the laundry, got the three boys dressed, fed, and on the bus. Then I started the laundry, cleaned the kitchen, and was just heading to the fridge to prepare my morning drink of almond milk and liquid chai latte mix when my neighbor and best friend, Talia, appeared at my back door.

She entered the kitchen without knocking, which was usual, but what wasn't usual was her attire. Her normal skinny jeans and snug t-shirt had been replaced by what appeared to be workout clothes, and her usually perfectly done hair was pulled back in a low ponytail. Uh-oh, here we go…again.

"Good morning, Freya! It is gorgeous outside!" she announced. She always mentioned the weather when she was trying to throw me off the scent of something else.

"What's his name?" I sighed, needing no prompting whatsoever. We'd danced to this song many times.

"What? Whose name?" she asked, a little too innocently.

"Tal." I stopped pouring my milk, looked her in the eyes, and waited. A few seconds passed before she released her breath and hopped up enthusiastically onto one of my breakfast bar stools.

"His name is Lars. He's the new Zumba instructor at the Y… please, please, please, can we go to his class? It's at 9:00." I don't think she paused to even take a quick breath. I smiled and shook my head, then glanced at the clock on the counter. 8:15.

"You're lucky," I said.

"I know," she replied without hesitation, then seemed to consider this. "…um, why am I lucky again?"

"Because you happen to have caught me on the first day of the rest of my life, and I think a new workout is the perfect way to begin."

Alright, brand new day, let's see what you've got.

EPISODE 3
Possibilities

The unexpected trip to the gym with Talia proved to be more than worth it. Besides the fact that I was impressed, and a little relieved, with my best friend's current choice of crush, I got a great workout and relished the endorphin rush for quite some time afterward. So far, I still felt different, as if I was finally awake, and I intended to stay that way.

I wanted desperately to mention my interest in becoming an FBI agent to her, but I was afraid her preoccupation with Lars would hinder her response. Although, I have to say, he was quite something. If it hadn't been my first day out of a forty-year coma, I might have felt my pulse quicken when the Vin Diesel-esque god corrected my form during class. I did notice Talia give me a dirty look, like it was my fault I was sucking so badly at Zumba that he felt the need to stop instructing and do something about it. She could have at least pretended to be having trouble if she wanted him to touch her, too. Did she really have no clue how to initiate a relationship? That was Flirting 101, for Pete's sake. Who was the eligible single gal in this friendship, anyway?

After the class, Talia mustered the courage to approach him, at my insistence, to tell him how much she enjoyed the workout. He seemed genuinely moved by her comment, and actually gave her a quick hug. As she made her way back to me, she could barely contain her giddiness. She wanted to stay for a while, so we decided to pretend we knew how to use the weight machines, which were located in full view of Lars' next class. We claimed a machine that I'm convinced was designed by that Escher guy, and Talia sat while I played the role of "spotter." This was as good a time as any to bring up my latest news.

"So...I had a kind of epiphany last night, if you're interested," I started.

Without removing her eyes from the direction of Lars, the god of glistening biceps, she replied, "An epiphany? Do tell."

"I'm thinking about becoming an FBI agent." That deserved at least a glance, but I got nothing.

"Funny. Really, what was your epiphany?" she responded, sounding incredibly attentive, though I'm pretty sure I could have transformed into a giant purple gorilla and she wouldn't have noticed.

"I'm serious, Tal. Rip's going to get me into the training program."

I was suddenly more interesting than her new boyfriend, and she turned to me with confusion...and a hint of...was that fury? Finally, I had her undivided attention. Good thing; if I didn't get this out of me, I was sure it would burst out on its own, and I didn't think they would let a homicidal maniac into the FBI.

"You don't think I can do it?" I accused.

She cocked her head slightly, her confusion shifting to surprise, still with that whisper of lividness. "What?" she exclaimed. "Where did this even come from?"

I absent-mindedly fiddled with the weight adjustor behind her seat. Maybe it was more than a whisper. "I told you. Epiphany."

"Could you be a little more specific, please?" she demanded.

"Answer my question," I said flatly.

"What?"

"Do you think I can do it?" I repeated.

"That is not the issue here. You're talking about a complete upheaval of your fairytale life!" So much for whisper; she was now definitely angry. "Aren't you happy? You have everything, you know," she informed me, rather than asked. "Most women are envious of you to the point of insanity!"

I had wanted her complete and total attention, but I did not expect this reaction at all. "Why are you getting so upset?" I asked in a hushed tone, hoping she would follow suit.

The patrons who actually looked like they belonged here were starting to stare.

"Upset!? I'm not upset!" She was upset. "What will happen to me? To us? You'll be Miss Super Cool Secret Agent, and what will I be?"

I realized maybe I hadn't approached this the right way. Talia's life consisted of making sure her two ex-husbands paid their alimony on time, and...well, me. And I had just told her I was removing myself from the equation.

"Tal, this is something I really want, and it feels so right, just even thinking about it. I promise, I will still have time to hang out with you. I will make time. I don't need to see my husband, or my kids. All my free time will be yours," I pleaded. There was a smile starting at the corner of her lips now. I grinned back and waited for the storm in her eyes to subside.

She took a deep breath, and spoke at a more reasonable decibel. "I'm sorry. I just had a minor panic attack," she apologized. After another deep, cleansing breath, she said, "I think it's a great idea. They would have to be complete idiots to *not* want you in the FBI."

Thank God her self-diagnosed bipolar disorder sometimes worked in my favor. Deep inside the big ball of crazy that was my best friend, was an intelligent, insightful, generous person who just needed a trail of bread crumbs to find her way back to reality sometimes. I didn't have to guess why she had trouble making friends, but I couldn't live without her.

That bliss I'd been bathing in since the previous night washed over me again, and there was that smile, uncontrollable and radiant.

"I couldn't wait to tell you. I'm so excited about it, but I really wanted your input. I value your opinion above everyone else's. You know that, don't you?" I responded.

She immediately read between the lines. "So, what does Trevor think of all this?"

It was my turn to take a deep breath. "He thinks it's a bit of a passing fancy. Like that time I decided to learn how to play the guitar, of which he thoughtlessly reminded me."

Talia nodded. "Uh huh...sounds like him. He worships you, you know. He just thinks of you as this Martha Stewart-slash-Betty Crocker wife who wants nothing more than to cater to his every need, which you do every day. You've spoiled him. I think it's high time you let him know you are an independent woman who can have whatever she wants."

Wow. That statement might win her Best Friend of the Century, but she wasn't done.

"Let me ask you something," she said, but didn't wait for my consent. "If Trevor had told you he was absolutely against you doing this, and I had told you I thought it was a stupid idea, would you still do it?"

I knew the answer to this immediately, but I paused to marvel in my friend's ability to read my thoughts. I had asked myself that very same question. "Yes, I would."

She grinned from ear to ear. "Then what the hell are you waiting for?"

◼ ◼ ◼

We left the Y, though reluctantly for one of us, and headed home. I was anxious to call Rip and set up my first interview, or whatever I would be required to do. Whatever it was, I was sure I could handle it. I could handle anything today. I felt like the world was in my corner, maybe even the universe.

I ended up calling Rip while I was still sitting in my car, which was now in my garage. Talia had opted to run home to shower and get ready for the day, but made me promise to keep her posted.

When I got his voicemail almost immediately, I assumed that meant he was in an important meeting, so I sent him a quick text and was gathering my things to get out of the car when my phone rang. It was Rip. I answered, "Hey, handsome. Thought you were in a meeting."

"I was, but there is no better excuse to duck out early than talking to you. What's up?" It was so easy to remember why I had been attracted to him all those years ago. He always said the right thing. Why couldn't Trevor ever leave a meeting early just to talk to me?

"Can you do lunch? I want to talk to you about…well, what we talked about last night. Do you remember?" I asked.

"How could I forget? I thought Trev was going to need the Heimlich," he laughed.

I bristled. "Oh, please don't mention the Heimlich…ever."

"Sorry," he said. "I'd love to do you for lunch—I mean do lunch with you," he joked.

"Ha ha. You know, normally, I wouldn't allow such inappropriate remarks, seeing as how I'm a married woman, but I'm in such a good mood, I'll let it slide just this once."

"Madam, you are indeed a saint among women." I loved it when he broke into his Old World speak, and when he called me a saint.

—— —— ——

By the time I was polished and ready, it was time to meet Rip for lunch. He was already there, sipping on an iced tea, when I arrived at the bustling downtown café…my favorite café, and he knew it.

"I ordered you a Diet Rite," he said, pointing to the glass of cola at the place setting across from him.

I sat and took a drink, exaggerating how much I was enjoying it for his benefit. "Better than sex," I teased.

"Hmmm…I doubt it. But then again, my memory is failing me," he commented.

"Aw, is Prince Charming having a dry spell? Alisa not your fairy princess after all?"

He snorted a laugh between sips of tea. "She decided two twenty-two-year-olds were better than one forty-five-year-old."

I almost felt sorry for him. Almost. He wasn't losing any sleep over the little Russian girl, I was sure. There was always another slutty fish in the sea for Ty Ripley.

"You know, if I thought for a minute that you were hoping to settle down and have a few kids with Little Nikita, I might feel a slight pang of pity for you, but…" I stated, shaking my head slightly.

"I'll let you and Trevor take care of the whole 'Happily Ever After' thing. No woman can hold this stallion hostage for life," he replied. Suddenly, his cheeks grew red, and he took a quick gulp of his iced tea, as if to hide the blush. Blush? Ty Ripley was not prone to blushing, yet I had just witnessed this anomaly first hand.

Maybe it was just a sudden fever.

The sound of my husband's ringtone snapped me out of my thoughts. I answered, as Rip motioned for a waitress to refill his drink.

"Hey Babe, I'm sitting at Ariadne's with Rip. You wanna join us for lunch?" I asked.

"Actually, I was driving by and saw your car. I'm on my way in now," he replied.

"Awesome! See you in a minute." I put my phone back in its special pocket in my handbag, and looked up just as Trevor was coming in the front door of the café. I was a little surprised he had decided to stop, since he referred to Ariadne's as a "Chic Café" and balked every time I suggested grabbing a meal there, but I was thrilled to see him, as always. I stood as he approached our table and gave him a solid kiss. He held out my chair as I sat back down, and then sat down next to me, after giving Rip's hand a quick shake.

The waitress strode over to take our food order, and after Rip and I took our turn, my husband waved her away, saying he would not be eating.

"Why aren't you eating?" I inquired, after the waitress had walked away.

"I already ate," he quipped. I cocked my head in confusion. "What, a man can't stop and see his wife just because?" he asked. "Maybe I missed you."

I leaned toward him and we kissed again. "That is so sweet," I whispered. He held my eyes for a moment, but I couldn't figure out what he was thinking. Love, adoration, and…something else.

Rip apparently thought it was time to remind us of his presence. "So, Trev, your lovely wife and I were just about to discuss her acceptance into the FBI agent training program."

"What?" I exclaimed, louder than I meant to. "I'm in, just like that?" I refused to hide my excitement. I was officially a trainee. That was easy.

"I vouched for you, and when I told my boss you had applied before, he was intrigued. So, I dug out your original paperwork," he revealed.

"Are you kidding?" I asked. "From twenty years ago? How the hell did you find it?"

"Fifteen years ago, they took all their paper files and input the information into the government computer system. You had a file all along," Rip replied. "The next class starts on the fifteenth. Can I tell them you'll be there?"

"Seriously? Yes! Yes, I'll be there! This is so great. Thank you, Rip. You're the best!" At this, I stood up and walked around to him. He stood so I could give him a proper hug, which he readily returned. I couldn't believe it; this was really happening! And I couldn't have gotten this far without Rip. How could I ever thank him?

Then, I realized my bladder was even more excited than I was... typical. I hoped the FBI wouldn't care about my various lingerings from having three children. I prayed that the question, "Do you pee when you sneeze?" would not be part of the entrance exam.

I excused myself, and hurried to the restroom in the back of the café. I did my business, washed my hands, and quickly returned to our table. I desperately wanted the fifteenth to be here, to be now. How would I get through the next ten days without exploding?

When I returned to the table, however, the mood was not what I expected. The two men were sitting as far apart as they could while still in their chairs, looking away from each other, and obviously having just been arguing about something.

How dare they ruin my buzz! I was still deciding whether or not to confront them both, when Trevor stood and gave me a quick kiss. "I'll see you tonight, honey." And he was gone.

Rip chugged the remainder of his iced tea, and stood himself. When he came around to give me a friendly hug goodbye, he sighed. "Don't worry. It's nothing you need to worry about, I promise," he reassured, as he kissed me on the cheek. "I'll see you on the fifteenth." He smiled.

I was standing at our table alone when the waitress brought the food.

EPISODE 4
Falling Out

I couldn't believe what I had just heard. Was I dreaming? I reached down and discreetly pinched my thigh...ouch. Nope, not dreaming. Did Freya just say what I thought she said? If so, this might be the best night of my life so far.

Trevor wasn't taking her seriously, the jerk, so I stepped up to the plate, trying to hide my overflowing excitement.

"I remember you actually talking about doing it. Back in college, remember?" I reminded her. This was too much. How many times had I fantasized about me and Freya, partners in the field, kicking ass and taking names?

She brought up the government jobs fair we went to twenty years ago, where she talked me into filling out the FBI application, unwittingly sealing my fate. Her own application had been ignored, which always baffled me. She would make a great agent. She was strong, fit, smart, determined, fearless, funny, beautiful...well, I suppose the last two aren't really prerequisites to being in the FBI, but she did have an incredible sense of humor. And she was...beautiful.

Trevor was doing his best to keep her down, which I know stemmed from his unreasonable fear of losing her, but, to her credit, she was successfully ignoring him while she asked me question after question about becoming an FBI agent. I was on Cloud Nine.

The rest of the evening sailed by, and at some point, I noticed my date had migrated to another table, and was sitting on some young pup's lap. Shit, I'd forgotten she was even there. Thank God she wasn't one of those women who formed an immediate attachment, and refused to let go. I wasn't looking for a commitment. She seemed pretty content letting the two young men at the table fight for her attention. She eventually left with them, which was just fine with me. I was sure she could take care of herself, after what she'd done to survive in Russia before coming to the States. It was the two clean-shaven yuppies I was worried about.

I turned my attention back to Freya. She was in a considerably better mood since her return from the restroom just a few minutes earlier. She had been a little out of sorts at the beginning of the evening, due to a choking incident that happened with her youngest son, Rowan, earlier in the week.

Everything had turned out okay, but even I had held my breath when she told the story. I'm not so sure I would have handled the situation any better than she had. I loved those kids like my own—or what I imagined I would feel if I had my own—and I could only hope I wouldn't be paralyzed with fear if a crisis arose on my watch. She was beating herself up for something she couldn't possibly have controlled, and I felt the need to make it better, for her. Especially since Trevor was dropping the ball big time.

When she excused herself to freshen up in the ladies' room, Trevor was more concerned about his steak getting cold than his wife's well-being.

"What the hell is wrong with you?" I demanded. He stopped cutting his steak and glared at me.

"Excuse me?" he replied, matching my anger. "What's wrong with *me*?! Are you kidding? You know I only agreed to this weekly torture for Freya." He went back to dissecting his supper.

I shook my head in disbelief. I knew it, alright, but he didn't have to be such a prick about it. This whole charade wasn't going to work if he couldn't at least pretend not to hate me.

Six months ago, we were best friends. I trusted this man with my life, and he felt the same about me. We got together as often as we could, to stay connected, to talk about our lives, and, in a way, live vicariously through each other. I had the freedom of a bachelor that he sometimes missed, and he…well, he had everything I didn't.

And I don't mean that figuratively.

━ ━ ━

We had met at our usual place, a little hole in the wall I found during one of my assignments. It was safe enough, and out of the way, so we could really blow off steam without worrying about running into people we knew. We played a couple games of pool against a few locals, and then claimed a booth to finish our drinks. We had both had more than a few when he started talking about Freya. He knew how good he had it with her, but he started complaining, saying she was always frustrated with him for leaving his dirty laundry in the middle of the bedroom floor, and for not helping out more with the boys. Something about the injustice he felt struck him as funny, because he started laughing. I thought he was being ridiculous.

"So, why don't you help out more with the boys?" I asked.

He looked at me, and his laughter stopped. Then started again, as if he thought I was joking. For some reason, that infuriated me.

"I'm serious, man. Why don't you just pick up your laundry? Is it too much to ask after Freya cooks, cleans, helps the boys with their homework, drives them to all their activities, and still finds the time to put up with your ungrateful ass?" I said. I hadn't meant all of that to come out at once, but the alcohol in my system was severely affecting my internal censor.

He stopped laughing and just stared at me for a minute. I could have easily pretended I was kidding at this point, but for some reason, I stood my ground, knowing the shit storm that followed wouldn't be pretty.

"Just what are you trying to say, Rip?" he finally asked.

Yeah, what *was* I trying to say? "Never mind, dude. It's just the alcohol."

Too late. He wasn't going to let it go now. "No. Clearly, you have something to tell me," he said, slamming his hand down on the table. "Now, spit it out!"

"Come on, you know you don't deserve her. She's a frickin' saint," I replied, trying to produce a natural-sounding chuckle in an attempt to make light of the whole train wreck that was this drunken conversation.

"I knew it," he whispered, shaking his head, and almost knocking his beer over with the accompanying hand gesture.

"What?" I asked.

"You still have a thing for her. After all these years, you still—"

"What?!" I exclaimed with false shock. "You're drunk. You're not thinking straight."

"I've had four beers, Rip. I'm far from drunk, and I think I'm finally seeing *you* for the first time," he accused.

We sat there, staring each other down in silence for what seemed like an eternity. Then he spoke. "You think you're in love with her," he accused.

No, I didn't. I sat there, frozen, trying to figure out how this male bonding session could have gone so wrong. I couldn't move.

"You think you're in love with my wife," he repeated. "Admit it."

Still, I couldn't move, or speak. What the hell had I just done?

"Admit it!" he yelled this time, purposely knocking his beer bottle off the table with his hand. When I remained still and silent, he stood, reaching across the table with both hands and grabbing either side of my shirt collar. He was growing angrier by the second. Did he really only have four beers? I hadn't kept track. I had no reason to an hour ago.

As he lifted me off my seat, I couldn't keep quiet any longer. My response left me at a volume I couldn't control, and caused several bar inhabitants to look our way.

"No! I don't think! I love her! I *love* her! More than you do, you worthless sack of shit!"

His anger changed to shock and he released my shirt. I sat back down, and waited. For what, exactly, I don't know. He stood there, awkwardly leaning over the table.

"You don't deserve her," I said under my breath, but he heard.

He straightened up and stepped out of the booth. He started to walk away, but paused and turned after just a few feet. "Neither do you," he seethed.

I don't know why I said what I said next. I guess I figured since I had leapt across this ravine with my eyes closed, I might as well make sure I perish in the fall.

"She should be with me."

He turned away again, and left the bar without responding. I knew we were done.

We had kept up the façade of our friendship for Freya's sake, so he said, but I knew the truth. If he admitted we had a falling out, she would demand to know what happened, and he was bound and determined she *never* found out that her college boyfriend, and husband's lifelong best friend, had the hots for her.

━ ━ ━

When Freya had first returned from the ladies' room, she seemed better, but a little disoriented. I started telling a story I thought she would enjoy, but she remained unusually quiet while I relayed the hilarious tale of a fellow agent who was busted by his two wives. Normally, she would have found something like that just as funny as I did, but she sat with this blank look on her face, making me think she wasn't listening at all, until she dropped the bombshell that nearly made her husband choke on his wine.

What I wouldn't give to relive that moment over and over…and over.

━ ━ ━

Freya wanted to become an FBI agent. I couldn't stop smiling as I drove to work the next morning. By ten a.m., I was trying to stay awake during a meeting about some new computer-generated training we would be required to complete twice a year, when my phone vibrated with a text. Eager for something, anything, else to do, I pulled it out of my pocket and looked at the screen. Freya. My palms started to sweat.

I was close enough to the door to sneak out of the meeting. Once I was far enough down the hall, I hit number one on my speed dial. She picked up right away.

"Hey, handsome. Thought you might be in a meeting," she said in that silky voice.

Damn. I really did love her, and there was nothing I could do about it.

━ ━ ━

I met Freya for lunch at her favorite café, Ariadne's. We were just getting past the pleasantries when Trevor showed up, uninvited. Was he following Freya now? Or following me? This guy's insecurities really knew no bounds.

I was not deterred, even when he said something lame to his wife that she took as a sincere compliment, and they spent a moment in a lip lock. I was determined to do what I came to do. When I told Freya she had been accepted into the next agent training program that started in ten days, she stopped kissing her husband and hugged me. I had left out the part about anyone, really anyone, being able to sign up for the program. I hadn't really done anything but put her name on a list. The hard part came around the third week, which was when most people were weeded out, due to the physical and mental strain...and sometimes they just didn't pass the background check.

Freya excused herself and ran to the restroom, leaving us recent mortal enemies alone, again. What was it with her and public restrooms? I was planning on sustaining a nice, friendly silence during Freya's absence, but Trevor had other ideas.

"You're not seriously going to let her think she can become an FBI agent?" he asked.

"There's that word again," I grinned as I recalled our blowout at the bar. "'Think'. I don't have to think anything. Freya believes she can do this, and so do I."

"If you really love her, like you claim, you won't encourage this fantasy of hers. When she falls flat on her face, she'll have no one to blame but you," he informed me. "Of course, now that I think about it, it would solve one problem for me." He paused for a moment, but then reconsidered his previous statement. "But I can't stand the thought of Freya getting hurt."

"You're trying to convince the wrong person of that," I retorted.

"You're going to tell her she doesn't qualify to be an agent. Make something up, I don't care, but don't let it go any further," he ordered.

"I will not lie to her," I answered. "She can do this. You're just afraid she might find something else to live for besides you."

Freya came around the corner from the restrooms, and we immediately ceased our disagreement. Trevor kissed her goodbye and left as quickly as he'd arrived. I could tell she knew we'd been arguing, so I said my farewell before she could ask any questions.

She was going to be an FBI agent, if it was my last act on this earth, and her devoted husband couldn't do a damn thing about it.

EPISODE 5
For Better or Worse

I sighed. Not one of those frustrated wish-it-were-over kind, but the wow-I-have-a-new-lease-on-life kind, and the smile that accompanied it...well, let's just say I think it could have launched a thousand ships.

Forty-eight hours before, I had been a woman undone. I had experienced the near-loss of a child, and had been forever changed... and I didn't like it one bit. Just when I thought all I wanted in the world was to go back to the way things were before, I was shown what my life could be, what *I* could be. And the two men in my life would be there to support me during every step of my journey. Or so I'd deluded myself into thinking.

I was making supper for my family, an activity I had done thousands of times, but today, this day, I was preparing spaghetti and meatballs with more gusto than ever before. Blaise and Rowan were sitting at the breakfast bar, each hoping to be the first to get a taste, and Levi was doing homework on his laptop at the small table in the atrium. He was writing a paper on Marie Antoinette, and I was cheerfully informing him that, not only did she absolutely *not* say anything about eating cake, ever, but that she was simply a young girl who'd been forced into an arranged marriage and made to live far from her home where she was hated the moment she set foot on French soil.

"She was a wife and mother," I told him, "under dire circumstances and did the best with what she was given."

"But this website says—" he started, but I headed him off, lest he be sorely misinformed, like most of the American public.

"Find another website," I instructed him. "Search for 'Marie Antoinette did *not* say let them eat cake' or something like that."

He reluctantly complied.

Needless to say, this was a topic near and dear to my heart, and he knew he wasn't going to get away with a half-assed paper full of half-truths and outright lies. I read once that, for hundreds of years, history was put to paper by monks who believed women didn't have souls and were dirty, impure creatures. Since then, I'd always been a silent champion of women who, I believed, were essentially given the shaft when it came to the version of 'history' that was actually written down.

I couldn't help but think I was vindicating them, even just a little, by following my heart and pursuing my long-forgotten dream of being an FBI agent. I would not squander the precious time I had by regretting all the things I wish I'd done, and I definitely wouldn't let my sex limit my possibilities.

I had ten days to say goodbye to my old life, and prepare for my new one, and I was going to make every minute count. I felt sure my kids would want to nominate me for Mother of the Year by the time I started the training program.

Just as I was draining the pasta in the sink, my husband entered the kitchen through the door to the garage, seemingly exhausted from a long day, but a smile broke across his face when he smelled supper… spaghetti and meatballs was his favorite meal. He walked over to the sink and gave me a soft kiss, then did his usual rounds with the boys, starting with Rowan.

"Choke on any quarters today?" he asked the preschooler, ruffling his hair.

What the hell? My first instinct was to throw the full colander of steaming spaghetti at his head, but that would set a very bad example for my boys, so I settled for a lame and unsatisfying retort.

"Not funny, Trevor." When he glanced at me, wincing, I gave him a look that clearly told him his remark had cost him dearly…no naked time later, no matter how much foreplay he promised.

"Sorry," he said. Too little, too late, pal.

He stepped over to Blaise and they high-fived, their special routine, and Trevor asked him how his science test had gone at school. Well, I had forgotten about that, so good for him. He was replacing husband points with daddy points.

"I got a hundred," was the response. Not surprising. Perfect scores were the norm for our middle child, who craved being the best at everything he did. Sometimes, he even brought home above perfect scores. God bless whoever invented extra credit.

As Trevor made his way to our eldest, still revered as the hero of the household, Levi was holding his head in one hand, elbow firmly planted on the table, while he scrolled on the laptop with the other hand. His face was less than serene.

"Whatcha working on, bud?" Trevor asked. Levi looked up as if he'd just noticed his father's presence for the first time.

"Hey, Dad," he started. "Report on Marie Antoinette. Mom's making me work for this one." Perfect scores were not a priority for this child. The quicker he could get an assignment done, the better, quality be damned. He must get that from his father, I thought to myself.

"Ah," Trevor replied. "Let them eat cake!"

Levi looked up at me, as if to say, "See, I was right!"

"Trevor, I just told Levi that she never said anything of the kind," I exclaimed. "The whole 'let them eat cake' thing was someone's Hollywood version of the truth."

"Really?" he asked, then just shrugged. He leaned over Levi's shoulder, placing a gentle hand on the other one.

"Listen to your Mom, Lee. She's the smart one," he whispered loudly, then stood and beamed at me, hoping to see that I had softened since his quarter remark. How could I not with that dazzling smile? I pretended to glare at him, but then broke into a smile in return. He might just get to sleep in the bed with me after all.

After stuffing ourselves with pasta, meatballs, garlic bread, salad, and brownies and ice cream—no, honey, I'm not pregnant, really— Trevor offered to get the boys bathed and in bed. That wasn't so unusual, but afterward, he found me in the master bedroom folding laundry, and he picked up a towel, his sincere attempt at a tri-fold causing me to bite my bottom lip to keep the snicker from surfacing.

"You're incredibly helpful this evening," I said, implying a question.

"Well, I had a bit of an epiphany myself this week...today, actually," he answered mysteriously.

A few minutes went by, and he continued to make more work for me by poorly folding towel after helpless towel, but I said nothing. Clearly, he was waiting for me to coax an explanation out of him. Alright, I was in a pretty good mood, and still floating in a pasta coma that promised to last well into the night, so I decided to play.

"Would you like to elaborate, or do I get to guess?" I asked.

"Well, I realized that maybe I haven't been the best husband."

I stopped folding and looked at him, but he was reaching for yet another defenseless towel to almost fold. I decided to make it last as long as I could.

"'Maybe'? Usually epiphanies are a little more...certain," I teased.

"I'm serious, Frey," he responded. "I remember when we had Levi, and we had that big discussion about how we're a team and, and... we're in this together," he stammered. Suddenly, I didn't want to play around anymore. He was really trying to connect with me as we stood across our king-sized bed from one another, sorting Superman undies.

"I remember," I started. "We agreed that we were partners, and no matter how tired we were at the end of the day, we would be...what did we call it? 50/50 parents, right?"

He smiled, happy we were on the same page.

"Yeah." He took a deep breath. "So, I realized that maybe I'm not living up to our agreement." He opened his mouth to continue, but couldn't find the words.

"You know, I *do* realize how tough your job is, and that *does* count for something," I offered, and I meant it.

He thought about that for a moment, then responded.

"You know, I've been telling myself that for years, but I can't justify it anymore. I want to do my share...plus, I like being here with the boys...with you. You've made our home a sanctuary, and I don't show my gratitude for that nearly enough."

Whoa. I found myself thinking of the old horror flick *Invasion of the Body Snatchers*, but couldn't remember for the life of me how to tell a pod person from a human. Wasn't it something about a seam on the back of the neck? I shook my head back to reality.

"I don't know what to say, honey," I whispered. "It would be wonderful if you could spend more time at home, but you don't have to give up your 'guy time' with Rip. I know how much that means to you."

My mention of Rip made him cringe, but I pretended not to notice. I was hoping he would break down and tell me what was going on between the two of them, but that didn't seem to be on his agenda. I let it go this time, but I was determined to find out what that mysterious argument was about, eventually.

"I'm not married to Rip," he said. "Plus, we still have our weekly dinners with him."

"But you don't want me tagging along every—" I argued, but he cut me off.

"Don't worry about my 'guy time'...please," he interjected. "I get plenty at work."

His job as a day trader *was* horrendously male-dominated. It involved a 45-minute commute to the city and miserably long hours, but he loved it, and I refused to be one of those wives who whined and complained about my husband's choice of profession. After all, it was my choice to stay at home, and it was his salary, which he worked his ass off for, that allowed it.

And now it was my choice to go back to work, and I was confident he would be just as supportive as he was when I gave up my career to raise our boys.

I guess I hadn't woken up completely yet, but I was about to.

"So, I wanted to talk about this FBI thing..." he said, abruptly changing the subject.

"Yes?" I asked, tentatively. We hadn't really discussed it in private yet. I didn't want to admit I'd been avoiding it, but...

"Are you going to put the boys in daycare after school? I was just wondering if you'd thought that far ahead...and if you'd looked into cost..." he said, trailing off.

I made a sincere attempt to not be offended by this. It was a valid question, after all.

"Okay," I started. "First of all, Rip said the training hours are eight to two, so I don't even have to worry about after-school care until I'm a full-up agent," I said, my voice even and emotionless.

"Second, by the time we need care, I will have a paycheck, so cost won't be an issue," I assured him. "I was thinking about The Learning Treehouse downtown—" I informed him, but he didn't let me finish.

"Isn't that the most expensive one in town?" he accused.

"Because it's the best," I replied. "Besides, we only need care for Blaise and Rowan."

We stared at each other across the bed for a few seconds. His eyes were alive, almost angry, and I had no idea why. This was the best thing that had happened to me in a long time, and I thought he would be just as happy for me as I was. Isn't that what love was all about, wanting the other person to be happy, no matter the cost? And I didn't think the cost was all that much…at least not for him. His life wasn't about to change drastically. He would still go to work all day and come home for supper, which would magically appear on the dining room table, not to mention his clean socks and underwear magically appearing in his dresser drawer.

That reminded me of something else we hadn't discussed yet.

"I'm going to hire a cleaning lady." I was no longer in the mood to beat around the bush.

"What?!" he exclaimed, to which I gave him a 'the-boys-are-sleeping' look, and he took a breath and lowered his voice.

"How much is that going to cost?" he demanded in a loud whisper.

At that, I threw the jeans I was trying to fold back on the bed in frustration.

"What the hell is wrong with you?" I asked. "We could afford daycare and a cleaning lady *now*, and you know it. So, what's really bothering you?"

He hesitated, then the words came fast. "Maybe I don't want you to do this. Maybe I like our life the way it is. Maybe…" he stopped, clearly afraid to say what he was thinking.

"Just say it," I encouraged.

"Maybe, I'm a little hurt you didn't ask me first."

I think I stopped breathing for a second.

"Ask you…as in, your permission?" I probed.

"Well, yeah," he answered, then saw my eyes on fire. "I mean no, not permission, exactly…more like approval." This only stoked the fire.

"So, all this talk about 50/50 parenting and wanting to help out more around the house…you are offering to lower yourself to these menial tasks as long as I stay home and be your indentured servant forever?"

"Come on, Frey, you're being overly dramatic," he reasoned. "We are equal as parents, but as far as keeping our home running smoothly, well, I pay the bills and you take care of all the little daily stuff. I thought that was our agreement. I'm willing to make the sacrifice of being home more and helping out with housework. I'm asking for you to make a small sacrifice in return."

"What happened to 'I love being here with you and the boys'?"

"I do," he insisted, "but—you're not listening to what I'm trying to say—"

"Oh, I hear you!" I shouted, ignoring his gesture to lower my volume. "You think washing a dish now and then is the same level of sacrifice as me giving up a dream I've had since college!"

"Come on. You don't really think you can be an FBI agent, do you?"

And there it was. The moment I realized I had no idea who the man in my bedroom was.

EPISODE 6
Phase 1

I had been to Rip's office in the government building a few times before, but I had a butterfly or two when I walked through the main entrance into the massive lobby for the first time as a trainee. I ran my fingers across the cool brick wall on the way to the elevators, and smiled. I felt as though the building itself was welcoming me. That it had been waiting for my arrival for a long time. The butterflies ceased to flutter, and I confidently pushed the button to summon the elevator.

Rip was standing right in front of the doors when they opened onto his floor, causing me to jump about a foot in the air. He loved doing that to people. Sometimes, he was more boy than man... another one of his endearing qualities. He was grinning from ear to ear and held a steaming Starbucks cup in each hand.

"You know I don't drink coffee," I reminded him, when my heart had resumed beating.

He dipped his head in a goofy sort of bow, and responded in his best British accent. "Milady, your chai tea latte with soy milk and a sprinkle of cinnamon," he said, as he handed me the cup. My favorite indulgence. This *was* a special occasion, I thought, deciding whether or not to accept it. Rip stayed frozen in his half bow, waiting for me to release him.

"As you were, good sir knight," I played, but not attempting an accent. I wasn't about to start this monumental day by embarrassing myself...too much.

"How did you know I was on *this* elevator?" I inquired, happily taking the cup of sweet, delicious nectar.

Just then, I noticed some commotion over Rip's shoulder. An elderly woman was standing in the middle of a small crowd, complaining loudly and pointing toward Rip and me. She waved her arms in alarm, and then clutched her chest as she relived her recent terror.

"I didn't," he confessed. "I thought I gave that old bird a heart attack, but she's alright…just a little upset." He put a hand on my back and gently led me toward his office, attempting to leave the area before the woman could positively identify her assailant.

"A little upset?" I laughed. "I think you poked an ornery bear with a stick."

"All the more reason to turn tail and run," he responded, quickening his pace.

━ ━ ━

I spent a few minutes with Rip in his office before I was supposed to report to the Training Center two floors above. Trevor had canceled our last weekly dinner with Rip, saying he didn't feel well, so I hadn't seen Rip since our lunch at Ariadne's. I didn't bring up my argument with Trevor, and Rip didn't ask how my currently bedroom-banned husband was, so I pushed it down as far as I could, along with all the emotions associated with it. Trevor would come around.

Rip was responsible for all the training of new agents in the state, but I wouldn't be in his presence officially until I was through Phase 1, which was fine. For the time being, I was still just an old friend, sitting comfortably in his office, shooting the shit.

This may be the last time I'm allowed in here for some time, I thought. Unless I really screw up. The idea of Rip scolding me, and meaning it, struck me as funny, but then I sobered. I was determined to not give him any reason to.

Then, as we both stood, he gave me a friendly kiss on the cheek and said, "Now, go get 'em."

I gave a mock salute and performed an abysmal about-face, and skipped out of his office. It was like my first day of kindergarten, when everything was new and exciting. In just a few minutes, I would be an FBI Trainee fully engaged in the first phase of the agent training program. I might have thought I was in a movie or, more likely, dreaming, except for the fact that everything around me—potted plants, cubicles, people—were all so sharp and clear. If I had been dreaming since my new and improved vision had kicked in on that fateful night, I decided right then and there, I never wanted to wake up.

I checked in at the Training Center and gave the agent at the desk a firm handshake, never wavering my eye contact with the rather short, stout man…one of the many tips from Rip on how to survive the first day. The man seemed pleased, and gestured toward the classroom across the hall. The room was empty. I was the first one to check in. Score one for me.

◼ ◼ ◼

So it began. The next two weeks were filled with all the 'unpleasant but necessary stuff', as our primary trainer, Special Agent Moss, called it. She would disappear for hours while we filled out form after form, completed one computer training module after another on our current knowledge of operational security, strategy, and crisis reaction, and waited to be called out for our mandatory appointment with the Agency Psychiatrist. It was tedious and a little boring—okay, it was positively mind-numbing—but I never complained.

The twenty-two hopefuls quickly dwindled to twelve by the end of the second week. One young man, who had arrived the first day in a "Men in Black"-type suit, hadn't even returned the next day. I thought he was trying to be funny, but it became immediately clear he had neither seen the movie nor had a sense of humor when I poked him and laughed, "Are you the best of the best of the best?"

He avoided me the rest of the day. I dismissed the possibility that his withdrawal from the program had been due to my comment. Besides, if he was that sensitive, he wasn't cut out to be an agent anyway. I vaguely wondered what could possibly have scared off nearly half the group at this point…the fear of getting carpal tunnel?

When I was called for my psych evaluation the morning of Day 11, I left the doctor's office an hour later fairly sure I was much saner than he was, and confident I had passed with flying colors. Confident because the fifty-something, balding giant of a man had spent the fifty-five-minute session asking my opinion on how to deal with his seventeen-year-old son, who was rebelling big-time and had moved in with his eighteen-year-old boyfriend. Although I insisted I had no words of wisdom for his particular situation, he kept pushing, until I was forced to resort to a few generic statements about accepting him for who he is, letting him make his own mistakes, and loving him no matter what, etc. I was pretty impressed with myself as the supposed superior brain in the room scribbled furiously while I spoke...seriously, he was taking notes? I knew I was good, but I had no idea I was *that* good.

I returned to the classroom to find it empty except for Agent Moss, who was closing up all the computers. I walked over to my station and sat down.

"I can close it up for you, if you want. I dismissed everyone for the day," Agent Moss offered. She was so nice, it freaked me out a little. I guess I expected a female agent to be...well, a bitch. I would have understood completely. She had conquered a man's world, and didn't want any company on her pedestal, but Agent Moss was not what I expected at all. I really liked her, and was anxious to pick her brain, but hadn't found the right moment.

"That's alright," I replied. "I wanted to finish up my security clearance application, if that's okay. I'm almost done with it."

"You are?" she seemed surprised.

"I just have the previous address section left," I responded, logging in to my computer.

She walked over to me. "Did you bring all the paperwork you need for that?"

Oops. What had I missed?

"Um...what paperwork?" I asked innocently.

"All the stuff with your old addresses on it?" she replied.

I relaxed. "Oh, I don't need anything but my noggin'," I said, comically tapping the side of my head.

"You haven't moved around much, huh?" she assumed, smiling.

"Well, I didn't as a child, but since college, I have had seven moves," I counted. "I was in the Air Force for four years," I added, as if this was an explanation.

"You have nearly ten addresses, and you have them all memorized?" She pulled up a chair next to me, much to my dismay. I didn't like people watching me type. It made me nervous, and I hit more wrong keys than I normally would.

"Uh, yeah." I scooted my chair over a tad to make room for her.

"Impressive."

"Not really," I dismissed. "I've always had a good memory for anything with numbers in it...addresses, phone numbers, birthdays, stuff like that." I located the security clearance application file and opened it. She stared at the screen. I hesitated.

"Well, come on. I want to watch your brain at work," she coaxed.

"Are you sure you don't have something more exciting to do, like, I don't know, floss?"

She immediately covered her mouth with her hand. "Why, do I have something in my teeth? Shit, that's embarrassing," she exclaimed, while she pulled a small compact mirror out of her suit jacket pocket and peered at her teeth in it, making funny faces as she did so.

"No, no, you don't. Sorry..." I apologized. "I was just making awkward conversation...a bit of a nervous typer, I guess." I chuckled, glancing at my hands hovering over the keyboard.

She sighed with relief and put the mirror away.

"I'll leave you to it, then." She stood to leave.

"You don't have to leave," I pleaded. "I'll just be a few minutes."

"Take your time." She walked across the room, and we went about our respective business for the next ten minutes, my fingers clicking away on the keys until my application was complete. When I stood to leave, I arched my chest to stretch my back and released an involuntary grunt that got Agent Moss's attention.

"You okay?" she asked.

"Just not used to all the sitting," I replied. I started to gather my things as she hunched back over the computer she was trying to shut down, but something stopped me.

There was that feeling again. *Don't leave. Keep talking.* I wasn't going to ignore it. It had served me well last time.

"Can I ask you something?"

She turned to me, curious. "Sure."

"Did you always want to be an agent?" I started.

She took a deep breath. "Really?" It was a big one to start with, I admit.

I nodded.

She looked around the room, then cracked her neck, first left, then right. Another deep breath. Did she not know the answer, or did she not want to tell me?

Finally, she spoke. "My dad was an agent. It just seemed…natural. By the time I was ten, I knew it's what I wanted."

"So, how long have you been an agent?"

"Twenty-one years."

"Are you kidding?" I responded, sincerely shocked. "Okay, woman to woman…how old are you? Because I was guessing around thirty-eight."

She grinned and blushed just a little. "I'm forty-five."

Holy shit. Not only was she nice, but now she was a hot forty-five-year-old, which is much more annoying than a hot thirty-eight-year-old, especially to a mediocre forty-year-old. And still, I wanted nothing more at that moment than to continue the connection. I decided to go for broke.

"Did you ever…regret it?" I asked tentatively, hoping she wouldn't suddenly transform into the bitch I had expected on the first day.

"Sure." That surprised me. "I thought about giving it all up to find Mr. Right and have some kids…always thought I'd be a mom…but, it just didn't happen, and now…well, now, it's a little late for kids, but I haven't given up on Mr. Right. Not yet, anyway."

"But it's been worth it? I mean, if you could go back, would you turn down the FBI?"

She smirked, thinking hard. "I used to be able to answer that question, but now…"

"What's changed?"

She gave a heavy sigh, and glanced at the ceiling, obviously weighing whether or not to tell me what she was really thinking.

"You."

"Me?"

She took a deep breath before she began. "When I heard a forty-year-old mom was going to try to be an agent, I didn't expect—well, you."

Here we go. *Freya, I'd like to introduce you to Agent Bitch.*

She leaned in closer to me. "If you tell anyone I said this, I'll deny it, but…well, I'm known in the bureau for my good instincts, which is why I get the newbies who come in thinking they're going to be drop-kicking drug lords the first week." She laughed at her own joke, while I leaned away, afraid I had tapped a powder keg.

She noticed my unease, and backed away.

"Anyway…I've got a good feeling about you. If you can handle the physical and psychological aspects of the job like I think you can… you'll be a field agent, and a damn good one, in six months." She stood upright again, and turned to push a stray chair under the table.

"I won't tell a soul." I didn't know how to tell her she had just reaffirmed my entire existence, but I had to say something. "Thank you." I hoped that was enough.

At the risk of pushing my luck, I asked, "So, what does…all that… have to do with whether or not you regret being an agent?"

"I don't regret being an agent. I just kind of wish I had done it the way you are. You know, perfect husband, perfect kids, and *then* become an agent, when I finally had some brains."

This made me laugh. "Well, I think 'perfect' is a relative term, and I still feel like I've gone completely insane sometimes, but so far, it's the fun kind of insane."

"I know exactly what you mean." She looked down at the floor and then back at me, taking a breath. I sensed the deep conversation was over.

"So, when does the training get hard?" I asked. "'Cause I gotta tell you, if there's much more sitting, I may have to rethink this life-changing decision of mine." I was kidding…sort of.

Agent Moss smiled. "Don't worry. The *real* training doesn't start until Phase 2."

"So, Phase 2 is when the fun begins?" I joked.

She chuckled. "Oh yeah. Just not for you."

EPISODE 7
Frustration

It had been two weeks since I'd finished Phase 1 of the FBI Training Program, which consisted solely of filling out forms and completing virtual training modules on the computer. I was so anxious for Phase 2, I could taste it, but I had hit an unexpected brick wall: my security clearance.

It was a mystery to me why it was taking so long. The four years I had spent in the Air Force should have garnered me Top Secret clearance before I even walked in the front door. No entity does a more thorough background check than the federal government, and I'd already been through the whole rigmarole once. The only new information was my marriage and my kids, and although it was a span of fifteen years, I still didn't understand what the problem could be.

I told myself it was a possibility my time in uniform was actually delaying the clearance. I had worked for a two-star general at one point, and had been required to read everything he did, most of which made no sense to me. But, that was more than seventeen years ago, and, although I had been in the Intelligence field, the world had changed so much, I couldn't imagine that the information was the same, even if I had retained any of it in my overwhelmed brain.

The problem was that I wasn't authorized to begin Phase 2 until the stinking clearance was granted. All I could do was try to enjoy the unexpected time at home, and be patient. Rip called me every morning to update me and tell me to sit tight. He had no idea what the holdup was either, but he was almost as frustrated about it as I was, I could tell. He just kept saying that every clearance was different, and it was no indication as to whether or not it was going to be approved.

"Most likely," he huffed through the phone on the morning of the thirteenth day of waiting, "someone is on vacation, and it's sitting on their desk."

I sighed deeply as I said a forlorn goodbye to Rip and set my phone on the kitchen counter.

"Be patient. This is going to happen," were his final words to me.

I took a deep, cleansing breath and turned around to see Talia coming to the back door. She was dressed and ready to Zumba her little heart out with Lars, and she was ecstatic—as she'd been every morning these past two weeks—to see me still home, which meant I was going to Zumba too. Oh well. There were worse things than staying fit while Lars, Keeper of the Sexy Six Pack, shouted words of encouragement inches from my face, the sparkling sweat carving little tributaries into his cheek as it meandered down from the top of his bald cranium.

Seeing him every morning these last two weeks…well, let's just say that Vin Diesel was threatening to bump Keanu Reeves out of first place on my 'If I suddenly need a new husband…' list.

Trevor and I had called a cease-fire two days into my waiting game, but were far from back to normal, and it was nice to have a gorgeous man pay attention to me…especially when that man addressed me as "Goddess Freya" every day. Damn. He was beautiful *and* smart.

Freya was the name of the Norse Goddess of Love and War, and Leader of the Valkyries, the Choosers of the Slain, girl gladiators who rode over battlefields on winged horses, taking the souls of noble warriors killed in battle and transporting them to Odin's Hall, Valhalla, to feast for eternity. Yeah.

That hunky historian might actually be good enough for my Talia, if she ever snapped out of her trance long enough to flirt a little. She was so enamored by him, in fact, that I was a little worried about her. She'd never, ever had trouble communicating with the opposite sex, verbally or otherwise.

It didn't help that he did seem to pay a lot of attention to me during his class, but I was certain it had nothing to do with physical attraction. I really had no coordination, and I was inclined to think he saw me as someone who needed a lot of extra help in the Zumba department. I was more of a jogger, and any other activity that required no more than a simple 'left, right, left, right' motion.

Talia was so good at, well, everything resembling aerobics, that he barely glanced her way anymore. I could only tell her to suck so many times, but she refused to start the relationship with a lie.

Relationship?

I said, "Tal, it's not a relationship until he actually knows your name, and he'll never know it if you don't tell him!" This just got a shrug in response. So unlike her. Then it hit me...this was not another one of her casual crushes. She was more than smitten with Lars. She was in deep, deep smit...dare I say it? She was in love...?

Alright, Universe. Freya, Goddess of Love and patron of young lovers, accepts your challenge.

After the intense workout on this, Day 13 of my sentence in Purgatory, I decided it was time Lars and Talia joined the ranks of the legendary couples in Asgard, the realm of the gods and goddesses.

I located Lars at the front of the room, standing in the middle of a small, sweaty crowd of adoring women, and patiently listening to the overflowing praise about his class. This was a daily occurrence. Shameless, all of them, and the ones I recognized were all married, acting like love-struck teenagers. Was I the only adult here? Seriously.

I shook my head to regain focus on my newfound mission. I fixed the waistband on my workout shorts, and tucked the stray wet hairs behind my ears before I headed straight for the only man in the room, firmly grabbing Talia's arm on the way. This was happening.

Hold on to your spandex, Lars.

▬ ▬ ▬

"What do you mean, there's a problem?" I was growing increasingly agitated.

"Agent Ripley, I can't discuss the specifics with you," said the young, male voice on the other end of the phone. "All I can tell you is that Freya Douglas' security clearance has been flagged for upper-level review for a...um...discrepancy."

"Discrepancy?" I repeated, but at a slightly louder decibel. "What the hell does that mean?"

"Sir, I already told you, I can't—"

"You can't tell me the specifics, I know," I finished for him. "How long have you worked for the Bureau, Danny?"

"Uh, it's Donald. I started three weeks ago…sir."

I couldn't help but smile. I could feel my heart rate coming down a little, and decided I didn't want to take my anger and frustration out on this nervous man-boy…anymore.

"Can you tell me whose desk it's on right now? Is that information I'm allowed to know?" I asked, in the friendliest tone I could muster.

He stammered a second, and then blurted out a name. I didn't want to believe it.

"Are you sure about that?"

"Y-y-yes, sir, positive."

I took a deep breath and processed the information.

"Thanks," I quipped, and hung up the phone before he could respond. I'm sure he was grateful, after I'd spent the last ten minutes ripping the kid a new one. Ah, he needed a little toughening up. I was frickin' Mary Poppins compared to some of the other agents he would have to deal with. Especially the one I was about to pay a surprise visit to.

▬ ▬ ▬

I stood in the elevator as it ascended to the top floor of the FBI office building, listening to an instrumental version of Madonna's "Like a Virgin," and filling in the words in my head. When the doors opened, I stepped out to a secure entry with two very large guards blocking the door. I showed my access badge and put my thumb on a scanner on the wall until a beep accompanied by a green light proved I belonged there. The guards stepped to the side, and the one on the left punched in a code on a keypad below the door handle. A loud buzz sounded and then a click to indicate the door was now unlocked. The guard opened the door and moved away to let me through.

On the other side was a second entry point, this one with two guards, and an agent, all three packing, and the agent with a handheld metal detector. After a thorough pat down, I was allowed access to the super-secret sanctum through this second door. I entered the secure area, and knew exactly where I was going. I turned left down the long hallway, and then made a right. The fourth cave on the left was my destination. I knocked, but didn't wait for a response before I burst through the bullet-proof door.

As I approached the large, and much nicer than mine, desk on the opposite side of the much bigger than mine office, the inhabitant turned in his high-backed chair to face me.

"Just get it done or I'll find someone else," he said harshly into his cell phone as he came into my view. I glared at him to get off the damn phone.

"I don't give a shit, Larry. Now, you're going to be on the next plane back to Moscow if you can't handle this." He was a real warm fuzzy, this guy.

I started drumming my fingers on his desk, loudly.

He avoided making eye contact with me, but cleared his throat in frustration.

"Listen, your expenses are none of my concern…yeah…I'm hanging up now, Larry," and he did.

He took his time raising his eyes to meet mine.

"What the hell do you want?" he demanded.

"You know damn well what I want, Trevor," I responded, equally frustrated. "Why are you blocking your wife's security clearance?"

EPISODE 8
Ulterior Motives

I decided it was time Trevor and I had it out, before our estrangement got any…stranger.

I was feeling pretty good about my mediation skills, after practically setting up a lunch date between Lars and Talia myself earlier that day, while making Lars think it was all his idea. Okay, I guess that's more coercion, technically, but, either way, I was confident I could get the Trevor who loved and adored me to return. Then we could murder the new cold, insensitive Trevor together. Ah, romance.

I decided to make his second favorite dinner—I didn't want it to be too obvious I had a diabolical plan—and was just putting the beef strips in the fridge to marinate when the boys got home from school.

I had to admit, it was nice to be there for them, as I watched them spread their homework out on various surfaces in the kitchen. I would miss this when I was officially a working gal again.

Rowan's homework was to find something that started with the letter of the week, and bring it to school the next day…this week's letter was "L", so we quickly found a small, stuffed lion and put it in his backpack. He was happy and skipped off to play in his room.

Blaise was learning about slavery in America in the 1800s and had to do a timeline worksheet. As I hovered for a second, glancing over his shoulder, it was obvious he didn't need any help from me… thank the Maker.

I wandered over to Levi in the atrium, where he was typing up his final draft report on Marie Antoinette. I was very impressed with it, having read it a few nights before, and I think he was too. He had found a ton of information on the *real* French queen, and had given, I thought, sufficient proof that the famous phrase accredited to her was a case of ugly rumor becoming history. I gave a deep, satisfied sigh and smiled at him, giving his shoulder a gentle squeeze as he typed. It felt good when they actually listened to me and valued my advice.

By the time Trevor made an appearance, homework was done and put away, supper was minutes from being ready to eat, and I had showered and even put a little makeup on, a very rare occurrence.

Trevor walked in and tossed his keys in the basket hanging on the wall. He sighed with fatigue and gave me a half-hearted, "Hi."

As he emptied his pocket of his cell phone, wallet, and some change, and placed it all on the kitchen counter, he must have noticed the mood in the house had changed, because he suddenly looked up. He looked at me, not smiling, but quizzically, and looked around the kitchen.

"Are we celebrating?" he asked.

"Just you coming home," I responded mysteriously.

He suppressed a grin, but I could see it in his eyes. "What's going on?" he asked in a suspicious tone.

I walked toward him and put my arms around his waist. "Well, homework is done, it's *not* bath night, and I made beef and broccoli for supper."

He raised an eyebrow, a recessive trait only Rowan had inherited from his father, and waited.

Finally, I cracked. "I thought…after supper…we could talk about…um—" I struggled to form my plan into words. To my surprise, he let out a sigh of relief, and wrapped his arms around me.

"Okay," was all he said, but his eyes spoke volumes. He leaned down and kissed me gently, and I felt a jolt of electric current run through my entire body. I loved that he could still do that to me.

▭ ▭ ▭

Finally alone in our bedroom, Trevor started kissing me, and actually managed to get my shirt off before I stopped him. Men. No matter how long I'd known him, it still surprised me when he translated 'talk' to mean 'sex'. It had to be so much easier to be a lesbian. A woman would never make that mistake. It just reconfirmed my belief that the whole Venus-Mars thing was right on the money.

I gently pushed him away. "Trevor. Talk first, then…well, we'll see."

He laughed and kissed me one more time. "Alright. I've just… missed you."

He really needed to stop saying random awesome things like that, or I would never be able to get out what had been weighing on my mind these past weeks.

"I've missed you too, but our relationship…our marriage and partnership, is more than physical. Right?" I asked.

"Of course. I just meant…" he trailed off, unable to find the words.

"I know," I reassured him. And I did.

We sat on our bed, and I started.

"I want to be an FBI agent. I'm *going* to be one. It feels right… like I was meant to do this."

I paused, waiting for him to comment. When he didn't, I continued.

"I need to know that I have your support in this." I took his hand in mine, but couldn't bring myself to look at him just yet. "I know you're worried I might fail, and how that would affect me, but I've never been more sure of anything in my life…at least, not since you asked me to marry you." I knew I was cheating, but his silence was making me nervous. I decided to wait until he responded.

So, I waited.

And waited.

Sixty seconds seemed like an eternity. Then, he inhaled.

"I was a jerk. I know that. I had no intention of making you feel like…like you shouldn't pursue your dreams. I was just…scared, I guess. I love our life, and I didn't want it to change, but I didn't consider that, as happy as I am, maybe you aren't as happy…I mean as you could be."

The words coming out of his mouth were more beautiful than anything I'd ever heard in my life. I was dumbstruck, so he kept talking.

"I want you to be happy. And if that means more eating out, and hiring a cleaning lady, then…that's what we'll do."

"And if I fail, and decide next month that I want to take voice lessons and start an 80s band…?"

He turned to me and, in a split second, I was sitting in his lap. His physical strength was such a turn on; I felt that electricity shoot through me again.

"Then, I'll turn the garage into a recording studio and grow a mullet…but you won't fail. You've never failed at anything you really wanted to do." He kissed my forehead.

"Thank you," was all I could say in response, and I meant it with every fiber of my being.

We hadn't just murdered Trevor the Jerk, we had disposed of the body and left no evidence behind. Good riddance.

"I'd say that's…enough talking," I said, with renewed enthusiasm, and pushed Trevor back onto the bed. It was nice when Venus and Mars were in alignment.

▬ ▬ ▬

Trevor decided to take a shower before going to bed, so I snuck downstairs for a little post-coitus snack. I stepped into the dimly lit kitchen, and headed for the fridge. Just as I grabbed the door handle, I noticed Trevor's phone on the counter. The screen was lit up. A text had just come in.

I opened the fridge. Then I closed the fridge, nothing turning my fancy. I finally decided on a whole grain bagel, which I toasted and topped with a generous serving of Nutella…my favorite late-night snack. I was letting the bagel cool, when Trevor's phone vibrated and lit up again. Another text?

I slowly walked over to where his phone was lying, and picked it up. I instantly realized that it wasn't Trevor's phone. At least, not the phone I remembered. My mind raced for a second, but I took a deep breath and told myself he must have just gotten a new one, without me…and for free. Nothing had shown up in our finances, and I was meticulous with our money. So…it must be a new…*work* phone. That was it. I took another deep breath, and grinned at my paranoia.

Silly Freya, making something out of nothing.

I was about to set it down—I wasn't the type to read his texts, especially work-related ones—when something on the lit-up screen caught my eye. It was the number the text had originated from.

Talia's number.

No, that's not right. I looked again, scanning each digit carefully. It was my best friend's number...on my husband's secret phone.

I let out a nervous laugh, feeling the butterflies awaken in the pit of my stomach. I was being paranoid again. Wasn't I? I mean, talk about the oldest cliché in the book.

I moved my eyes to the body of the text and read.

Spoke to AR...has assignment changed? Will continue mission until told otherwise. AM.

EPISODE 9
Distraction

I felt a little nauseated. I read the text again, but that just increased my confusion. I read it a third time, this time dissecting it one word at a time.

Spoke...to...AR...

AR? Who the hell—?

...has...assignment...changed?

Assignment? Since I was certain Trevor and Talia were not taking a Creative Writing course at the community college together, this word birthed several tangent thought streams, none of them good.

Will...continue...mission...

Mission? This did not seem to be a secret love note from a mistress, but then, what exactly was it?

...until...told...otherwise. AM.

AM. Anatalia Mitchell. That was the only part of the message that was easy to figure out, but only on the surface. What the hell was I looking at? It was so formal and encrypted, I couldn't help but think it was...official in some way.

Why was my best friend sending a seemingly official text to my husband, whom she'd barely spent ten minutes with in three years, at 10:30 at night?

My mind reeled. I couldn't form a coherent thought and, within seconds, my brain was so noisy, I slammed my eyes shut in an attempt to quiet it and focus. I suddenly felt a little dizzy, and my nausea increased tenfold. The forgotten bagel still on the counter, I turned and, almost robotically, carried the phone up the stairs, into the master bedroom, and straight through to the master bathroom, where Trevor was toweling off. I walked right up to him. He smiled at me, but his smile waned when he saw what was in my hand.

"You got a text," I said, not recognizing the sound of my own voice.

He dropped the towel on the floor and took his phone from me.

"Thanks," he said hesitantly. He pushed the small button to restore the screen, and was as still as a statue, staring at the text.

Not being one to intentionally prolong my own suffering, I dove headfirst into the pit of hungry crocodiles. "That's Talia's number."

His eyes locked on mine then, first shocked, then confused, but it was…what was it? It was forced. Forced confusion. I wasn't having any of it.

"Explain," I stated.

He set the phone down on the bathroom counter, and quickly slid on his clean boxers. I waited. "It's not Talia's number," he finally replied. But it had come after too long a pause. Too much time to think of a lie.

"Yes. It is."

He shimmied past me and left the bathroom. I watched him put the phone on his dresser. Noticing I hadn't moved—I couldn't—he returned to me, and wrapped both arms around my neck. He stared into my eyes. His were ice blue, and so…sparkly. I felt my anger subside just a tiny bit. Damn him.

"Baby, I promise you, I did not get a text from Talia."

I thought about that word. 'Promise'. I would never use that beautiful word for evil, but I suddenly wasn't sure about this man I had just been intimate with. He had proved time and again in the past weeks that he had a side I hadn't been aware of before. A dark side. I had married Anakin Skywalker, but now he seemed to be turning into Darth Vader.

If I didn't think there was a possibility he was hiding something from me, something big, I would totally be into it.

"I know her number, Trevor. She's my best friend."

He sighed in a slightly condescending way, which elevated my anger back up to Mount Vesuvius level, and released one nervous chuckle. "Sweetie, is it possible you don't really know her number?

I mean, you just select her name in your phone, right? You don't actually dial the number by hand. No one does that anymore."

"That's true," I admitted, "but that doesn't mean I don't know her number."

He grasped my shoulders and tried to penetrate the wall behind my eyes. "Freya, listen to me. That text was from a client of mine. He works with Rip—Adam Michaels. He even mentioned Rip…AR? Agent Ripley." He gently released my shoulders, but continued his assault on my eyes. He smiled. "I have to admit, I do love it when you're jealous. It doesn't happen very often, but it just makes me feel good…like you love me so much, you don't want to share me."

He turned and sauntered back into the bedroom, stopping at his dresser for an old T-shirt. As he pulled it on over his head, he sat on the end of the bed. He seemed so…comfortable. Like a man with nothing to worry about. Not like a man who was hiding a mistress. Or a secret identity. I started to think I had been acting irrational.

"I wasn't accusing you of cheating," I clarified, "the text itself is too business-like." I had to think about this before I continued. "It just didn't make sense. A text like that coming from Talia," I concluded.

"Of course not," he agreed. "Because it didn't come from Talia."

I finally willed my legs to move, and joined him on the end of the bed. He put his arm around me.

"Let's just forget about it, and go to sleep, huh?" he offered. "I know I'm exhausted after…well, you know what you did," he teased, leaning down and kissing my shoulder. His lips left a tingly spot on my skin that lingered for a moment. Did he purposely drag his feet across the carpet before touching me, or was he simply made of electricity?

I just wasn't ready to let it go.

"412-555-8789."

"What?" he asked, his lips so close to my face still, I detected just a hint of garlic from supper on his breath.

"Talia's number."

He sighed, normal this time, and stood up. "Alright, let me put this to rest once and for all." He strode over to his dresser and picked up his phone. He pushed the restore button and read off the screen. "412-555-8987…is that her number?" he asked.

I couldn't believe it. I had gotten it wrong. I had misread the numbers and had created this whole uncomfortable situation in my head. My stupid, overactive imagination. Curse my creative brain.

"I'm so sorry," was all I could say. I blushed with embarrassment. Trevor put the phone down and came back to me.

"Don't be. It's resolved now." He started kissing my shoulder again, and moved to my neck. "You are so sexy when you're jealous…"

Could he really be getting in the mood again so soon? Men.

"Well," I interrupted, "what about the wording? Why is one of your clients using words like 'mission' and 'assignment'?"

"I told you," he said between kisses, which were getting steadily wetter, "he's a friend of Rip's. All those secret agent types talk like that."

Shit. That made perfect sense.

One more thing.

"Is that a new phone?" I asked, trying not to sound accusatory.

"Yeah…company made us all get the exact same one last week… stupid idea…people are already picking up the wrong ones in the restrooms," he said absent-mindedly.

I took a deep breath, and closed my eyes. After shutting down the part of my brain labeled 'Unfounded Paranoia', I turned to face Trevor, who had slid his hand under my sleep shirt and was firmly massaging my breast. Our lips met and I welcomed the current that vibrated through me.

When was the last time this happened?

Shut up, Freya, this gorgeous man wants to pleasure you…again.

Apparently, Venus and Mars were still slow dancing in the sky. God love 'em.

■ ■ ■

The next morning, I was in such a great mood, the whole night before was a blur…except for the really good parts. It was Saturday, so I let the boys sleep in. Trevor had to go in to the office for a few hours, and then he said he could spend the rest of the weekend with us. I just smiled like a good wife, and slapped him in the ass before he stepped out to the garage.

I was enjoying my first cup of almond chai when Talia burst through the back door. I swear, she didn't just walk, she bounced everywhere she went. She subsequently bounced over to the table in the atrium where I was sitting and plopped down in the chair across from me.

"Good morning, Tal," I greeted. "What are you doing here on a Saturday? Shouldn't you still be in bed?" She wasn't a party girl, but she was addicted to Netflix, and tended to have Friday night movie marathons. It was a little sad, because she never wanted company for these extravaganzas, but preferred to be alone with her remote, her Dr. Pepper, and a giant bowl of peanut M&Ms. How she stayed so thin, I'll never know.

"Ha, ha. Very funny," was all she said.

I set my cup down after a long, satisfying draw, and considered her for a moment. "Lars has a class this morning, doesn't he?" I asked. How had I missed the workout garb? It must have been all that bouncing.

She gave me a sheepish grin. She didn't have to say anything.

"Sorry, can't go. The boys are still asleep and Trevor had to work this morning."

"On a Saturday?"

"Just for a few hours, Miss I-don't-have-to-answer-to-anyone-but-myself," I jibed.

She gave me a sour look while she redid her ponytail.

"Stop pouting," I said, feeling like her parent. "You're a big girl. Go to the class by yourself."

"Oh, I intend to," she informed me. Suddenly, her cell phone buzzed and she pulled it out of her hoodie pocket. I noticed something was different.

"Did you get a new case?" I asked, suddenly having flashbacks of the night before.

"I got a new phone, duh. Remember, I dropped my old one in the parking lot last week and it dumped all my contacts?" I vaguely remembered something about Talia dropping her phone, but didn't recall it warranting getting a new one.

"Oh yeah," I said leadingly, hoping she would give me more information. She didn't disappoint.

"I told you this, didn't I?" she inquired as her fingers became a blur, replying to the text that had caused the initial buzzing. "I took it to the place where I bought it, and they couldn't retrieve my contacts, so they said I could get a new one because I'd bought the insurance— thank you for making me do that, by the way..." she strayed, glancing up at me.

I nodded and she returned her gaze to the tiny screen in front of her.

"...anyway, I decided to get a new number too, because of that creep I met at that speed dating fiasco last month...you know, the one who called me, like, ten times in one hour?" She shuddered at the memory. Now *that* rang a bell.

She finished her reply text, and put her phone back in her pocket. She looked up at me and smiled, then cocked her head in question.

"Didn't I tell you about that?"

I squinted as if to say I wasn't sure. I realized I hadn't tried to call or text her in over a week. She was always just a few steps away, if I needed her. I didn't require technology to contact someone who lived practically in my backyard, and who rarely left her house.

I felt even sillier about my suspicions of Trevor the previous night. Even if Talia had texted him, which I was 110% sure she hadn't, I wouldn't have recognized the number in the first place.

Oddly, however, I was glad that I had accused Trevor when the alternative might have been ignorant bliss. I refused to be one of those clueless wives. I preferred informed bliss.

Suddenly, my phone rang behind me on the kitchen counter... Rip's ringtone. I stood and took two giant steps to retrieve it, hitting the answer button just as Jack Black was starting the chorus of "Tribute." It was Rip's favorite song, and it always made me smile when I heard it.

"Hello, good lookin'!" I said, more enthusiastically than I intended.

"Hey, beautiful. You're in a good mood this morning," he commented. "Well, I'm about to make it even better. Your clearance came through. You start Phase 2 on Monday."

EPISODE 10
Kill Shot

Monday morning had finally come. I reported to the same classroom where I'd spent two weeks before, sitting in the same uncomfortable chair, staring at the same computer screen. The room was empty, save the dozen computers occupying the perimeter.

I went back out to the registration desk, and the same short, stout agent was there. I asked again if he was absolutely sure I was in the right place. He gave a frustrated and blatantly condescending sigh, and nodded, peering at me over the rim of his glasses.

What was this little man's problem?

Just before I turned around, I gently grasped his vibrant teal-green tie in my hand—I think I heard him swallow hard—and said, "By the way, this color is incredibly sexy…matches your eyes." Then I winked and left him standing there, staring at his tie.

As I spun on my heels to return to the classroom, Agent Moss was there, her arms folded across her chest, and a smirk on her face. I froze and stared at her, wondering what she was thinking. Her hands dropped to her hips.

"Trainee Douglas, I'm here to take you to your small arms training."

Small arms training. Sounds fun.

She waved her hand for me to follow, and I fell in step next to her. We hadn't gone ten feet when she said, just above a whisper, "I'm impressed. You had quite an effect on him. I don't think Agent Biggs has smiled since he lost his tongue."

As I walked, I looked quickly behind me to see the short agent blushing and grinning after me. I returned his smile, happy that I had made his day.

Then I realized what Moss had just said. Suddenly, I was horrified. I stopped walking and stared at her in disbelief.

"What?"

She pulled me along, and my legs managed to move, although I hadn't instructed them to. "He was undercover. Deep in the mafia scene. Some moron blew his cover, and Tony the Moose had one of his goons cut out Biggs' tongue. A subtle message for the FBI."

Holy Shit.

"Holy shit," I decided to share. My mind raced. We were still walking.

Where was this small arms training, anyway? Tony the Moose? Was Al Pacino in that one? Was his sidekick a squirrel? Cutting out someone's tongue was considered subtle*?*

Agent Moss chuckled. "Having second thoughts?"

Oh, hell no. She wasn't going to scare me away that easily.

We stopped at the elevators and Moss pushed the button. They both immediately opened and I followed her into the left-most doors. Once inside, she again took charge and pushed the button labeled 'B'.

The basement.

By the time the doors opened to the sub-level, I had more or less recovered from the horrors of Tony the Moose and Agent Biggs' lack of tongue, but I was sure they would both show up in my dreams that night. I took a deep breath and straightened my blouse. I didn't have time for distraction.

I was about to hold a gun for the first time.

The indoor shooting range was pretty much what I expected. I guess I had seen so many of them on TV, it was almost…familiar.

Agent Moss walked me over to the front desk, where a very tall, skinny gentlemen—I didn't assume he was an agent, due to the fact that he was wearing a Halo T-shirt and wore his hair to his shoulders—scanned her badge and had her sign in on the futuristic computer screen that was recessed into the countertop. Well, it looked futuristic to me.

Before we proceeded through the doors, she smiled at the gamer geek and pointed to his shirt. "You know, I like your Skyrim shirt better."

He grinned and looked down at his shirt, as if he'd forgotten which one he was wearing. I imagined his collection of gamer T-shirts to be vast. "Dragons? Really?" he teased her.

Her face contorted to mock anger. "Dragons are cool!" She poked him in the chest.

He put his hands in the air, pretending her finger was a gun. "Hey, hey, put that thing away! I'll wear Skyrim tomorrow, I promise!"

She backed off and started laughing.

He just shook his head. "Agent Moss, you are a geek in agent's clothing," he informed her.

"You say the sweetest things, Johnny."

Although I was enjoying this little exchange, I was anxious to get in there and see what I could do with a firearm. I hadn't realized I was actually bouncing up and down on my heels ever so slightly, like a child waiting for her turn on the swing.

Moss noticed.

"Alright, Douglas, don't pee yourself. We're going."

Once we both had our protective goggles and ear plugs in place, Agent Moss walked me over to the third lane and set a 10-cartridge magazine on the counter. Then she gently placed the 9mm handgun next to it. It was beautiful.

Just then, something occurred to me.

"Don't I need to take some kind of gun safety course before I actually handle a real gun?"

Agent Moss nodded. "Yes. I'm going to give you the short, short version of Gun Safety 101 right now, so listen up."

I straightened up and gave her my full attention. So far, I liked the fast-paced training of Phase 2.

She picked up the gun and started pointing to parts of it, as I attempted to commit it all to instant memory. "This is the barrel... the chamber...the safety...the trigger..." she rattled off. Then, she picked up the magazine. "The magazine goes..." she started, as she popped it into place, "right in here like this."

I heard it click.

"Then you disengage the safety," she motioned, but didn't actually do it, "and...just point and shoot. Pretty easy, really."

She handed the gun to me, all the while pointing the barrel away from us and downrange.

I felt the weight of it in my hands. It felt good. A wave of heat swept over me.

Without thinking, I whispered, "Hello, baby."

Why did I say that? I suddenly felt a tingle replace the heat wave, and shivered.

Moss grinned at my intimate comment toward the deadly weapon. "Nice," she said, nodding slightly and chuckling under her breath.

A gentleman had claimed the adjoining lane and was now shooting sporadically, so Agent Moss had to raise her voice to be heard.

"Never point it anywhere but at your intended target," she yelled, "and you can't let the end of your barrel go past this line." She pointed at a red line drawn on the small counter and up the sides of the cubicle we were in.

Something told me that I already knew that. I must watch way too many cop shows.

"That's called the Firing Line," she continued.

Uh-huh. Knew that too.

I stood there, motionless, for a second, waiting for her next instruction. When none came, I glanced at her, raising my eyebrows.

She raised her eyebrows back, and motioned for me to go ahead.

I smiled and took a deep breath. After flipping the safety off, I raised the gun to eye-level and instantly found the sight and my target at the far end of the lane—a paper silhouette of a human form.

You'd better run, dude.

I was already taking another slow breath and preparing to shoot on my exhale, when Moss yelled, "Always shoot on your exhale... it's when you're the most steady."

I applied the slightest amount of pressure to the trigger, exhilarated at what I was about to do. More pressure. More. Just a tiny bit more. The world around me faded, and all sound muffled to near silence.

Breathe in slowly...it was just me and my gun...and my target... exhale, and...

"Oh, and just discharge one at a time, so we can assess each—"

The world returned, and I was still staring at my target. A tendril of smoke was creeping out of the barrel of my gun, and the handle felt warm.

I remembered to breathe.

I turned to Moss, who was focusing down range, her mouth hanging open like she had been saying something, but had been cut short. Her eyes were wide with shock.

Had she been saying something? I couldn't remember.

That's when I realized the entire range was quiet. So quiet, it was unsettling. Where had everyone gone? I leaned back to check the other stalls, and there were still three or four others there, but now, they were all leaning back in their stalls staring at me with disbelief.

Crap. What did I do?

Something stupid, I was sure.

I gently laid the gun down, and wiped my sweaty hands on my pants. I looked up nervously at Agent Moss. Might as well face the music now.

"Okay, what did I do?"

Moss blinked a few times, and then turned to me. "You fired your entire magazine. Did you do that on purpose?" she asked.

"I did?" I picked up the gun and popped out the clip. Empty. Huh. I didn't remember pulling the trigger more than—wait, I couldn't remember pulling the trigger at all.

Must be all the adrenaline pumping through me.

"You…you said you'd never shot a gun before, right?"

"Never. Never even *held* a real one," I replied.

She didn't respond, but pushed a red button on the wall of the cubicle that I hadn't noticed before, yet I instinctively knew it was to bring the target closer so you could count your hits.

I really needed to stop watching all those *Law & Order* reruns.

As the target neared, I saw one, and only one, hole.

Damn.

It was smack in the middle of the silhouette's head, though. That had to count for something. Right?

The paper victim stopped moving about a foot from us, and Moss reached up and pulled it off the metal hook. She scrutinized the head wound for a second.

"So, I got one good shot in, right?" I asked, laughing nervously.

She put two fingers through the hole my bullet had made, but still didn't speak.

Exactly how bad was it? I couldn't possibly be the only trainee to hit the target just once. I went from nervous to frustrated in a split second. She was overreacting. Was she trying to make me think I'd done something wrong just to mess with me? Was the whole range in on it?

I was hoping my age and sheer life experience would garner me a little respect, but I guess I was going to be treated like any other newbie. So be it. I could handle it.

Finally, Moss sighed, and spoke, but still apparently pretending to be in a state of mild shock. "You hit the target more than once."

"I did?" That was a relief. I leaned over the target and tried to find another hole, but couldn't. "I don't see any other holes," I informed her.

"They all went through *this* hole," she said, motioning to her finger poking through the head shot.

Intrigued, I stared at the hole, and tried to figure out how in the world anyone could tell exactly how many bullets had gone through the same contact point. Glad that wasn't *my* job.

"*This* hole..." Agent Moss said, thinking hard before she continued, "this hole was made by all ten of your rounds."

What?

"You not only hit the target, Douglas. You got an identical kill shot...ten times."

EPISODE 11
Secrets

I walked into the secure office without knocking, and with an unusual sense of urgency. The bastards had started without me.

As the door opened, I caught bits and pieces of the conversation already taking place.

"…twenty years…assigned to watch her…"

"…Moss's report…small arms…off the chart…"

"…incredible…she has no idea...no memory…all these years…"

As I entered, the three men turned, ceasing their conversation. Trevor looked angry more than anything else to see me there. The other two, Agent Hart, who I knew to be a trustworthy and seasoned old dog, and Director Pixley, both nodded a silent greeting. Hart handed some paperwork to the Director, who tucked it under his arm. And here I thought I was fifteen minutes early.

"Agent Ripley," Pixley greeted me, "I have a 2:30, so we started right away. Douglas said he texted you."

I nodded in frustration. Oh, he had texted me alright. Thirty seconds before I had burst through the door, which, I realized, was becoming a habit with Trevor and me. I was still out of breath from sprinting to his office.

Pixley was the kind of man who could decide on a whim to put any one of us on patrol duty at the local mall, just for fun, so I didn't quibble about the late text. He hated whiners.

"Douglas was just filling me in on the situation we have here," Pixley said.

Was he? How reassuring. I remained silent, waiting for a hint that it was my turn to speak.

Pixley continued. "He says his wife is now an agent trainee, due to your manipulation of government policy and resources."

He says WHAT? Why I ever wanted to step in front of a bullet for this guy was beyond me. After glaring at Trevor, I responded in the calmest voice I could muster.

"Sir, I assure you, Freya—I mean Trainee Douglas—checked all the required boxes to get this far. Her security clearance even came through last week with no issues."

Trevor was suddenly in my face, pointing a finger into my chest. "No issues!? You called a buddy at the State Department and her clearance was magically approved! Explain that, Agent Ripley!"

I guess we were no longer on a first-name basis. I could point a finger too. "*You* were trying to keep it from getting *to* the State Department! Explain *that,* Agent Douglas!"

His finger pointing turned into outright shoving with his whole hand. "I was trying to save her from being humiliated when she fails! Because I love her!"

"If you loved her, you'd let her do this! Someone has to support her!"

This stopped him in his tracks for a second while he gathered his thoughts. How could he think she would fail? It just didn't make sense to me.

Just then, Director Pixley stepped between us and pointed to two chairs. We sat reluctantly, still fuming at each other.

Pixley perched himself on the edge of Trevor's desk, and sighed like a disappointed father. "I don't know what kind of triangle you boys have going here, but I don't like it." He scratched his bald head. "Now, Agent Douglas, if your wife being a trainee—and possibly an agent—is going to affect your ability to do your job... both of you," he pointed at each of us accusingly, "then normally, I wouldn't see any other option but to cut her FBI career short, right here and now."

I started to protest, but he cut me off.

"However, in light of the information I've learned today, I think it might be...in the FBI's best interest to...keep Mrs. Douglas under close surveillance. And what better way than to make her an agent?"

Information? What information? What exactly had they been talking about before I entered the room? It got even more confusing when Trevor spoke up.

"Director, you can't be serious? I *live* with her. What better surveillance is there than that? I've been on this assignment for almost twenty—"

"Yes, but you're here all day, aren't you? Working as a full-time agent all this time, as if you didn't have a Priority One assignment at home. You should have briefed me on this last year when I took this position and became your boss. Seems to me you *haven't* been doing your job." Director Pixley folded his arms across his chest and scrutinized Trevor with superior eyes.

Trevor was stunned. Nothing offended him more than being told he wasn't succeeding in something. And even my total confusion at the whole conversation couldn't squelch my satisfaction of watching him being knocked off his throne. I grinned for a second until I realized I was being left out of something. Something big.

"Sir, what information are you referring to?" I demanded.

He didn't seem concerned with my tone, although it bordered on insubordination. "Agent Ripley, since you weren't privy to it when it was prudent, I don't have the authorization to bring you into the loop. I'm sorry." And he did seem sincerely sorry he couldn't tell me.

Okay, what the HELL is going on?

"Sir, I don't understand—" I stammered, but he stood and put his hand up to stop me.

"That's all the time I have, gentlemen. See to it Trainee Douglas makes it through the program as quickly as possible. I want her a full-fledged agent within three months."

And with that, Pixley abruptly walked toward the door. He stopped a few feet from the exit and turned to us.

"You two are going to have to leave your differences in your pants, or I'll have you both reassigned to Antarctica…together…just the two of you. Do I make myself clear?"

Although I was sure we didn't have an FBI office anywhere in Antarctica, I didn't doubt he could make that happen.

We both nodded vehemently.

Pixley opened the door and was gone, Hart following close behind. I turned to Trevor. His face was red and his eyes furious. The fact that we'd had a major falling out no longer mattered. I needed answers, and clearly, he had them. But we both needed to calm down first.

"Trevor," I said, my voice even, "what the hell is going on?"

He closed his eyes and released a heavy sigh. When he opened them, his anger seemed to have faded, giving way to...sadness. I didn't push him to answer me right away.

He walked over to the big leather chair behind his desk and slowly sat. Then he looked up at me and smiled. "Rip," he began, measuring every word, "this was never supposed to happen."

"What was?"

"Freya. Wanting to join the FBI. Shit." He took a deep breath and blew it out like he was in pain. "Becoming an agent."

I sat down in one of the chairs in front of his desk, and let him regain his composure. Maybe if I didn't say a word, he would accidentally tell me everything. I could dream.

"You know, I blame you for all this," he said, but chuckled lightly under his breath.

Me? Still, I didn't respond.

Elaborate, Trevor...that's it, keep talking.

"If you hadn't been around all these years, making it sound so exciting to be an FBI agent, and...and making her remember..."

"Remember what?" I asked, seriously considering the possibility that I had walked through a dimensional crack and straight into Bizarro World.

He shook his head as if to sort out the thoughts rolling around in it. "You brought up that stupid jobs fair back in college, when she applied to the FBI," he reminded me.

"So, you're blaming me for something that's been going on for twenty years, because I brought up a long-forgotten dream of hers just a few weeks ago?"

"She was never supposed to remember any of it. The procedure was tricky, but...it should have been permanent amnesia..." he uttered, barely above a whisper. I think he'd forgotten I was there.

"Trevor, what are you talking about?" I asked. "I've known Freya longer than you have. She's never had amnesia...Trevor!" I pounded my fist on his desk and he snapped out of his hypnosis, looking at me with renewed intensity—almost fear.

"Rip, if anything happens to Freya and me, you have to take care of the boys." He grabbed my wrist and squeezed so hard, my fingers went numb for a second.

"Trevor, tell me what's going on! Is Freya in danger? Are you in danger? The boys? Please, tell me!"

He grabbed both my wrists. "Promise me!"

"Of course...of course, Trevor...Jesus! I'm their Godfather! I won't let anything happen to them, I promise."

I was really freaking out now. I had come in here not ten minutes ago, pissed at Trevor, and absolutely positive I was right about... well, everything. All of a sudden, I wasn't sure I was even on the right planet. I didn't even know who the hell this guy was sitting across from me, and I had once known him better than I knew myself.

Trevor was holding his head in his hands now, muttering to himself. He had really lost it. I knew I wasn't going to get anything else out of him, at least not today. Whatever was going on was really messing with his head and, for a split second, I was thankful that I was clueless.

What do I do now?

I stood to leave Trevor to his breakdown, when it hit me like a lightning bolt. I was so dizzy, I had to sit back down.

There were two things I *did* know.

The first, thanks to Director Pixley, was that Freya was going to be an FBI agent, and sooner than I, or even she, ever dreamed.

Second, thanks to Trevor's reaction, I suddenly knew I had to protect her. In fact, the energy that coursed through my veins confirmed that this was my new mission, assigned or not.

I didn't know why, or from what, but that didn't matter.

I had to protect the woman I love.

EPISODE 12
Memories

My first assignment. I couldn't believe it. The last three months had gone so fast, it was almost a blur...almost. Since the day I had apparently, in the words of my fourteen-year-old son, Levi, "*owned the firing range*," I had been treated like some sort of prodigy. From then on, I had had one-on-one training, mostly with Agent Moss, or Agent Ripley—which is what I had to remember to call him when we were on duty. He seemed to hover even when he wasn't my instructor for the day.

It had been intense. Like nothing else I had ever done...except maybe childbirth. That was the only thing I'd done in my life that I could compare it to. It was like being in active labor for nearly three months straight...but with an epidural...an epidural turned way down so I could still feel the pain.

Every morning began with hand-to-hand combat training with an incredibly intimidating, and experienced, agent named Hart. He had a deep, raspy voice that sounded like Darth Vader with a sore throat. It was kind of sexy. He didn't intimidate *me,* but I made him think he did for the first week or so. I could tell it was important to him, so I went with it. He prided himself on coming off as tough and unrefined, and I really liked him. Maybe because he was so different from the people in my previous life...that life where the highlight of my week had been the sometimes heated coupon exchange at Lucy Pevler's house.

That seemed so far away now.

Trevor had made it clear, however, that he did not like Agent Hart, especially after I came home with my third injury. I assured him I was just fine, and that I was glad they weren't treating me like a baby, or worse, an old woman. I could handle Agent Hart and the training, and I was going to prove it, no matter how many bruises and sprains I got.

Hart was amazingly fit, and whipped me into shape faster than I was sure Lars even could.

Lars. *Talia.*

I'd been standing for a long time. I shifted my weight to my other foot, and wondered how they were doing. Their first lunch date had gone well, if a little awkward according to Talia, as most first dates are, and they were seeing each other on a regular basis now. I hadn't had a chance to talk to Talia in a few days, and I realized I missed her.

I chuckled softly. It struck me funny that I was thinking of her at a time like this.

I stood under a rarely-used bridge out in the middle of nowhere, waiting. I was almost a bona fide FBI agent. This was the last box to check. My first real assignment.

It was a benign exchange with a long-time FBI informant, so the danger level was next to nothing. The biggest risk, I mused to myself, was probably being hit by a meteorite, as the bridge was the only structure I could see for miles in every direction. Of course, if I had to wait much longer, I was in danger of becoming dehydrated…okay, maybe just thirsty, but it was a concern. Just then, my stomach made a low, rumbling sound. Great. My Nutella bagel was long digested, and it was nearly lunch time.

I took a deep, cleansing breath.

Relax, Freya. FBI agents don't bitch about being hungry or thirsty. Stay focused.

I reached down and grasped the handle of the firearm holstered to my hip. It felt heavy and reassuring, like an old friend. It made me feel confident and strong, even though Rip had made me give him my magazine before we got out of the car, saying it was important to get used to the feel of just the gun on my body first.

I knew that was a bunch of crap. He was clearly nervous about giving me a loaded weapon.

Rip was standing just ten feet away, hidden by the supports of the old, crumbling bridge, but ready to spring into action and save the damsel in distress—me—if need be, so the weapon strapped to my personage was strictly a self-esteem booster at the moment.

I was a little nervous, I admit, but just enough to heighten my senses. I listened to the silence around me, only to realize it was anything but. A dragonfly buzzed by my left ear. A small patch of tall grass that had survived in the shade of the bridge rustled in the breeze. A hawk screeched far above my head, looking for its lunch.

Lunch. There was that rumbling in my gut again.

Where the hell is this informant? He has no respect for other people's schedules.

A voice behind me made my heart skip a beat.

"Is that your stomach?" Rip said, clearly amused at my bodily noises.

I closed my eyes and willed my pulse to normalize. "Shhhh…" I replied, "I'm trying to commune with nature."

He giggled. "Yeah? Well, I think your stomach scared all the nature away."

"You don't have anything to eat, do you?" I asked, seriously considering the grass at my feet as a possible snack.

"I'm sorry, Agent Douglas, I must have forgotten your treat bag. I thought I was your handler on this assignment, not your nanny."

"Wait, you're my *what*?" I asked, not liking the sound of the word 'handler'.

"Handler. It means—" he tried to explain, but I didn't need the definition. I watched TV.

"I know what it means. Can't we just say 'partner'?"

He didn't respond right away, but I thought I heard him intake a sudden breath.

"If that makes you feel more important," he finally said.

I turned toward where he was concealed, feigning shock and anger. "Oh, so being Mr. Big Super Secret Agent Ty Ripley's partner is such an honor, that I can only pretend to be your equal?"

All I heard was a snort from Rip's hiding place.

I smiled and leaned against the bridge, having resisted the urge up until that moment because I didn't want to get my new kick-ass jacket dirty. I may be the new-and-improved Freya, but I was still me, after all. I crossed my arms and inhaled. It had been a while since I had been outdoors and just...been. I let my breath out slowly. It was a beautiful day.

My next question left my mouth before I had given it permission to. "So, what does a girl have to do to earn such an honor, your majesty?"

Suddenly, he was next to me, leaning against the bridge. I nearly jumped out of my skin.

"How the hell do you do that?" I asked, when my feet were back on solid ground. I was standing in front of him now, delivering my best incredulous face.

He just smiled. "Years of practice, my dear."

Agent Ty Ripley needed to be taught a little lesson. And I was free at the moment. I gave him a little shove right between his pectorals.

He cocked his head and raised an eyebrow at me, his eyes playful. He gave me a gentle shove back.

I pushed him, harder this time, on the shoulder.

He raised both hands and pushed *both* my shoulders, and I staggered backward slightly. He grinned mischievously, stood upright, and straightened his sport coat, ready for my retaliation.

I made a big production about pushing up my jacket sleeves, and ensuring my sunglasses were straight, before I made my move.

He set his feet shoulder-width apart and motioned for me to come forward.

I chuckled, and stepped forward, effortlessly pulling my useless firearm from its holster and pointing the barrel directly between his eyes.

He froze for a split second, looking shocked that I would do such a thing. Then, he relaxed and started laughing.

I gave him my 'I win' smile, and he put his arms in the air in mock surrender.

"Okay, I give," he laughed.

Just as I was relaxing my gun arm, he brought the back of his hand around in a blur and knocked the pistol out of my hand. I watched it hit the dirt and slide away from me, coming to a stop about ten feet from us. Before I could protest, he grabbed my right arm and attempted to spin me around and immobilize me, but, thanks to my sparring buddy, Agent Hart, I knew how to thwart that move.

I tried to take a step backward, but my foot hit a softball-sized rock buried in the ground. I immediately lost my balance and realized I was going down, and I couldn't stop it. Panicking, I grabbed Rip's free arm, and took him with me. I tried to control my fall, but our arms were wrapped around each other's like a pretzel, and the half a second we had until impact was not enough time to untangle them. I hit hard, my tailbone taking the brunt, and then Rip landed full-force on top of me.

We lay there, panting for a few seconds. Rip raised his head off my shoulder, and his eyes found mine. He looked worried.

"Are you hurt?" he questioned, his tone anxious.

"Yes, jackass!" I responded, irritated. I was sure my jacket was ruined after that.

I waited for him to move…to get off of me, but…

I looked into his eyes, about to order him to let me up, but his expression caught me off guard. He was staring so intently at me, that I had an instant flashback of the first time he had been on top of me like this…well, minus the bruised tailbone. It felt like a hundred years ago. My anger subsided and I found myself unable to resist returning his gaze.

He was so wonderful…sexy…trouble…familiar…*trouble*… sweet…sexy…did I already say that? He was leaning in for the kill, and my good wife instinct should have stopped him in his tracks, but suddenly, I had been transported to twenty-two years earlier.

▬ ▬ ▬

Rip and I had been friends our entire freshman year in college, and had finally taken the leap to being 'an item' during the summer before our sophomore year. It was the day before classes were going to start up again, and we had gone to the park for an old-fashioned picnic lunch. One thing led to another and, in no time, we had abandoned the food and were engaged in a pretty awesome make-out session. The fact that the park was practically deserted and that we had purposely searched for a spot that was secluded and not in view of any of the walkways, was a plus. We laughed at the possibility of our first time happening in such a public place, but it was a perfect afternoon, and it had all felt so right, him and me.

I lay down on the grass next to the trunk of the huge oak we had camped under, and Rip slowly climbed on top of me. I could feel his hardness through his button-fly jeans, and felt a delicious tingle travel through my entire body in response to it.

Although we had been kissing pretty hot and heavy for about ten minutes already, something about that first, slow-motion contact while peering into each other's souls was otherworldly. I was instantly so aroused, I was annoyed that we were still clothed, and it seemed to have the same effect on Rip.

He began to work his body into every nook and cranny of mine, shifting and arching until it felt as though there was nothing between us, not even a molecule of air. His lips were so intoxicating; I didn't want them to leave mine, until they began to travel down my neck.

I wanted to touch every inch of him. I let my hand travel down his back. He turned his hips slightly, and I slid my hand between us. As I undid the buttons of his pants one at a time, he lifted my shirt. He began unhooking my bra, when—

A car came barreling down the hill toward us. It screeched to a halt just a few feet away from our horizontal forms, and suddenly, we were choking on the cloud of dust kicked up by its tires. I heard four car doors slam, and four figures came into view. They were all armed.

Wait. That didn't happen. Rip and I made love under that tree, without interruption. It was one of my favorite memories. I often referred to it when Trevor wanted to be intimate and I wasn't in the mood. It worked every time. I loved having sex with my husband, but in almost twenty years, he had yet to beat that perfect afternoon with Rip under the oak tree.

So, what the hell was happening?

The blood pumping through my veins was so disorienting, I felt dizzy. My vision went fuzzy, then black, and my heart raced. I blinked hard several times, trying desperately to see. I couldn't feel Rip on top of me anymore, but I was sure I was still on the ground, half sitting up now.

Where was he?

Then a tunnel of light appeared and, after a few seconds, I could make out the four forms in front of me again. I was relieved at this, until—

Someone laughed. I didn't recognize the voice, but it wasn't friendly.

My vision was gradually getting crisper, and I located Rip, still on the ground next to me, looking just as stunned as I felt. We were back at the deserted bridge, where we were supposed to be waiting for someone...

He turned to me, and I instantly knew he was confused and scared, which made me even more terrified.

If Rip was afraid, then we were in deep shit.

The smallest of the four men—yes, I confirmed, they were all men—holstered the pistol he was carrying and walked toward us. The other three kept their weapons trained on Rip and me. Neither one of us moved.

"Looks like we interrupted something, boys!" the little man joked. He approached me and squatted down, grabbing my chin and forcing me to look at him. He would have been a good looking guy, if it wasn't for that evil glint in his gaze.

Rip moved to stand, but the other three men simultaneously cocked their pistols and refocused their sights on him. He sat back down in the dirt.

Why isn't he pulling his gun?

"Hey darlin'...looked like your boyfriend was having a little trouble undoing your bra...maybe I can help," offered the tiny demon. He reached up to touch the front hook of my bra, and I flinched and slapped his hand away.

That's when I noticed my blouse was unbuttoned, and my bra was half undone. Horrified, I put myself back together, then looked over at Rip, scrutinizing his appearance. His shirt was unbuttoned as well, and so were his jeans, although there was only one button, not five.

My reality started to mix with the memory, and I felt dizzy again. *Oh my God. What had we been doing?*

The small man was laughing at me, standing over me now, with his hands on his hips.

"Who the hell are you?" Rip asked roughly. I was so relieved he had finally joined the party. Maybe we had a chance of getting out of this after all.

The little leader wasn't as amused with Rip as he seemed to be with me. "Oh, we know you were expecting Leon...your snitch." He sauntered over to Rip and kicked dirt in his face with his steel-toed boot. Rip recoiled and didn't look up at the bully. I was losing confidence in his ability to rescue me, and fast.

"Leon isn't gonna be your snitch anymore, cop!" he continued. Something struck him as funny then, and he said, "He isn't gonna be anyone's snitch, is he boys?"

They all laughed on cue.

Then he motioned for the other men to get us to our feet as he backed away. The biggest of the four thrust me to a standing position and held me there, while the other two each took an arm and pulled Rip up.

The leader walked right back up to Rip, standing on his tiptoes and still having to crane his neck to make eye contact, and pulled a gun. He casually pointed it at Rip's head. "We're taking your girlfriend," he said, watching Rip's eyes fill with panic. That seemed to satisfy the man's evil desires, and also appeared to give him an idea.

"You're gonna hafta finish what she was doing to you," he gestured down toward Rip's groin, "all by yourself, big guy...but you're probably used to that, aren't ya?" He rested his gun hand on Rip's shoulder and put his other hand on my shoulder, pushing us to turn and face each other.

"Now, kiss her goodbye," he said, and laughed as he walked back to the car.

The goons pushed us together so our faces were inches apart. Rip still seemed very out of it, like he'd been in a coma and was just waking up. He searched my eyes, and I knew he was desperate to find a way to save me.

I tried to tell him that I would be okay…that I didn't need him to save me…that I was the Goddess Freya with some seriously mad skills and I would stay alive…but I couldn't even convince myself of any of that. My eyes started to water, and I was powerless to keep a tear from rolling down my cheek. I swallowed hard, and whispered the one thing I knew I had to say, just in case I never saw this beautiful man again.

"I love you."

My words seemed to hurt him, and as the lackeys carried me to the car and shoved me between them in the back seat, I couldn't erase the pain in his eyes from my mind.

As the car careened down the dirt road, farther and farther away from Rip, my thoughts turned to my children.

EPISODE 13
Confusion

Why hadn't I told her? The woman I lived and breathed for had just told me she loved me, and all I could do was cringe…not with disgust, but with the pain that now, just when I might get the chance to make her happy, I was losing her.

I could still feel the heat of her body beneath me. The past ten minutes seemed like a dream…first a dream, then a nightmare.

I watched, helpless, as the car sped away, getting lost in its own cloud of dust.

I had failed.

As I sat on the ground, covered in the same dust, my mind was still swimming, as if I'd been drugged. I didn't understand what had happened. Freya and I had been screwing around when, admittedly, we should have been paying attention to our surroundings, but Leon was late, and since that was a common occurrence, I wasn't concerned. He had been my most reliable inside source for four years.

I guess my number two source had just been promoted.

I shook my head and tried to stand…nope, not yet. I pushed the wave of nausea away. I needed to focus.

One minute, we were horsing around like two colleagues, and then I had inadvertently made her fall…I was still pissed at myself for that mishap. I was so worried I had hurt her, but she always proved to be tougher than I gave her credit for. When I realized she was okay, I meant to get up, get off of her so she could stand and assess the damage. I knew she would be homicidal if her new jacket had received so much as a smudge…damn, she looked good in that jacket.

Then, all of a sudden…

I could still see the memory I had been transported to…that day in the park, under the oak. I had dreamt about that day nearly every night since—well, I couldn't pinpoint when the dreams started, but they tortured me on a regular basis.

But this time, it wasn't a dream…it had seemed so real…felt so real. I was twenty-three again, and about to make love to the woman of my dreams, in a surreally beautiful setting, when the car—wait. We *had* made love that day. The car had been in the present, not the past. The car had snapped me—us—out of our…

Jesus.

I knew something strange was going on here. It hadn't been just a little trip down memory lane. Freya and I had both experienced it, of that I was certain, based on the way she had so easily started caressing and undressing me. We were literally reliving our first time, and if we hadn't been interrupted, we would have—

My pulse quickened.

I have to get out of here.

I quickly buttoned my shirt and my pants, took a deep breath and held it. Slowly, I stood, eyes closed. When I was fairly sure I wouldn't hurl, I started back toward the car on the other side of the bridge, concealed by a gentle slope in the terrain. As my mind cleared and stomach settled, I broke into a run. I skidded into the driver's side door, and got in as quickly as I could.

I began to sort it all out in my head while I drove like a bat out of hell. There was no sense in trying to chase after them, as there were a dozen different routes out of here and back to the city, and they had a good ten minutes head start. The goons who took Freya were just kids, and if they wanted her dead, they would have taken care of her right then and there, and then killed me. I was sure they were acting under orders, working for someone who wanted an agent alive for— what? Collateral? A trade? Whatever the reason, I was sure I had at least twenty-four hours to find her before—

Don't think about that.

I knew every gang and 'unsanctioned organization' in the state, and I'd gotten the midget's license plate number. I would find her.

What made me nervous was the recent revelation that I didn't know everything about Freya's past. I didn't know why she was so special— well, I knew why she was special to me, but why had the FBI been watching her for two decades? I had put the question together from the conversation that had been taking place when I entered Trevor's office for that fateful meeting three months ago, but I still had no answer.

Ever since her mysterious stellar performance at the shooting range, and my orders to accelerate her training, I had stopped trying to get answers from Trevor. I attempted several times to get something, anything, out of the FBI database, but it just led me to one dead end after another. She definitely had an old file, but there was nothing in it but her name and date of birth. Why keep her in the system? It definitely raised more questions than it answered.

Desperate for information, and keeping all the Hollywood versions of the lives of FBI agents out of the running, I spent every waking moment trying to decipher what Freya could have possibly done twenty years ago, presumably while we were dating, to deserve so much attention.

I was sure the little man and his 'peeps' had no idea who she was, and as I sped through the city streets, nearing the FBI building downtown, I discerned one thing. Freya was either more dangerous, or *in* more danger than even her kidnappers realized. I prayed for the former, imagining that she was a Cylon who would be activated before the unsuspecting boys arrived at their destination, but I feared the latter, and that whoever was threatened by her existence these past twenty years was the kind of person, or persons, who could snuff us all out with the snap of his, or her, or *their*, fingers.

I parked and raced into the building, calling the last person I wanted to talk to at that moment, but the only one who would understand the urgency of the situation, on every level. He answered on the first ring.

"What?" he asked, annoyed. I couldn't get used to *not* being friends with this guy.

"Trevor, Freya's been taken," I said, my voice shaky. "I'm walking in right now."

A true professional agent, he immediately pushed his personal feelings aside—I was just imagining this of course—and replied.

"Come straight to my office."

▬ ▬ ▬

When I walked in, Trevor was standing behind his desk, loading his pistol. I got the feeling I suddenly had a new partner.

"What happened?" he asked, not looking up.

I walked over to his desk, but remained standing. I couldn't sit. Sitting meant I wasn't actively looking for Freya, and I wouldn't sit until she was found. Not until she was safe in my arms…

Shit, what was I thinking? She was still a married woman.

But she loved me. I would hold on to that, and figure out the rest later.

I leaned on Trevor's desk with both hands and filled him in. I told him everything, except her last words to me. That part was only for me, and wouldn't help find her anyway.

I don't know why I told him everything else. Maybe I wanted to see his face when I told him his wife had very much wanted to get my clothes off. Maybe I knew I would have to tell him eventually. How else could I explain why I let these creeps take her without a fight?

Trevor was now frozen in place, staring at me with blank eyes. I could tell he was processing it all, just as I still was, but I couldn't tell whether or not he was contemplating using one of the fresh bullets in his firearm on me. I waited for him to respond, but not long before I pressed, "Say something."

He breathed and looked down at his gun again. He shook his head and laughed. "What do you want me to say? Congratulations?" He finished loading the gun and thrust it into the holster already secured to his waist.

He looked up at me. "She's still *my* wife."

I closed my eyes and tried to focus. "Trevor, you don't understand. Something…happened…to us. We didn't intend to…do…what we did…it was like…a vivid flashback, but even more real." I found his eyes and pleaded with him. "It was like a drug-induced memory recall…" I realized I wasn't explaining myself very well. I tried to start again.

"Trevor, whatever happened between you and me, I would never…" Nope. This wasn't going well. I gave it one more shot.

"You know how the government picks random people...school teachers, accountants, pilots, *college students*...to test the latest mind control technology—"

"What the HELL are you talking about?" he accused. "Are you saying some covert branch of the government *made* you seduce my wife?"

Yeah, that did sound ridiculous.

"I'm saying I never would have consciously made a move on her," I said honestly. "You know how I feel about her but, believe it or not, our friendship still means something to me. I may be a prick for being in love with another man's wife, but I would never, will never, be the kind of guy who lures her away from her family." My clarity was finally back. I knew what I needed to say now.

"Trevor, I'm saying that there is something else going on here, or has been going on for twenty years. Freya and I had a very real flashback. Like *amnesia* patients when they recover a strong memory." That got his attention, but he still wasn't offering any information.

"If we're going to find her, you need to tell me what you know," I demanded. "Has Freya ever had amnesia?"

He retrieved the jacket from the back of his chair, and quickly put it on, then rounded his desk, pausing next to me. "We'll talk in the car."

That wasn't good enough. I grabbed his arm, as he made for the door. "Just give me *something*. I'm losing my mind here."

For a second, the old Trevor, my lifelong best friend and confidant, was back. He seemed genuinely concerned about my well-being. He sighed and lowered his gaze. I knew anything he told me could get him fired—or worse—but I didn't care. I released his arm.

"Has Freya ever had amnesia?" I asked again.

He leaned in, as if someone else might be listening—although we both knew this section of secure offices was the only part of the building that wasn't bugged—and said, just above a whisper, "You both have..."

EPISODE 14
Fear

Am I dead?

I had a serious headache, so I assumed not. I opened my eyes, but there was still darkness. I tried again…and again. I blinked my eyes so many times, I couldn't tell when they were open and when they were closed anymore. I gave up and relaxed my eye muscles, assuming they were closed.

As the realization of my situation swirled around in my head, my heart raced and I felt like it would leap right out of my chest. I started to sweat and, suddenly, I couldn't breathe.

So this is what fear feels like.

Real fear and uncertainty of whether or not I would survive the day…the hour. It was new to me. I had felt fear when Rowan was choking on that damn quarter, but not like this. I had to get a hold of myself. Rip would find me, of that I was absolutely sure…eventually. I forced the thoughts of my precious little boys to the back of my mind, and concentrated on steadying my heart rate. A minute later, the sweating had stopped and I was taking deep, cleansing breaths. Better.

Remember your training, Freya.

First, assess my surroundings. Where the hell was I?

I felt around with my hands…the floor was cold tile…cold, wet, sticky tile. I tried to wipe my hands on my pants, but the sticky wouldn't come off. Gross. I had no idea where I was being imprisoned, but I could definitely cross off a suite at the Hilton from my list of possibilities.

Seriously, though, why couldn't it ever be a suite at the Hilton? Criminals were such barbarians.

I was kneeling. I stuck my arms out and felt around for a wall, but only found emptiness. I slowly tried to stand, and that's when I realized my right foot was chained.

Shit. There was that instant head-to-toe sweating again. My breath quickened.

No. You can do this.

I followed the thick links to the wall behind me, and found the metal ring the chain was attached to. It was mounted securely into the cement wall. I couldn't budge it.

I reluctantly felt around the wall, terrified of what I might touch, but...nothing.

I slowly stood, careful to keep the chain from wrapping around my leg, and took a tentative step forward. After four steps, I was pushing the limits of the chain and had to stop. I reached out and walked in a semi-circle as far away from the wall as the chain would let me, and my hand hit something.

It was solid, smooth plastic and, as I ran my hand along it, it seemed to span the whole length of the room, although the chain stopped me from confirming that. The only thing I could compare it to was a car windshield, but it was much longer.

Just then, I heard someone coming...make that two someones. A muffled conversation was coming from the other side of the wall, but I wasn't sure exactly from where until a door opened just across from where I was chained. The light coming in was so bright, I slammed my eyes shut and knelt back down on the floor in an attempt to escape it. My head pounded.

"Shit, she's awake," I heard a voice say, nervously. "I ain't goin' in there."

I opened my eyes slowly, spots still swimming in front of my eyes, and saw that my blouse was stained with blood.

What did they do to me?

I hadn't felt any pain, except for my incredibly sore tailbone, and I knew what that was from. Rip's eyes flashed in my mind, but I pushed them away. Thinking about him and what had happened... well, it wasn't going to help me get out of there, so I focused on searching for any wounds on my body, ignoring my guests for the moment. They were hesitating in the doorway anyway, arguing about who should go in first.

Nothing. I barely had a scratch on me. My hands had dried blood on them, but not from me. I suddenly realized what I had stuck them in on the floor earlier. But it wasn't my blood…and if it wasn't mine, then…

Wait. My headache. I slowly reached up, trying not to get the blood from my hand in my hair, but found nothing. The pain in my head was all internal, apparently.

I shuddered at the possibilities running through my brain. The blood had still been wet when I'd accidentally discovered it. Had they been keeping someone else in here just before me? Someone else who had lost a lot of blood? Enough to…

I closed my eyes and struggled to control my breathing. I knew I had to focus and think of a way out. I would not become the damsel in distress. I was not a weak woman who needed a man to rescue her. I was the Goddess Freya, and I would wield my power…whatever that was. I didn't know how much time I had before my captors decided I was no longer needed. Why I was still alive was a mystery. A mystery I would have to solve later. I needed to get rid of the chain binding me to the wall. I wondered if one of my reluctant visitors had a key.

Why the hell were they still hovering in the doorway? It was almost as if they were…afraid.

Afraid of what? Me? I had to test that theory, ridiculous as it seemed.

"What are you afraid of, boys?" I interrupted their argument. "Come on in…I won't hurt you." My throat was so dry, my words came out rough, like I'd been at a Styx concert the night before. If only. The possibility of dehydration was no longer a joke.

They both went silent and froze, staring at me. My eyes were adjusting to the light and I was able to focus on the two men…or should I say *boys*. They couldn't have been more than twenty, either one of them, and they were dressed like white wannabe gangsters, with the chains around their necks and stupid hats on sideways. I prayed my boys would never succumb to that pathetic fad.

I noticed one of the young men, the meatier of the two and rather muscular from the bumps and contours I could make out under his dirty T-shirt, had a pretty serious black eye, and under a large rip in the thigh of his overly-baggy jeans, was a bloody bandage in dire need of changing. The wound was still actively bleeding. For a split second, I forgot myself and my maternal instinct took over my brain.

"You should really have that leg looked at."

The look of fear on their faces increased tenfold at my statement. Not the response I was expecting at all. I put the mom part of my brain in a time out and regained my composure.

What exactly are these two so afraid of?

Since they weren't making any movements to enter the room, I decided to stand. What difference did it make? If I was going to die here, I was pretty sure standing up wasn't going to change that. I raised up my torso and put one foot on the ground. My tailbone twinged at the motion and I stopped. Looking up at my two new friends, I noticed they had backed away from the door now, regarding me as if I was Calypso turning into a thousand sand crabs right in front of their eyes.

It didn't seem as though they knew my stopping in mid-stand was because I was in pain. Okay, assuming they were afraid of me, for whatever reason, they must think I'm doing it for effect...to put them on edge even more. And it was working.

I completed the maneuver, slowly stretching my spine to my full five-feet-ten-inches. I scanned the room, looking for anything that might help me escape. The windshield I had felt earlier was actually a sneeze guard for an old, now empty, ice cream shop display case, and there were a few bar stools left over from its glory days...but I couldn't reach them with that blasted chain on my ankle. There was nothing else in the room, which I now suspected to be a tiny free-standing building. Maybe we were at an abandoned fairgrounds...or drive-in theater...my mind reeled.

The muscle boy pushed his companion toward the door. "Get in there! The boss wants to know who this bitch is. Check her for ID," he ordered, pushing him farther into the doorway, but the young man resisted, thrusting both arms outward and bracing himself in the door frame.

"So she can mess me up too? No way, man!"

What?

"You have a gun, moron!" the bigger man reminded him. This seemed to convince him it was safe for a second. He reached inside the doorway with one foot, but then retreated again.

"Dude, so did you!"

My head pounded again as I tried to follow the scene playing out in front of me. My hand flew involuntarily to my temple. Suddenly, I had a flash of...something...a memory? It was muscle boy, and he was frisking me for any hint of identification, but he was really enjoying it. *Really* enjoying it. In fact, he was attempting to get to third base when I'd had enough of his tentacles on me. I swung my whole body around, so quickly, he was caught completely off guard, and came around with one elbow right into the side of his head—the black eye. Then I spun back around and slammed my right foot into his left thigh with such force, the heel of my boot ripped his jeans and sliced open his thigh at the same time—the bleeding wound. As the hooligan fell backward in my memory, I heard something small, but heavy, hit the floor and slide into the darkness of the corner.

His gun.

Wait. *I* had injured the young man, when he'd had a gun and...all those muscles. I had kicked his ass, and he'd run, bleeding and scared to death of me. Bleeding. The blood on the floor, on my blouse, and now, on my hands. It was his.

How did I do it? My brain must have accessed the intensive training sessions with Agent Hart and my instincts had kicked in, but why couldn't I remember anything else? Just then, I realized that my last memory, besides the flashback, was of the large man from the bridge putting a blindfold on me in the car. I had just said goodbye to Rip.

No. I hadn't said goodbye. I'd said something else...

I shook the memory loose, determined not to get distracted. It was probably just the adrenaline and stress of the situation...my memory loss. I'd read that was common. I think.

Or maybe they had drugged me. That would explain why I'd been asleep—or unconscious—and the headache. Now I was pissed. I prided myself on my healthy lifestyle, and I never, ever put man-made chemicals into my body, if I could help it. How dare they!

The pounding subsided and I looked up at the boys with renewed clarity…and a plan. I was no doctor, but I was a mom, and judging by the amount of blood on me and on the floor, and the fact that the kid's thigh was still bleeding heavily, I knew he was going to die without medical attention, and soon. He should be feeling weak by now.

And I was positive that his gun was still in the corner.

EPISODE 15
Escape

The two young men were still arguing just outside the door to the small building I was being held captive in. I was chained to the wall and needed to...not be. I had to coax those boys inside somehow.

'Come into my parlor,' said the spider to the flies...

"Listen, gentlemen," I started, interrupting their bickering. "My back is killing me. Can I get one of those bar stools to sit on?" I motioned toward the two stools near the ice cream bar, covered in cobwebs.

They just stared at me for a second. Then the smaller one nudged the other.

"She's talking to you, Jax."

"Shut up, Case."

I noticed the bigger one's thigh wound was now soaking through the makeshift bandage and he was getting paler by the minute. I had to make this happen fast.

"Seriously...boys...I have a bad back...leftovers from having my last baby. Just slide one of those stools over here. Please." I was hoping that mentioning my children would appeal to something inside of them, some compassionate part buried deep in their memories. I mean, they had to have mothers, right? I had a fleeting thought that Hitler and Jeffrey Dahmer both had mothers too, but I quickly dismissed it. Doubt would not help me escape.

Neither one of them moved. I switched gears slightly.

"I'm really sorry about your leg," I said, with as much genuine concern as I could muster.

He looked down at his bleeding thigh and I swear his face instantly grew one shade whiter. I really didn't want him to die. He was just a kid.

"I'm not a doctor, but I have bandaged a cut or two in my day. You need a clean bandage and you need to wrap it really tight. You're losing too much blood."

Come on, kid. You want mommy to kiss your booboo and make it all better, don't you?

His friend was now looking at me with glossy eyes. It was working on *him*, at least. I kept going.

"You look pale. Please, let me help you." My concern was genuine now. He was as white as a ghost, and was leaning against the door frame for support. I decided I had to take charge of the situation if I was going to save him. I pointed to the other delinquent.

"You...Case? Bring him here. He doesn't have much time." I was surprised when Case immediately did exactly what I'd said. The dying boy, Jax, didn't protest either.

Case helped Jax sit down, propped up against the wall right next to where my chain was secured, but he looked like he would pass out at any second. Case just squatted next to his friend—brother? I suddenly noticed a family resemblance in their faces. They had the same nose and chin. Good. That could only help my situation.

I kneeled back down on the floor and moved to unwrap the bloody bandage, when I realized my palms still had blood on them.

"Do you have anything I can clean my hands with?" I asked Jax, urgency apparent in my voice. He looked to be in shock, and just shook his head ever so slightly. I don't think he could've told me his name at that point.

I looked around the room. I noticed the outline of a sink in the dark corner I hadn't noticed before. If it was still hooked up to a water line...

"Case," he looked at me like a frightened little boy as I spoke, "I need to get to the sink to wash my hands. Do you have the key for this chain?"

His eyes grew wider at this, as if he was remembering I was supposed to be a prisoner. He was close enough for me to grab his shoulder.

"Case, look at me." He did. "Case, I want to save Jax. Help me save Jax. I promise I won't run." At least not until I'd done everything I could for the injured boy. After all, *I'd* inflicted the wound with my 'ninja skills', as my boys would say.

Case seemed to snap out of his shock and started rooting around in his brother's jeans pocket. He came out with a small key.

Jax moaned in apparent protest, but we both ignored him. Case gave me the key like an obedient child. I slid it right into the padlock that held the chain onto the metal ring in the wall, and it took me a minute to unwrap the chain from around my ankle. I started to stand, but Case stopped me, grabbing my arm. His eyes pleaded with me.

"I'm just going to wash my hands, Case. I'll be right back." He released his grasp and I quickly walked to the sink, praying water would come out. I turned the knob and heard a sputtering noise, like my old 1980 Cougar used to make when I turned the key, right before it came to life. I held my breath.

Water started to trickle out of the spigot, and I exhaled with relief. It wasn't a lot, but it was enough. I washed the blood off my hands, and dried them on the cleanest part of my pants. It was the best I could do. As I walked back to the boys, I took off my jacket. I didn't even want to think about the condition of my new, favorite item of clothing. I laid it carefully over the sneeze guard, hoping it could be saved too.

I returned to Case and Jax, and kneeled.

"Take off your shirt, Case," I instructed.

He looked at me with total confusion.

"I need a clean bandage for the wound. Give me your shirt."

I wasn't sure how clean it was, but it would have to do. He quickly took off his shirt and handed it to me. Now, I needed something to clean the cut…and Case needed something to do.

"Case, is there any alcohol here?"

He looked around, not really comprehending what was going on.

"Not in here, Case. Out there," I pointed out the door. "Do you have any alcohol? Not beer, but…whiskey?"

The mention of whiskey registered with him and he stood, but hesitated, looking at me for more instruction. He was like a puppy learning to fetch the Sunday paper.

"Go get the whiskey, Case, as fast as you can…run!" He left the little shack in a flash. Turning back to my patient, I started to tear up the white T-shirt while I assessed the wound. When I was satisfied with my strips of cloth, I slowly, carefully began to remove the soiled rag that was currently loosely wrapped around Jax's thigh. He moaned. Thank God. He was still with us, but barely.

The cut my boot heel had made was jagged and ugly.

I thought of my purse. My favorite yellow handbag full of useful items that I'd left in the front seat of Rip's car at the bridge. I always kept a small bottle of manuka honey in there for emergencies. It was the best natural antibiotic for cuts, and with four boys, I had used it on a regular basis. I also thought of the lip balm I never went anywhere without. My lips were so dry, they hurt. I silently cursed the unofficial rule that an FBI agent must be unencumbered. In other words, no purse. Why did it have to be so difficult to be a woman sometimes?

Case came tearing in the door, with a half-empty bottle of single malt whiskey in one hand. He knelt next to me, handing me the liquor, but looking nervously at his brother. The bottle didn't have a lid.

"Have you two been drinking, Case?" I asked, my mother tone really coming through.

He looked at me and shook his head. "No, ma'am. Not today." Good boy. I handed the bottle back to him.

"Take a swig. You need it." I told him. He gave me a half grin and complied. Then he gave the bottle back to me. I took a small swig myself, for courage, and then poured a generous amount on the cut. Jax made a horrible noise, like a cow going to slaughter, but then relaxed. I poured a little more, and this time, he barely flinched. I rubbed a little whiskey between my hands, and went to work re-bandaging his thigh. I was pretty happy with my wrap job, but this boy wasn't out of the woods yet. I was afraid I hadn't gotten to him soon enough. His eyes were closed now, and his breathing was very faint and shallow. Maybe he had lost too much blood.

I wracked my brain, but could only come to one conclusion. He needed a doctor.

"Case, you have to take him to the hospital."

Case suddenly found his voice. "What? But, didn't you just save him?"

"I did what I could, but he's lost a lot of blood, and he needs fluids."

Case picked up the whiskey bottle from where I'd set it on the floor, and put it to his brother's lips. "We'll just give him a drink…" He was desperate.

"Case, he's unconscious. You have to take him to the hospital or he'll die."

Case sat on the floor, and hung his head, letting the bottle fall out of his hand. It rolled to the wall and stopped. The sound reminded me of something else hitting the floor and sliding…the gun!

Shit. I'd gotten so wrapped up in saving this kid, I'd nearly forgotten my escape plan.

Case was crying now. I felt bad for these two boys and wondered how they'd ended up here. My maternal instincts were too strong to dissuade. I mentally made a change to my plan.

"Come on, Case. We'll take your brother to the hospital together. Do you have a car?"

I stood and, as casually as I could, sauntered over to the corner. My foot hit something and I bent over to pick it up. The gun felt so good in my hand, I paused for a second, but startled at the sound of Case's voice, and quickly put the firearm in my empty holster. I was fairly sure I no longer needed it, but just in case we ran into any trouble outside…

"Jabba's gonna kill us…all we had to do was watch you while they were gone..."

Gone? 'They' were gone. Perfect. Time for us to go, too.

"Case, we need to go now! Do you have a car?"

He just sat there, looking at the floor between his legs. I crouched down and forced him to look me in the eyes. He looked much younger to me now than he had when I'd first sized the two of them up.

"How old are you?" I asked, not able to keep the compassion out of my eyes. He gazed back at me, as if the only thing he wanted in the world was someone to care about him.

My plan had worked a little too well.

"Seventeen."

Just three years older than Levi.

I tried to justify why I had encouraged a minor to drink whiskey, but it just made my temple throb. I needed to focus. I pulled him to his feet and hastily removed the gun from the front of his pants, but he didn't even seem to notice. I hoped he didn't have any hidden weapons that could get him in trouble. I slid his pistol's barrel halfway down the back of my pants, flinching as it scraped my bruised tailbone.

Case took a deep breath in through his nose, and then turned to me. "I'll get the keys."

I hoisted Jax up as gently as I could, but all those muscles, and the fact that he was dead weight, were very heavy. I half-carried him outside and had to squint for a few seconds while my eyes adjusted to the sunshine. Then I saw the car.

No way.

A 1980 red and white Cougar. My baby from high school…but it couldn't actually be mine, since my first car had become scrap metal after the engine block froze. Still, I couldn't help but smile.

I made my way to the car, and noticed on the way that we were at an abandoned track of some kind. I vaguely remembered something about an old greyhound racing track just outside of town that had closed over eight years ago, before Trevor and I had moved there. The track was still pretty much intact, and the small concession shack I had been chained to was just outside the old main entrance. The car was parked in the 'VIP' parking spot just twenty feet from both.

I reached the old beauty and laid Jax in the backseat. I buckled both seat belts over him as best I could, and then checked his pulse.

Weak, but there.

Hang in there, kid.

Case appeared, running toward me from the old box office directly in front of the car, keys in hand. He started to get in the driver's seat, but I headed him off.

"Oh no you don't…you've been drinking." I snatched the keys from him and climbed behind the wheel.

As he ran around to get in the passenger side, he threw his arms in the air. "So have you, lady!"

He got in and I put the key in the ignition. "Yeah, but at least I'm legal."

He didn't have a retort for that.

I turned the key, and the car purred to life like a very happy kitten.

Definitely *not* my car. As I fastened my seat belt, I noticed Case wasn't doing the same.

"Put your seatbelt on."

When it was clear the car wasn't moving until he did as I commanded, he reluctantly buckled his seatbelt.

I put it in reverse and backed out of my 'VIP' parking spot. Then I slammed on the accelerator and sped out of there. I was a woman on a mission. I had two juvenile delinquents—and possibly runaways—in the car. One was sitting next to me, and his brother—nearly dead due to an injury *I* gave him—was bleeding in the back seat, while I prayed their crime boss—the jackass who kidnapped me—and his muscle-bound henchmen wouldn't pass us on the road.

I had never felt more alive.

EPISODE 16
Jabba the Hood

Trevor and I immediately got a hit on the license plate, and couldn't drive fast enough to the well-known, but officially top-secret, headquarters of a local crime boss named Bastien Evers.

Bastien was born on a small island in the South Pacific—so small, it wasn't even tourist worthy—and had come to America when he was fourteen. He was smart, but with no adults in his life to guide him, he had fallen in with the street crowd, the pickpockets and petty thieves, and had worked his way up through the ranks to the very top. Now, nearly twenty years later, he was the big cheese, and with his power, he had grown fat and lazy...gluttonous in fact. His easily four-hundred-pound girth was accredited to his addiction to American fast food, and there was an underground rumor that he hadn't left his chair in six months, because he couldn't. I took that to mean either he was actually physically stuck in the chair, or he couldn't lift his own weight anymore. Then again, it very well could be both. I tried not to think about how he was relieving his bodily functions if he couldn't get to a bathroom. Regardless, it had garnered him the nickname, "Jabba," which he seemingly took as a title of royalty.

Trevor took a left turn too sharply, and my head hit the window. I scowled at him, but he didn't notice. He had refused to elaborate on Freya and I apparently both having had amnesia, which I was still trying to convince myself was a lie, and I finally had to let it go, in the interest of finding Freya as soon as possible.

As we parked in the back lot of the specialty bookstore, the front for Jabba's real business, Trevor didn't bother paying attention to the parking spaces, and I didn't complain. We both hopped out, not having said one word to each other since we'd left headquarters. I decided to let him lead. She was his wife, after all, as much as that thought made me cringe.

Trevor got to the back door and paused, pulling his gun from its holster and clicking the safety off. He pointed it in front of him and moved to open the door.

I guess we're going in strong.

I put my hand on his arm, lowering his weapon to point at the ground.

"Trevor, what are you doing? Jabba's not the enemy here...he probably doesn't even know about Freya being kidnapped. The jerks who had us at gunpoint...I didn't recognize any of them, and they didn't act like Jabba's guys. Let's be smart about—"

He cut me off. "Until my wife is safe, everyone is the enemy."

His eyes had a fire in them I'd never seen before...and I'd seen this guy in hand-to-hand combat, fighting for his life. I suddenly got the feeling he was lumping *me* in the 'enemy' category with the rest of the world.

I sighed heavily, and retrieved my gun, unlocking the safety, but only, I told myself, to shoot Trevor's gun out of his hand if he got carried away inside.

He gave me a nod, careful to make eye contact as briefly as he possibly could, and I reluctantly returned the nod. He slowly checked the door...unlocked. We ducked inside.

We had entered through the employee entrance, and silently crept down a long narrow hallway. We passed a room that looked like it should be an employee lounge, based on the soda machine and full-sized fridge I could barely see on the opposite wall, but it had so many boxes piled up, some to the ceiling, there wasn't room for anyone to...well, lounge. Then there was a bathroom, surprisingly clean, and next to it was a small meeting room with a long table and several mismatched chairs. It was neat and tidy, as always. Jabba may be an obese slob, but he was also a clean freak and had had the same meticulous cleaning lady for eight years. I knew this because, oddly enough, Janice was also *my* cleaning lady.

We knew Jabba and his crew would be upstairs, in the loft of the old bookstore. That's where Jabba lived, and where his throne was. Literally. He'd bought it online a few years ago, some leftover prop from a movie set, and he loved it more than a mother could love her child.

We approached the bottom of the stairs, just before the heavy red, theater curtain that separated the bookstore from the rest of the establishment, and still hadn't encountered any of Jabba's goons, or 'Bounty Hunters' as we jokingly called them at headquarters. The joke was two-fold, as most of them were barely adults, and all of them were relatively harmless, except for the fact that they were low-grade criminals.

One thing we hadn't discussed yet, Trevor and I, was what Jabba could possibly have to do with all this. Kidnapping wasn't his thing. I was secretly hoping he knew something, if only to get Freya back safely, but I was doubtful. The whole mess was nagging at the back of my consciousness as we slowly ascended the stairs.

Jabba was unlike any other criminal I'd ever met. We called him a 'Crime Boss', but in reality, he was more help to us than hindrance. Jabba had appeared on the FBI's radar three years before, when there was talk on the street of a new drug lord in town. What we discovered throughout that investigation surprised everyone at the bureau. Not only did we uncover the drug lord and nail him, but it turned out not to be Jabba.

Not even close.

It seems Jabba's mother had been a drug addict when he was still living on his little island. He was too young to understand why she was 'sick', but he knew enough to stay away from the drugs himself, and did a pretty good job of keeping his younger brother away from them too…for a while. One day, his brother's curiosity got the better of him, and Jabba wasn't around.

His mother, apparently overwhelmed by the whole situation, and—one can only hope—blaming herself for her son's death, overdosed on heroine the next day.

So, fourteen-year-old Jabba hopped the next boat to the east coast, and ended up in our little mecca, presumably scared and alone. He blamed drugs for taking his family away from him, and vowed to never, and I mean, NEVER, have anything to do with them.

It seemed our resident Hut was a crime boss with morals.

He also, we found out soon after that, never steals from pregnant women, mothers with children in tow, the elderly, or the mentally or physically challenged, and he holds all his 'subjects' to the same standards.

I wouldn't call him Robin Hood, but he was damn close, and you had to give the behemoth credit for running his below-the-law business the way he did.

Plus, he was Trevor's #1 informant, and had been for two years. His specialty bookstore was legit, and made a small profit, but most of his wealth came from behind the red curtain, and as long as we allowed it to happen, he would help in any way he could to keep our city drug free.

In this crazy, mixed-up world, that seemed like a pretty good trade-off.

We reached the landing, and could hear voices coming from the room directly in front of us. The Throne Room. The door was cracked, and before we could formulate an entry plan, Jabba's booming voice bellowed from the other side of it.

"Come in, gentlemen! But holster your weapons first, please!"

Trevor lowered his weapon but didn't put it away. I grabbed his arm, and when he glared at me, I met his glare tenfold. He hesitated, but then conceded and flipped on the safety before he slid it into the holster. I did the same, and we pushed the door open and entered.

Jabba was sitting on his throne, which faced the door, with a large napkin tucked down the front of his quadruple extra-large Hawaiian shirt, and was just finishing up a Big Mac. There were at least eight young men and women of various ages milling around the room, some relaxed on the overstuffed couch, watching a rerun of *Psych* on the 52-inch plasma TV, a few playing video games on yet another giant screen, and several plopped in the far corner on dozens of pillows reading. Although I merely glanced, I was sure one of them was engrossed in *Oliver Twist*. Appropriate. One beautiful young girl was attending to Jabba, and seemed very happy to do so. She cleaned up the McDonalds bag and stood next to the throne with a soda cup as big as her head, waiting for his majesty to feel parched.

As he put the last bite—which would have been four bites for a normal human—in his mouth, he pulled the napkin out of his collar and wiped his mouth and hands, smiling at us the whole time. He finished chewing, far from thirty mastications by my count, and swallowed. He turned his head toward his attendant and she put the straw to his mouth. After sucking down enough Root Beer to drown a Saint Bernard, he thanked her sweetly, and then addressed us, still smiling.

"Why do you enter Jabba's palace with your weapons drawn, friends?"

Jabba spoke in the third person, which normally would have made Trevor smirk at me, but he was not in the mood today, it seemed.

"Your boys kidnapped an agent this morning, Jabba. It seems you've become bored with petty crimes," he snapped.

Jabba was genuinely confused and shocked by Trevor's accusation, which didn't surprise me one bit, but I knew I wasn't going to get through to Trevor. I only hoped Jabba could convince him.

"Agent Douglas, you know very well Jabba does not condone such acts. Why do you accuse Jabba of this? What evidence do you have?"

"We have one of your cars at the scene," Trevor stated.

Jabba had an inkling of recognition at that, and took a deep breath in, looking at the ceiling. Finally, he responded. "The 1978 Caddy."

"Yes," I answered. "Jabba, there were four men in that car this morning, and they took a female agent at gunpoint."

Jabba rubbed his chin thoughtfully. "Four men?"

I nodded.

He sighed. "This morning, Jabba's 1978 Cadillac went missing... along with *six* of Jabba's wayward brothers."

"Six?" I blurted out, before I could process what Jabba had said. He was claiming six of his men went rogue and kidnapped an FBI agent without his knowledge? This was one of the oldest excuses in the book, but I was inclined to believe him.

"Jabba believes four of them have bad juju. They were not content being in Jabba's family. They are greedy and not right in the head."

Just how crazy do you have to be for someone like Jabba to call you 'not right in the head'? I was getting an increasingly bad feeling about this, and I could sense Trevor was too.

"And the other two?" asked Trevor calmly.

"The other two were motivated by financial hardship alone. They are good boys, and will be welcomed back into Jabba's palace, if they have not already done something...unforgiveable."

"Like kidnapping an FBI agent?" Trevor asked, a slight edge in his voice.

"Jax and Case are not the brains of this treason, friend. Jabba believes Logan and his brothers in crime were given a job outside of his purview...and they were offered a lot of money to do so."

Something in Jabba's coded language struck me. "Jabba, what do you mean 'brothers in crime'? Were these four young men in prison together?"

Jabba smiled and pointed a ginormous finger at me. "You are close, Agent Ripley. They were just boys when they met under dire circumstances."

"Just boys...they were in Juvenile Hall together?"

He grinned. Talking to Jabba was like working your way through a labyrinth.

Trevor asked, "If you knew all this, Jabba, why didn't you stop them? Or call us?"

Jabba looked sad now. "Apologies, friends. Jabba found out only a moment before you arrived in his court. Sister Lila overheard their evil plan this morning and was concerned for brothers Jax and Case." He motioned to his personal attendant, and she gave a shy smile, but made eye contact with me for only a split second.

"Wait," I asked, "why are you so worried about these other two boys?"

Jabba looked at Lila and she gave a nod, giving him permission to respond on her behalf.

"You see, friends, the poor young boys believe they are acting under Jabba's orders. They have been deceived by Logan and his evil intentions."

"Lila, do you know who gave the boys this job?" Trevor asked gently.

She just nodded and gave the same shy smile. We waited for a name...or anything...but she remained silent.

Just then, Jabba began signing to her. I had no idea he knew sign language, and I could tell it was a surprise to Trevor too. So, Lila was deaf...

Wait.

But then, how did she overhear the plan in the first place? Something wasn't right here.

"Jabba," I started, carefully choosing my words, "how did she overhear the plan if she's deaf?" I thought it was a valid question, but both Jabba and Lila gave me an offended glare.

They returned to their silent conversation, Lila responding with lovely, flowing, feminine sign language. It was beautiful to watch. When they were finished, they both turned back toward Trevor and me. Jabba clasped his hands in front of him, which seemed to be quite a task as his arms barely reached across his girth.

"Friends. Lila is not deaf. In fact, her beguiling ears perform better than yours or Jabba's. She is, however, speechless, in a permanent sense. Her last boyfriend saw fit to separate her from her instrument of speech." He paused here, to make sure we were understanding him.

We both must have looked puzzled—I know I was—because he rolled his eyes slightly and sighed. He leaned forward a little... probably as far as he could, and spoke just above a whisper, and in a tone that reminded me the whole third person thing was all an act.

"Her tongue, gentlemen. He tried to cut out her tongue."

When he was sure we were following, he leaned back again... about the same as putting your seat on an airplane from its upright position to recline.

"He did not succeed fully, but the damage was done. She heard about Jabba's happy family, and came here, where she is now safe from cavemen like Tony the Moose."

Trevor and I looked at each other with intensity. We both recognized that name. He was number one on our bad guy list. He liked cutting people's tongues out, and every agent in the bureau would like nothing more than to cut out *his* vile tongue…with a rusty spoon.

I thought I was catching on to where Jabba was leading us.

"Jabba, did Tony the Moose send the boys on this job?" It was perfect. Of course, that meant Tony had Freya, and that thought made my stomach churn, but at least it was a step closer to finding her. Then I noticed Jabba was shaking his head.

"No, Agent Ripley. Jabba fears you will not like what you hear, but in the interest of maintaining our amiable relationship, Jabba has no choice."

Trevor was growing impatient with Jabba's riddles. "Jabba, just tell us, please! This agent…she's in danger!"

"Peace, friend." Jabba spoke so calmly, I actually felt a little more peaceful…but just a little. Then, Jabba closed his eyes and took a deep, cleansing breath, as if he was meditating. He opened his eyes and gazed at us. His concern was evident, but there was also fear in his eyes. But fear of what? This hooligan, Logan? Tony the Moose? What he was afraid of was not clear…until he revealed the name we had been waiting for.

"Lila overheard Logan telling the three others that the job came straight from your Director Pixley."

EPISODE 17
Information

Trevor and I were both frozen in time, speechless.

Director Pixley had hired a mentally unstable juvenile delinquent to kidnap Freya?

Why?

I couldn't believe my ears. Jabba was certain, however, that his lovely mute informant

had overheard correctly.

Had he targeted Freya specifically, or was Logan just supposed to grab any agent? No, the young man hadn't even hesitated when he took Freya, so I could only assume the decision had already been made for him. I suddenly had a skullcap headache.

What the hell is going on here?

Then, I remembered Leon for the first time since that morning. Logan, whom I assumed was the shorter of the four men who had taunted me and tried to touch Freya—both of which I planned to make him pay for—had practically boasted about killing Leon when he had us captive at the old bridge. What had really happened to my most trusted informant? Had Pixley ordered the boy to kill him, which is what I had assumed his fate had been that morning? Maybe Jabba knew something.

"Jabba, this agent, she and I were meeting someone this morning when your boys showed up instead. Do you know anything about the other man?"

"Apologies, Agent Ripley, but Jabba does not know."

We needed to find Leon, and fast.

■ ■ ■

We started with Leon's place, a dive of an apartment in a dilapidated complex unofficially known as 'Hooker Hill', for obvious reasons. The actual name was 'Highland Hills', but the sign was so old and faded, the letters couldn't be deciphered.

I smiled as we leapt out of the car and headed toward Leon's one-bedroom catastrophe, remembering a few years back when Freya had been determined to raise money to clean up the complex. Not surprisingly, she had trouble getting her manicured and tummy-tucked 'friends' to help out. Most of them just wanted to pretend the place didn't exist, but she was on a mission, and there was no discouraging her when she was so focused like that.

She organized a fundraiser, and had a whopping two hundred bucks to show for it at the end of the day…most of which was from me and her friend, Talia, and she had eventually been forced to take another route. She petitioned the city to do something about the 'problem' as she euphemized, but unbeknownst to her, the city actually owned the whole complex—under a made-up name of course—and blocked her at every turn.

In time, she gave up, though very reluctantly. I felt so bad for her. She was such an idealist, one of the many things I adored about her, and had these grand plans to help all the 'poor young girls' who were trapped in the would-be human trafficking that was going on.

I would never tell her the city secretly owned Highland Hills—I wasn't allowed to call it the other name in her presence—because of the *reason* the city secretly owned Highland Hills…so they would have a place to entertain VIPs who were into that sort of thing, which was a surprising number of them, apparently. It was definitely not something the Mayor wanted common knowledge, and I liked my job, so I kept my mouth shut.

We reached Leon's door and Trevor put his hand up to stop me in my tracks. He pointed to the door. It was hanging open, the doorknob broken and dangling from the hole it should have been occupying. We drew our weapons and, this time, I led.

The living room was a mess, but no more than usual, and Leon was nowhere to be seen. We silently made our way to the bedroom, and heard a noise, like a lawn mower or one of those espresso machines.

And there he was. Asleep on his bed. A bed that had no covers but did have stains on the mattress that made me think of an 80s horror movie. I was so relieved to see him, though, snoring away, that I sat down on the potential health hazard and sighed with relief, holstering my weapon as I did so. I roughly shook him until he stopped snoring and opened his eyes. He rubbed them for a second, and then looked around frantically, as if he had no idea where he was.

"What the—!" he exclaimed. "How did I get here? What did you do to me?"

"Leon, you're in your apartment. You must have been having a pretty intense dream," I teased.

That didn't seem to calm him down at all.

"Rip? What's going on? I was on my way to meet you and…" he trailed off, lost in thought.

"Yeah, you never made it, but four *nice* young men came in your place," I said irritably. I was through playing games. We needed to find Freya before nightfall. "Leon, what happened? Did Logan pay you off?"

He looked hurt by my comment. "Logan? Man, that dude is psycho. I'm telling you, I was on my way to the old warehouse to meet you, and—"

"Warehouse?" I interrupted. "Idiot. We were supposed to meet at the old bridge north of Halloway."

"Well, yeah, at first, but then you texted me to go to the warehouse instead."

Shit. Was Pixley playing with all of us? I suddenly felt like we were being watched, and when an FBI agent had that feeling, it was usually true.

"Leon, what time did you get the text from me?"

He stared at me for a minute, rubbed his eyes, and then pulled his iPhone—courtesy of the United States government—out of his jeans pocket. "Let me see…" he scrolled through his messages.

How many friends did this guy have? I thought I was the only one who could stand the smell.

Then he nodded. "Here we go…8:45 this morning…I wasn't even awake yet, man. Have some respect for other people's schedules."

I smacked him hard in the back of the head and his greasy dishwater brown hair fell in front of his face. He deserved it. I snatched the phone out of his hand and read. Damn. The text had inexplicably come from my phone, and there were just a few people I knew of who had the technology to hack into an encrypted government cell phone.

I stood and tossed his phone onto the mattress.

"You know your front door is broken?"

That surprised him. I quickly made a decision.

"Get cleaned up, Leon. You're coming with us."

Trevor smacked me, but I ignored his protest. I had a strong feeling Leon was still in danger, and it was my job to keep him alive. He had to come with us.

"Aw man, I wanna go back to sleep!" he yawned. "Why do I have to come with you?"

"Because I think whoever went out of their way to keep you from making our meeting this morning may have drugged you, and then broke your doorknob to get you in here. We're going to take you to the lab and have your blood tested."

He laughed at this, and Trevor and I both knew why, but I let him tell us anyway.

"Rip, you know drugs have no effect on me."

He was right. His numerous attempts at becoming a drug addict—this guy had a past no one would blame him for wanting to block out—all failed miserably until, finally, he had to accept the fact that he was, somehow, immune. He couldn't even get drunk, the poor bastard. He was like Captain America, except smelly, undernourished, and not very brave.

I like to think I had something to do with the fact that he was now proud of his super power, although I advised him to never tell anyone from the seedy underbelly, where he usually hung out. It could be dangerous information in the wrong hands, and he was an FBI informant, which was not an inherently safe job to begin with.

He closed his eyes and banged the center of his scrawny chest with his fist. "Constitution of iron, dude!"

I grabbed his fist and pulled him to his feet. That's when the smell really hit us, and even Trevor recoiled. He wasn't usually bothered by something like body odor, but this was an extra special blend of stink, stank, and stunk. Apparently, the only way Leon could block out his bad memories was by never bathing...effective, because one whiff and I swear I lost 1989.

I covered my nose with my other hand, and pulled him toward the bathroom. I flung him through the doorway, and closed the door between us.

"Dude! Take a shower, and hurry up!

━ ━ ━

We left headquarters and Trevor drove, making it impossible to *not* put our seatbelts on, and we headed for Jabba's once again. Leon, who smelled a lot better, had tested positive for drugs alright. Whoever wanted to keep him away from the bridge that morning had given him a massive amount of...caffeine.

That's right. Caffeine. Enough to keep any normal human awake for a month, if it didn't stop your heart first. Because Leon was...special... his system had been overloaded, causing him to skip right past the caffeine high and right into the caffeine crash. Whoever drugged him had either been trying to kill him in a unique and creative way, or knew Leon's secret. And that made sense if Director Pixley was behind it all.

He still had a lot of the popular drug coursing through his veins, and the rate at which his mouth was now moving was proof of that. I was starting to wish Logan *had* killed him. The guy wouldn't shut up.

We pulled into Jabba's employee lot for the second time that day, and escorted the still-talking Leon inside. Jabba had agreed to take Leon in, temporarily, to maintain our friendly relationship, but he was always eager to recruit new family members. I strongly suggested Jabba *not* try to adopt him, but I knew Leon would be safe in the 'palace' for the time being.

After a wham, bam, thank you ma'am drop off of our snitch, Trevor and I left Jabba's with an eerie quiet emanating throughout the car.

"Where to next?" I finally asked, knowing what he was going to say.

"Pixley." Yup. Just what I thought. We didn't have any other leads anyway. Jabba hadn't heard from Logan since we had talked to him last, nor had we been able to locate the Cadillac. Might as well march into the Regional Director of the FBI's office and point-blank accuse him of hiring a known criminal to kidnap an agent on her first assignment.

It was a life-changing day for both of us.

I checked my watch. 4:15…six hours since the punk, Logan, had taken Freya. It seemed like a lifetime. Then, something occurred to me.

"Hey, don't you need to go home for the boys?" I asked, not that I thought he had forgotten, but…okay, I was a tiny bit worried that his three children had slipped his mind. I was their Godfather, after all, and I was allowed to worry, but I don't think Trevor saw it that way. His hands clenched the steering wheel so tight, his knuckles went white. He responded without looking at me.

"You'd love that, wouldn't you?" he said bitterly. I remained silent. He had a right to be angry. I *had* tried to seduce his wife that morning, consciously or not.

He gave a labored sigh and relaxed his hands slightly.

"Talia's there. I talked to her this morning, right after you called me."

That made me feel better. Talia was like an eccentric aunt to those boys, and Freya loved her like a sister.

———

I had to run to keep up with Trevor as he sprinted into Headquarters, but I wasn't about to scold him. Freya's time was running out, and we needed to know what Director Pixley knew. We reached the secure area, and impatiently went through the entry process before we were allowed in. The Director's office was centrally located, no outside walls, and was reinforced with twelve inches of concrete on all four sides. It was nearly as safe as the President's bunker. The guards outside his door were not the biggest, or the most muscular, but you just knew if you had to fight them, you would lose. It was something about the steely-eyed glare that never left their eyes, and the fact that they were required to have extensive black ops and sniper experience, to have been a trained assassin—not necessarily for our side—or to possess black belts in at least two of the martial arts. All the above was ideal, and it was smart to assume these two gentlemen had checked every box.

After our pat down, which was not unlike being fondled by a Terminator, we were escorted in. Director Pixley sat at his desk, smiling at us as we entered.

"Gentlemen! Still haven't found our new Agent Douglas?" He tsked his tongue and shook his head, looking at his watch, then back at us.

"A little behind schedule too. You boys are off your game today."

I nearly bumped into Trevor, he stopped so abruptly. I quickly moved to stand next to him, and joined him in his confused glare at the director. Then, slowly, it began to sink in. After a moment of silence, I found my voice.

"Director, you had Frey—Agent Douglas kidnapped…as a test?"

I knew the answer. What I didn't know was who he was testing—Freya, or us.

"Of course I did." He wasn't smiling anymore. He stood and walked around to the front of his desk, buttoning his suit jacket. He sat on the edge of his desk and studied us for a moment.

"This whole situation is completely unorthodox. I had to make sure we were doing the right thing, allowing her to become an agent." He crossed his arms in front of him.

"After what I've read in her file…well, it was risky, but the only way I could think of to keep her close…still, I had to make sure she could cut it, didn't I?" He asked this rhetorically, assuming we agreed with everything he was saying. I knew I was more confused than anything.

"Sir—" I tried, but he cut me off.

"I'm disappointed in you, Agent Ripley. I expected you to be able to handle those boys. The chances of her actually being abducted were supposed to be low with you on the job. What happened?"

I was pissed. I didn't owe this jackass an explanation. I just needed to find Freya.

"Sir, do you know where she is?"

"St. Matthias Hospital, in the emergency room."

At that, Trevor and I both startled, and the director suddenly realized he needed to clarify.

"She's fine, gentlemen! She's not the one in need of medical care."

"Sir—"

He raised his hand before I could continue. "I still can't tell you anything about her file," he informed me.

He walked back around to his chair, unbuttoned his coat, and sat. Trevor hadn't moved since we entered, and I was so frustrated with being treated like a child who couldn't keep a secret, I couldn't form a coherent thought.

"Of course…" Pixley sighed as he swiveled back and forth in his white, high-backed leather chair.

Probably baby seal, I thought maliciously.

"If you happened to obtain her file on your own…"

He opened the top right-hand drawer of his desk and pulled out a very thick manila envelope. He dropped it on his desk with a thud, snapping Trevor out of his trance.

"Director, I don't think it's wise to share information with Agent Rip—"

"Stop right there, Douglas."

Yeah, stop it, Douglas! I'm about to find out what's going on!

Pixley didn't say any more, and Trevor had been silenced. I suddenly regained control of my legs, and made my move.

I stepped forward, grabbed the envelope off the director's desk, and walked out.

EPISODE 18
Wonder Woman

Case and I entered the emergency room, dragging the dead weight of Jax between us. Luckily, I still had my badge on me and was able to *not* get tackled to the ground by the hospital security guard when my gun set off the alarm. It was my first official, "Agent Douglas. FBI," and I couldn't help but smile when the guard recoiled slightly at my badge flash.

Once the boys were in the capable hands of the doctor and a gaggle of nurses, and I had convinced the skeptical male nurse that I did not require any medical attention myself, I took a few selfish minutes and went into the ladies' room. I couldn't believe what I saw in the mirror. My hair was a wreck, my white blouse was covered in dried blood, and my slacks were ruined—muddy, bloody, and torn. It was no mystery why the nurse had assumed I was a patient too. I looked like I'd been through hell and back.

So why couldn't I stop smiling?

Staring at the disaster that was my reflection, I felt myself coming down from the adrenaline spike I'd been functioning on for the last few hours. I regarded the stranger in the mirror, and immediately decided that I liked her. She looked like she'd seen a thing or two.

Suddenly, she frowned at me. She was trying to tell me something.

Horrified, I realized she wasn't wearing my new jacket.

I looked down, praying the real me had remembered to grab my favorite article of clothing from the tiny food shack, but alas, neither one of us was wearing the awesome yellow, faux leather jacket with brushed nickel buttons and gorgeous satiny merlot lining.

Damn. I looked back at my new friend, and we both took a deep breath and then shrugged at each other. It didn't matter, in the grand scheme of things. I was alive and had escaped a kidnapping, albeit a severely botched kidnapping, but a bona fide, you-can't-make-this-shit-up kidnapping nonetheless. I was on top of the world.

Except for one thing. The persistent nagging from my maternal instinct to check on the two young men who had accompanied me to the hospital. I sighed. I *was* genuinely concerned. I cleaned up as best I could and went back out to the waiting room.

Quite some time later, as I returned to my seat after asking the curvaceous nurse at the desk, again, if there was any update on Jax's condition, and was told, again, in an overly-friendly tone that there wasn't, I realized I hadn't called Rip. Funny. I hadn't even thought of it until that moment. Instinctively, I reached for my cell phone next to my gun on the holster, but it wasn't there. The kidnappers must have taken it while I was unconscious, I thought.

I didn't have to ask twice to borrow the sexy, young male nurse's phone. He had been flirting with me since I'd brought Jax and Case in over an hour before. He couldn't have been more than thirty, and I looked like I'd been in an episode of *Dirty Jobs*. Maybe Nurse Fabian had low standards…or maybe it was the gun. Chicks with guns were hot…even old chicks.

I looked at the phone and realized my hands were shaking. Understandable, I told myself. I hadn't eaten since early that morning. I tried to dial the sensitive touch screen buttons, but I hit a wrong number, and had to start over. I dialed again and put the phone to my ear, willing my hand to stabilize.

Finally, I heard ringing.

One ring.

Two rings.

Three rings.

Voicemail.

I was reluctantly returning the phone, when it rang in my hand, and I almost dropped the damn thing. Taking a breath, and assuming it was for the cell's owner, I handed it to him, said my thanks, and started to walk away. I heard him answer with a tentative, "Hello?"

I discreetly reached into my bra, finding the secret pocket where I kept my emergency credit card—Rip's advice, which was about to save my life—and consulted the sign on the wall for the cafeteria, when…

"Uh…Agent Douglas?" It was Nurse Pretty Boy.

I turned and looked at him. He wasn't holding a triple-decker bacon cheeseburger, so he'd better have a good reason for distracting me from my task at hand.

"It's for you."

Rip.

He was holding the phone out for me to take, a confused look on his chiseled face. I started toward him, and suddenly felt an odd chill and a wave of disorientation. My mind was swimming. I reached out to grab the nurse's shoulder for support and he put an arm around my waist. I took the phone from his other hand and held it out for a second, waiting for my vision to completely normalize. Then, the episode passed as quickly as it had come.

"Are you alright, Agent Douglas?"

I nodded and chuckled weakly, releasing his shoulder and regaining my strength. "Do you have anything to eat?" I asked, barely above a whisper.

The confusion in his eyes doubled, and he shook his head. He slowly released me. "Sorry….you look a little pale. Do you want me to get you something?"

Tempting, but I needed to hear Rip's voice. I waved him away and answered the phone. "Rip?"

His voice was urgent on the other end. "Freya!? Thank God! Whose phone are you on?"

"A nurse in the ER let me borrow it." He didn't need to know the male nurse who answered happened to resemble Owen Wilson and was into Cougars. I looked back and noticed Nurse Hottie was still standing there, watching me. Didn't he have people to…nurse? The reference made me think of a mother nursing a baby and I laughed so loud, I startled myself. I was feeling a little strange.

"I'm on my way. Just stay there," was the last thing I heard Rip say, before my hand loosened its grip on the phone without my permission. The room was spinning and I tried to get to the nearest chair to sit, but the edges of my vision went black, and then the chair was gone. I heard shouting and people running toward me. Then the floor slammed into my head.

▬ ▬ ▬

I opened my eyes, and the first thing I saw was Rip's face. I reached up and touched his cheek. He was smiling at me, so I smiled back, but then I noticed the worry in his eyes. Suddenly, I remembered I was forty…and married…not to Rip. I had no idea where I was. I tried to sit up, but the IV in my arm tightened and I flinched at the pain. I panicked a little.

"What the hell happened? Why am I in this bed? What's in this IV?" I demanded. I was still trying to sit up, but Rip put a gentle hand on my shoulder.

"Calm down. You're fine. You just passed out."

Oh great. At least *that's* not embarrassing at all. An FBI agent passing out on her first assignment. I felt like a college freshman throwing up after one beer.

Not cool. Not cool at all.

Rip must have read my mind. He pulled his chair as close to my bed as he could and took my hand. His touch immediately relaxed me.

"You have absolutely nothing to be embarrassed about, Freya. You were dehydrated, and, I imagine, coming down from a pretty intense adrenaline rush from all that happened." He was beaming at me now. "I just talked to that punk, Case. He told me everything that happened after he and his brother, who's going to be fine, by the way, were told to watch you. He thinks you're frickin' Wonder Woman, and I happen to agree."

He chuckled, and then just gazed at me like…like…an overprotective lover.

"I guess that makes you Batman."

Who said that? It had sounded suspiciously like me. And from the way Rip was now blushing for the second time in his life, I realized it *had* been me.

Apparently, I wasn't in full control of my faculties just yet.

Rip noticed my expression change. He leaned in even closer to me, now looking sad. "Listen, Frey. About what happened...at the bridge...I mean before Logan and his eunuchs showed up..."

"Logan?"

"Oh yeah, that was the short kid's name...long story. I'll explain it all later, when you're out of here."

I nodded. "Sorry, you were saying..." After pushing the whole thing as far to the back of my mind as I could all day, I was ready to deal with it. Plus, I was anxious to hear his interpretation of the strange events that had taken hold of us that morning.

He hesitated, ordering his thoughts, and I waited patiently.

"It was so...real...but...I thought we were back in college again... when we were still together..." His voice broke on the last word, and he had to stop. He looked down at his lap and then closed his eyes and took a deep breath, but I noticed the hand that held mine was trembling.

"Rip, I know what you're saying. It was like...we were transported back in time...and all I could think about was...you and me..." It seemed I couldn't get through it either. "Rip, please look at me."

He slowly raised his head and locked his eyes with mine. He looked so vulnerable, I didn't want to say what I was thinking. But I had to.

"Rip...Trevor...and the kids...I can't just..."

He looked away, nodding and smiling, but it just made his face look even more devastated. "It's okay, Freya. I understand. Really, I do. I don't want to hurt Trevor and the boys any more than you do. I just...I just needed to know...needed to hear...when you said..." He made eye contact again, and this time, I felt a rush of heat that started in my chest and jolted through me, up to my head, and down to my fingertips and then my toes.

Whoa.

When I said...what did I say? My head was fuzzy again as I struggled to remember.

"When you said..." he seemed to gather all his courage to gaze into my eyes again. "When you said you loved me...it was like I'd been waiting a thousand years to hear it. But I understand. It was the stress of the situation and the whole psychedelic time travel…you were still in the past when you said it…I get it—" I had to stop him right there.

"I *do* love you."

He stopped, his mouth hanging open as if he was trying to form his next word, but it never came.

I sat up slowly, minding my IV cord, and looked deep into his hypnotic gray eyes. This was going to get complicated, but I was no longer the Freya who lived in a bubble. I would say what I was feeling, dammit, and deal with the consequences as they came.

"I love you. I wasn't lost in the past when I said it. I was afraid I might never see you again, yes, but that's why I had to tell you. I love you. I've always loved you."

For the second time that day, I had said three little words that should have been music to Rip's ears, but, because of our unique circumstances, seemed to rip his heart in two. I didn't know what else to say. Those smoky eyes were now boring through mine like laser beams.

"Freya, I have loved you with every molecule, every fiber of my existence, for over twenty years. You are the only woman I want to be with."

Tears were streaming freely down my face, and I didn't try to stop them. Maybe this whole 'be honest with yourself' thing was a mistake. I felt more miserable than ever. All I could do was try to convey everything I couldn't put into words through my eyes. He had always been eerily good at reading my eyes. He gently wiped a tear from my cheek, and the path he made with his finger tingled for a second. Then, he leaned in and kissed my lips so softly, it sent a shiver down my spine. He broke away, but it was painfully obvious he didn't want to.

"Why did we ever break up, anyway?" he asked, I assumed rhetorically.

I smiled tragically at him, but then I realized something. I *couldn't* remember why we had broken up. Suddenly, my head hurt.

"Why *did* we break up?" I asked. "I think my brain is still a little clouded. Help me remember. I'm afraid I have partial amnesia after hitting my head." I was only half kidding.

"You hit your head?" He was worried again. "They didn't tell me you hit your head."

"Well, I assume that's what happened when it collided with the floor," I responded, trying to be funny, but he didn't laugh.

He stood and helped me lay back down, which I didn't fight. My head was really pounding now. He was so concerned, I couldn't help but be a little nervous.

"Did the doc say if I have a concussion or anything? I have a mongo headache."

Rip looked around the room, and located my chart hanging on a nail next to the door. He walked over and retrieved it, paging through until he found what he was looking for. "No. It says here they checked you for a concussion and it was negative." He continued to read silently for a moment.

"Is there something else?"

He started at my question, but then forced a smile. "Just a lot of mumbo jumbo." He put the chart back on its nail and returned to me. "Do you want me to get the nurse to give you a Motrin or something?" he asked.

I nodded, and he turned to go, but I couldn't stand the thought of him leaving. "Wait. Don't go. I'll buzz her."

He turned and smiled at me. It was such a beautiful smile, with one side of his mouth just a little higher than the other the way he always did, and his silvery-gray eyes were all shiny from his unshed tears…and he looked sort of like he was glowing.

There was something seriously wrong with me. The room started to sway a little and I closed my eyes. Then, I had a flash of being in a hospital years before. I was covered in blood but I wasn't in any pain. I looked over to the bed next to mine, and saw a young Rip, unconscious and also blood-soaked from head to toe. The doctor was yelling instructions at his medical team, trying to revive him. I screamed his name. Back then, I called him Ty…

"Are you okay?"

I opened my eyes, and there he was, his glossy eyes worried and… yes, he was definitely glowing. Then, it passed. The room stopped moving and Rip stopped radiating light…mostly.

"My head is really killing me," was all I said before I pushed the call button and asked sweetly for an ibuprofen, watching Rip the whole time as if he might disappear in a poof of smoke or something. He smiled mischievously at me.

"So, *Batman* and Wonder Woman?"

"Yeah, I always thought they made a better couple. Superman's a little *too* perfect for her, don't you think?"

He nodded his agreement, not attempting to hide the sparkle in his eyes at the fact that we were indirectly referring to ourselves as a Superhero couple, but then his smile faded, and he looked at me with concern again.

I wanted to reassure him. "I'm fine, ba—" I froze in mid-word.

His eyes sparkled a bit. "You were going to call me 'babe'. You used to call me that all the time, before…" He didn't need to say any more. We both knew something wasn't right.

"Frey, do you really *not* remember us breaking up back in college?"

I took a deep breath and closed my eyes, trying to see beyond the headache, and past all the traumatic goings on of the day, and thought hard about Rip and I…in college…in love…then, I was with Trevor…what happened before that? Why couldn't I retrieve it?

"I can't remember, but I assume it's just a side effect of, well, everything that happened today, culminating in the unprovoked attack on my head by the ER floor. I'm thinking of pressing charges," I joked, trying to hide my real feelings.

What other memories had I lost? Would I ever get them back?

"Tell me what happened, and maybe it will come back to me." I tried to sound casual.

He took my hand in his again, and seemed uncomfortable with what he was about to say. "That's just it, honey…"

Honey? He used to call me that. Cliché, I know, but when he said it, it was like he was calling me 'Aphrodite'. He continued.

"…I can't remember either."

EPISODE 19
Freya's File

I left the hospital exhausted, emotionally and otherwise. Trevor had come to take Freya home, and the last thing I wanted was to feel like a third wheel. I was too tired to think about all that had happened. I walked into my apartment and tossed my keys, missing the bowl on the small hallway table and watching the keys get some air before crashing to the floor. I sighed.

I'll get those later.

I took my jacket off and threw it on the back of the couch as I entered the living room. Janice had been there that morning, so the place was clean, but I wasn't much of a neat freak. I only hired the cleaning lady after Freya had stopped by and commented that the place smelled too much like 'bachelor'.

I dropped onto the couch and stared at the envelope I had taken from Pixley's desk. Freya's Super Top Secret file, that the Director had practically handed to me himself, was pulsing in my hands. The small part of my brain that was still functioning knew, somewhere deep down, that the pulsing was actually my body throbbing from extreme fatigue, but it still seemed like the envelope had a life of its own. The secrets inside were practically screaming to get out.

I was so spent from the day I'd had, and from fearing for Freya's life, I didn't know if I had the energy to open it. But I was positive sleep would not be possible until I knew what was in that mystery file. It may hold the answers to the strange flashback Freya and I had simultaneously experienced.

I took a deep breath and slowly broke the seal.

I pulled out the two-inch stack of papers and laid it on the glass-top coffee table. I put my elbows on my knees and ran both hands through my hair, then leaned back for a few seconds, staring at the pile. I wondered if I would regret what I was about to do. What if the woman I loved and thought I knew was…well, someone else? The curiosity was too much. I had to know.

I reached for the top sheet when I realized something. If I was going to figure out what Freya had been through, I needed to start from the beginning. I picked up the whole pile and flipped it upside down.

The very first paper, the oldest one in Freya's file, was an assignment order. It looked just like the one I had signed when I joined the FBI all those years ago…right before Freya had started dating Trevor…

Suddenly, my head started to pound, and the words on the page became blurred. I had a flash of a memory and grabbed my head with both hands, trying to hold it in.

▬ ▬ ▬

Freya and I were in my car, a shiny, red, two-door Grand Am, and she was laughing at something I'd just said. She looked so beautiful, that I couldn't take my eyes off her. She was wearing a brown dress that hit her every curve just right, and had her hair pulled back in a low pony tail so I could see her sexy neck. She scolded me, smiling, and pushed my face away so I would watch the road. She had always been the sensible one.

I laughed, and turned my attention back to the road. We were driving down a busy street at night…a city street that could have been anywhere…New York City, Chicago, L.A., Minneapolis? There was nothing from my vantage point to suggest exactly where we were, but the young me knew where he was going, it seemed. Everything was right with the world.

Then, Freya shouted at me, and my smile disappeared. I glanced in the rearview mirror and saw a black car with blacked-out windows approaching fast. It had European plates.

"How the hell did they find us so fast?" Freya asked me.

Then she hiked up her dress and retrieved a gun from a concealed holster on her hip. She leaned out the window and started shooting.

■ ■ ■

I opened my eyes, and the lights in my apartment flickered. I was still sitting on my couch, leaning back against the cushion. I blinked a few times, as the throbbing in my temples ceased.

What the hell was that?

I rubbed my temples and sat forward again. It took a moment for my eyes to focus. Then, I picked up the form that had signed Freya's life into the FBI *over* twenty years ago…but that didn't make sense. It was dated March 22, 1991, when Freya was just a sophomore in college. Maybe it was just a typo…but, even if I could write it off as an error, I couldn't ignore the fact that she hadn't even applied to the FBI until a year later, and then she'd been rejected.

I remembered her disappointment when she'd received the letter. It was some shit about how there were no field openings that would fit her particular skills, etc., etc. I had told her it was a bunch of crap, and that it was their loss. She seemed to recover pretty quickly, and started talking excitedly about pursuing her second choice of joining the Air Force, and her spirits had lifted considerably by that evening when I had taken her to see the newest *Indiana Jones* movie…that would be the one with Sean Connery, not the one with aliens. It had been out for a few years, but if you didn't mind waiting a while, the campus would eventually show 'new' movies for free, and, well, college students are poor, so we usually waited.

After the movie, we had gone back to her little apartment, which was practically *our* little apartment for as much time as I spent there too, and we'd had an incredible night together. As she fell asleep in my arms, I had thought that my life couldn't possibly get any better.

A shiver ran down my spine as I remembered, and my groin throbbed.

Down boy.

I needed to concentrate. I went back to the paper, and scrutinized every line on the page. March 22, 1991. I just couldn't convince myself that it was a simple error. My suspicious nature wouldn't let me. But, if the date was correct, then, what the hell did it mean?

We had started dating in the Fall of 1990, after pretending our mutual feelings for each other were strictly platonic for the first year. We had met in August of 1989, when we were both freshman, but at twenty-three, I was older than most of the seniors, and hadn't made many friends, until I met Freya, who was barely…what…she had to have been seventeen…in the small Forensic Science 101 class.

But, wait. She wasn't only seventeen when I met her, was she? The dates started to swim around in my head. That would have made her only sixteen when she graduated high school. That didn't sound right. It was a long time ago, but I'd always been good at remembering dates. I was sure we had met in August of 1989.

I was, however, certain of the memory of my first impression of her. She was a beautiful young girl, which was the first thing I noticed, of course, but after talking to her for only a few minutes, I was surprised at how quickly we connected. It was immediately clear how smart she was and I could tell she had what some call an 'old soul'. I was hooked after five minutes. It was love at first conversation.

I smiled at the memory of our first encounter. Then I frowned. I had to focus. I took a deep breath and closed my eyes, hoping that would help me sort out all the dates.

She had applied to the FBI in November of 1991. I was sure of that. It was our third, but last year of college. She had taken classes every summer and a more than full load during the regular semesters to graduate in three years, and had convinced me to do the same, although my grades couldn't compare to hers. The combination of her intelligence, her drive, and her ADD, although there wasn't a name for it back then, made her a force to be reckoned with. I was convinced, even then, that she could do anything…

…which was why it was a shock when she received the rejection letter in February, 1992.

The rejection letter. I quickly flipped through the pile, and couldn't find anything that resembled the letter I remembered.

Strange.

I went back to the form in my hand, wondering what other mysteries I would find. Realistically, incorrect dates didn't really tell me anything, other than whoever filled out the form might have been a complete idiot. Wrong dates were put on forms all the time, I had to remind myself.

The rest was all pretty normal, from what I remembered on my own initial assignment form...but, wait, another incorrect date. This time, it was Freya's birthdate. The day was correct, July 1, but the year was wrong. It said 1971, but she was born in 1972.

Wasn't she?

Suddenly, I didn't know for sure. All the dates were now doing battle in my head. It was like the WWE in there.

I was starting to think the form had been typed up by a moron, plain and simple. But the Director back then, Baron Sheelds, had signed it, big and bold at the bottom, and he had been known for his attention to detail. He was the Director who had ordered all FBI forms to be redone, made more efficient with less redundancy. Why would he sign a form with so many errors?

Then, I noticed one final oddity. The signature block where Freya's smooth, classic script should have been...was blank. She'd never signed her own enlistment form into the FBI. So, was she in the FBI, or wasn't she? I mean, I knew she was *now*, and she'd signed the same form just a few weeks ago, albeit an updated version, but twenty-one years ago...? A sharp pain tore through my head, and I closed my eyes for a moment.

I set the form down on the table, and reached for the next one in the stack. As I tried to pick up one sheet, several came with it, all connected by perforations that had never been broken. Irritated, and tired beyond belief, I pulled and pulled until the last connected sheet came up. I laid the six-page spread flat on the table, shoving the rest of the file back to make room. It was a medical scan of some sort. As I tried to make my eyes focus, I read the top. Above the computer-digitized waves that spanned all six pages, it said 'Freya Tamar McKenna', her maiden name, and below that it said 'Initial CAT Scan of Proposed Subject, Project RVW-19710701'. It was dated '5 Apr 91'.

The next item on the pile was another CAT scan, this one dated a month later, '2 May 91', and titled 'Post-Implant CAT Scan of Proposed Subject'. This one had a handwritten note at the bottom that said 'Implant successful. Subject ready for reinsertion and test'.

Then I noticed something, and pulled the first scan out to double check. In the top, right-hand corner of both scans was a stamp, faded, but legible. It was a company signature...'Winkle Labs'.

That sounded vaguely familiar to me. I rubbed my temples and closed my eyes, navigating through my memories to find this one specific clue.

Winkle Labs...Winkle Labs...Winkle...

Freya and I had done an experimental study in college for a little extra money. The pharmaceutical company that sponsored it was Winkle Labs. I remembered because Winkle seemed to use unwitting college students for a lot of its studies back then...and it was a funny name. I couldn't remember when, though...was it April? Then it all came flooding back to me. The study was during our Spring Break. I remember we laughed at how romantic our break was going to be, volunteering to be lab rats for the week. The exact dates eluded me, but it could have been April.

Why the hell was a CAT scan...no, two CAT scans from a standard drug study, using college students as guinea pigs, in an official FBI file for an eighteen-year-old woman who wasn't in the FBI? And what had we tested during that study? I tried to focus, tried to bring that memory to the front of my brain, but it just made my entire skull throb with pain.

Think, Rip, think, dammit!

I couldn't think anymore. I needed to sleep, no matter how much I wanted to keep reading. I decided to forego the bedroom and just get comfortable on the couch.

I was so tired, I don't even remember taking my shoes off, but when I woke up hours later, they were on the floor, kicked off and left to land one perched on top of the other. I rubbed my eyes and slowly sat up. I glanced at my watch...6:12 am.

As the events of the day before came flooding back, I attempted to organize my thoughts, as well as all the information I had read but couldn't process the night before. I remembered one thing.

Winkle Labs. I knew that's where I would start.

I stretched my neck, cleared my throat, and stood to head for the shower, when I noticed something about the coffee table.

It was empty.

I frantically looked around, but Freya's file was gone.

EPISODE 20
Darth Vader Returns

Trevor was being so nice to me, I didn't know if I would ever get around to telling him *everything* that had happened that day…or if I'd have the guts. He'd rushed into my hospital room like I'd been in a tragic car accident or something, and stayed until I was released. Rip had left soon after Trevor arrived, and they pretended not to notice each other, but I could have cut the tension with a chainsaw.

I didn't know if it would be easier to tell my husband I had strong feelings for his best friend if they were still *acting* like best friends, but either way, this was not going to be a picnic.

Picnic.

Don't think about the picnic, Freya.

The word alone made me tingle all over.

How could I tell Trevor about that? I asked myself on the car ride home from the hospital. *It would destroy him.*

I realized I was being selfish, determined to tell Trevor that I loved Rip *and* him. What was I expecting him to do? Jump up and down for joy just to be in the running? Was I really that conceited? And, no matter what his reaction, what was I going to do after he knew, assuming he didn't make that decision for me and take himself out of the picture? Eventually, I was going to have to choose between my husband of fifteen years, with whom I had three beautiful children, and the man who had been my first real love, and was not only my husband's best friend, but *my* best friend as well, and that was the realization I had been avoiding.

Who did I love more? I wasn't sure at that point, and worried that I may never know. What if I chose the wrong man? I was playing with people's lives, and no matter who I chose to be with, all our lives would be irrevocably altered. What would my children think of me if Daddy moved out and Uncle Rip moved in? How could I even be thinking of ending my marriage after one strange, albeit intense, encounter with Rip? Just yesterday, I had been content with the way things were. Was I ready to throw my life into a Category 5 tornado?

It was overwhelming, and I was suddenly nauseated and dizzy. Through the haze, however, I kept focusing on one fact. If life experience had taught me anything, being honest right up front was a lot less painful in the long run, and I had always been the type to rip the Band-Aid off in one swift motion.

Plus, Trevor and I didn't keep secrets from each other.

When we arrived at our house, Talia was eating popcorn, and sitting in the living room with all the lights off, watching *Tank Girl*...one of her favorites in my special collection that also included *Stargate, Judge Dredd*, and every *Mystery Science Theater 3000* ever made. She quickly turned it off when she saw us, and hurried to me, asking if I was alright. I assured her I was just fine, and she gave me a heartfelt hug that aggravated my tailbone, but my microscopic flinch went unnoticed. She quickly excused herself, after Trevor and I both thanked her profusely for watching the boys, and she brushed past my husband to leave through the back door in the kitchen. (The boys and I actually called it 'Talia's Door'.)

She stopped next to me and whispered in my ear. "You're my hero."

A few seconds later, I heard Talia's front door open and close. I wondered if Trevor had told her what I'd done to my young captor. But, if *he* knew, Rip must have told him, and I'm pretty sure that was against the rules.

I shook my head slightly. I didn't have the energy to analyze Talia's comment. I just wanted to go to bed.

After Trevor escorted me into each of the boy's bedrooms to gently kiss their sleeping heads, he practically carried me into the bedroom and tucked me into our king-sized bed. I didn't protest. I was kind of enjoying it.

He sat next to me on the edge of the bed, and smiled down at me. Then, his smile faded. "I was so worried about you," he said, with such concern in his voice, I felt sorry for him. I grabbed his hand and squeezed.

"I'm so sorry. I should have called you as soon as I was safe, but I was so single-minded…I just needed to get those boys to the hospital." I hoped I wasn't revealing too much, but I was gauging his reaction too, trying to discern how much he already knew.

He squeezed my hand back, unfazed by everything I'd said. "You're safe. You're here. That's all I care about." He leaned down and kissed me gently. He tasted like coffee. He always inhaled the stuff when he was stressed, and I guess it had been a somewhat stressful day for both of us.

He stood and began emptying his pockets, placing the contents on his dresser. Then he chuckled. "You know, I didn't think that pretty boy nurse was going to let me take you home. He seemed very protective of you." He was clearly amused, as opposed to jealous.

I replied, "That kid was flirting with me from the minute I walked into the ER, and I was covered in blood and looked horrendous!" We laughed together. "Maybe I reminded him of his mother," I added. I laughed at this, but Trevor shook his head.

"First of all, you and 'horrendous' have never been in the same country together, and anyone who's legally considered an adult would never think of you as their mother." He sat by me again, and this time the kiss was filled with passion. That tingle went through me. Apparently, the tingle wasn't going to give me any indication of whose team it was on, Rip's or Trevor's. Thanks for nothing, blasted tingle. Even crazed *Twilight* fans could make a decision. We pulled apart, and Trevor was peering into my soul. I felt the need to lighten the mood a little.

"Well, he came in handy though, when I needed a phone to call Rip—"

"You called Rip?" he asked, his smile fading fast. His eyes flickered with jealousy. Or maybe it was my imagination. As far as I knew, he had no reason to be jealous of Rip…yet.

"Well, he *was* my partner for the assign—"

"He's your partner now?" he accused. "When were you going to tell me that?" Jealousy and anger now, and I wasn't imagining either one. He knew. How much he knew, I was unsure, but he knew enough to be suspicious.

"How much did he tell you?" I risked asking, hoping I would like the answer.

He stood and walked away from me, stopping at the foot of the bed. He seemed to be having trouble looking at me. That's when I realized. He knew everything.

"Rip told you about the...what happened at the bridge...didn't he?" He looked at me. The answer was clawing its way out of his eyes. Why in the HELL did Rip feel the need to tell my husband, his best friend, that we had almost...that we had almost...

Band-Aid, Freya. Rip if off like a Band-Aid.

...that we had almost gotten naked together under an abandoned bridge in the desert? I may be in love with Rip, but at that moment, I wanted to run him over with my minivan. How dare he! I would have to deal with him later.

I tried to sit up, wincing at my bruised tailbone. Trevor was suddenly concerned again, and came to my side. He helped me prop myself up in a comfortable sitting position.

"What did those goons do to you?" he asked, almost to himself, as he arranged the pillows behind my back.

Before I could stop myself, I answered. "You can thank your buddy, Rip, for this one. When he fell on top of me, I hit—"

Trevor abruptly stood, and walked back to the foot of the bed, pacing. Okay, that was a stupid thing to say, in light of what was going on, but Rip and I had just been horsing around at that point. It wasn't even part of the...well, the part that Trevor clearly didn't want to talk about. Why couldn't he just tell me that he knew and give me a chance to explain that it wasn't real?

"Why didn't you say anything?"

He glanced up at me like a wounded animal, but didn't respond.

"Why have you been so nice?"

His face changed to confusion, but he still didn't speak.

The words came fast, and I felt my face heat up. "If you knew that Rip and I had almost had sex in the desert, why aren't you livid? Why didn't you pack your bags and leave me? How can you just stand there and try to pretend I didn't almost cheat on you?!" I was mad now, and I didn't know why. I was the one in the wrong, and I was yelling at him.

He was silent for a moment, and then rubbed his face with his hand, as if he was trying to rub the whole situation away. Then, he took a deep breath. "How can you ask why I didn't leave?" he asked quietly.

It was my turn to look confused. He let an infinitesimal smile escape. "I love you, Freya. I love you so much...I could never leave you."

I was taken aback by his honesty. The statement itself rivaled the sappiest lines from all those cheesy movies I hated, and maybe any other woman would be swept away by it, but to tell the truth, it rubbed me the wrong way. I felt like he was really saying that he would never let *me* leave *him*. The look in his eyes was unsettling. He could read me like a book, and he knew I had received his message loud and clear.

We stared at each other for a moment. The natural thing to do after your husband tells you he loves you is to reciprocate the statement, and that's exactly what he was waiting for. And that's exactly why I couldn't say it. There was nothing natural about the way he was looking at me...like he owned me and there was nothing I could do about it.

I still wanted to explain what happened at the bridge. He had to know it was not something Rip or I intended...it was a sort of simultaneous glitch in our psyches...or something.

"Did Rip tell you we weren't ourselves when it...it happened. We were having some sort of surreal flashback of when we were dating back in college. It was almost like a drug-induced hallucination, it was so real—"

He cut me off as he came back to sit by me on the bed. "We don't need to talk about that right now. The point is, nothing happened. Not really. You didn't intend to cheat on me, and you didn't cheat on me. That's all I need to know." He leaned down and kissed me on the forehead. "I'll let you get some rest."

He smiled at me, and he was the old Trevor again, the Trevor I knew, the Trevor I loved.

Then he left the room, turning the light out as he went.

"Trevor." It escaped my mouth without my knowledge, but I knew what I wanted to ask him. I heard his footsteps stop. He didn't come back, but responded from the hallway.

"What," he replied curtly.

"Why did Rip and I break up?"

It was met by silence, but I had to know.

"Back in college, before I met you. One of us must have told you how we broke up."

I counted the seconds of uncomfortable quiet…five, six, seven, eight.

"You really don't remember?"

"No. Please, I just need to know."

I heard a heavy sigh. "He cheated on you." His footsteps sounded again, and the old wooden stairs creaked under his weight as he quickly descended.

He was lying. I knew with every cell in my body that he was lying. If he didn't know the answer, he would have just said he didn't know, but why lie about it?

I sat there in the dark for what seemed like an eternity. My mind reeled. I thought of *Stepford Wives*, the weird original, not the even weirder remake, and wondered if there was a Fem-Bot out there somewhere that looked just like me, but with bigger boobs. The Trevor I had just met was capable of it, I was sure. Or maybe it was the painkillers coursing through my veins. Whatever it was, I didn't feel like myself at all, and it was freaking me out.

Why didn't Trevor want to hear the explanation? If I thought *he* had 'almost' cheated on *me*, I would want—no, *need* to know every sordid detail, no matter how it would devastate me. Of course, sweeping traumatic events under the rug, and trying to pretend they didn't happen, was standard procedure for him. He had reacted the same way when Rowan choked on the quarter…and when I announced I wanted to be an FBI agent. But, then there was the obvious lie…for what reason? To make me hate Rip?

I thought of the attempted reenactment of the Sex under the Oak extravaganza, and smiled. I remembered every second of it, but at the time, I had forgotten I was married, that I was a mom, that I had lived more than twenty years since that day. I had been nineteen again. Nineteen and terminally in love with Ty Ripley.

I wrapped my arms around my chest and sank down in the bed. I closed my eyes and let the pain pill take me. It seemed like only seconds, and I was deep in a dream.

Ty...

EPISODE 21
The Brain Room

Trevor vehemently denied breaking into my apartment and taking Freya's file. In fact, he seemed genuinely upset that it was missing, and blamed me for the whole thing. When he told the Director that I had "let it get stolen," Pixley seemed more bored than concerned, which screamed to me that he had not only orchestrated when the file came into my possession, but he had also controlled when it left.

I got the message that Pixley was sending. I was only supposed to get a sneak peak, and if I was stupid enough to fall asleep with the file right out in the open, then, well, I didn't deserve to know what was in it. If I was a decade younger, I might have had the presence of mind to copy the whole damn thing to a flash drive the minute I'd walked into my apartment. But my brain just didn't work that way. I was starting to think I was getting too old for this shit.

It would seem I was being left to my own devices to find the information I so desperately needed. Why Pixley couldn't just call me into his office, sit me down, and say, "Agent Ripley, get comfortable, because I'm going to tell you everything you've ever wanted to know about Freya Douglas…would you like a vodka tonic?" was beyond me. Why couldn't *anything* ever just be easy?

If only I could ask Freya herself.

Clearly, she was more in the dark about her past than I was. I realized my passion to find out the truth wasn't just to satisfy my own curiosity. I needed to find out who Freya was…for Freya.

Several attempts to call up the twenty-year-old memory of my inexplicable break-up with the love of my life had failed miserably… although I did succeed in giving myself a whopper of a migraine.

It seemed that if the flashbacks, or whatever they were, continued, they were going to come when they were good and ready, and not a second before. Needless to say, I was going to avoid operating heavy machinery for the time being, just in case...and maybe roller coasters.

I decided to check the FBI database one more time, although I'd done so exactly seven times already, with no luck. This time I had something new to type into the search box...Winkle Labs.

To avoid any passersby viewing my computer screen, I went down to the 'Brain Room', or the central database computer room, where all of the updates and repairs to the system were done. There were generic computer stations there, kind of like at the public library, and there was never anyone there but 'The Brain' herself.

Ainsley Krese was very possibly the smartest alleged full human on the planet. I say 'alleged' because there was speculation by the Trekkie sect that she was an android. She had helped make several modifications to the NASA computer system ten years before, when she was just fifteen years old, and one NASA official had been overheard telling another that she was smarter than their computers. She had never received any formal computer training—she had been recruited by the FBI before her sixteenth birthday, and had never graduated high school—but, there was a rumor she was building a working replica of Optimus Prime in the old renovated warehouse that she lived in...and I believed it.

We called her 'Brainsley' or just 'Brain' and she didn't seem to mind. In fact, it was a bit like trying to communicate with an alien. Brain's first language was computer. She spoke to humans only when she absolutely had to, and I was no exception.

I stepped through the door and closed it behind me. I was in a small room with a second door and an access panel. I scanned my FBI identification card and heard the lock on the door disengage. I pushed the heavy door and immediately heard the loud humming of all the computer equipment and technological gadgets inside the massive room. I couldn't name them all if my life depended on it...heck, the only things I recognized were the computer monitors...and the chairs.

Brain was there, in the far right corner, sitting facing the door at the main access terminal that controlled the whole building, more or less; interoffice security systems, internal and external surveillance cameras, every desktop computer, the cash registers in the commissary, even the sprinkler system. She stopped typing and held up two fingers without looking up.

She wanted me to go to Terminal #2.

As I headed toward my assigned cubicle, I couldn't help but be awed at the speed Brain's fingers were moving on the keyboard. I couldn't tell what she was doing, but she was always making modifications, improvements, and/or upgrades to the system. She seemed so at home in her custom-made ergonomic chair, that it was almost like she was part of it...part of the machine she now so intimately conversed with.

Her funky, cat-like purple glasses had slid halfway down her nose, but she didn't seem to notice, and she had a lovely face that she never masked with makeup of any kind, her amber eyes sparkling as they reflected whatever it was she was doing on the computer screen. Her black curly hair was always pinned back in some way, away from her face, although tendrils escaped and cascaded along her cheekbones, and her voluptuous little figure was accentuated with her eclectic thrift shop fashion style. I didn't understand it, but I had heard several female agents say that she was one of the few women on the planet who could mix and match colors and patterns, and make it work. It was just so... her. All I could see from my vantage point as I settled in at Terminal #2 was a dark yellow blouse that matched the darkest flecks of her eyes, and her signature purple and orange knit fingerless gloves that stretched to her elbows.

Freya had caught a glimpse of her once, as they passed each other in the ladies' room, and had said she was "hauntingly beautiful." I thought that assessment was spot on.

Suddenly, she noticed I was staring at her, probably with a stupid grin on my face due to my daydreaming, and the click clack of her fingers on the keys stopped for just a second. I could have sworn I saw a slight blush as she quickly looked back to her monitor. Embarrassed, I looked away too, cleared my throat for no particular reason, and sat down at the computer she'd assigned to me.

I might as well get this done, so I can get on with my day, I thought to myself, convinced I would find nothing but disappointment on the screen in front of me.

Just for the hell of it, I typed in Freya's maiden name and waited for the screen to change. I wasn't surprised when the form that materialized was blank except for the name and birthdate.

I went back to the search screen and typed in "Winkle Labs." I waited. And waited. Suddenly, a message I'd never received before appeared. It said: "This terminal is not authorized to access this information."

Hmm. So, Winkle Labs triggered something that I needed a higher security clearance to access. It was a roadblock, but a roadblock was progress. It was better than a blank screen.

Just then, I heard music. It was ethereal and Enya-ish. I looked around for a moment and then the music stopped. I heard Brain quietly say, "Hi," into her cell phone.

I turned back to my screen, unsure of what to do next. I heard rustling behind me, and Brain was standing, gathering her things to leave. I looked at her, and she glanced over at me. She stopped gathering, and released a small, quick sigh. I think she'd forgotten I was there.

"Lunch."

Brain had just spoken to me. I was stunned for a moment.

"You have to go."

Four more words from the hauntingly beautiful android. I finally realized she was waiting for me to respond. I nodded. "I'm done here, anyway."

She surprised me when she engaged me in conversation a third time. "No luck?"

I was so flabbergasted, I had to swallow hard before I could answer. "Uh, no...I guess access to Winkle Labs is above my pay grade."

Shit. Why had I mentioned Winkle Labs? So much for staying under the radar with my self-appointed assignment. I took a deep breath and reminded myself that Brain never talked to anyone. Maybe she would keep my secret...but, then, do I have to tell her it's a secret in the first place? What had I just gotten myself into?

"Um...I don't want...if you could...just not...if you..." I stammered. She had gone back to gathering and, without looking up, rescued me from my own verbal noose.

"I won't tell," she stated, sounding almost bored. She slung her large purse over her shoulder and headed for the door. She reached for the knob.

"Um…I thought I had to leave…?" I asked, confused.

She froze and, moving nothing but her lips, said mysteriously, "Go back to your girlfriend's file."

I didn't register what she was saying at first. "Excuse me?" I replied.

She turned to me and smiled. She was even more breathtaking when she smiled. I was beginning to see the validity of the whole android theory.

"You assume what you're looking for will be tucked neatly inside a text box. Look outside the boxes."

She began to turn the knob, but stopped.

"You may need to try a different terminal. I don't think that one is working properly." She motioned with her head ever so slightly toward her workspace…the central access terminal…and I saw her ID sticking out of the card reader slot. She was still logged on.

Then she left.

EPISODE 22
Too Many Secrets

I sat down slowly in Brain's chair. I inhaled as deeply as I could and then blew it out through my mouth. I stared at the screen. She had left it on the search page. My fingers hovered over the keys. I knew what to type, but I was apprehensive…nervous even.

Why was Brain helping me? As far as I knew, she had never spoken more than four words to anyone else in the building…so, why me?

I decided to take advantage of the opportunity before me and stop questioning it. It was what it was…and it was all I had at the moment. I gave my neck a quick snap right, then left, the popcorn sound filling me with satisfaction. Then, I braced myself, and typed 'Freya McKenna' in the search box.

The same blank screen I had seen seven, now eight times, stared back at me. I frowned.

What was it Brain had said? Think outside the box? Not something I was inherently good at, but nearly twenty years in the FBI had taught me some tricks.

Question: What do you see?

Answer: A file for an FBI agent.

Question: Is there anything unusual about it?

Answer: Yes.

Question: What?

Answer: It's void of information, save name and birthdate.

Question: Is it really?

I grunted with frustration as I always did when I was forced to run through the mental exercise I had learned in a training seminar years ago…one that claimed it could teach anyone how to see *every* clue in a case, not just the obvious ones. It was meant to heighten one's awareness of his or her surroundings, but after two weeks of 'close your eyes and visualize the scene', my end-of-training critique form made one recommendation: lose the two-week waste of time and just email the mental exercise questions to every agent in the bureau. It was tedious, but the only thing that I had taken away from the seminar that had actually worked for me a time or two.

I took a breath and focused.

Where was I?

Question: Is it really void of information?

Answer: Yes.

Question: What do you see when you focus only on the background?

Wait. That one was for when I was at an actual physical crime scene and was having trouble finding any leads. Jokingly, I thought to myself, *I see a blue pixelated screen.* I chuckled at my funny, but then gasped with an epiphany. What if I did consider the question in a more literal sense?

I made my eyes focus on the background of the screen, outside the boxes.

Outside the boxes...

Outside the boxes!

That's what Brain had said! Not 'think outside the box', but '*look* outside the *boxes*'. Being literal was working for me. I decided to make it my theme for the day.

I scanned the page on the screen, focusing on the blue space around the mostly empty text boxes. I started in the top left corner and worked my way across and down. As I approached the bottom right corner, my heart sank. There was nothing there.

Just to torture myself, I worked my way back up, ending at the top left corner.

Nothing.

Okay, Brain. What am I missing?

In a simpler world, Brain would have invited me over to her all-knowing terminal and shown me everything I had been so desperately searching for, all the time giving me her dazzling rarely-seen smile. Of course, in a simpler world, I wouldn't be here, secretly digging through the FBI database looking for twenty-year-old information that I had nowhere near the clearance to access through proper channels. In a simpler world, I would have married Freya twenty years ago, and my biggest problem would be what to get her for our anniversary.

Ouch. I let the sudden wave of sadness wash over me. Sometimes it was easier than trying to suppress it…and maybe it was one of the things motivating me to keep going.

As it passed, I realized the emotion left behind was anger. Anger at the FBI for having so many secrets. Anger at the fact that one of the oldest and biggest seemed to involve Freya and me. Anger at the way everything had to be so covert, and wrapped in a million layers of encrypted code.

I had a fleeting thought and checked my watch. 12:22. Brain had been gone just over twenty minutes. I assumed she took an hour for lunch, like most people, but then again, she was not most people…I couldn't assume anything. I needed to get the information and get the hell out of there.

I thought about the theme of my day. Maybe I still wasn't taking Brain's words as literally as I should be.

Look outside the boxes…look outside the boxes…look…outside… look…look…

Look.

I had noticed when I'd first sat down that Brain's cursor was an eye…wide open, lidless, and staring at me with an intensity that almost said, "It's about time, dummy!" I was just now realizing the importance of that all-seeing symbol.

I had been looking at the page with the wrong eyes…or eye.

I grabbed the mouse with renewed hope, and placed the eye in the top left corner of the screen. Slowly, I dragged it across the top, one imaginary row after another, watching closely for any change to the eye…anything at all. I was nearing the bottom right corner and my mouse hand was starting to sweat. I slowed the cursor, staring back at it with determination. I would not leave here as clueless as when I'd arrived.

Suddenly, the eye winked at me. I stopped the mouse and froze. Maybe I had imagined it. The soulless eye scrutinized me, giving no indication that it had closed its invisible lid for a microsecond. I cautiously lowered my right hand back down to rest on the mouse ever so gently. A few seconds later, I moved the cursor to the right, slowly, about an inch.

Nothing.

I reversed direction and willed myself not to blink as I bore a hole through the eyeball on the screen.

Wink.

I gasped quietly.

The eye looked at me innocently, denying it had just flirted with me a second time. I slid the mouse just a tiny bit, an infinitesimal distance. Time slowed...or seemed to. Or I was having a stroke.

The eye closed.

I lifted my hand as quickly as I could and held my breath.

The eye was still closed.

I allowed myself to exhale and leaned back in the chair, running my hands through my hair with relief. I imagined this must be how a brain surgeon felt after successfully removing a tumor. Thank God the only fine motor skill I had to worry about mastering was pulling a trigger. I enjoyed my victory for a moment, then sat up and cracked my knuckles. I slowly placed my index fingertip on the button of the mouse. Fingertip only...

Click.

The screen cycled through what seemed like a million pages, as if the computer was uploading the entire central database while I watched. It reminded me of the opening song for *The Big Bang Theory*. Then, it stopped.

The screen I was now looking at contained only three icons.

Heaven. Hell. Purgatory.

I didn't know what I'd expected, but that couldn't have been farther from it. I stared at the three choices for a moment, contemplating...

Which one first?

I was a fan of getting the bad out of the way first, so I clicked on the little red devil.

The page materialized and I frowned. At first glance, it was a list of numbers...all eight digits long, filling the screen in eight columns.

Numbers were not my thing, and I suddenly felt like I may be way out of my league. I scrubbed my face with my left hand and tried to think. I looked back at the endless sea of numbers.

Okay, I can do this. What do all the numbers have in common?

The first thing I noticed was that every single number on the page started with a '19'.

Suddenly, the eight digit numbers that had looked like some sort of encrypted computer language at first seemed very familiar. They were dates. Year, month, day.

That was easy. I smiled. A small victory is still a victory. I started scanning each number and realized my victory was short-lived, however. None of the dates were ringing a bell. They were listed chronologically, and the first, and oldest, number on the screen was '19120822'. A hundred years ago. I clicked on it.

It was a personnel file for someone named Clyde Conway. I scrutinized the information in front of me, and found that Clyde's birthdate was August 22, 1912. Then I saw a box labeled 'Nickname'. Clyde Conway's nickname was Casanova. Casanova Conway *did* ring a bell. He was a legendary agent who was the first documented member of the FBI to turn to the dark side. He was caught working for the Nazis during World War II and was summarily executed for treason. His natural charm and charisma had garnered him the name 'Casanova', but it proved to be doubly true when it was discovered he had a wife and kids in D.C…and a wife and kids in Germany.

I paged back and clicked on the next file. This one also belonged to an agent I'd heard of…because he had also been charged with treason. The next file, and the next file…all agents who had been caught, convicted, and executed for betraying their country. I didn't need to look any further to realize I had indeed entered Hell…the place in the FBI database where agents who'd turned bad rotted for eternity. Because of my nature to always second-guess myself, I did a quick glance to make sure Freya's birthdate was not listed, and then moved on.

I paged back to the three icons, and clicked on 'Heaven'…a small, ethereal angel complete with gown, wings, and halo.

Again, eight columns of eight-digit numbers stared at me. I noticed at the bottom of the screen that there were in fact thirty-one pages of the same. Hell had only had eight pages...I guess that was a good sign. If Hell was agents who'd gone bad, then what the...*heck* would Heaven be?

I clicked on the first file, '18781224'. I didn't recognize the name, but this guy was no double agent. He had earned so many awards, four of them posthumously, that there was a link to an extra page just to list them all. As I went back to the file list, I had to go to page twenty-eight just to get to the 1970's. Freya's birthdate was not listed. Purgatory it is. I clicked on the picture of the clock face with zeros where the numbers one through twelve should have been. The place with no time.

I quickly paged forward until I saw 1970 as the first four numbers of the file names, and slowed down, scanning for 19720701. It wasn't there.

Shit.

Now what?

I was about to abandon the whole thing when something struck me. I remembered the CAT Scans that had briefly been in my possession. And the enlistment form I had found at the top of the pile that was Freya's secret file. The form had said Freya's birthdate was 1971, not 1972. The CAT Scans had also had a file number of 19710701. That number *was* on the list.

I clicked on it, and there it was. Freya McKenna's file. And it was teeming with information. My heart skipped a beat.

I looked at my watch, and realized I didn't have time to read it. My hour was almost up. I pulled the tiny flash drive I'd bought that morning from my pocket, plugged it into the side of Brain's computer, and smiled. There might be hope for me yet.

EPISODE 23
A New Ally

I don't think I'd ever driven to Freya's house faster. I couldn't wait to show her what was on the flash drive, but I wasn't sure if it was because it might solve the mysteries of not just her past, but also mine, or if I was hoping it would somehow provide a way for us to be together. It didn't matter. Either way, she had a right to know what was going on, and to be told the secrets that had been kept from her all these years…and it seemed right that I was going to be the one to tell her. I just hadn't worked out how I was going to do it. Trevor was an agent, and that meant his whole life was constantly under surveillance, including his home computer. I couldn't just plug in the flash drive and access an FBI file. Someone would know. Freya had just bought a new laptop for Blaise, and I was praying it was still off the grid. But then there was the possible issue of the file being encrypted. I had thought of that half way to Freya's. It might not open on a civilian computer. I'd decided I would cross that bridge when I got to it.

As I turned down their street, I saw Trevor's car just starting to back out of their garage. I panicked, and quickly veered into Talia's driveway, which wound around behind her house and would keep me from being seen, I hoped. I pulled in as far as I could, and then hopped out of my car. I ran, half crouched, back to the edge of the house and peeked around. Trevor's car sped by, and he made no indication that he'd noticed me at all. Good. I definitely didn't want him around when I dropped this bombshell on his wife. I didn't expect to run into him at this hour. It was nearly eleven. He must have decided to go in late, given what Freya had been through.

What a good husband, I sneered to myself.

I headed back to my car, wondering if I should go ahead and leave it where it was just in case Trevor decided to come home early. Before I could make a decision, I passed by Talia's kitchen window and something caught my eye. I stopped and, at the risk of being a peeping Tom, pressed my face closer to the glass, so I could focus. There were papers spread out on the table, but there was something familiar about the extra-long, connected sheets of paper cascading across the surface...they looked almost like...

The CAT Scans. I pushed my face as close to the window as I could without breaking my nose and focused my eyes.

Holy shit.

Freya's CAT Scans from her secret FBI file were on Talia's kitchen table. I cupped my hands around my face to block out the sunlight obscuring my vision, and realized that Freya's *entire* secret FBI file was on Talia's kitchen table.

Click.

I froze.

"Turn around slowly," came the familiar female voice, but with a new, hardened tone.

I turned around, and Talia was standing there, pointing a gun at my head, and looking all too capable of pulling the trigger and getting on with her day. Still, I realized I was smiling.

"Something funny, Agent Ripley? This isn't my Annie Oakley Halloween costume, you know. I'm actually pointing a real gun at you."

"I'm sure it's real," I chuckled. "But this is hilarious, if you think about it, in a sad, sadistic sort of way."

"What the hell are you talking about?"

"You *and* Trevor. The two most important people in the world to Freya, and you're both..." I shook my head, chuckling at the irony.

"Both what?" she asked, sounding agitated.

"You know what you are."

"*I*...am just doing my job."

I chuckled again. "Well, that's a relief. I'm sure Freya will be glad to know you've been paid to be her best friend," I said, forgetting why the situation had struck me funny at all.

Talia didn't respond, but her expression softened...even if her grip on her revolver didn't.

"Whose side are you on?" I asked. "Are you working for Trevor?"

It was her turn to chuckle. "Trevor? No, Trevor didn't hire me."

"But he knows who you are. Doesn't he?" I pushed. She'd been living right under his nose for nearly three years. He had to know. He was a prick, but he was a damn good agent.

She lowered her revolver. "Let's talk inside...your car."

She made a quick motion of cupping her ear and nodding ever so slightly toward the house. I got the message. Her house was bugged.

"Okay...after you." I motioned for her to go ahead, but she was no rookie. She waved her gun to indicate she would follow me to the car.

I climbed in behind the steering wheel, and she got in the passenger seat. She gave a deep sigh, and I glanced in her direction. She was looking at me like a mother who had caught her son stealing money out of her purse. She laid the gun down on the dash, and I frowned.

"It's not loaded, anyway," she shrugged.

Well, my instincts were definitely dulling in my old age. "Are you kidding?"

"Maybe." She winked. "What do you know about the file?"

"Not much," I replied curtly. "I had only read a few pages when you took it from my apartment."

This took her by surprise. "You had the file in your possession? Who gave it to you?"

Now I was confused.

"Wait, you mean you didn't break into my apartment while I was asleep on the couch and take the file from my coffee table?"

"No." She was telling the truth.

Okay, I could cross Talia off the list...if she had been on it in the first place. I realized that she must have stolen it from whoever took it from me, or the mystery person gave it to her. My head started to spin. My money was still on Trevor, but before I could ask her, I heard a soft giggle.

"Asleep on your couch? Who are you, Fox Mulder? Don't you have a bed?" She smirked at me.

I couldn't help but grin in return, but I pretended to get defensive. "It had been a long day, alright? Haven't you ever spent the night on your couch?"

"No. You have anything else in common with Mulder I should know about?"

I gave her a perplexed look, and she raised both eyebrows at me a few times, all the while grinning at me mischievously. It took me a minute. I had to access the part of my brain that held the old episodes of *X-Files*…processing…processing…then, I remembered Mulder's insinuated penchant for porn.

My confusion changed to disgust.

"Believe it or not, Talia, or whatever your real name is, not all men are into that sort of thing. I'd much rather watch The Cooking Channel."

She regarded me for a moment. Then she took a deep breath and shook her head.

"You don't believe me?"

"Oh, I believe you. That's the problem. It's just a shame, that's all…" she trailed off.

"What's a shame?" If she was saying it was a shame I didn't like porn, then I was going to tell Freya to find a new best friend…but wait, she needed to do that anyway, I reminded myself, seeing as how her current pal was a big, fat phony.

"You're quite a catch, Agent Ripley. It's a shame you're hopelessly in love with a married woman."

I suddenly choked on nothing, gasping for air. When I regained my composure, I noticed she was smiling at me.

First Trevor, and now Talia. Did the whole world know?

"What are you talking about? She's my best friend's wife—" I stammered.

She waved a hand in my face. "Save it. I know about your falling out with Trevor, and why…but anyone who's seen you and Freya in the same room together knows you two are *much* more than friends."

"You said, 'you two'…has Freya ever told you how she feels about me?" I didn't realize until I said it aloud, but I sounded like the awkward seventeen-year-old me, interrogating all of Amanda Mavus' friends trying to find out if she wanted to go to prom.

"She didn't have to."

"What do you mean?"

She sighed loudly, and I just knew it was one of those 'why are men so dense?' sighs. "You're wrong."

"About what?" I had been wrong a lot lately. She was going to have to be more specific.

She looked in my eyes now, conveying that what she was about to tell me would either make me very happy, or very sad...or both. "The two most important people in the world to Freya? They aren't Trevor and me."

"You think they're Trevor and *me*," I stated, more than asked. The thought had crossed my mind, based solely on the fact that I'd known her longer than either of them, but it was nice to have it confirmed.

"No. I think her three gorgeous boys share the number one spot...but you are definitely number two."

I got a tingle just then, and I couldn't stop the unmistakable shudder that swept through me. Talia had no idea how she had just made my day, my week, my month...hell, my millennia.

I tried to extinguish my smile, but after a few attempts, just decided to work around it. I still wanted answers.

"Okay, so you know a lot about *me*. Who the hell are *you*, really? And who hired you?" I demanded, if it's possible for one to be demanding whilst grinning from ear to ear.

"All I can tell you is that I'm here to keep Freya safe. She is my assignment." She didn't break eye contact as she said this.

"How did Trevor find out about you?"

She took a deep breath. "All he knew is that someone else had been assigned to protect Freya, and we communicated via text only. He didn't know it was me until she saw a text I'd sent him. She recognized my number, and confronted him."

I had to smile. That sounded like my Freya. "How did he react?"

"I got one text: 'Get a new phone number.' He didn't have to tell me it was stupid of me not to have a separate phone for our communications. I got a new number that night, and Freya pretended to buy it…but, she's so much smarter than he gives her credit for."

"No shit."

"If you had no idea that I was undercover, then what are you doing here?" she asked, as if it had just occurred to her.

I stared into the rear view mirror. "I was hiding from Trevor."

"Why?"

"I decided it was time to tell Freya everything I know…so far."

"Were you planning on handing her the file for some light reading?" she joked.

"That thought occurred to me, but I found something else… something more…I think."

I hope.

I reached into my pocket, and she leaned back, throwing one hand in the air, and the other reaching for her gun.

"Calm down," I reassured her, retrieving the flash drive from my pants pocket. I held it out in front of us. It was amazing how something so small could hold the key to my past, and possibly my future.

"Where did you get this?" She had relaxed again, but I couldn't help but be impressed by her reflexes. I was sure that if she'd wanted to take me down by now, she could have.

"Staples. Down on Grand Avenue…cost me forty bucks…" I glanced at her and she was giving me a glare, but she pursed her lips to keep a smile at bay. I had to release a laugh before I gave her a serious answer.

"I was…*granted* access to the FBI database, and I found it in a folder called 'Purgatory'."

At that, she tried to grab the flash drive out of my hand, but I reflexively recoiled. I wasn't ready to give it to her just yet.

"You found Purgatory? Who told you about it?"

"No one…I just…found it," I answered honestly. I had done all the hard work myself, after all. She took a few deep breaths, but the intensity in her eyes persisted. She gave me a look, and I could tell she didn't believe that I had just stumbled upon a secret file folder that could only be opened through an invisible link by accident. It also hadn't escaped my attention that if she knew about Purgatory, whoever she was, she had a higher security clearance than I did.

"What's on it?" she asked excitedly.

"I don't know yet. I need a computer that's off the grid to look at it."

We stared at the little bugger for a moment.

"I'll be right back." She got out of the car and ran into her shed that was across the driveway from the house. I watched the doorway of the small storage unit and, within seconds, she reemerged, carrying something. As she climbed back into the car, I got a good look at the small laptop in her hands. It was covered in alternative rock stickers. I gave her a sideways glance, furrowing my eyebrows.

"I know a guy…he makes computers untraceable…for a living… he's very good at it…anyway, I—"

"Does your friend also know how to make it possible to view FBI files on a civilian computer?" I asked, just trying to torture her a little.

"Trust me." She nodded toward her open hand, half-rolling her eyes at me, and I placed the flash drive carefully in her palm. We looked at each other, and both took a deep breath.

She plugged it in to the side of the laptop, and we watched the screen in anticipation. When the first box appeared, she clicked 'Save'. That only took a minute, and then she unplugged the flash drive and handed it back to me. I hadn't expected her to do it that way, but I didn't protest. I had a good feeling about trusting her…at least for now. Plus, I reasoned, it was probably a good idea to have the information in more than one place, just in case we needed it.

She opened the saved file on the laptop, and an error message came up…something about the computer not having administrative permission to view this type of file. My heart sank. Then, Talia started to type furiously, opening system files I didn't recognize, getting error message after error message, and then, suddenly, there it was. Freya's file. I was stunned…and starting to like Talia more and more.

We both scanned the screen. It was a standard personnel file for Freya Tamar McKenna, a.k.a. the love of my life, and at first glance, didn't look to contain anything unusual. As I scrutinized, however, the same errors I had noticed in her paper file were popping out at me. Her birthdate was listed as July 1, 1971, not 1972. The file said she had joined the FBI in March of 1991, just like the old enlistment form I'd seen, when she was…well, if she was indeed born in 1971, she would have been nineteen.

What kind of moron recruits a nineteen-year-old to be an FBI agent, plucking her right out of college to do so, no less? I was fairly sure that even twenty years ago, an FBI agent was required to have a bachelor's degree, or four years as a cop. At nineteen, Freya had neither.

And what about my memories? Did I just imagine that we dated, graduated college, and then…well, there was a big chunk that was a little fuzzy, but it couldn't have been more than a few days…or weeks. Could it? Suddenly, she was with Trevor in the Air Force and I was in the FBI, alone.

As Talia focused on the laptop, I tried to recall my earliest memory of Trevor and Freya being together, and instantly, my head began to throb. I closed my eyes, and massaged my temple for a few seconds.

"Look at this!" Talia suddenly exclaimed.

I opened my eyes and followed her finger to the screen. In a larger text box there was a notation that said: 'RVW Program. Winkle Labs. Successful integration and test. Recommend field duty.' It was dated 13 May 1991, followed by the initials 'GLM.'

"It confirms the information on the CAT Scans," Talia said softly, almost to herself.

"Yes, but it doesn't make any sense!" I snapped. "I would have sworn on a stack of Spiderman comics that Freya was born in 1972, not '71." I was beyond frustrated now, and really wanted to talk to Freya. "I know that Winkle Labs used to do drug testing on college students, and Freya and I were part of one during our Spring Break in '91, but—"

"Wait," she cut me off, putting a hand on my shoulder. "*Both* of you were part of a Winkle Labs experiment? The RVW Program?"

I shook my head. "No, I mean yes…NO, I don't remember anything called RVW, but we were part of a routine drug test, not an experiment. Talia, what do you know?" Something was causing my pulse to soar, and I didn't like it one bit.

"Rip," she said gently, as a friend would before telling you your dog died, "RVW stands for Rip Van Winkle. It was the code name for a top secret government experiment. Winkle Labs was hired to test young subjects to be sleeper agents."

I stared at her, dumbfounded. She was talking about shit that I'd only seen in movies.

"Rip," she was looking at me more seriously than when she'd been pointing a gun at my head, "you and Freya were both implanted with an experimental technology...to create assassins."

EPISODE 24
I Am Reborn...Again

The boys were at school. Trevor was downstairs doing God knows what, and had insisted he didn't need to go in to work until later that morning, although I had told him I was fine and to please stop fussing over me. The truth was, I needed some time alone to think...and I had to admit, his company was the last thing I wanted, but he just smiled and kissed me on the forehead before he trotted downstairs.

I had been ordered to stay home the rest of the week—company policy when you actually pass out, no matter the cause—and I was warm and cozy under my covers, feigning content.

I had tried to convince myself the conversation with my husband the night I had come home from the hospital had not been as odd as I remembered...that it had been a product of my state of mind at the time, compounded by painkillers coursing through my veins, and my preoccupation with Rip. Trevor had been his usual chipper, wonderful self since then, which only seemed to confirm my theory. So, why was it still hanging there in my head, like an inoperable tumor?

Before I got out of bed, around 10:45, shamefully, I took a few minutes to attempt at meditation to clear my head. Talia swore by it, and had tried to teach me several times, but, although it's easy enough for a single, childless gal to spend all day breathing, some of us had other people to take care of nearly every minute of the day. Shit, I was just lucky breathing happened to be an automatic thing, or I was sure I simply wouldn't have time for it.

So, I took a few deep breaths in...and out...in...and out...in... suddenly, a loud clanging noise came from downstairs. Trevor must have dropped a dish. Oh God, I hope he wasn't trying to empty the dishwasher again. He put everything in the wrong place, but I would still smile and thank him for…for making more work for me, but, at least he was trying to be helpful…I guess. I shook my head and closed my eyes again…breathe…Rip came to mind. His steel gray eyes. That ever-so-slightly crooked smile that produced a sexy dimple on his right cheek. His dark brown hair that was just starting to lose its pigment right above his ears. His fit, muscular body, and that tight, round—

Bang. Bang, bang, bang!

Trevor was fighting with the child lock on the silverware drawer again. Why couldn't he just open it slowly and push down on the damn thing, like everyone—Bang! Deep breath…

What was I thinking about again? Oh yeah, Ty Ripley…

I opened my eyes in horror, and shook my head. And shook my head again. I had to stop thinking about Rip. I had a husband, and three kids with said husband. I had built a life with the man downstairs… who had apparently now left the refrigerator door open based on the fact that I could hear the high-pitched ping, ping, ping of the "hey, stupid, you left me open!" sensor.

Breathe…in and out…in…and…out…Rip had worn an eggplant-colored shirt last week with his dark gray blazer…it looked so good on him, my heart had actually skipped a beat when I saw him—

Stop it, Freya!

I opened my eyes, and let out a defeated sigh. I had come to one conclusion: meditating was stupid. I had to make a decision, and deep breaths weren't helping one bit. I just had a crush on Ty—I mean Rip…residual feelings from when we dated back in college, I tried to convince myself. But, we hadn't just dated. We were madly in love, and had professed that fact to each other on several occasions. We were going to be together forever…so, what the hell happened? My headache rushed in to save me from that thought process, and I slunk back down under the covers.

Trevor came in to kiss me goodbye and to pretend to order me to stay in bed as long as I wanted, and I was so glad he was finally leaving. His lips against mine were cold and flat…no tingle.

What am I going to do about this?

When I heard the garage door open, then a moment later close, I threw back the covers and hopped out of bed. My morning ritual of almond chai was long overdue. I ran my fingers through my hair...ouch, knots...and padded down the hall in my slippers, not bothering to put a robe on over my pale pink tank top and short little sleep shorts. I didn't need to look nice for anyone at the moment, I thought to myself, but when I passed the mirror in the hallway, I paused, bit my bottom lip as I stared at my forty-year-old self, and quickly ran back into my bathroom. I whipped my hair into a low pony tail and then brushed my teeth. I wasn't living in anarchy, after all.

Trevor had sweetly, and annoyingly, instructed me not to do any housework while he was gone, but seriously...he had to know me better than that. So, I grabbed dirty laundry on my way down the stairs, threw in a load, poured my almond chai heaven, and sat down in my atrium. I took a deep breath, then began sipping—okay, maybe chugging—my creamy beverage, and watching a squirrel race around the trunk of a tree in my yard, when my daydream got really out of control and I imagined Rip walking up to my back door. I shook my head a few times and blinked my eyes. I had to get control. I looked again, and realized Rip was actually there, coming up my back steps. I hadn't seen him since the hospital...

He was wearing a dark gray T-shirt—the dressy kind, not the 'going for a run' kind—and dark, dark jeans. My stomach did a quick somersault.

I noticed his car wasn't in my driveway...or anywhere along the street that I could see. Weird. I shrugged it off and bounded to the door, flinging it open and causing him to screech to a halt. His hair had that irresistible unkempt look. He looked at me with surprise, then relaxed and smiled.

"I take it you aren't going to work today, Agent Douglas?" he grinned, as he scanned me from head to toe, raising his eyebrows at my skimpy pajamas, and looking away quickly when he noticed I was also braless. Was he...blushing...? He seemed to do that a lot around me lately. I was shocked at his reaction, but crossed my arms in front of my girls just the same. He had seen me naked a hundred times, granted 99 of them were twenty years ago, but…

He had walked in on me stepping out of the shower once, a few years back, and had apologized profusely several times. I remember instead of immediately shielding his eyes and retreating, he had stood there, awestruck and frozen, gazing at my naked body, and only then found my eyes before realizing what he was doing. Thinking about that now, I realized that's when our relationship…changed. Just a little, tiny, microscopic amount, but I noticed, and I was sure he had too. Our three-way dinners had become more and more awkward after that.

I realized I was staring at him now, and blocking him from coming into my kitchen. He flashed a quick smile and I backed away to let him in. He moved past me and our shoulders brushed each other. There was a jolt of electricity and we both stopped and exchanged a quick glance. I closed the door and turned to him.

"Are you okay?" he asked, and I could still see a hint of that blush on his cheeks. A sudden searing pain in my head made everything go black. I reached up and held my forehead. I thought of Trevor for an instant and had a flash of something…a memory? I opened my eyes, and a very young Trevor was sitting next to my hospital bed, typing furiously on a computer, state-of-the-art for 1991, and I could see a wire hooking the computer up to an IV bag, and a thick tube from the bag to…oh my God…the tube was inside my head. As he typed, I was experiencing vibrations and short bursts of light behind my eyes.

What the hell was he doing in my head?

I tried to move, but couldn't. I tried to scream, but no sound came. Trevor must have noticed I was awake, because he suddenly stopped typing and turned to me. The vibrations and light show abruptly ceased. He leaned down, and his twenty-year-old face had an unsettling expression of evil victory, like he had just figured out how to become the Supreme Overlord of the planet Earth.

He leaned in closer to me and whispered, "Now, you'll be mine forever." He kissed me then, but I couldn't have returned it even if I'd wanted to, and his touch made me sick to my stomach. He smiled. "Go to sleep, Princess. When you wake up, we can start our life together…" He turned and started typing again and, like a neon hotel sign on the fritz, my brain buzzed and hummed. Then, the world went away.

I opened my eyes, and I was sitting at the table in my atrium, my head in my hands.

"Frey…are you okay, honey?"

I started at the sound of his voice, moving my chair and making that "fingernails down the chalkboard" kind of squeak on the tile floor. I looked up, and Ty was sitting across from me, donning a very worried look.

Thank God.

"Freya?"

"What happened?" I asked tentatively.

He reached across and took my hand in his, gently caressing it with the other. "You said you felt strange, and then you almost passed out."

I chuckled. "It seems that happens a lot on your watch."

He smiled, and it was so sexy, I almost forgot what we were talking about. "My watch? Am I your babysitter now?"

"I thought you were my handler, remember?" I joked, referring to our conversation at the old bridge before we'd tried to rip each other's clothes off.

"I thought you wanted to be my partner?" he reminded me. I just grinned and shrugged, as if I would have to think about it. His face grew serious then. "You had a flashback, didn't you? Just now? Tell me what you saw…"

Of course he knew. We'd had a joint flashback just the other day, after all. I hesitated, but he was staring at me so intently, telling me we were in this together. I took a deep breath, and told him everything I could remember. By the time I was done, he looked more than worried. He looked almost scared.

"He's dangerous, Freya. I don't know how he ties into all this, but—"

"He's still my husband, Ty." My words may have masqueraded as loyalty to Trevor, but my Freudian slip revealed everything.

"Ty?" he asked, the red returning to his cheeks for a microsecond.

I tried to downplay it. "I've been married to this man for fifteen years, Ty—"

Damn! I did it again!

"—and we have three children. What am I supposed to do? Divorce him because I'm having some sort of mental breakdown?" *Divorce Trevor? Why did that sound so good?*

He reached for me again, shaking his head vehemently. "Freya, no…you're not having a breakdown." He looked at our hands intertwined for a second, then he swallowed hard before he continued. "I came here to tell you something. Something very important about the flashback at the bridge, the one I had in my apartment, and the episode you just had—"

"What one in your apartment?"

"It was about you and me, and we were…" He paused.

"Having knock-down, drag-out sex?" I guessed.

He was stunned silent for a moment, struggling to continue. "Uh… no…unfortunately," he smirked at me. "We were kids again, and we were driving somewhere, and then, you pulled out a gun, and—"

"I'm sorry, WHAT?!" I didn't let him finish, due to the fact that I was sure I was having some sort of breakdown *now*.

"No, no, it was all good. You were shooting at some *bad* people, I know that. I don't know how I know, but I do."

"What are you talking about?" *Was everyone going crazy?*

He leaned closer and spoke just above a whisper. "Freya, I found your FBI file…from twenty years ago."

"I know, you told me that before I started the training program… that they'd transferred everything to computer—"

"No," he stopped me. "Not that file." He took a deep breath and said it fast. "You were *in* the FBI twenty years ago. With me." He studied my expression. I was dumbfounded. He wasn't making any sense. I must have looked at him like he was losing it, although I wasn't sure who was more unstable, him or me. He held up one finger. "Hold on…one minute…" He stood, and backed toward the door. "I'll be right back."

I didn't move for the thirty seconds it took him to run outside, around Talia's house, and then return the same way with a large folder in his hands.

Where on earth did he get that?

He came in through the back door, and sat back down at the table facing me. He looked at me apprehensively as he slid the folder across the surface. I glanced at it and saw my name on the outside. I looked up at him, and then opened the folder, slowly. My heart was pounding all of a sudden. It was like I was slowly cranking a jack-in-the-box...dreading that moment when...POP!

I read the first page...a form of some sort that said someone named Freya Tamar McKenna had joined the FBI in March of 1991. I swallowed to keep my heart from crawling up into my throat, and found Ty's eyes.

"This isn't me..." I didn't sound half as convincing as I'd hoped. I didn't even believe what I was saying. "...is it?"

He looked a little sad now, and I really hated that. I gave him a compassionate look in return, to try to tell him everything would be fine, but...I didn't even believe it. I returned to the file and started paging through, more and more shocked at what I saw. Then, I got to some sheets that were connected, and Ty helped me lay the first one out so I could get a good look at it. Before I could absorb any of it, he pointed to the stamp in the corner that said "Winkle Labs." That rang a bell somewhere deep inside my brain, and I looked up at him, wide-eyed.

"Do you remember Winkle Labs?" he asked carefully.

All I could do was nod. My mouth was so dry...I remembered my almond chai, and took a good, long sip through the straw before I let my eyes wander back to the papers. It looked like a brain scan. My brain scan. And there was a second one.

"I remember the drug study we did, that one Spring Break."

"It wasn't a drug study."

"What do you mean?" I knew what he meant, but it was crazy. I was thinking about things that only happened in movies...super classified, high-tech, *Total Recall* shit.

"Are you feeling okay?" Well, that question seemed out of place.

"Yes, I'm fine. Tell me what it was...really."

"They told us we were testing a drug to treat depression, do you remember?"

I nodded.

"That's how they justified the brain scans. They said they had to test the dopamine levels before and after we took the drug, but the pills we took were placebos…probably just sugar. It had nothing to do with depression."

I gave him a stern, motherly look. "Just tell me. I can handle it."

"Are you sure you're feeling okay?"

"Yes…why do you keep asking me that?" I was getting angry with him, and I didn't like it, but he was being so frustrating. He knew I hated people who beat around the bush.

"Freya. They were testing a brain implant that would cause normal people, i.e. college students, to be sleepers…"

I'd heard the term 'sleepers' before, but I still gave him a confused look. He wasn't saying what I thought he was saying. This wasn't happening…then, he pulled the trigger.

"Freya, you and I were part of a secret experiment to create sleeper assassins."

Bang.

I stood slowly, fighting the nausea and disorientation. He'd shot me right in the common sense and logic…where I lived. He stood too, acting as though he was ready to catch me when I fainted, which I guess was warranted, since we'd already done that one-act play this morning. Suddenly, things started to make more sense. My flashbacks that had seemed like visions of someone else's life, my unusually stellar performance at the shooting range, my renewed desire to become an FBI agent after all these years…

"Assassins….you and I…are sleeper assassins."

"Yes…well, we were. Are you okay?"

That damn question again. I stood abruptly, livid now, though I wasn't sure why.

"STOP…asking me that…please. I'm fine." Just then, a sensation I could only describe as a short circuit of some kind tightened my brain for a second. I staggered slightly and grabbed my head, but Ty was there, wrapping his arms around me to keep me safe…like he always was.

I looked up at him, no longer angry, and suddenly, I had the strangest feeling come over me. I wanted to kiss him. The urge was so strong, like Arnold Schwarzenegger strong, that I couldn't fight it. I had to kiss him right away. It had been so long, I couldn't stand it anymore. He was looking at me with such intensity, and a little confusion...

"Freya, what...?"

"Ty," he was clearly in ecstasy whenever I called him that, "I missed you so much." I moved in closer. His eyes were as intoxicating as ever...those beautiful slate eyes, and then...

His lips were enveloping mine. Over and over, we kissed, adjusting our heads to make each one a unique and exhilarating experience. He was holding me so tight, I never wanted him to let go. This was happening and neither one of us had the strength, nor the desire to stop it.

We moved in tandem into the living room, where I eyed the couch...but he had other ideas. As soon as our feet hit carpet, he was gently laying me down onto the floor.

Yes.

EPISODE 25
Talia's Secret

We lay on my living room floor together, wrapped in a blanket that had been draped over the back of the couch. Our clothes were strewn all over the room, but we were in no hurry to retrieve them.

I had a 1000-piece puzzle in my game closet that the kids and I used to love to put together on rainy days. One day, we realized we'd lost one tiny piece, and we all agreed, it just wasn't the same, so we put the puzzle away and there it sat, acquiring dust. I couldn't bring myself to throw it away, because it had brought us so many happy memories. One day, months later, when we decided to rearrange the living room furniture, I found the missing piece underneath the entertainment center. I was so excited, that we dusted off the puzzle, and it became our favorite rainy day activity again.

In a way, that was how I was feeling as I lay there next to a very naked Ty, albeit on a much larger scale…like he had been the puzzle piece I thought I'd lost, but was there all the time, waiting to be discovered, and to complete my picture…and make me utterly, blissfully happy. Well, maybe that was a little strong for the puzzle, but Ty was definitely responsible for my current glow.

We'd been talking about the whole secret government experiment thing for the last fifteen minutes, trying to agree on our next step. There was nothing like earth-shattering sex to clear your mind.

"Is there a way to…remove the implants?" I asked him.

"I don't know," he said, sounding disappointed in himself for not having all the answers.

I craned my neck to make eye contact, my head still resting on his chest. "We're going to get through this, Ty. We have each other now."

That seemed to cheer him up and he gave me a wonderful squeeze and kissed me on the top of the head.

"What are we going to do about Trevor?" he sighed, trying really hard to care.

I didn't even want to think about that now, since, technically, I'd just cheated on the guy. I assumed he'd have a problem with that.

"We have to find out what he's done...everything...from the very beginning," I answered. "I mean, if my flashback has any basis in reality, then...I think I should be afraid of him."

"Are you?"

"What? Afraid of him? I don't know...I don't think anything can get through the ecstasy right now." I started to caress his bare chest...just a little hair...I liked that.

"Well, I hate to admit it, Frey, but no matter what he's done to you and me, he does love those boys more than anything. We have to be very careful about how we proceed."

"Okay," I agreed, sitting up and turning to him. "Any ideas? Are you proposing I pretend I'm still content being Mrs. Trevor Douglas, and continue to...perform my wifely duties?" I was dead serious, but my choice of words made him chuckle, and I broke into a smile at the sight of that adorable dimple.

He sat up just then, and I could almost see the light bulb above his head glowing brightly. "What if I can convince Pixley to send Trevor on an assignment for a while? I was planning to tell him everything I know tomorrow anyway. Orchestrating your kidnapping aside, he's got a reputation for doing the right thing, and I have a good feeling about trusting him."

I nodded in agreement, staring at him. "Okay, two things in there that I need clarification on. First, how can Pixley send Trevor on an assignment? He's not an agent..."

My last word came out very slowly, as I watched the light bulb flicker, and Ty's face instantly went from "I have a great idea!" to "Oh shit, I forgot you didn't know that!"

"TREVOR'S AN AGENT?!" I screamed at him, but before he could speak, I put my index finger over his lips. "And second, Pixley arranged my kidnapping!?" I removed my finger so he could defend himself on both counts.

"I'm so sorry. I was going to tell you about all of that when I came over this morning, and then, you had the flashback, and I was having second thoughts about dumping more on you, and then you jumped me, and I—"

I shoved him in the chest. "I didn't jump you! I'm a lady...ladies don't 'jump'...they seduce."

"Okay, then you seduced me, and I kind of forgot everything else." He was grinning like a fool, and looking at me like he had just made love to Angelina Jolie.

"Trevor's an agent...Trevor...agent...holy shit..." It was just hitting me, and I tried not to hyperventilate as I stood and looked for my clothes. I wrapped the blanket around me, ignoring Ty's protests that he was now "exposed to the elements" of my 72-degree living room, and searched for my panties. "How could I not have known that...how long have you known? WHERE ARE MY PANTIES?!" I asked, as I accepted defeat and sat down hard on the coffee table.

Trevor cleared his throat, and I glanced at him. He was looking above my head. I followed his gaze up and saw the ceiling fan... and my purple unmentionables hanging from one of the blades. Impressive, but he wasn't going to distract me that easily.

"How long have you known, Ty?" I asked again, as I stood on the coffee table and reached for my undies, absent-mindedly dropping the blanket, much to his delight. I snatched the panties, and then gave him a questioning look. He hadn't answered because he was gazing at me stretching my naked form to reach the ceiling fan.

Men.

I gave him a look of daggers, and he snapped out of it.

"Since he joined fifteen years ago."

I froze, panties in hand, staring at him with contempt.

He stood, quickly recovering his jockeys and whipping them on. "Freya, I couldn't tell you. Can you understand that, now that you're an agent yourself? You got the briefing...I would have lost my job."

Dammit. I did understand, although I really wished I could force myself not to at that moment. I had been lied to about so many things the past twenty years, but this was the first thing that Ty had kept from me. It hurt a little, but I knew I had to forgive him. He hadn't betrayed me, he had just made a commitment to his job, and had kept it. I had to respect that. Of course, I could also apply that compassionate logic to Trevor keeping the same monumental secret from me, but...no, he wasn't going to get off that easy. His reasons had nothing to do with loyalty to anyone, of that, I was absolutely sure.

"I really was living in a fog, wasn't I?" I accused myself, more than posing a question to Ty, as I stepped into my skivvies as ladylike as I could. "I mean, I knew something was a little off between Trevor and me since...the choking, but..."

I hadn't told Ty about my crazy in-body experience at the restaurant that night, and wasn't ready to yet, so I moved on.

"Director Pixley had me kidnapped on my first assignment. Is that standard procedure? Some sort of test? Did I pass?" My mind was reeling now, wondering what I had really gotten myself into joining the FBI...again. I'd always thought of the 'bad guys' as people *outside* the office.

"No, it's not usual, but he does have the authority to 'test' a new agent however he wants. And if it were up to me, you would get an A+."

"So, you didn't know...before?"

He froze, one leg in his jeans, and his gray eyes sucked me in. "No...no, honey, I had no idea, I swear."

I gave him a small smile of relief, and located my tank top, pulling it on over my head.

"It's my fault you were kidnapped, though," he added sadly.

"What are you talking about?" I asked, as I scanned the room for my shorts.

"I guess Pixley assumed I would take care of the four hooligans and you wouldn't actually be taken. He didn't figure on an intense memory recall of our first time rendering me...well, useless."

Useless. I remembered using that word to describe myself once... when I was telling Ty about Rowan choking. He had refused to let me believe I had been useless, and I wanted to do the same for him.

I located my shorts, snatched them up and turned to him. "You were not useless. I was never in any real danger, apparently. Plus... I'm glad I was taken." This garnered a wide-eyed stare. "I know now that I can handle myself in a situation like that. It was the best training exercise I've ever done, and even though I passed out afterward, I'm still proud of myself."

His jeans were on and he had just slipped his gray t-shirt on over his head, when he walked over to me and gave me a bear hug. I would never not revel in the feeling of Ty Ripley's arms around me. He broke away enough to find my eyes. "Not as proud as I am."

"What the hell did you two just do?"

We both jumped at the sound of Talia's voice coming from the doorway to the kitchen. We snapped our heads in her direction simultaneously, but remained wrapped in each other's arms. Talia was tapping her foot, hands on hips, and looking at us as if we'd just stolen money from the church collection plate.

We couldn't speak, so she continued. "Rip, what the hell? Was this part of the plan?"

Wait a minute. Plan? Talia was part of all this too?

Was there anyone in my life who hadn't been lying to me?

She glared at Ty. "Have you told her *anything*, Romeo?"

He let his arms hang down now, but not because he wanted to. He had to defend himself, and he talked with his hands. "Everything but...about you...!" he stammered, throwing his arms out to his side.

She suddenly looked at me sheepishly, mouthing the word, "Oops."

"Et tu, Talia?" I interjected sadly. "You'd better start talking, girlfriend," I said in my stern, Mom voice, but I turned to Ty before Talia could respond. "And YOU!" I shoved him in genuine anger now. "What ELSE have you been lying about?" He didn't fight back, and looked at me like an abused puppy.

"Frey, I just found out about Talia a few hours ago...OUCH, Freya!"

I rounded on Talia, who looked like she was preparing herself to be shoved into the next room, her eyes closed and face all screwed up, and asked, "Is that true, Talia?"

She opened one eye at me. "Yes, it's true. We're on your side, Freya."

I had to laugh at that. My side? What exactly was my side? I liked to think it was the side of good and right, but then I remembered I had just cheated on my husband, and realized there was no such thing, not really. At least, if Trevor turned out to be an evil mad scientist, my team would prevail. The mad scientist never wins, after all.

I looked back and forth between my two best friends in the world, and let out a heavy sigh. Talia opened her eyes and relaxed a little, and Ty came away from the far wall, where I had shoved him, and approached me slowly.

Wow. I could command a lot of power in my underwear, I thought. *Go Goddess!*

"If there is anything else you two aren't telling me, spill it right now!"

They looked at each other, and seemed to be communicating telepathically for a second. I took the opportunity to put my shorts on, although I really wanted to take a shower, and put some actual clothes on, but I was terrified that if I left the reality bubble that was currently in my living room, it would pop and I would never find out what was going on. I knew I wasn't the Freya who had been naively happy being Trevor's concubine for the past fifteen years... not anymore. Something was very different, but it felt like I was heading in the right direction... toward the real me, and I knew these two were going with me.

Then Talia asked Ty, "Did you tell her about Trevor?" He nodded. She sat down in my antique chair just inside the living room doorway, and leaned back, crossing her legs. "And the whole brain implant..."

"Yep, yep, covered that...everything we know anyway."

"...and the sleeper assassin thing..."

"Yeah."

"...and me being undercover..."

"You took care of that one, yeah."

"...and...um...oh yeah, the whole alien DNA and her kids..."

"WHAT?!" I demanded, sure I hadn't heard her right.

Talia started to laugh. It was quiet at first, just a girlish giggle, but then she lost it completely, and almost fell out of the chair.

"Not funny!" Okay, it was a little funny, but I wasn't in the mood. I gave Trevor a sideways glance, and noticed he was trying not to laugh, but I think he was more entertained at Talia's reaction to her own joke than he was of the joke itself.

Talia held her side with one hand as she began to calm down, shoving the palm of her other hand out toward me. "I'm sorry…I couldn't resist, Frey…sorry." She took a deep breath and composed herself. "Actually, there is one other thing that you should know, and *Ty* here doesn't know about it either, yet." She was serious. "We might want to sit down for this."

She was so serious; neither of us said a word as we followed her back into the kitchen and sat down at the atrium table. My chai was still sitting there, and I had never enjoyed a good long pull of it more. Then, Ty and I looked at Talia, waiting for her to talk. She took a few deep breaths before she started.

"I have some information that I suspected was true this morning, but I had to verify it before I could tell you both. Freya," she looked at me like she was about to confess to a murder or something, "the man who was responsible for yours and Rip's involvement in the Rip Van Winkle experiment—"

"Rip Van Winkle? As in the man who sleeps for a hundred years? And they were making *sleeper* assassins? That's hilarious!" I was actually finding that funny, and the other two were looking at me as if I'd gone insane, so I cleared my throat awkwardly and motioned for Talia to please go on.

"Anyway, the man in charge had the initials…GLM."

My jaw hit the table, and I couldn't breathe. "Are you kidding?" I managed to squeak.

"The initials from the CAT Scan?" Ty was clearly not following, but I knew exactly what Talia was saying.

"There's more," she answered me, ignoring Ty. "He's the one who hired me to keep an eye on you three years ago. He's been lying to me, which is a breach of our contract. So, that's why I'm telling you everything I know."

"He hired you?" I couldn't believe what she was saying. It couldn't be true.

"Wait," Ty interrupted. "Who's GLM? Why is this bad?"

I was speechless, trying to process it all. This might be too much for my brain to handle…after all, it had been quite a day. I had cheated on my husband, found out I had something in my head that turned me into an assassin, and that Talia and Trevor were secret agents…oh yeah, and my new boss had arranged to have me kidnapped. Nope, I couldn't take any more. My head started to throb, and the room began to spin. Talia could see I was in no condition to answer Ty, so she did it for me.

"GLM stands for Gerard Lochlan McKenna."

Before the last name registered with him, Ty turned to me. "Hey, your brother's name is Lochlan, isn't it?"

I was sure my eyes were a pool of hysteria, and I watched as his joined mine in Crazy Town. He looked back to Talia, his mouth hanging open. She nodded.

"GLM is Freya's father."

EPISODE 26
Trevor Gets His

Trevor hit the floor, already unconscious, blood trickling from his nose. Talia and I just sat there for a minute, stunned. When I could think again, I was flipping between shock and pride as I stared at Freya, who was standing over her husband, breathing as if she'd just run a mile. The last thirty seconds had been a blur.

Talia, Freya, and I had been sitting around the breakfast table in the atrium, discussing the fact that Freya's father, with whom she'd had no contact with for nearly twenty-five years, had been involved in the RVW Program. Not just involved, but somewhere at the top… and worse yet, he'd recommended Freya for the risky implant and authorized her activation, whatever that meant, after the experiment had apparently been a success. Talia believed that my being implanted as well may have just been because we were attached at the hip back then. That didn't fuel me with self-confidence, to say the least. She wasn't trying to be mean…just offering her theories, but I gave her a hard look anyway.

We were so wrapped up in our conversation, and I know my ears were ringing from all that had transpired in the past few hours, that we hadn't heard the garage door open. Trevor burst through the door, like I imagined he always did, and before he noticed us across the room, he yelled, "Frey! I'm home! Are you still in bed, you lazy—"

That's when he saw us, and the emotions that cycled through his face were numerous. Surprise, confusion, anger, realization, shock, back to anger. There could be only one reason the three of us would be huddled together in a seemingly secret meeting, and he clearly had no idea how to respond to it. Then he noticed Freya was still in her pajamas—sexy little pj's to boot—and his expression was unreadable, like his brain couldn't process what his eyes were seeing. He started toward us with a purpose.

"Freya, whatever they told you, it's not true! Rip is trying to take you away from me! And this BITCH—" he had pointed to Talia, who stared back at him like he was an insignificant fly on the wall, and that's when Freya's fist had collided with his face. She had moved so fast, I didn't even realize she was standing until Trevor's eyes were rolling back into his head.

Talia had immediately leapt out of her chair, and was checking Trevor's pulse when I came around.

"Freya? Are you okay?" I started toward her.

She turned around, and I almost didn't recognize her face, she was so angry. I grabbed her shoulders and tried to make her look at me. Her pupils were dilated, and her cheeks flushed.

"Freya!" I shook her urgently. Her blood was pumping so hard and so fast, I could feel it through her skin. I tried to guide her back toward her chair, but she resisted.

"LEAVE ME ALONE!" she insisted, a little above her normal decibel level, but she seemed to be talking to no one as she tried to push me away.

I glanced back at Talia, who nodded and came to Freya's other side. We headed for the living room, each of us with one of Freya's arms in our own. Six feet from the couch, she suddenly went limp, and I caught her full weight and picked her up, carrying her the rest of the way. I laid her on the couch, and sat on the coffee table. Talia stood at the foot of the couch, and we both watched her nervously. Her eyes were closed, but it was as if she was in an intense dream state, and we could see them jerking back and forth erratically under the lids.

I didn't know what to do.

In the time it took me to exchange apprehensive looks with Talia, Freya was sitting up, holding her head. I tried to make her lie back down, but she grabbed my arm, giving me a determined look.

"I'm fine."

I believed her. She sat up, and we waited patiently for her to regain her bearings.

"Did I kill him?" she asked, taking deliberate deep breaths to slow her heart rate.

I let out a snort. "I don't think so, but he's going to have a whopper of a headache when he wakes up. Why?"

"That's what I was thinking…that I was going to kill him. I *wanted* to kill him." She took a deep breath, continuing to handle the crazy day with strength and grace. She looked up at me, and smiled sadly. "I wanted to kill the father of my children."

I didn't know how to respond…how to make her feel better about that. I cocked my head slightly and compassion flooded from my eyes. She swallowed, and then seemed to rally. She smiled again, a little brighter, and leaned forward to give me a quick, but soft kiss.

"It's okay, Ty," she patted my knee. "There are some things you can't fix for me." She stood, a little shaky, but stabilized quickly. "Now, I need to clean up before my boys get home from school in…" she looked at the clock on the wall, "…forty-two minutes…" She seemed lost for a second, and placed her hand across her forehead, as if it would help her think clearly, and sighed slowly. "I have to figure out what I'm going to tell them about their father—"

I finished the thought for her, "—who we will remove from your kitchen floor…Talia?" She was already heading out to the garage.

"I'll get some rope to restrain the bastard."

I looked back at Freya, who seemed like she may need to be restrained as well to hold in all the emotions she was feeling. Freya found my eyes and smiled, but it was just short of the euphoria I was feeling. I couldn't even imagine what was going on in that gorgeous head of hers. I gently put my hands on her shoulders.

"We made love on my living room floor," she stated.

"Yes we did."

"I've loved you forever."

"Not as forever as I've loved you." I had no idea what I was saying, but I meant every word. She giggled at my nonsensical profession of love, but then, her forehead started to crinkle with worry, and she frowned.

"Why can't I remember why I ended up with Trevor?"

I took her face in my hands and gently lifted it to make her look at me. I searched her eyes, getting lost in them for a second. A loud crash came from the garage, and a muffled, "God dammit, who put that there?" let us know that Talia was having a little trouble finding the rope. Freya was trying to find answers in my eyes...answers that weren't there.

"I can't remember either. But, we'll figure it out...together." I leaned down to kiss her, adrenaline making my veins feel ten times bigger than they really were, and then—

Click.

This just wasn't my day.

We turned and saw Trevor, wiping the blood from his nose with one hand, and pointing a gun at my head with the other. He looked so different, his hair sticking up in odd places, and his eyes wild, like his evil twin might look if he had one. I took a step toward him to shield Freya.

"I wouldn't," was all he said, a strange confidence lacing his tone. "Freya, are you alright? He didn't hurt you, did he?"

What the hell was he playing at?

My heart was trying to pound through my chest as at least a dozen moves to disarm him flashed through my brain, but all of a sudden, my mind was clouded. It was as if just being near Trevor disoriented me. All I could think of was to keep Freya safe. I tried to clear my head and focus. I quickly chose one maneuver, and mentally ran through it, preparing myself to kick my former best friend's lying ass...when Freya slowly moved around me. I instinctually tried to stop her, but she grabbed my arm, and shot me a look that told me she needed to do this. I hated the idea, but I had a feeling she could handle herself, as she'd already proven. She stepped out in front of me.

"Trevor. What's going on?" she asked him, as if he were a child throwing a tantrum.

"Freya, come stand behind me...you'll be safe."

She took another step toward him. I reached for her arm, but she avoided it.

"Trevor. Tell me what the hell is going on." She said it sternly.

He tilted his head slightly, and smiled at her, but the madman was still there. "Freya, it's alright, I forgive you. Now, come here." His tone was very condescending. She hated to be spoken to like that.

"You forgive me…?" she asked, the rage starting to build in her voice.

"Of course I do. You're my wife. I love you. Now, COME HERE!" This jackass didn't know Freya at all if he thought she was going to obey him like a puppy, gun or no gun.

"Exactly what do you forgive me for, Trevor?" She sounded so calm, and was careful to stay out of his arms reach.

"I'm not an idiot, Freya. I know what you and Rip did…but it's not your fault. He seduced you with his lies about brain implants and government conspiracies, and I—"

"What are you saying, Trevor? That I don't have a brain implant? That I wasn't an assassin for the FBI?"

His forced laughter wouldn't have convinced anyone he was telling the truth. "Of course not! Listen to yourself, Freya! An assassin? You're a housewife, not a—"

"I'm an FBI agent, Trevor…just like you."

My eyes bugged out of my head as I stared, frozen, at Trevor, waiting for him to hang himself. He laughed for real this time, like she had just told him the funniest joke he'd ever heard. "Just like me? You're not a real agent, Freya. You only got through the program because I let you. You're done with that now." She was circling him with her arms crossed, and he actually seemed nervous. And he was the one holding the gun.

"I'm done with that?"

He whipped his head around, trying to follow her, and keep the gun trained on me. "You didn't think you were going to continue pretending to be an agent, did you? You can go back to doing what you did before. You can be my wife and the mother to our children again."

Her eyes narrowed at this. "So, I was just pretending to be an agent?"

"Of course. None of it was real."

I couldn't stand it. "Freya, don't listen to him! You're a real agent, and you earned every bit of it—" I was surprised when it was Freya who stopped me with a hand in the air and a quick glance. I realized she had a plan.

"And I'm not a real agent, like you are?"

"Of course not. I just let you believe you were..." It finally dawned on Trevor that he had just admitted to lying to her all these years. He was speechless for a few seconds while he worked out his next lie. His tone lost its superiority complex, and switched to over-the-top pleading. "Freya, I couldn't tell you I was an agent. You know the rules—"

She was coming around from behind him, still circling like a vulture. "I know the rules, because I'm an agent too."

"Yes, yes, you're an agent. I didn't mean...I just said that because..." And he had nothing. Unfortunately, his gun was still pointed at my head, although his attentions were elsewhere at the moment. The move I had chosen was still hanging there, in my frontal lobe waiting to be used, but I didn't want to sabotage what Freya was doing. She was getting him to confess.

"And because I'm an agent...a real agent...I also know that you don't have a clip in your gun." And that's when Talia charged him from behind, jumping over the threshold into the living room like a cheetah, but somehow, he was ready for her. He swung around and slammed the barrel of his gun right into the side of her head. She hit the floor and was motionless. I moved to take him down, but Freya beat me to it.

She spun around so quickly, she was almost a blur. She clocked Trevor with a strong roundhouse kick to the head, and he went down. The gun flew out of his hand, and I immediately retrieved it. Freya checked Trevor's vitals, to make sure she hadn't killed him, since I guess that might have been construed as a bad thing, but when she straightened, she kicked him in the ribs.

"He'll live," she spat.

I was in love with G.I. Jane.

Then she stepped over to check on Talia, who was already stirring and trying to sit up, but Freya made her lie back down. She pointed to a throw pillow on the floor, and I picked it up and handed it to her. She gently placed it under Talia's head, but the quirky neighbor, who was really Freya's secret bodyguard, was white as a ghost, and sweat was forming on her forehead. She had a concussion. Suddenly, Talia pointed into the kitchen, and mumbled one word before she lost consciousness again.

"Rope."

I grabbed the rope from the kitchen counter and tied up Trevor's hands and feet, while Freya called 911 for Talia. He had hit her with such force, we were afraid to move her to transport her to the hospital ourselves. You don't mess around with head injuries.

"I want him out of here." Freya nodded toward her husband's lifeless body as she walked over to stand next to me. I nodded in agreement. She was shaking, so I tried to embrace her, but she stopped me.

"Did you cheat on me?"

Where the hell had that come from?

"What?"

"Back in college. I asked Trevor if he knew why you and I broke up, and he said you cheated on me."

I was just beginning to realize how much Trevor had played us... all of us.

"I honestly don't remember, but I can't believe that I would've been that stupid."

I would never have cheated on Freya. I pulled her to me, and kissed her feverishly. When we pulled apart, she smiled.

"I didn't think so."

She suddenly turned toward the clock on the wall. The boys would be home in fifteen minutes.

"Where will you take him?"

I knew where we had to go. I didn't like it, but it was the quickest way to get answers, although I was risking getting in big trouble myself.

"FBI headquarters. He's going to tell me and Director Pixley everything." She nodded, allowing herself to breathe deep. "What are you going to do?" I asked.

"You mean after I take care of Talia, the boys, and get a shower?"

I raised my eyebrows and smirked at her. She reached back and pulled the band out of her hair, letting it hang around her shoulders. So sexy. I reached out and moved a thick strand from her face, and she grabbed my hand, holding it to her cheek. Then, we heard the ambulance approaching and the school bus barreling down the street at the same time. I had to get Trevor out of there.

"Are you okay?" I asked.

She gave me a sweet smile and a tiny nod. "I will be. Can you come back…tonight?"

I actually had butterflies in my stomach. I couldn't remember the last time I had had that sensation. "As soon as I can," I responded.

"Good. I need you to come with me."

"Where?"

"To see my father. I'll need someone to keep me from killing him."

EPISODE 27
The KGB Babysits

I hadn't seen him in twenty-five years, since he'd walked out on us. I was fifteen, and my little brother, Loch, was just five years old. My mother didn't seem devastated, but more…relieved when he left. That spoke volumes to me, although I was just a teenager. We didn't talk about him after that, and we both did the best we could to raise Loch to *not* be like his dad. The general attitude was that we were better off without him. End of story.

My mother was an engineer working as a civilian employee for the Air Force, and three years later, right after I had left for college, she was transferred to Germany, where she met and fell in love with a local widower named Klaus Spang. They were married the next year, and she and Loch moved into the lovely apartment above his bakery, in a tiny village called Niersbach in the southwestern part of the country. Klaus was a good man and adored my mother, and soon after the wedding, he officially adopted Loch as his own. Loch, who was now almost thirty years old, had spent years traveling and exploring Europe after school, learning several trades and having a blast, courtesy of his adopted father, but he finally decided on becoming a chef. He was currently in one of the best culinary schools in the world, located in Cologne. Needless to say, I rarely saw them, but I made a point to call at least once a month. I missed them terribly.

I had already talked to my mother twice that month, but the happenings of the day warranted a third. I lied to her and told her I had received a letter from the IRS wanting to know my father's whereabouts, and that I wanted to flick this booger as quickly as possible. She just sighed, as if it didn't surprise her one bit that he would be in trouble with the government, and reluctantly gave me the last address she remembered. I knew the little town. It was a two-hour drive, but there was no sense in waiting. Ty and I were planning to leave the minute he came back from dropping Trevor off at FBI Headquarters, assuming that all went to plan. Right.

After talking casually about our lives for a few more minutes, she mentioned that Loch had met a young Belgian woman, and he was head over heels. I would have to interrogate him about that the next time we spoke. We each said, "I love you," and hung up. I took a deep breath, and stared at the address on the yellow sticky note in my hand. I hadn't heard Levi come up behind me.

"Whose address is that?"

I jumped, and my heart skipped a beat. He really needed to consider becoming a ninja. I put my hand on my chest and turned to him, smiling. When I caught my breath, I responded.

"It's my father's…your grandfather's address." I was so tired of all the lies, and saw no reason to add to the long, long list of them. He came to my side and we both regarded the sticky note for a moment.

"Are you going to see him?"

"Yes. Uncle Rip and I are going tonight."

"Is Talia coming over then?"

I nodded. Talia had only suffered a minor concussion, amazingly, and had been released after just a few hours. I had followed the ambulance to the hospital after Levi convinced me he was perfectly capable of babysitting for an hour or so, and after the doctor told her she didn't have to stay the night, she insisted she was up to playing nanny for a few days. Lars, who I'd called at Talia's insistence, and who'd been at her bedside within fifteen minutes of said phone call, had agreed to come over and help. It seems the two were getting pretty serious, and I found out he used to be a school teacher in Sweden, so I allowed it.

Lars had seemed very concerned and attentive, readjusting her pillow every five minutes and making her take sips of water. He was a good man, I could tell…like Ty. Talia promised she would only take the awesome painkillers the doctor gave her if she absolutely needed to. Lars and I had looked at each other with disbelief in our eyes, which she pretended to take as an insult. I had left the two to figure out the discharge paperwork when I realized, halfway down the corridor, that I'd forgotten my cell phone in her room. When I got back to the doorway, I stopped cold. Lars and Talia were having a conversation, but not in English.

When did Talia learn Swedish?

Wait. I was no linguist, but I was sure the language they were speaking was not Swedish. Swedish always made me think of the chef from the Muppets, and this didn't sound like him. I realized it sounded exactly like Ty's date on the night of our last weekly dinner, and she had been from…Russia.

Talia was speaking Russian…and very easily from the sound of it. There was a lot she still wasn't telling me, obviously…and why on earth would a Swede be fluent in Russian?

I shook my head slowly back and forth.

No. No more life-changing news today, I thought to myself. I announced my presence with a boisterous, and possibly over-done, "I might need my cell phone, ya think?" before I bounded into the room, snatched the phone off the counter next to the sink, and left. I didn't know if they realized they'd been busted, and I didn't care. I made a point to care later, after I got some answers out of my dear old dad.

Back in my kitchen with Levi, I was still a little concerned about leaving Head Wound Talia and her beefy Swedish/Russian boy toy, who I hardly knew, with my three precious gems overnight. But, although I knew they were keeping even more secrets from me, I also knew Talia loved my boys, and would never, ever jeopardize their safety.

"Just remember, she fell and hit her head today…" Okay, that was a distortion of the truth, but a necessary one. "…so she might not be her usual bouncy self. And Lars is coming over too…you remember him?

"Yeah, I like him…and Rowan LOVES him." That eased my anxiety a little. Kids usually had good instincts about new people.

"You'll be second in command, okay?"

"Yes, ma'am." He saluted me. Cute.

"So, why are you going to see Grandpa?" It was weird, hearing him call my father that. He'd never met him, but I'd told the boys about him…the little I knew myself anyway.

"I think it's time I ask him some important questions." Not lying, just not offering too much information that will freak Levi out.

"Like why he left Oma?"

I considered that for a moment. Twenty years ago, that would have been the first thing out of my mouth, if I had ever run into him on the street, which I hadn't, but now…

"No. It doesn't matter why he left. It was so long ago…it's more important that I know why he stayed away from his children. Does that make sense?"

He simply nodded. He was still standing there, wanting to continue our conversation. I realized it had been a while since we'd had time to just talk.

"And I'll ask him if he might want to meet his three handsome grandsons."

"Really?" That idea seemed to please him.

"Would that be okay? If I brought him home to meet you guys?"

"Yeah, that'd be cool. We've never had a grandpa. More Christmas presents." He was grinning at me now, waiting for my reaction. I messed up his hair, which, at fourteen, he hadn't started caring about just yet.

"Well, I wouldn't count on that. I might find him living in a cardboard box in an alley somewhere, or…I might not be able to find him at all." My tone had inadvertently changed to serious by the end of the sentence, and Levi picked up on it. He was my eternal optimist, though, and attempted to cheer me up.

"You'll find him mom. You're an FBI agent. You can do anything."

That worked. I grinned and gave him a quick hug. "Now, go ask your brothers what they want on their pizza. I'm calling to order it in two minutes."

At that, he skipped toward the living room, where his brothers were playing Rock Band, and screamed as if I'd just told him we were going to Disneyland. "Woohoo! We're having BJ's pizza for supper!" The other two joined him, and it sounded like a college frat party in there.

■ ■ ■

Ty showed up at around 8pm, right after Talia and Lars had arrived, Talia looking no worse for the wear. I didn't ask how many times in her life she'd gotten a blunt object to the skull, but I imagined this hadn't been the first time. At that point, she could have told me she was an alien from Venus, where they all have titanium skulls, and I would have believed her.

Rowan and Blaise had selected a board game to play with Lars, and had set it all up on the dining room table two hours before. Rowan met him at the door, and immediately took his hand, pulling him toward the dining room. Lars had expressed genuine excitement about it, skipping off with my three-year-old to select his piece for Star Wars Monopoly. Swedish Zumba instructor, Russian spy, Venusian spy, I didn't care...this guy was a prize. Talia was planted firmly on the couch, remote in hand, flipping between "What Not to Wear" and a marathon of "Firefly" on the Sci-Fi channel, when Ty knocked softly on my back kitchen door. I was alone in the room, unloading the dishwasher, when I looked up and saw his face.

I wasn't prepared for how elated I would be at the sight of him. It had only been six hours since I'd seen him last, but the time had dragged like waiting for a nearly empty bottle of ketchup to expel some tomato-ey goodness onto my cheeseburger. In between dealing with waves of overwhelming emotion at all the information my brain had been forced to absorb that day, and handling menial but necessary tasks, like laundry, dishes, and spending twenty minutes locating a matching pajama top and bottom for Rowan, all I had thought about was how Ty smelled. How he tasted. How he felt...his arms around me...his hands caressing every part of me...I felt a shudder flow through me before I closed the dishwasher.

I opened the back door, which I'd locked earlier just for peace of mind, and gave him a shy smile. He looked a little tired, but good. So good. He smiled, and that dimple peeked out at me, his eyes sparkling like I'd never seen before.

"Ready?" he asked. I nodded.

I quick said my goodbyes to the boys, and Lars and Talia, thanking them profusely and silently praying that they weren't enemy spies sent to kill me and my entire family. Then Ty and I went out the

WENDY HERMAN - 187

door. He had parked in Talia's driveway to keep the neighbors from talking, and as we walked around Talia's house, we hit a spot that was concealed from the road and any prying eyes. He stopped walking, and I slowed, then stopped, raising my eyebrows at him. He reached for my hand. As his fingers intertwined with mine, my heart raced and my stomach felt like it was hosting the Olympics in there. We looked at each other for a moment. Then, we were in each other's arms, and he was kissing me over and over, like he was going to war the next morning or something, and I melted into him.

As much as I needed to find my deadbeat dad and get some answers, a meteorite heading straight for us wouldn't have prompted us to stop what we were doing. We had waited too long. Been apart too long.

I pulled away, and gestured for him to wait a minute. I retrieved Talia's "secret" key hanging on a nail just above the ground behind a dense bush, and we went inside. I guided him down the hallway, and then pushed him onto the bed in the guest room, climbing on top of him.

For the next thirty minutes, he reminded me again just how well he remembered every curve, every contour of my body, even after twenty years.

EPISODE 28
Papa McKenna

We drove in relative silence, but it was comfortable silence… except for the occasional grin and blush we gave each other due to our little distraction at Talia's house. I couldn't believe how my life had transformed in the past twelve hours. Just yesterday, I had resigned myself to the fact that I was Trevor's wife until…well, until death do us part, and now…now, that mindset, that Freya, seemed like a world away, and I was so glad. I felt like a whole new section of my brain had suddenly woken up after twenty years.

I sighed, and glanced at the clock in Ty's silver Elantra…10:00pm. It was just before 11:30am that morning when I had made love to Ty…the first time. I felt my cheeks get hot again, as I imagined him naked, embracing me with such unbridled passion, first on my living room floor, and then in Talia's guest room…

We were like teenagers who'd gotten their first taste of the forbidden fruit, and now we couldn't get enough. I smiled, and put my hand on his thigh. He gave me a sideways glance and raised his eyebrows.

"Oh, no you don't," I responded to his nonverbal question. "I need you slightly on edge just in case you have to rough up my father for me." He pretended to pout. I slid my hand up his thigh a few inches, and he swallowed hard. "Then, we'll find a hotel for the night…"

"I can pull over right now…the road's practically deserted…" he said, his breaths uneven.

I looked out the window. We were on the freeway, and we were far from alone. It was Friday night, and everyone was headed into the city with us…except that we were going straight through to a small town about an hour on the other side. I gave him a "what the hell are you talking about?" stare, and he grinned. That damn dimple. I wanted to rip if off and keep it in my pocket forever. I removed my hand and he whimpered like a puppy. He was so adorable.

I was surprised by a sudden flood of anger and sadness at the twenty years we'd lost. Aside from my children, the time had been such a waste…I had been with the wrong man, and worse, the right one had been so close the whole time.

I reached up and ran my fingers through the graying hair just above his ear. I couldn't stop touching him. I was so afraid I would wake up and realize the last few months had been a cruel dream.

"You know, if you continue to touch me like that, I will pull over and take you right here, on the side of the busy freeway. We'll get arrested, and you'll have to call Talia and explain why we're in jail…" he teased.

I reluctantly stopped torturing him and placed my hands on my lap. "Talia would be easy to tell. In fact, she'd probably think it was awesome. I wouldn't know what to say to the boys, though. I can just hear Blaise…'Mommy, can I tell my friends you're a criminal now?'" I chuckled, but shook my head to get rid of the thought.

"What did you tell them about Trevor?" he asked. It was the question I'd been dreading.

"Promise me, you won't be mad," I cringed.

He glanced at me, surprise in his eyes. "Of course not, honey. I wouldn't have a clue what to tell them…at least, that wouldn't require intense therapy later in life, anyway." He laughed at his own joke, but then stopped abruptly when he realized I wasn't laughing with him. "You didn't tell them anything, did you?"

"I couldn't do it. Not yet. I told them he was out of town on business. They're used to that, so it didn't raise any red flags. I'm sorry. I chickened out, I—"

"Freya, it's okay. I think you did the right thing. We can figure out what to tell them together, after we know more about what's going on ourselves."

That made me feel so much better; I gave him a ravishing smile and took a deep, cleansing breath. But, there was something else we needed to talk about.

"So, you haven't said how it went…down at Headquarters. Did Trevor regain consciousness?"

He laughed, "Oh yeah! And was he pissed! I had gotten all the way into the parking garage, where Hart and O'Reilly—you remember him, the really tall, quiet guy—anyway, I had called Hart and given him the Reader's Digest version of what had happened, and asked him to meet me in the garage, so they start yanking Trevor out of the back seat of my car, and he wakes up and starts flailing like a kid about to get a shot. Even with his hands and feet tied, he got in a few good kicks. Luckily, Hart had brought a syringe full of…hell, I don't know what was in it, but he got it into Trevor, and two seconds later, he was a ragdoll again."

He had been rambling like he was talking to just another fellow agent about something funny that had happened at work, then he glanced at me and realized I was more than a little disturbed by his jovial account. His smile fell, and he put his hand on my knee.

"I'm sorry, Frey…I know, he's still the father of your children…I just…he's a bad guy, you realize that, right?"

"Of course I do. But it's more than that. I have a terrible feeling that we've only just discovered the tip of the iceberg with him. I'm afraid he's done some awful, evil things, and I don't know how I'm going to get through it…get my kids through it. How do you tell a child that his daddy is…a monster? I just think it may be a little too soon to be so…happy about it."

"You're right. I'm sorry." He was silent for a moment as he concentrated on changing lanes to get around a slow-moving eighteen-wheeler.

"I didn't mean to be a buzzkill, I just…so much has happened today, I'm still waiting to wake up in my bed and realize it's all been a dream…and a nightmare."

"Nightmare?"

I hadn't thought that comment through, as I noticed his expression change to desperate uncertainty. I put my hand on his thigh again. "Oh, not you…you're the dream part." He relaxed and winked at me. "Trevor's the nightmare…not to mention the whole top secret brain implant thing…" Something occurred to me just then.

"Ty, did you ever think that it might be a bad idea for the two of us to be alone together?"

This garnered a single eyebrow raise. I'd forgotten that he and Trevor both had that recessive gene.

"I mean, what if the implants go all ape shit, and we snap and start killing people? Not that that wouldn't be kind of cool, as long as they were all bad, but...I'm just sayin'."

"I think we're safe. It hasn't happened in twenty years, why would it now?" We were getting off the Interstate now, and it would be back roads the rest of the way to the little hole in the wall called Garrity.

I thought about his statement for a minute, before I voiced my thoughts. "Are you absolutely sure we haven't been...activated at all in the past two decades? I mean, how can we be sure? The memory would be...what? Stored in our implants where our conscious minds couldn't access it, or would it be erased immediately after it happened? I don't know how it all works, but...you would think the technology included a way to keep us in the dark when we'd been... awakened, I guess...right?"

"I don't know, but you're freaking me out now. We may never know, so stop thinking about it, it's just going to drive you crazy."

"Oh, I'm already there, baby. Join me, won't you, in Crazyville... we have cookies."

He laughed, and then gave me a super serious look and asked, "What kind of cookies?"

"What kind would you like?"

"Chocolate chip and Freya."

I glanced at him without turning my head, allowing the smirk to take over my face. "Later, big guy. Even goddesses need a rest period." I gave his thigh a seductive squeeze, though, keeping my delicious anticipation to myself about getting to our hotel room later.

We enjoyed a few minutes of quiet, as Ty turned the Elantra onto a highway, then a county road, and finally, an old highway in desperate need of repair...and decent lighting. We were almost there. I didn't have butterflies in my stomach. They were more like demon bats, accentuating the feeling of dread I had about seeing my father again, after so many years. And then, there was the possibility that he wouldn't be there at all...long gone to rot in some other tiny town who knows where?

My mother had mentioned once that she heard he had been forced into retirement, kicking and screaming, and consequently, out of spite, had vanished, where even the Army couldn't find him. I imagined if he was involved in more than just the RVW project, that his own brain contained several secrets the government may not want to get out, and he knew if they found him, they would likely kill him. The more I thought about it, the more it looked like the address my mom gave me probably was either no longer good, or never had been.

I was jolted out of my head by some serious turbulence. We had turned down a dirt road, and it had not been leveled...ever. I cringed at every bump—and there were a lot—feeling sorry for Ty's tires. I had grown up in small towns, though, so I knew something Ty didn't.

"Ty, if you speed up, it's not as bumpy."

He gave me a confused look. "Doesn't that just ruin my suspension faster?" His tone was light, but his face was clearly wishing his new toy was at least paid off.

"Trust me...speed up and the tires will skim across the top of the uneven dirt."

He still wasn't sure, and I could see his mental tires spinning, trying to figure out if I was making any sense.

"Ty, I've done it myself. If I'd driven as slow as you are right now, I not only wouldn't have made curfew, I would have needed new tires every time I had a date...now punch it!"

I guess he figured it couldn't possibly be worse, and he accelerated. As we neared forty miles per hour...forty-five...fifty, he sighed with relief, as the bouncing reduced considerably.

"I'm in love with a genius," he said, not looking at me, but meaning every word.

"Say that again..." I ordered.

"You're a genius." He flashed me his Superman smile.

"Not that part."

It wasn't fair of me, really, to ask so much of him while he was trying to navigate an unknown, dimly lit, severely grated country road going fifty miles per hour, but I couldn't help myself. Later, I would make a mental note to not risk our lives just to hear those three little words.

He reached over and took my hand.

"I love you."

I knew I would love the sound of it, coming from his mouth, but I didn't expect to feel my eyes tear up in response. I was turning into a real sap. If I started watching movies on Lifetime after this, I was going to have to kill myself, for the good of all mankind.

Ty dared to take a microsecond to turn away from the road as he said it, and looked into my eyes, so I had no doubt that he believed what he was saying was possibly the most important thing he'd ever, or would ever say.

I opened my mouth to respond in kind, and very happy to do so, when something caught my attention out of the corner of my eye... something on the road in front of us. So, instead of professing my undying love, I screamed, "LOOK OUT!"

Ty snapped his head toward the road, and took evasive action. As we drove down the ditch on the other side, and into a corn field, I thought I had felt something impact the vehicle.

Ty quickly turned us around so our headlights would illuminate the road, then he put it in park, and we both leapt out of the car. I was sure I had seen a person...a man, standing in the middle of the road.

"Did we hit him?" Ty asked me, as we clamored up the ditch.

"I don't know...we hit...something, but...I don't know."

We got to the road, and saw a lump lying right in the middle of it. We both froze, and I could feel my palms start to sweat. Then, the lump moved, moaning as it slowly stood up. The old man started to brush off his pants with one hand, and that's when we noticed the shot gun in the other. Ty moved to draw his weapon, which I hadn't realized he was wearing, but I motioned for him to hold off a minute. I stepped forward to address our victim...and possibly our murderer...out here in the dark, on a deserted country road. It really was too cliché.

"Sir, are you alright?"

"Jesus Christ, girl! What the hell were you two driving so goddam fast down my road for?"

"We're very sorry. We didn't see you—"

"NO SHIT!"

"Look, we just need to know if you're hurt, so we can—"

"I'm not hurt, so unless your goal was to kill me, you can clear your conscience and get on with your useless, boring lives, the both of you!"

This guy was a real ray of sunshine. Ty and I exchanged looks and shrugs, relieved we hadn't killed anyone today...yet. Ty stepped closer to the man, who was now limping toward us, holding his shotgun over his shoulder. He was wearing overalls, and old work boots with no laces. His hair was gray, overgrown, and unkempt, and he had a suspicious scowl on his wrinkled face. Ty didn't seem intimidated as he approached.

"We're headed for Garrity...can you tell us if we're going the right—"

"You're in it, but there's nothing for you here, so why don't you turn your luxury SUV around and head back to the big city where you belong?" He was just a few feet from us now, and I really scrutinized his appearance. He screamed lifelong bachelor/crazy old coot, and I was ready to be rid of him. I decided to ask him if he knew my father, and then, expecting him to say no, we could grant him his wish and get the hell out of Garrity.

"Sir—"

"Stop calling me 'Sir'! My name's Jerry!"

"Okay, Jerry—"

"You don't get to call me Jerry! Only my friends call me Jerry! You call me Mr. McKenna!"

"Okay, Mr.—" My heart stopped. Ty's jaw dropped open, as he stood frozen next to me, staring at the old man.

"You gotta be shittin' me..." Ty whispered.

The three of us stood there, regarding each other. Finally, I felt brave enough to ask.

"Dad?" It had come out sounding more like an accusation than a question.

The old man walked right up to me and stared me in the face. When I saw his eyes, I knew it was him. It was one of the few things I remembered about him. He had beautiful ice blue eyes, and my brother had inherited the same, but mine were dark brown, like my mother's.

When he didn't say anything, I reiterated, "Dad," but it still wasn't a question.

"Freya?" I don't know why I was surprised that he remembered my name. He was my father, dead beat or not.

I closed my eyes in shock and slowly nodded my head. He sighed deeply, like he used to do when I'd bring home B's on my report card. I hadn't expected an "I've missed you so much, my sweet baby girl!" and a warm embrace, but I guess I'd expected something related to... happiness, or at least *not* disdain. Instead, I got...

"Shit."

EPISODE 29
Newspapers

The old farmhouse my father was living in could have easily been confused for an abandoned building, even from the inside. He clearly did not have a cleaning lady. He was attempting to uncover a small couch for us to sit on, throwing piles of books and newspapers on the floor, while we watched, when I noticed his leg was bleeding just below the knee.

We *had* hit him with the car.

"Dad, you're bleeding."

He stopped what he was doing and looked down at his leg. "Ah! Just a scratch." He picked up one last pile and then motioned for us to sit. Then, he sat across from us, perched on the corner of the coffee table...at least, I think there was a coffee table under all those newspapers. I looked around the room at the sheer unlivable conditions, and thought of that TV show, *Hoarders*.

My father has gone crazy, I thought.

"Don't give me that look, young lady," he scolded me, pointing a finger in my direction.

"What look?"

He laughed, but not because he was happy about something. "Ha! Your mother used to give me that same look. You think I've lost my mind."

"Dad. What the hell are you doing here?"

He looked down at the floor for a second, as if contemplating whether or not to tell me the truth. I hoped I would be able to tell the truth from a lie.

"I *was* hiding, but if *you* found me...I guess I need to consider... relocating."

"Why?" Ty asked him, leaning forward on the tiny couch. "What are you hiding from?"

My father squinted at him. "Who the hell are you, then? You're not my daughter's husband, I know that."

Ty stammered for a second, so I stepped in.

"How do you know he's not my husband?"

"I was at your wedding, darlin'."

"No you weren't."

He ignored my response, studying Ty's face intently. "My God! You were the boyfriend...?" He studied Ty's eyes even harder for a second. "Yes, you were! Your face is the same...just...older."

Ty and I looked at each other and he smirked at me, revealing that dimple. I must have let a quick, dreamy look escape, because my father noticed.

"Ohhhh, so you two are together now. Where's Travis, then?"

"Trevor," I corrected him.

"Whatever," he said, rather insensitively. Not that I cared if he got my husband's name wrong, but my own father should know the name of the man I'd spent the past twenty years with. It was the principle of the thing. So, now I was annoyed with him.

"Dad. We have some questions—" I started, but he interrupted me.

"Yeah. Yeah. Figured you'd come looking for answers sooner or later. Hoped I'd be dead by then, but..." He chuckled.

"We know about the brain implants," Ty blurted out. I loved that he had gotten right to the point. I put my hand on Ty's knee, and nodded at my father. We expected him to start confessing right then and there, but...

"Congratulations." He just stared at us for a moment. "So, what's your question?"

"Dad, tell us what role you played in all of this. We know you had something to do with Ty and me being turned into government super soldiers. We just want to know what happened back in March of '91."

He sighed then, and seemed to be having trouble looking at us. He stood up and started to go through a nearby stack of newspapers, like he had forgotten we were there. He was mumbling to himself. I thought he really had gone over the edge, until he pulled a paper out of the middle of the pile, and handed it to Ty. Ty took it, but gave my father a confused look, to which he responded by gesturing for us to look at the paper. We glanced down, and realized fairly quickly that this was no ordinary newspaper. The name at the top was the first clue. It said, "The McKenna Memories."

As I scanned the front page, two words jumped out at me from the middle of the mass of words: Winkle Labs. It was written as if it were a newspaper article—the author was listed as "The Old Man"—but it was essentially the story of how my father first became affiliated with Winkle Labs. My eyes went to the top right corner, searching for a timeframe. It was dated Nov 4, 1989.

I looked up at my dad incredulously. "What is this?"

"I was starting to forget things, so I decided to write them all down...as I remembered them."

Ty and I glanced around at the hundreds of newspapers piled up all over the room. It hit Ty first.

"You mean...all these newspapers...are...your memoirs?"

"Yep."

I was still very confused. "Dad, how did you make all these papers?"

He jerked his head back, and said, "This house was the old town paper and press for Garrity. I bought the house, and got the old printing machine and a shed full of paper along with it. I taught myself how to use it, and after a few years, started writing."

Ty was just beginning to see what my dad was saying, and seemed almost giddy. "So, all these newspapers...Mr. McKenna...they are all your memories from your top secret job with the government? All the secrets you were sworn to keep...you wrote them all down in these newspapers?"

"Yep."

Ty and I looked at each other, wide-eyed. How could he give such a glib response?

I shook my head with disbelief, and stared at my father. "Dad... why?"

"It gave me something to do. A man can't be idle for so long without going a little crazy. After a while, the secrets didn't seem all that important anymore, and they were swimming around in my head, so I decided to let them escape, but not in a way that would get me noticed right away. I figured after I died, and the place was cleaned out, either someone would realize what the newspapers really were, or they wouldn't." He sat on the coffee table again, and leaned toward us, speaking just above a whisper. "Even if they did know what they had, who would believe them, right?"

We were awestruck...at least I was, by his audacity and arrogance. The secrets didn't seem all that important? He had authorized the government to turn his only daughter into a sleeper assassin when she was nineteen years old. How in the hell does that *ever* seem "not all that important?"

He broke the stunned silence when he snorted. "Seemed like a good idea at the time."

Suddenly, my throat was very dry. "Do you have any water?"

That got him standing again, and he headed for the kitchen. "Water? I don't buy that bottled crap...it's a scam, you know. Tap water was good enough for me, it's good enough for anyone..." he mumbled to himself as he disappeared around the corner.

I stood, and turned to Ty. "Do you realize what he's done? Putting everything down on paper?"

Ty stood too, and smiled at me. "All the answers we're looking for are here...somewhere."

I smiled back at him, and then the daunting reality hit us both. We looked around at all the piles. They were everywhere. The crazy old bugger had been writing entire newspapers of memories for years.

"Where the hell do we start?" Ty asked me.

I just continued to scan the room, trying to make sense of it all. I realized that if my dad had any kind of a system, the first choice would be chronological...at least, that would have been *my* first choice. I pointed to the pile he'd pulled the Winkle Labs paper out of, and Ty followed me to stand over it. He gestured to the pile with his hand.

"After you, milady."

I started to go through the pile, and quickly realized that my father and I did not have the same brain. The dates were all over the place. His system was not chronological, it would seem.

Between the papers were some old photos. One that caught my eye was a small black and white of a beautiful young woman holding a small child. I don't know why, but I put it in my pocket. Then I resumed rifling through the endless newspapers, before admitting defeat just a moment later. "Dad, how are these piles organized?" I yelled toward the kitchen.

My father returned, with no drink in hand, and cocked his head at me. "Organized? They're organized by when the gosh dang memories came to me, that's how they're organized. I'm not a library, sweetheart."

I looked back at Ty with an "I don't know why I'm surprised" look on my face, and he threw down the papers he was holding, frustrated.

Maybe, just maybe, we wouldn't have to spend the next three years reading newspapers.

"Dad, do you have any idea where the information on Ty and me… the implants, and the sleeper assassin thing…any idea at all what pile those papers would be in?"

Please, please, please, please…

He reached up and scratched his stubbly chin, screwing up his face like he was thinking really hard.

"Hmmm…don't think I've written that one down yet…" he replied.

"WHAT?" Ty and I exclaimed in unison. I was starting to feel like I was nothing more than a pebble in this guy's shoe…but I was done playing around.

"Okay, Dad. Here's an easy one. Why did you hire Talia Mitchell to watch me three years ago?"

If our knowing about the brain implants hadn't surprised him, this little chestnut definitely took him by surprise. Then he tried to pretend it hadn't.

"Don't know what you're talking about…"

"CUT THE CRAP, DAD!" I kicked over a pile of newspapers, letting the anger fill me. "I know what you did…*we* know what you did! We just want to know…why? Why did you offer up your only daughter, and her boyfriend, to some government experiment?" I gestured toward my man, who was staying unusually quiet. "And why worry about my safety now? Why hire someone to keep me safe? You haven't cared for twenty years. Why now?"

"Well, darlin'—" he started, but I wasn't done.

"And STOP with the small town country bumpkin speak! You're from Minneapolis, not Mayberry!"

He took a deep breath now, and his expression changed drastically. It was like watching Mr. Hyde turn back into Dr. Jekyl right before our eyes.

"Freya…" Finally…my father had emerged after an eternity of pretending he was someone else. "Sit down, both of you. I'll tell you everything you want to know."

EPISODE 30
Answers

My father had managed to find some beer in his fridge, and we were all enjoying the calming effect of fermented hops when I finally decided on my first question.

"Were you really at my wedding?" An odd choice, I admit, but I had to get the random ones out of the way before I could focus on the big stuff.

"Yes, I was. Your mother sent me an invitation. I stayed out of sight, but I didn't miss a moment. You looked so beautiful, but…" He stopped, reconsidering what he was about to say.

"But what?" I pushed.

He took a deep breath and decided to spill it. "I never liked that Trevor. There was always something…off…about him. I wanted to tell you not to marry him, but your mother wouldn't let me. Of course, she didn't know what I knew, and I couldn't tell her..."

"He was part of it, wasn't he? He was barely twenty at the time, but he had something to do with the implants?"

My father closed his eyes and took a few deep breaths.

"Dad. You said you'd tell us everything. I need to know."

He cleared his throat and nodded. "He was a brilliant young protégé who helped develop the technology. He knew everything there was to know at the time about the human brain and what it is capable of, but… he was…odd, to say the least. I noticed he took a liking to you right away…he had quite a crush, but you were always with *this* guy." He gestured to Ty, but not in a menacing way. He chuckled at the memory. "How did you ever find each other?"

Ty and I gave each other a puzzled look. He answered. "We were never apart…at least, not for long. Trevor was my best friend…since college...since he and Freya got together..." He seemed to be trying to string his thoughts together, so they made more sense to him, but it wasn't happening. I took his hand in mine. He smiled at me, but I could tell he was having trouble processing it all.

"What do you mean, you were best friends? You hated him!" my father exclaimed.

Ty perked up at this, and leaned toward my father, but kept hold of my hand. "When?"

"Well, you only saw him when you were 'on', if you know what I mean...when your implant had been activated. You wouldn't have remembered anything after you woke up and went back to your mediocre life."

"Dad," I was trying desperately to figure out how to make all the events line up. I needed the right question. "Did the implants fail?"

"On the contrary! They were a resounding success. You two were invaluable to national security. You—"

"Killed people," I finished for him.

He locked eyes with mine. "Yes. You were very good at it. Both of you. You were quite a team, until—"

Ty cut in. "Until what?"

"Until all the touchy-feely people in the government decided it was too risky to have you

roaming the streets."

"What does that mean?" I asked, growing impatient. I silently wished that all the information I wanted, all the memories I had lost, could be instantly downloaded into my brain, like the machine in *Matrix* could do. This was taking far too long for my ADD brain.

"We were given two options," he sighed. "Terminate you both, or remove the implants and throw you back into normal society."

The room was quiet for a moment. The government wanted to have us killed, because we were too good at what we did. And what we did was the job they created us to do in the first place. But, wait. Ty and I were not dead. And we still had our implants...or did we?

"Did they remove the implants?"

"Initially, they voted to terminate, but we convinced them it would be easier...less paperwork, if we just turned you both back into normal, boring human beings. Trevor was given the task of removing the implants."

"Trevor?" I repeated, nervous now at what I would find out next.

"But he couldn't do it."

"Couldn't or wouldn't?" Ty asked, now holding my hand with both of his.

"He said it was impossible. That you would suffer severe brain damage if he tried to remove them. But, he said he could wipe them clean, and then deactivate them. We knew the Senate committee overseeing the project would never go for it, so I fudged the paperwork, and as far as they knew, your implants were removed."

"Wipe them clean? You mean the memories of when we were 'on', as you called it, were all stored in the implant? And that's why we couldn't remember anything?"

He nodded and chugged the remainder of his beer, reaching down and picking up another and cracking it open. This discussion was definitely easier to handle with a little sedative in the system, so I didn't judge.

I had to admit, the technology was fascinating, even though it had altered my life irrevocably, and may have caused me to spend two decades with a man I never loved, but…it was still incredible to think that I had a device in my head that could turn me into a lethal weapon at the drop of a hat.

"How did you activate the implants? When we were needed for a mission, how did you turn us on?" I asked.

Dad raised his eyebrows at me. "Ah… it was the old cliché phone call, and a certain word that would act as a trigger, but cell phones weren't an option back then, and if neither of you were home to answer the phone, well…and what if someone else answered? There were too many variables…too many things that could go wrong, so we came up with a Plan B if the phone didn't work." He took another swig of beer, and then continued, more and more animated as he spoke.

"Trevor had already programed the trigger into the implants, so he added voice recognition. It had to be a specific word, but also spoken by a specific person, and only that person could activate you both. And if we couldn't get you by phone, we sent that person to you…physically."

"Who was that person?" Ty asked.

"Well, it was Trevor…shit." He was just realizing himself how diabolical Trevor really was. His eyes grew wide as the dark door opened in his mind.

"Trevor was the only person who could activate us?" I couldn't believe what I was hearing. Suddenly, my head began to pound. *Oh no you don't,* I ordered my brain. I will not check out of this moment. I had a million more questions. After a few seconds, the pounding subsided.

"We were just his puppets," Ty murmured, staring at the floor. Then he looked up at me, his eyes burning with rage. "All these years, he manipulated us, not just with the lies, but…he was literally inside our heads!"

I felt tears well up in my eyes. My strength was waning, right along with Ty's.

My father interjected just then. "Now, wait a minute. When he deactivated the implants, he assured us the trigger was turned off as well."

"DID HE!? The psycho brain scientist assured you? That's reassuring, JERRY!" Ty was losing it. I tried to say something to calm him, but I couldn't think of anything. He stood and started to pace the room…as well as he could with all the piles of newspapers.

"What are you saying?" my dad asked, his genuine confusion scaring me a little. He really had no idea to what lengths Trevor had gone to coordinate the life he wanted, but it was all coming together for me.

I maintained my gaze on Ty as I spoke. "Dad, Trevor didn't turn the implants off. He reprogrammed them." Ty looked at me, his mouth falling open. I knew what his eyes were asking me. Would we ever really know all the damage Trevor had done? How could we?

My dad shook his head. "What the hell are you talking about? He couldn't have…someone would have known—"

"And what if they all turned a blind eye, Dad!" I turned to him now. "Or they were in on it? Or he somehow convinced them he had done what he was supposed to do? I know what he's capable of…"

My dad thought about that for a moment, and then his eyes lit up with revelation. "Trevor had money!"

"What?" I asked.

"He had money. His parents had died the year before, and they left him a small fortune."

"He paid the other scientists off?" Ty was coming down from his anger.

"Maybe."

"Could Trevor have reprogrammed the implants to give us false memories?" he asked.

"Son, I have no idea. The technology was not my department."

I needed to lay it all out...get my ducks in a row, as it were, so I began to think aloud. "Trevor somehow made me believe I was in love with him. And he gave Ty the memory...memor*ies* of being best friends...but why? Why would he want to be best friends with a man who hated him? And why did he want *me*?"

"Oh, he fell for you the moment he saw you, Freya. And you were nice to him. I saw the effect it had on him, but I kept telling myself it was an innocent crush. I knew how you and Ty felt about each other..." Ty sat down and squeezed my hand, as my dad continued. "Men like Trevor...well, he didn't get much attention from the opposite sex, until you tried to be his friend...you always wanted to be everyone's friend...and he took it the wrong way. I don't think you noticed, but he confided in me once."

"What?" I responded. "What did he say?"

"His real mother had died when he was ten. He'd loved her very much. Then his father remarried a cold woman with whom he could never form a bond...she wouldn't allow it. Then, when they died... well, it all affected him...shaped him. He was a lonely young man who craved attention from nice, maternal women, like his mother had been, and he desperately wanted a family to replace the one he'd lost...and you came along, and you were everything he ever wanted, so he said..." Dad suddenly clammed up, perhaps thinking he'd said too much. Or realizing that he should have seen Trevor as the sociopath he was back then, and maybe he could have saved his daughter the heartbreak she was now going through.

"He told you that?" I couldn't believe the Trevor my dad was describing. "Dad, Trevor is nothing like the introverted science nerd you're talking about. He's confident, successful...hell, until two months ago, I thought he was the perfect husband and father...and aside from all the lies, he was...perfect..." I trailed off, something in my brain opening up.

He *had* been perfect...too perfect.

"Of course he was all of those things, *after* he had you on his arm. You were the one thing he needed to have the life he'd always wanted. Once he had you, he could be whoever he wanted to be. You fit the missing piece in his psyche. It makes sense...psychologically. He reinvented himself to be the Trevor you know, but he's still—"

"He's still a lying, crazy bastard who manipulated Freya and me to be part of his life." Ty said this with an eerie calm.

Dad smiled at him. "Yes. And I'm sorry about that. If I'd known what was going on, I would have done something." He really meant it, and that made me feel even worse.

I got the distinct feeling that he was full of regret, this old man who had been my dad a hundred years ago. Regret, not just about his family, but about a lot of things. I was starting to see how creating the newspapers had been a cathartic process for him, releasing all those memories, good and bad, after keeping them locked up in his brain for so long. I actually felt a little sorry for him, sitting across from him now, and seeing how the life he chose, the life of a covert career with no one to go home to at the end of a long day, had really aged him.

"The only thing Trevor ever gave me that was real was my boys." I felt the tears rolling down my cheeks, and didn't care.

"I've been meaning to ask you about that..." Dad started.

"They're just fine, and they want to meet you," I said, thinking I was finishing his sentence.

"No, that's not what I was going to say, but I'm glad they're doing well...your mother sends me pictures, you know...she's a good woman...you're like her, Freya. No, anyway, I was going to ask who the surrogate father is, if you even know...you didn't go to one of those God-awful sperm banks, did you?"

I waited for him to start laughing at his own joke, tasteless though it might be, but he didn't laugh. In fact, he looked very serious as he waited for an answer.

"Dad, what are you talking about?"

"Sweetheart, it's okay, I know about Trevor's…condition. He told me about it himself, twenty years ago."

"What condition?" Ty was stiffening beside me, as if he was guessing what my dad was going to say.

"You were his best friend and he never told you? Freya never told you?"

"Dad, I have no idea what you're talking about. Trevor is the boys' father, I swear."

Dad opened his mouth to respond, but froze for a second, waiting for his brain to tell him what to say. He seemed very nervous all of a sudden, and stood, pacing. I couldn't move while I tried to prepare myself for what I was about to learn. I wagered a guess in my head, but immediately dismissed it. It couldn't be *that*.

"Trevor can't be the father, Freya."

"Why not, Dad?" I asked, each word a dagger through my heart.

"He was born with a deformity…in that area," he started, and I frowned at his inability to say the word "penis," although I knew full well it was a product of his generation. "It was repaired when he was two, supposed to be an easy fix…but the surgeon cut too deep…"

"Dad, just say it." I had to hear him say it, or I would never believe it.

"He's sterile, Freya."

EPISODE 31
Bottomless Pot of Secrets

Trevor was not the father of my precious boys.

My life was becoming a soap opera. I had shut down my emotions to avoid a complete and total blackout when my father told Ty and me that my crazy, soon-to-be ex-husband was sterile, and had been his whole life.

Talia's joke about the alien DNA was starting to sound less and less ridiculous.

I told both men that I couldn't handle any more bad news. I was so exhausted, I just wanted a bed. When my dad informed us that the nearest hotel was back in the city, over an hour away, I felt my face start to tremble. I was losing control.

He offered his guest room, and we had little choice but to accept. We followed him to a back room, where an old built-in bookcase concealed a set of stairs going underground…but not the kind one would imagine. They were beautiful, wooden stairs, and the light coming from the other end was inviting. We descended and found my father's real home. He had spent the past decade creating a subterranean paradise beneath the old print shop and dilapidated house. It was complete with home theater, fully stocked bar, and a cozy guest bedroom and bath, in addition to the master suite on the other end, which was simple, but beautiful. It seemed there was no end to the secrets this man kept.

As my dad walked us into the guest bedroom, Ty excused himself to use the bathroom, and left us alone for the first time. There was an awkward moment, and Dad made to leave, but I stopped him.

"Dad." He turned and looked at me questioningly. "I have to know…" I was having trouble spitting it out.

"What?" he asked, not irritated or curt, but almost…fatherly.

"Did you volunteer me—us," I gestured toward the bathroom where Ty was hiding, "…for the RVW project?"

"No, honey. You volunteered yourselves…both of you. You knew what you were signing up for. After the implants were put in, we had that memory erased…it was necessary. Do you understand?"

"I understand you could tell me anything and then just claim my memory had been erased…"

He winced at my words, and I was kind of glad. I wanted to hurt him after everything that had happened, but…if I'd known exactly what I was doing back then, that changed everything. If Ty and I had willingly volunteered to be guinea pigs for the implants, then…I would have no one to blame but myself. For everything.

"Why did you let me, Dad?"

This surprised him, and he sat on the bed next to me, a smirk on his face. "There was no talking you out of something you really wanted to do, Freya. You were an adult—"

"I was nineteen. Hardly an adult."

"Yes, well, you were nineteen, going on forty. You had always been very mature for your age." He leaned toward me and put a gentle hand on my shoulder. His eyes were sincere. "You were so right for the RVW program, Freya. You were perfect."

"How can you say that? I was perfect for an *assassin*? How are you even qualified to be the judge of what I was or was not suited for? You hadn't been in my life for over five years. You didn't even know me." I was fighting the sobs. I didn't want to cry in front of him.

He took a deep breath and swallowed hard before answering. Ty came out of the bathroom just then and paused in the doorway when he realized he had interrupted our conversation. Then he saw how upset I was, and the look on his face told me that he would take my father down, if I wanted him to.

I squinted at him and shook my head ever so slightly to let him know I was okay. My father glanced at him, but then returned his attention to me.

"I don't want to overwhelm you right now, but…just know that the technology was not perfect. There were some side effects, and some of your memories, or lack thereof, are not what you think. I did know you...very well. Besides being your father, it was my job to know. I was responsible for making sure the chosen subjects were unique in their ability to adapt and overcome in any situation. You were...*are* an extraordinary woman, Freya, and I'm not just saying that because you're my daughter." He chuckled softly at his last comment, but he wasn't winning me over that easily.

"So, how, exactly, were you qualified to decide if I would make a good killer?" I had turned the corner from upset to pissed off.

"I'm a psychiatrist...one of the top in my field...or I was, thirty years ago...can't imagine the human mind has changed much, though."

"You're a shrink?" Ty asked.

"You...are a psychiatrist...? How did I not know that?"

He shook his head. "It was best that you didn't know what I was... involved in. I told you I was an accountant once, when you were around twelve, and you didn't question it."

An accountant? I didn't remember that either.

"Dad, why keep that a secret?"

"My life was very complicated, Freya. I got involved with the government early on in my career, shortly after your mother and I were married, and...let's just say the people I worked with, and the projects I was a part of...well, I thought your lives would be easier if you didn't know." He patted my leg and stood, smiling. "Now, get some rest. We can talk more in the morning. All this confessing is exhausting." He arched his back and stretched his arms out in front of him. "I think I'll turn in too...oh, and don't try to go upstairs without me."

Ty and I both looked at him, waiting for an explanation.

"I've got an alarm system, and you don't want to set it off." He pointed to the stairway door. "Let's just say the clean-up is a bitch." At that, he nodded good night, and left the room.

Ty walked over and closed the bedroom door. For the first time in a long time, I cried. I cried until I was sure my body could no longer manufacture tears. And Ty was there. He held me in his arms, and never let go. He didn't say a word while I let every betrayal, every deception, every fear flow out of me like a tidal wave. At some point, we laid down on the bed and fell asleep.

When I opened my eyes the next morning, still wrapped in Ty's strong arms, I felt renewed. I counted my blessings. Ty; my boys; Talia; my mother and brother, thankfully a million miles away from all this— how and when I would tell them everything was a decision that would have to wait; and the biggest blessing of all, my unwavering sense of self. Despite everything, I knew who I was, and I wasn't about to let anyone tell me otherwise.

I was Freya. Goddess, Warrior, Mother, Lover. My father was right. The qualities that apparently had made me the perfect assassin, would also keep me out of the loony bin as I pieced my life back together. I could handle anything life chose to hurl at me. And handle it, I would.

I got up slowly, trying not to wake up Ty, but pausing to gaze at his beautiful face for a second, then snuck into the bathroom to freshen up. I washed my face, brushed my teeth, and took a hot shower. When I emerged, I felt like a new woman, ready to take on the day, with Ty at my side.

Ty was just stirring when I opened the bathroom door, and he smiled when he saw me wrapped in a towel. I stood in the doorway and just gazed at him. He sat up on the bed and ran his hands through his dark hair, yawning, which produced the dimple that had one job and one job only…to make me happy. I smiled so big, I'm sure the light that emanated from me was visible from space.

"Well, you are in a good mood this morning, my warrior goddess."

My whole body suddenly felt warm, as I watched him stand and begin undressing for a shower. I had never been the praying sort, but before I could comprehend it, I was thanking God for making this amazing man just for me. I decided then and there that I would thank the Maker for my blessings on a regular basis. In fact, I was going to start appreciating everything in my life that was good…starting with Ty.

"Thank you."

He stopped unbuttoning his shirt and smiled that crooked smile that stopped my heart. "For what?"

"For saving me."

His smile faded, and he walked over to me, wrapping his arms around my shoulders. I couldn't look away from his stormy eyes. "*I* saved *you*?" he said.

I responded by curling up one side of my mouth ever so slightly.

He slowly shook his head back and forth, but didn't break eye contact. "For twenty years, I've had half a heart. I always knew it was you who had the other half, but I never dreamed—" He suddenly stopped, and I realized he was choking up. He looked away, but I caught his eyes. He was having trouble gaining his composure.

I put my hand on the back of his head and brought his lips to mine. His hands came up to hold my face, and he kissed me passionately. My stomach started doing an Olympic gymnastics routine.

"*You* saved *me*, Freya." He gave me a soft kiss then, and my breathing became erratic. "Tell me you love me," he whispered, so close that I could feel the vibrations from his words on my lips.

"I…love…you."

He closed his eyes, drinking in the delicious words, although I was sure I would never be able to do them justice.

I finished unbuttoning his shirt for him and let it fall to the floor, where my towel soon joined it. Ty got his shower about twenty minutes later.

When we emerged from our bedroom, the door to the stairway was wide open, so we assumed my dad was already up. As we ascended, the smell of eggs and bacon wafted down to us, urging us upward.

He had tidied up the kitchen enough to cook a decent breakfast, and he looked very different than he had the night before. He had showered, shaved, and was wearing jeans and a button-down shirt. My first thought was that he had decided it was time to come out of hiding.

"Well, you look like a new man!" I exclaimed.

He smiled as he carefully slid some eggs onto a plate and handed it to me. "I'd like to go home…with you, if that's alright."

I had been about to take my first bite, and it hovered in the air now, halfway to my mouth. I stared at him, disbelief filling my eyes.

"For how long?" Ty asked, after noticing that the ability to speak had left me.

"As long as you'll have me."

Suddenly, I came back to earth, setting my fork down on my plate instead of finishing the motion to my mouth. I was no longer hungry, but…something had made me smile. I realized it was the fact that my father had addressed Ty as if he were my husband…my other half, capable of making decisions that affected not just the two of us, but my boys as well. It had solidified what I had already begun to sense. Ty and I were now a family.

That realization spread through me, and I knew that whatever the day held, I would be able to take it in stride. My dad wants to live with me—us—after being absent from my life for twenty years?

Bring it on.

We ate breakfast, and gathered our things to leave when I noticed something different about the living room. It was empty, except for the old couch and coffee table.

"Dad," I called toward the stairs where he had gone down to pack a bag. "Where are all the newspapers?"

I could hear him coming up the stairs. "Safe. I don't know when I'll be back here, so I put them where they won't be disturbed, and where I can get to them if I need to."

I took a deep breath. All of this top secret, covert stuff was still very new to me, and sometimes, it scared me. Was I doing the right thing? I pushed the thought of my boys' safety out of my head…or tried to. I took another deep breath, and reminded myself that I had only done what was necessary. And I would continue to do what I had to in order to find out the truth. That was the only way to ensure their safety.

My father climbed into the backseat of Ty's car after depositing his single suitcase in the trunk with our bags. As Ty pulled away from the old house, I found myself staring after it, trying to comprehend that my father had been living there, just a few hours from my own home, for the past ten years.

I remembered an important question that he still hadn't answered, and decided that now was a good time. He was trapped in this vehicle with us for the next two hours, and as far as I was concerned, he was going to answer every question I threw at him during that time.

"Dad—"

"Hold on, Freya," he cut me off. "Ty, stop here for a minute."

"Is something wrong?" Ty asked, looking in the rear view mirror at our backseat passenger as he slowed to a stop in the middle of the dirt road about half a mile from the shack.

"Just one more thing I need to do before we leave." I turned in my seat to see my dad pull a small black box out of his jeans pocket. There was a red button on top.

No…it couldn't be…

My mouth fell open as my father pushed the button. Behind him, outside the back window, a large explosion erupted from the house, launching flames a hundred feet in the air.

EPISODE 32
Malfunction

Ty was more than happy to drive fast over the grated dirt road. Even with him masterfully handling the SUV going nearly 75mph, however, we could still feel the heat from the explosion inside the car…and we had to be a mile from the house by now.

I was frozen with shock.

"WHAT THE HELL DID YOU DO THAT FOR?" Ty screamed above the noise of the road and the fire still raging behind us.

"JUST DRIVE!" my father yelled.

So, Ty drove, minding the speed limit once we were on a proper road, just to avoid any chance of us getting pulled over. Once all evidence of the burning house had fallen below the horizon behind us, I realized I was trembling.

I may be a warrior goddess, and former assassin, but I didn't know how much more drama I could take. I suddenly feared for my boys. What had I dragged them into?

My fear turned to anger, and I decided to direct it at my dad. I grabbed the garage door opener from the center console, and turned and threw it at him in the back seat. Lame, yes, but it made me feel an infinitesimal amount better, and was therefore worth it.

"Ouch! Freya?!"

"Why?" I unleashed on him. "Why did you blow up your house? Why did you leave us twenty-five years ago? Why did you hire Talia? Why did you suddenly care about me three years ago?"

All the questions in my head were pouring out of my mouth, and I couldn't stop them.

"Freya, listen…I wasn't…you don't understand…" He stammered for a moment, but I wanted answers.

"ANSWER ME!" I was overtaken by boundless rage, and before I could control myself, I had unbuckled my seatbelt and was climbing into the back seat, hitting my dad over and over. He didn't fight back, but raised his arm to deflect my blows, which was ineffective for the most part. I couldn't even stop myself when I noticed my dad's nose was bleeding. Still, he didn't retaliate.

I hadn't realized Ty had pulled over, but suddenly he was yanking me out of the vehicle through the front passenger door, which had to have been difficult, since my front half was in the backseat.

I knew I should stop fighting, but something in my brain had switched off…or on…I didn't know what was happening, but I could no longer control my actions. I was screaming for Ty to let go of me, resisting his grasp with all my might, although my common sense urged me to calm down. He was much stronger than me, and managed to pin me against the outside of the Elantra, but still I fought, my arms and legs flailing, and my head thrashing back and forth. I could hear his voice, far away, trying to reach me, but my vision was dark.

"Freya! Freya, look at me! Freya, can you hear me?!"

I engaged the force that had taken hold of my brain, trying to regain control. Suddenly, Ty's voice became clearer, and then my vision started to return, a tunnel of light at first, then I could see Ty's face come into focus…slowly. I realized I was still kicking and clawing at him. I also realized I was back in the driver's seat of my own mind, and I was able to stop fighting.

I focused on Ty's face, and that calmed me, although his expression was anything but calm. His cheeks were flushed, and his nostrils flaring. His eyes were on fire, but started to extinguish when he noticed I was coming back to him.

"Freya!" He took such a deep breath, I thought he might take all of the air in the vicinity with him. He was breathing heavily, and he lowered his head, still holding my shoulders against the car with his hands, and I realized he was laughing. He raised his head and looked at me.

That smile. That dimple. It brought me back to reality quickly.

What had I just done?

He saw my rising panic, and his grin disappeared. He moved in closer to me, his gray eyes penetrating and reassuring.

"It's okay, Freya…it's okay." He sighed. "You're okay." He smiled again, but this time it was slightly forced, like I wasn't the only one he was trying to convince.

Just then, my dad came around from the other side of the car, holding a handkerchief to his face that was quickly filling with blood. He walked past us and headed toward a small gas station about a block down the road, presumably for the restroom. I engaged Ty's eyes, and gave him a quick, but strong kiss. Then I went after my dad.

"Dad!" He didn't turn around. "Dad, wait! Dad…I'm sorry!" He turned around at that.

"It's okay, Freya," he said, his words muffled by the bloody hankie. "I'll live…I just need to get cleaned up."

He turned and resumed walking in the direction of the gas station. He waved a hand in the air, as if to tell me to just let him go. I figured if he collapsed to the ground, I'd help, but until then…I guess he knew what he needed to do. I would have to find a way to make it up to him later…or did this make us even for all the deception over the past twenty years?

Nah…not even close.

I turned back toward Ty and he was already in the driver's seat of his car, starting the engine back up. I hopped in the passenger side, and we drove the twenty seconds it took to get to a parking spot in front of the gas station. He shifted the vehicle into park, and sighed. I realized my breathing was still a little heavy, and I attempted to calm myself. After three deep breaths, Ty glanced at me.

"You okay?"

I looked at him. "I'm so sorry, Ty…I don't know what happened—"

He had reached out and was holding the side of my face when he broke in. "It's alright. It wasn't your fault."

"What do you mean, it wasn't my fault?"

He looked at the steering wheel for a second, letting his arm fall to his lap. "I had sort of a flash…while you were…kicking your dad's ass." He grinned at this, then chuckled slightly, but his expression quickly turned back to concern.

I crawled out of my pity party and put my hand on his thigh. "What did you see?" I asked, just above a whisper.

"It was…you…and you were…spazzing out, just like now, but it was much, much worse." He turned in his seat to face me completely, and grasped my hand that was on his thigh.

"Freya, I don't think your dad has told us everything he knows about the implants."

"Yeah, I got that vibe too."

"The flashback was so quick, but…one thing I do know is that your…" he searched for the word.

"Spaz attack?" I offered.

He grinned at me. "Yes, your spaz attack…actually *attacks*…they happened twenty years ago too, and they got progressively worse… something was wrong with your implant. It was short-circuiting your brain or something…it was…scary."

I was trying to hold it all together. "Well, wait a minute. How do you know I wasn't just venting built-up anger this time, and my dad was just unlucky enough to be in the right place at the wrong time? I mean, normal people lose it once in a while…right?" I looked at him hopefully, praying he would agree with me…whether he agreed with me or not.

He grabbed my head with both his hands, his eyes frantically searching mine. "Because…when you…"

The thought occurred to me to offer "spazzed out" again, but I knew it wasn't the time to joke around.

"…your eyes…" he sighed as he gazed into my eyes. "…the pupils get so large in those beautiful, intoxicating, chocolate-brown eyes…they turn black."

He waited patiently for me to respond. I swallowed hard, and mentally added this new bit of information to my list.

"Black?" I repeated in the form of a question.

He shook his head. "I don't know why, but I know it's not supposed to happen, even when we're activated. Freya…we need to get that thing out of your head."

"Great idea, Ty. How do you propose we do that?"

"Well, there's only one person who can do it…without killing you."

"What about you? We need to get yours out too!" I wasn't going to be the only freak with a malfunctioning brain implant.

"Okay, there's only one person who can remove them without killing *us*."

I nodded, satisfied at his correction.

Suddenly, the back car door opened, and my dad climbed in. His nose had stopped bleeding and he looked just as healthy as ever. He handed me a bag of snacks. I opened my mouth to apologize, or something, but he cut me off.

"I'm fine, and I probably deserved that…but if you do it again, I'll have to use the Vulcan neck pinch on you." His tone was playful, but there was an edge to it, like it was entirely possible he actually knew the Vulcan neck pinch, and he wasn't afraid to use it.

"Don't worry, it won't happen again…as long as you tell us why you felt the need to incinerate your house and all your belongings," I responded, determined to get the truth out of him.

My dad buckled his seatbelt, and sighed. "Protection. I knew I'd stayed in Garrity too long, but you two showing up…well, it was time to play dead…again."

"Who are you hiding from, Mr. McKenna?" Ty glanced at him in the rear view mirror.

"You know, you used to call me 'Jerry'."

"Who are you hiding from, *Jerry*?"

"Let's just say, the current administration would love to get their hands on what's in *my* brain."

"What makes you think they won't look for you at your daughter's house? Especially when said daughter used to be a government-controlled assassin?" I thought it was a valid question.

"I'm hoping they'll think I'm dead long enough for us to figure this all out."

"Dad, why did you hire Talia three years ago? Did something happen then that made you feel the need to have me watched?"

He took a deep breath, and I knew he was going to tell me the truth this time.

"Yes, I hired Talia three years ago, because the previous…person I'd hired to protect you…well, he got a better offer…you never knew him…but my point is, I've been trying to keep you safe for twenty years…and unfortunately, staying away from you myself was an integral part of that plan, but now…"

"Now?" I asked.

"It's time we put an end to it…and see if we can't give my grandsons a normal life."

A normal life. A few months ago, I thought that's what I had, but it had all been fake…orchestrated by Trevor, the puppet master of my life…of *our* lives.

It was time to cut the strings.

"So, are we going to your house now?" my dad asked after a minute or two.

Ty put the car into gear and backed out of the gas station lot. "Not yet."

"Where to, then?" my dad asked, seemingly enjoying his little adventure so far.

Ty and I looked at each other, sure of what we had to do, and replied in unison.

"Trevor."

EPISODE 33
Trevor's Cell

I don't know what I expected to find when I entered FBI Headquarters, holding Freya's hand, her father trailing behind us, but it wasn't to be frisked and searched to the point of embarrassment. The guards at the entrance had been doubled since the day before, and it seemed that everyone was being considered a possible security threat, and several people without proper ID were being turned away.

What had we missed while we were in Garrity? World War III?

When I tried to lighten the mood by asking the guard why the "TSA search" was necessary, he ignored me, focusing on his very thorough search of my personage with a stone face.

Eventually, we were let through, and Freya's dad had even produced some identification card I didn't recognize that got him cleared without a strip search. I made a mental note to interrogate—I mean *ask*—him about that later. One thing I did know was that there was a lot he wasn't telling us, and I could sense that Freya felt it, too.

We had been so in sync, her and I, since our unexpected reunion, that I felt exhilarated and more alive than ever. In fact, I had no idea a person could feel this good, even with everything that was going on, I just couldn't be knocked off the cloud I was walking on. I had loved Freya my whole life, but had always known I could never have her…and then, BAM! Suddenly, she was mine again…and I was going to do anything and everything in my power to keep her.

I couldn't tell her, but I was secretly delighted that Trevor may not be the father of her children. If what her father told us was true, then…it just seemed to make the whole situation easier somehow.

The only reason she had contemplated staying with the bastard was because of their children. If that reason was now off the table completely, then he had no claim whatsoever on her or the boys.

I just had to know...how the hell had he done it? If he wasn't the father...then who was? And how on God's green earth had he managed to impregnate his wife with someone else's sperm? My head started to hurt when I thought about the possibilities.

I clutched Freya's hand tighter as we made our way to the detention area in the basement. Trevor was still locked up, and would remain so until we got some answers. I had spoken to Director Pixley briefly on the phone earlier that morning, and the FBI's newest prisoner hadn't given up any information...yet...but he was growing more and more unstable by the hour. It was just a matter of time before he cracked. And I wanted to be there when he did.

We approached the secure entrance to the detention area, and I turned to Freya.

"Are you sure you want to go in?"

I knew I didn't really have to ask, but I was worried the sight of him might be very confusing for her, considering what she had been through in the last few days...and the past two decades. She smiled at me, and nodded.

"I've never been more sure of anything." She was calm, and her confident gaze steadied my own heart rate. I silently hoped seeing him wouldn't freak *me* out, after learning what a diabolical son of a bitch he really was. He was the guy I had told my deepest, darkest secrets to—as much as men do. Except for the one about loving his wife...that admission had been an accident, but I had loved him too...like a brother. Had he programmed that or had it been real?

We scanned our badges and were allowed entry, and once again, Jerry's strange ID card garnered him immediate access as well. What the hell was that card of his? An FBI Fast Pass?

I opened my mouth to ask him about it, but he suddenly spoke to the young guard.

"What's with the body cavity search downstairs? Someone try to kill the President?" He chuckled at his own dangerous joke, but the guard just stared at him blankly for a second. Joking about killing the President at FBI Headquarters was likened to saying the word "bomb" in an airport.

"I…I don't know…sir," he stuttered. "I've been down here since o-six-hundred."

Now I was curious. "You didn't hear any alarms or anything?"

"No, sir."

I didn't have time to validate the sense of foreboding I was getting from the nervous guard, so I shook it off.

"Are you new?" Freya asked the young man. Leave it to her to make friends. I smirked to myself and turned to the secure monitors that showed each of the twenty or so cells on the other side of the 12-inch thick lead door we were about to go through. As Freya chatted up the guard, I found Trevor's cell, and froze for a second.

What the hell?

Trevor was curled up in a ball in the corner of his cell, barely visible in the shadows, but the audio was clear as a bell…he was crying.

Crying?

I'd known the man for twenty years, had considered him my best friend for most of that time, and I'd never seen him cry. Not once. I'd never thought how odd that was until now. Now…that he was bawling like a newborn baby.

Before I could prepare Freya for this new surprise, she was standing next to me, staring at the screen just as I had been doing… stunned at what she was witnessing.

"It's weird…I've never seen him cry…in twenty years…" she said, trailing off.

I turned to her. "He never cried in front of you? Ever?"

She looked at me, her eyes growing more alive with every new revelation. "That's strange…isn't it? He *never* cried…even when the boys were born."

Before I could censor it, it came out. "Well, if they aren't his, then…" I immediately regretted it. I gave her an apologetic look, but she didn't look angry. Her expression hardened, determined, and she pointed at the screen without breaking eye contact with me.

"That sad sack of a man is not my husband." Then she softened a bit and her eyes sparkled with mischief. "It's time for the puppet master to be controlled for a change." She walked to the door to the cells, and then glanced back at me to see if I was coming.

"Excellent," I whispered, and joined her.

"I think I'll stay put," Jerry chimed in. I started at the sound of his voice behind me. I'd forgotten he was there. Freya had a way of making the rest of the world disappear when I was with her. She turned to him and nodded.

"Don't you think your experience with this kind of thing might make you useful in there?" I was surprised he didn't want to go, but he just shrugged at me.

"I'll watch on the monitor. You don't need me in there...plus, if he recognizes me, it might open a whole other can of worms."

"Fair enough," I commented, but gave him a look that said, "We'll talk later." He just grinned at me like a school boy. He was enjoying himself and it made me uneasy.

"Don't be long, though," he pointed a finger at us. "I'm hungry."

Freya cocked her head at him, and he shrugged at her too. It was going to take a lot of patience to get any real answers out of Jerry McKenna, and I was dreading trying.

I pushed the thought away and turned to the rookie guard, whose sole job was to protect the rest of the world from what was behind the door in front of us, and nodded. He punched in a code on the console next to the door, leaned in for an eye scan, placed his hand on the screen for a fingerprint ID, and then punched in another long code. We heard a loud click and the door popped open a fraction of an inch. I opened it the rest of the way and led Freya down the maze of corridors to the end of the hall, hearing the door close with a loud thud behind us.

Trevor's success at essentially hiding from the FBI within our own walls for twenty years had garnered him the special suite, reserved for those unique criminals that the government was...well, afraid of. The fact that he had worked on a sleeper assassin program when he was barely twenty, and then married one of the assassins, after allegedly reprogramming her government-sanctioned implant for his

226 - JUST KILL ME

own nefarious purposes was...troubling to say the least. Add to that the fact that he had been a trusted agent, given the highest security clearance in the building, second only to the Director himself, and the staggering amount of information he had been given access to, and it was enough to get him fifty years in the electric chair. As far as I was concerned, he was lucky he hadn't been sent to a mining colony on Mars...but I was still hopeful.

Pixley had been hesitant to hold Trevor, only knowing what he'd been told by his boss, and his boss's boss, that Trevor had been assigned to watch Freya twenty years ago, and that the marriage had been part of the cover. If that were true, I would have to tell Freya. I hadn't mentioned it, frankly, because I'd forgotten about it temporarily. There had been a lot going on, after all.

When I'd called Pixley on our way to Headquarters, he'd been ready to release the bastard for lack of evidence, until I told him what we'd discovered in the past twenty-four hours. He was silent on the other end of the line as I told him everything...well, I might have left out the part about Freya and me...being together, but that was not his business as far as I could see. He agreed to keep Trevor locked up until we got there, but couldn't guarantee he could keep him unless we could get him to confess something...anything. I was sure I could get him to crack, and then he would never see the light of day again.

As we stepped into an elevator at the end of the hall and I pushed the arrow down button, I turned to Freya.

"There's something I need to tell you about what Pixley was told by the suits in DC." The words came faster than I intended.

"What?" She didn't look at me, so I continued.

"They say Trevor was given the assignment of watching you... indefinitely...and that the whole marriage...thing...was part of the cover."

She was quiet for a moment, then sighed heavily. "Well, that makes sense."

"Really?"

"No," she sighed again. "But...it does tell me that someone in Washington has been protecting him for twenty years for some reason...the question is, are they still?"

"We'll figure all this out. I promise."

She turned and gave me a sweet smile.

"You're taking it very well..."

At that, her smile vanished. "I don't feel the same, Ty."

I waited a second for her to continue...to clarify what she was talking about, but she seemed unable to find the words. "What do you mean?"

"Two days ago, I was this...person...I thought I knew exactly who I was, but I was living this half-life as Trevor's..." She closed her eyes. "I know it was just yesterday when we..." She paused and smiled, as if thinking about our first encounter. Then she opened them and looked into my eyes. "I'm sorry...my point is, I'm Freya. For the first time in twenty years...I'm finally me again." She laughed and looked down at the floor, shaking her head. "It's so strange. I really believed I had this picture-perfect life, but...it's like I was locked inside a part of my own brain...that you opened yesterday..." She looked at me again, and grinned at her unintentional pun.

I felt my cheeks get hot. She was the only person on the planet who could make me blush.

"I keep thinking I should be devastated at the time I lost being Trevor's puppet wife...all the time I could have been with you...but I refuse to let him dictate my emotions anymore. I'm just so happy to be...whole again. For the most part, I feel...relieved."

She wrapped her arms around my neck, staring into my eyes with those chocolate pools of hers. I wanted nothing more than to kiss her a million times, but the sound of a throat clearing loudly startled us both. We turned toward the elevator door, and realized it had already opened. The guard was standing in the hallway, waiting for us to exit, and appeared to be annoyed at our personal moment. He rolled his eyes as we released our hold of each other and I guided Freya to step out of the elevator first.

We had entered the sub-detention level. There was only one cell on this level, and it was currently occupied by the puppet master himself. Once the guard had called upstairs and spoken with his counterpart, and scrutinized our identification badges as if he were looking for clues left by the Freemasons, he turned to a keypad on the wall, and typed in a code. The cell door in front of us buzzed and popped open. Inside was another door, this one with a small window. The guard did not enter with us, but punched in another code on the same pad in the hallway, and the second door buzzed.

I took a deep breath, and opened the door.

Trevor was sitting up now, but still in the back corner of the small, otherwise empty room. He didn't look up when we entered, and we just stood there, staring at him for a few seconds.

"I haven't done anything wrong..." he said softly, as he raised his head. When he saw that it was Freya and me, his mouth fell open, and he made to stand.

I immediately drew my weapon and trained it right at his head. "Don't, Trevor."

He put his hands in the air in surrender, and sat back down on the floor. He looked terrible, his face revealing his earlier sob session, and his hair sticking up on end...the Trevor I knew would have been mortified if he'd seen himself in a mirror. He looked up at us, pleading.

"Rip...it's not what you think...you have to believe me...you're my best friend...I could never lie to you..."

"You were never my friend. It was all some sick fantasy world you created."

"That's not true...well, yes, it's partly true, but...wait...you remember?"

Sure, Trevor. Let's go with that. I didn't answer him.

He turned to Freya, desperation filling his eyes. "Frey, this is all a big mistake—"

"Yes, Trevor, it is a mistake. Our marriage, our life...you."

"Don't say that, Freya. We have a great marriage...we—"

"We didn't have a marriage. I was your prisoner."

"Freya," Trevor begged, "you are my wife. We have three beautiful boys...you can't just throw all that away because you think you still love...*him*," he said with contempt.

I rolled my eyes. "Uh, *him* has a gun pointed at your head, moron."

I waited for Freya to bring up the whole "sterile" thing, but she seemed to be avoiding it. I guess it was our Hail Mary play.

"How could you do this?" Freya asked, but maintaining control of her emotions. "How could you…turn me into your…live-in prostitute? All these years…why me? Why did you have to steal *my* life?"

He closed his eyes tight at her words…they were clearly cutting him deep. "I don't know what you're talking about, Frey…I love you…you love me…we fell in love and got married…we have three children that we raised together…we have the perfect life—"

"Yes. We did. It *was* perfect," she agreed. He smiled as if he was getting through to her, but his imagined victory was short-lived. "It was perfect, because it wasn't real."

He acted the tortured victim. "How can you say our life together isn't real? We have a great marriage…you are a wonderful wife, and you've always told me what a good husband I am…"

I snorted quietly at his expression. Then I noticed Freya was actually considering his words…or seemed to be. She was looking at the floor, her eyes scanning as if she was reading something. Trevor started to stand, and I tensed, gun still in hand. I looked at her without turning my head and saw her nod slightly, telling me it was okay to let him get to his feet. I didn't like it, but I let him stand. I wanted to shoot the superior, smug look right off his face.

"You *were* a good husband, when you were around…"

"I wasn't around much, I know…and I'm sorry about that…my job…" he stammered.

"Your job," she repeated. "Your job as an FBI agent?"

"Yes, and you know I couldn't tell you I was an agent, no matter how much I wanted to."

"But Ty…he could tell everyone that he's an agent…?"

He gave me a cold stare, but spoke to Freya. "It's 'Ty' now, is it?" He looked back to Freya. "*Ty's* position in the bureau isn't a Top Secret one."

He was right about that, although I was just realizing I had no idea why his position had to be kept a secret…his position as…as… what *was* his job? I suddenly had no idea what Trevor did for the FBI. Had I ever known? Why had it never occurred to me before? The questions swam around in my head, and I suddenly felt a little woozy. Trevor noticed as I fought the tunnel vision.

"You okay, Riptide?" he asked, in a mocking tone of concern.

Riptide? Why did he call me that? And why did it seem to open up a black hole in my brain?

"You remember what I do, don't you, *buddy*? What my job is at the FBI? Think hard..."

I tried to focus on what he was saying, but a voice in my head screamed, "DON'T LISTEN!"

Freya turned to me. "Ty? What's wrong?"

"Nothing...I'm fine...he's just trying to manipulate you, Freya... don't listen..."

I wasn't fine.

The next thing I knew, the world went black.

EPISODE **34**
Ty's Time Machine

The voices were muffled, but I could tell they were agitated…
arguing. My vision was returning slowly, but blurred with every
overwhelming wave of nausea. I felt my leg twitch, and suddenly,
two blurry figures were hovering over me.

"Is he awake?"

"Of course not, it was just a reflex," the other man, taller and
younger, answered in a distinctly Russian accent.

"But his eyes are open."

"That's not an unexpected physiological response to the stimuli
we're implanting."

"English, please."

"It's normal."

The two turned their backs to me, seemingly disinterested once
again, and resumed their measured argument.

"How do you expect to get clearance for this? It was not part of
the original plan…"

"Nothing that has happened since Day 1 was part of the original
plan," the Russian retorted.

"True, but this is very unorthodox…this is a human being we're
talking about."

"A human being who will be a mental mess if we don't put
something in there—"

"You're talking about giving him false memories—"

"Yes, to fill empty space—"

"Empty space that YOU say was caused by the implant
malfunctioning."

232 - **JUST KILL ME**

"I told you, I already fixed the malfunction…but I couldn't restore his memories."

"Why not let him wake up and have amnesia for the rest of his life?"

"The technology is very complicated, but I'll try to put it in terms you can understand—"

"Thanks so much. Should I get my crayons and take notes?"

A heavy sigh of frustration. "When a person has amnesia, the memories are still in the brain, the conscious mind just can't access them…"

"Right…"

"Because the implant essentially operated as a second, sort of mini-brain, the gaps the malfunction created are literally empty space. The memories were deleted. They're gone…forever." He paused to make sure the other man was following, and he got a small nod to continue. "The brain will interpret this empty space as brain *damage*, and—"

"And that's bad."

"Yes…it could be."

"Could be?"

"It could cause his brain to shut down completely."

"And you're risking everything…your job, his life, to give him memories that aren't really his…and hope his brain doesn't reject them and shut down anyway."

"Yes."

"And you are just planning to appoint yourself as official memory maker? You're going to make up the memories yourself?"

"I'm the only one who can manipulate the technology to such detail."

"And you're going to do all this…out of the goodness of your heart."

A chuckle. "Yes. That, and a possible ground-breaking, career-making success story in the field of memory fabrication that would guarantee me a place in the history books."

"Of course."

"Look, the bottom line here is, either way, there's a chance his brain is already fried. Why not at least try to give him a life, real or not?"

I lay there, listening, my eyes closed now. I was frantically searching my memories, desperate to find the empty spaces the two men were talking about. I concentrated on my earliest recollection as a child, and went from there. Elementary school, middle school (ugh!), high school, enlisting in the Marine Corps, then college, and meeting Freya. I couldn't find any holes that hadn't been there before, like the missing memory of Freya and I breaking up, but that didn't calm me down. It was entirely possible I wouldn't know if I had missing memories, because they would be…missing. But I *did* have missing memories, and I *did* know about it. Maybe they were talking about my gaps with Freya from twenty years ago…but how did they know? I had only told Freya…

My head began to throb with pain. The whole situation felt wrong.

I decided to fight, and opened my eyes, locating all the tubes that were hooked up to various parts of my body, and devising a plan to pull them all out at once, if possible. That's when I noticed it. The thickest tube, about an inch in diameter, coming from a large machine, and going into my head. It was just like Freya had described in her flashback of Trevor reprogramming her to love him and not me.

Panic rose inside me, and doubled…no tripled, when I realized I couldn't move anything but my eyes. I tried not to make any noise as I heard my heart rate increase on one of the many machines I was hooked up to. The nurse monitoring the machines punched a few buttons before mentioning the change aloud. I closed my eyes to hide the fact that I was conscious.

"Doctor, his heart rate just jumped."

I dared to open my eyes again, and caught a glimpse of the young man standing over me, checking all the wires and connections, before I slammed them shut again, afraid he would look at my face. I had seen enough to know that—aside from the obvious—something wasn't right. It was Trevor, and he was young…very young, but that wasn't the shocking part. The man I'd heard speaking with a Russian accent was also the man leaning over me now.

Trevor was Russian.

I knew now that I was having a flashback, but for the first time, I was aware that I was having one while it was happening, and therefore, aware that it wasn't real, or at least that it wasn't in real time.

The last thing I remembered was being with Freya inside Trevor's jail cell, and Trevor calling me "Riptide." He'd never called me that

234 - **JUST KILL ME**

before, that I could recall, and the mere sound of the word had made my head spin...something about *his* voice saying *that* word.

The bastard had used the activation word on me!

But then, why didn't I just kick his ass when my ninja skills were turned on? It must have been a word that triggered something else. He must have programed my implant to not just turn on and off...but to control my behavior as well.

And it only responded to his voice.

Suddenly, I felt a tugging sensation inside my head, and then searing pain. I tried to scream, but no sound came. I tried to open my eyes to see what was going on, but there was only darkness. When the pain subsided, I saw a tunnel of light. It got bigger and bigger, and made me think of *The Wizard of Oz*, when Glinda the Good Witch made her first appearance in her pink, glowing orb of light. I remembered watching that movie on TV when I was a child. It was so amazing and magical, I couldn't take my eyes off the screen, even during the short commercial breaks. I didn't want to miss a second.

The light was filling my vision now, and I could see a blurry silhouette. As it became clearer, I realized it was Freya. She was glowing like Glinda...and so beautiful. But, her face was tense. She was worried about something. Her mouth was moving, and a moment later, my hearing came back with a pop that startled me.

"Ty! Ty, can you hear me?!"

"Why are you yelling? I'm right in front of you..."

She sighed and smiled.

I was lying on the floor, my head in Freya's lap. Talk about a great way to wake up from a nightmare. She was stroking my hair, and smiling at me still, but something was missing in her expression. Her smile was shallow...like my waking up was just a minor victory.

As I regained my bearing, she let me sit up, slowly. That's when I felt like I might be able to talk without hurling.

"What's—" *Uh oh*...(deep breath)...*nope, I'm okay.* "What's... going on?"

"Who's Glinda?"

I looked up at Freya, and she was raising both eyebrows at me.

"Glinda...the Good Witch?" I ran my fingers through my hair as I tried to figure out how she knew what I'd been thinking before I came to.

She softened considerably. "From *The Wizard of Oz*?"

I nodded, but had to close my eyes to keep the tunnel vision at bay.

"You were dreaming about Glinda the Good Witch from *The Wizard of Oz*?"

"Um...sort of..."

She shook her head and laughed.

"How did you know I was thinking about that movie?"

"You mumbled her name right before you woke up."

I chuckled softly.

"Just don't ever do that during sex," she ordered.

I looked at her and we both smiled. Then, I was rudely brought back to our current situation, and remembered I had some important information.

"Frey, I have to tell you something about Trevor..." I lost my train of thought as I realized where we were.

Trevor's cell. But...no Trevor.

"Where's Trevor?"

She stopped smiling. "The bastard escaped."

I felt like I'd been sucked into a parallel universe. Trevor couldn't have escaped. He would've had to have outside help...holy shit.

I found Freya's eyes.

"No," was all I could muster. I didn't need her to say it. I could read her mind these days. She pursed her lips and sighed. How could I have been so stupid?

Trevor did have a man on the outside.

And we had driven him there.

EPISODE 35
The Russians Outnumber Us

"Freya, I had a flashback while I was unconscious. I saw Trevor, and another, older man, and they were talking about…empty space in my memories that needed to be filled, and…well, we already know what the prick did to us, but there's something else…" I looked up at her, and she was furrowing her eyebrows, trying to prepare herself for whatever it was I was about to hit her with. There was no delicate way to say it. "Trevor was speaking with a Russian accent."

I could tell by the change in her expression that there couldn't possibly have been anything further from all the speculation swirling around in her head. She was quiet for a moment, and I let her take it all in. Suddenly, her eyebrows raised and she looked at me with wide eyes. She looked scared.

"Freya, I know it's a lot, but—"

"No," she cut in. "That's not it. I just remembered something…something I hadn't told you yet, because…well, because I didn't want to believe it myself at the time, so I filed it away, but…"

"What?"

"I overheard Talia and Lars having a conversation…in Russian."

Any remaining symptoms I had from my episode were whisked away like raindrops on my North Face jacket, and before I could stop myself, I barked at Freya, "WHAT?! Before we left yesterday!"

"When Talia was in the hospital, so…yeah, I guess that was just yesterday, wasn't it?"

"How could you forget to tell me something like that?!"

"Well, you can see why I couldn't deal with it—"

"You do realize we left our three children with those two…those two possible…bad guys?" I hadn't meant to raise my voice, or sound condescending, but I couldn't seem to stop.

"You don't have to patronize me, I wouldn't have left the boys with them if I wasn't sure…wait, *'our'* children? "

"What?"

"You said 'our' children…"

"I did?"

"Yes, you did."

"Oh…um…sorry."

"You're sorry you said it?"

"No, that's not what I meant, I'm sorry…I'm sorry I yelled at you…"

She grinned in such a way, her eyes intense and sparkling, that my frustration melted. I knew that look. I'd seen her give it to Trevor a million times over the past fifteen years, and had always fantasized about it being directed at me. I remembered thinking the bastard didn't deserve her, but I was realizing that I was far from worthy as well…and yet, she still wanted me.

Right about that time, the young guard, who had finally come to after being hit on the head by Jerry (and with his own gun, no less, but we tried not to rub that in…he'd had a bad enough day), had come down to the sub-detention level and found the other security agent unconscious right outside the elevator. After the medics had taken his cohort away, and he had verified that Freya and I were both friendlies, he let us out of Trevor's cell. He was shaking, and looked like he might be reconsidering his career choice. I knew I should say something to make him feel better, but I wasn't very good at that. I had always been the guy who reveled in making the greenhorns feel worse when they screwed up. Freya came to the rescue.

"What happened, Jasper?"

That's right. I'd forgotten he was Freya's new best friend.

He scratched his head, and winced. "Mr. McKenna was watching you all on the monitor, and then suddenly he said he changed his mind, and wanted to go down to the sub-cell…so I opened the doors, and he went through. I waited two minutes, and Hal hadn't called me for confirmation yet, so I called down there, but he didn't answer. Just as I was reaching for the alarm, Mr. McKenna was back at the door, pounding on it like crazy. I let him out, and he screamed at me to give him my gun…that the prisoner had escaped and was heading up the elevator. He was so convincing…" He hung his head in shame, and Freya put a gentle hand on his shoulder. "When I came to, I sounded the alarm, and then I found Hal unconscious right out here…" he finished as we stepped onto the elevator to go up to the main level.

"Is he alright?" Freya asked, genuinely concerned.

"I think so, ma'am…"

"Are *you* alright?"

"Yes ma'am, just a bump on the head, and a bruised ego…" He tried to smile, but his face was pale and glistening with sweat.

We were all silent as the elevator doors opened and we stepped out, Freya first, then me. As Jasper stepped out, he felt the sore spot on his head gingerly, and took a deep breath.

"I know the Bureau prides itself on realistic training exercises, but I've never been knocked out before." He managed a slight chuckle. "I'm guessing I failed this one miserably."

Freya and I froze, and then both turned to face him.

"What are you talking about?" I asked, trying to work through the total confusion. I knew there had been something odd about his behavior earlier, and now he looked more confused than we did. His mouth fell open, but no words came.

"Jasper, why would you think this was an exercise?" Freya asked.

"Umm…well…the phrase…Mr. McKenna said the phrase…it's an old one, but it's still on the list…" he stammered.

"What phrase?" I insisted.

"When he asked if someone had tried to kill the President…it's Exercise Launch Phrase Tango."

Freya and I looked at each other.

Freya looked back to Jasper. "Jasper, are you sure he said the phrase word for word?"

"Yes, ma'am. I was top of my class in memory recall. I can recite all twenty-six phrases verbatim."

— — —

After a quick visit to Director Pixley's office, who had immediately sent two teams in search of our missing agent and Freya's dad after young Jasper had regained consciousness and sounded the alarm, he ordered us to go home, and we didn't argue. I did want to ask him one thing before we left, though.

"Sir, any idea what Mr. McKenna's magic all-access pass might be? Jasper said it just came up on his scanner as 'Immediate Access'."

"Jasper mentioned that to me too…seems Mr. McKenna has himself a Platinum Card."

A Platinum Card. The card only elite government employees who require not just anonymity, but invisibility are authorized to carry. They can come and go without an electronic footprint. Essentially, they're ghosts.

We had decided to tell Pixley about our suspicions that Trevor was not American, but kept the part about Lars and Talia to ourselves. Normally, I would have insisted I go after Trevor myself, but we were both anxious to check on the boys and, to be honest, I was tired. Exhausted. I couldn't imagine how Freya was still functioning, given what she'd been through on such a deep, personal level. It had been an unparalleled few days, and my brain was still sorting through everything that had happened. If I had a nickel for every life-changing, jaw-dropping event we had endured over the past thirty-six hours, I could pay off my Elantra.

We decided the speed limit was just a suggestion as we careened toward Freya's house, especially after Talia failed to answer her cell phone. The good feeling Freya had about Talia and her Swedish boy toy was fading fast.

"Drive faster," she said, staring straight ahead.

"You got it, babe," I replied, and hit the gas. I tried to change the subject to take her mind off the boys, or at least, come at it from a different angle.

"What I don't get," I started, glancing at her as she turned to look at me, "is why all the Russians? I mean, that plot's been done to death. Cold War. We won. They lost. End of story. And that was more than twenty years ago now."

She contemplated my remarks for a moment, before responding. "I've been thinking about that too…when I heard Tal and Lars in the hospital, I mean, it was strange, to say the least, but does it really mean anything? Except that they have secrets? Who doesn't have secrets? God knows we have our secrets..."

I grinned. "Yes, but we have the luxury of not remembering any of our secrets."

"True," she smiled back. "What I'm saying is it might just be a minor detail in all this...the fact that three of the people involved are secretly Russian...okay, that sounded a lot more convincing in my head." She sighed and laid her head back on the seat.

"It's just one more complication we don't need right now."

"Amen," she responded, picking up her head and pointing a finger toward me. "You can bet that will be the first question out of my mouth when we get to the house, though."

"'Why don't you answer your damn phone'?"

"Okay, the second question..."

About twenty minutes later, we pulled into Freya's driveway, and Lars was outside playing three-on-one football with the boys. Talia was laid out on a patio chaise under the shade of the house, watching and laughing every time Lars let the boys tackle him to the ground.

I heard Freya take a breath, probably her first one since her fifth failed attempt to contact Talia, and she had the door open and a leg out before I put the car in park. The fact that the Russian spies we'd asked to babysit hadn't kidnapped the boys...or worse, in no way made them trustworthy in my mind. They were still in for a whopper of an interrogation session.

After Freya hugged the boys to the point of suffocation, and then chastised Talia for not having her phone on her at all times, to which Talia rolled her eyes like a teenager being scolded for staying out past curfew, we all went inside. We had forgotten that if we confronted the two right away, the boys would be there, listening to every word. The interrogation would have to wait.

Levi immediately started to set up a video game, and he and Blaise were arguing over what to play. It was Rowan who voiced what Freya and I had been waiting for, standing at his mother's side.

"Mommy, did you find Grandpa?"

That's when the other two looked up at Freya, waiting for her response.

"Um…" She glanced up at me. We hadn't discussed what we would tell them about good ole Papa Jerry. I gave her a miniscule shrug, and she gave me a mild "You're no help" look. "Well, we did find him, but he…can't come over yet."

"Why not?" Blaise asked.

"Well, he's got some business to take care of first, honey," she euphemized.

I tried to hide the scoff that escaped me with a fake clearing of the throat, but I still got a quick glare from Freya.

The boys were disappointed that we hadn't brought home a grandpa, but it was eventually forgotten as the heated video game ensued, the boys agreeing on a Nerf gun battle. I even took a turn against Rowan, and let him win, temporarily forgetting that our lives had been in turmoil, and selectively forgetting what might happen to these three great kids when they would inevitably have to be brought into the know. I silently prayed for guidance from the Man upstairs, something I'd been doing a lot more lately, that I would be able to help them through all this.

We ordered Chinese take-out for supper, and after eating far more than my share, I helped put the boys to bed, volunteering to read a story to Rowan. He spent the fifteen minute session correcting my pronunciations and telling me my voices were all wrong, but it was still more enjoyable than I expected it to be. As devoted an "uncle" as I was, I had never done bedtime. I closed the book and he instructed me to give him ten hugs and ten kisses. He was so authoritative, a quality he got from his mother that I couldn't refuse. His cheek tasted like soy sauce…hmmm, had Freya asked me to wash his face after he inhaled his chicken chow mein? Oops. Oh well.

Ten hugs and salty kisses later, I was leaving his room, and met Freya in the hallway just leaving Blaise's room. I moved to embrace her, but she held up a finger to stop me. Just then, Levi walked between us, coming from the bathroom, and headed into his bedroom.

"Good night, Uncle Rip."

I swallowed hard, glad we hadn't been busted by the teenager, who would have required answers then and there.

"Good night, buddy."

Freya glanced after him. "You need me to tuck you in, Lee?"

"Good night, Mom," he replied over his shoulder, and closed his bedroom door behind him.

Freya cocked her head slightly (adorable), and smiled at me. "Guess not," she said.

Even though all three bedroom doors were closed, Freya pushed me backwards into the bathroom. She closed the door behind us, and surprised me with an aggressive kiss, wrapping her arms around my head. I felt like I'd just touched an electric fence on a dare, like I had more than once as a boy, but it was the exhilarating kind of shock... the kind you didn't ever want to end. We forgot where we were, forgot what we'd been through the past few days, forgot that she'd lost a husband, and I'd lost a best friend, forgot everything but each other. When she backed away to pull my shirt off, I looked into her eyes...and something was wrong.

They were black.

EPISODE 36
Talia and Lars Come Clean

I grabbed her shoulders and shook her gently to make her look at me, but she just started unbuttoning my pants. I wanted her, more than anything, but not like this. Her touch was so electrifying, though, that I closed my eyes for a split second, unable to prevent myself from enjoying it. I hesitated too long, and her fingers traveled around to my back, just inside the waistband of my jockeys. I shivered. She started to slowly remove my pants, and…

My eyes shot open, and I knew I had to stop her, as much as I loathed the thought. I shook her again.

"Freya. Freya, look at me."

My pants were now down around my knees, and she was reaching for the jockeys when I grabbed her hands. She looked at me, confused, with those unsettling dark eyes.

"Freya."

I decided to take a chance and, holding both her hands in one, I reached with the other for the sink. I turned on the cold water, and let it run over my fingers for a few seconds. Then I flicked some cold water right in her face.

She blinked several times, and I let go of her hands so she could wipe her eyes. When she looked at me again, her eyes were back to normal, but now they were filled with surprise and anger.

"Ty! What the hell?!"

"Are you okay?"

"No, I'm not okay! Why did you do that?"

"I was trying to bring you back…"

"Back? What are you talking about?"

"Frey, you were spazzing out again…but this time, it was a good kind of spazzing out…in fact, if you have to spaz out, this is definitely the kind of spazzing out you—"

"Ty! Stop saying that word!"

"Sorry…"

"I wasn't spazzing out. I remember pushing you in here and kissing you, and…" Just then, she looked down at my pants. "Whoa…how did your pants get like that?"

"You did that."

"No, I didn't."

"Yes, you did."

She paused for a moment. "And you stopped me." She sounded surprised…and a little impressed.

I nodded.

Suddenly, there was a knock on the door.

"If you two are doing what I think you're doing in there, shame on you!" Talia's voice, just above a whisper, sounded through the crack of the door.

I quickly put myself back together, and Freya opened the door. Talia stood there with a mischievous smile on her face, leaning against the doorframe, arms crossed.

"What do you have to say for yourselves?" she asked.

"We were doing exactly what you think we were doing," Freya said dryly.

"Sorry I interrupted, but you might consider doing the dirty deed in the downstairs bathroom, so the boys don't hear you," she joked.

"We plan to do it in *every* room, but first, we have to talk to you."

Freya left the bathroom, grabbing Talia's arm and pulling her along with her, and headed down the stairs like a woman on a mission. I was still stunned by the "every room" comment, and had to take a few deep breaths before I could follow.

□ □ □

I had no idea what had happened in the upstairs bathroom, but I pushed it to the back of my brain as I led Talia by the arm down the steps and into the dining room. She gave Lars a mock "save me" look and he stopped picking up toys in the living room to follow us.

He's picking up? If this guy really is a spy, he's downright diabolical, I thought.

Ty was close behind Lars, and after we were all seated at the table, I opened my mouth to lead the questioning, but Talia cut me off.

"What are you two going to do? Ty can't stay here. That might be a little hard to explain to the boys in the morning."

I had been focused on the task at hand, until Talia threw that wrench at me. I looked at Ty and my heart skipped a beat. How did he get better looking by the minute? It was very distracting. He grinned at me, and that accursed dimple peeked out just to torment me. I opened my mouth, but wasn't sure what to say.

"Uh, we hadn't really discussed that yet," Ty offered.

"We'll figure it out…" I said, not looking forward to doing so. "What we really want to talk about is why you two can speak fluent Russian."

That got everyone's undivided attention. Ty was beaming at me, and I couldn't imagine having to turn him away later…couldn't bear the thought, but I had to concentrate.

Instead of answering my question, Talia started speaking to Lars… in Russian. I wasn't sure if she knew Ty spoke the language as well, or if she was just playing with us.

Ty translated aloud, "I think our nice evening has just turned into an interrogation, my dear."

Lars chuckled and responded, in Russian.

Again Ty translated, "Is it time, then?"

Time? Time for what?

Why had I left my firearm in the lockbox in my bedroom?

Talia nodded, but neither of them made a move for a concealed weapon, so I talked myself out of the take-down move I was running through my head, assuming Ty and I could even 'take' Lars together. I was staring at his enormous biceps when Ty spoke.

"Just tell us the truth. The deception ends here. Either you're on our side, or you're not. If you are, let's talk…if you're not…well, then we have a problem."

Damn that was sexy. Shit…focus, Freya!

"We're most definitely on your side, and the Russian thing is really nothing to get your panties in a bundle about..." Talia started, but I wasn't going to let her downplay this.

"Okay," I said, "but..."

"*But*...I learned Russian a long time ago, when I was...in the CIA."

"I KNEW IT!" Ty broke in, startling us all.

"You were a CIA agent?" I asked.

"Yes. Until 2004. Then I left and became sort of a gun-for-hire. Your dad found me through a friend, and I took the job to protect you three years ago."

"Well, that last part I already knew, so...you had no knowledge of anything else before my father hired you? Anything about me or Ty?"

"No...nothing but your name and address."

"Why did you leave the CIA?" Ty wanted to know.

"Tired of the bullshit."

Ty and I both instinctively nodded, as if we knew exactly what she was talking about. Then I realized, I *did* know exactly what she was talking about. I was living the "bullshit." I turned to Lars.

"Where did you learn Russian, Lars?"

He cleared his throat and glanced at Talia, then back at me. "Goddess," he started, in his thick Swedish accent, "I was KGB."

"I'm sorry?!" Ty turned his whole body to Lars, subconsciously reaching for a gun on his side that wasn't there. Had we both sat down to an interrogation of two possible Russian spies unarmed? And with my three children snoring upstairs? We were idiots.

Lars brought his hand up in defense. "That was a long time ago, Agent Ripley."

Ty remained tense. "Talk."

Lars took a deep breath. "My family was poor. The KGB came to my town, promising money and excitement, and I went with them. I was barely sixteen. I did what they told me, bad things, but I have money to send home to my parents, my sisters, until Russia...wasn't Russia anymore. Then, an American comes, recruiting, asking who will turn on the Russians, and I went, because the KGB was not good to me, and I believed America was where I was supposed to go. I worked for the CIA, and one day, I met my own goddess..." He looked up at

Talia then, a faraway look in his eyes, and she smiled at him, and… blushed. Wow. Talia was blushing.

"Best day of my life when Talia and I were married…" He reached across the table for her, and she gave him her hand. I was so shocked, it almost escaped my attention.

"Wait," I snapped out of it, "you two are married?"

"For six years now," Talia said dreamily.

Ty was able to think past the intensely romantic moment we were in. "So, are you still CIA?"

"No, Agent Ripley," Lars replied, not breaking eye contact with his…wife? Wife. "I retired four years ago, when my beautiful wife became pregnant."

Talia wasn't one for sappy sentiment, and finished for Lars before I could ask another question, the main one being the obvious absence of a child in their lives. "Okay, folks, here's the synopsis. I got pregnant. We were ecstatic, and both decided to retire…God knows we have enough money to live comfortably for the rest of our lives, but then…I lost the… pregnancy, and our plans all fell apart. Lars had already officially retired from the CIA, so when Jerry found me and offered me this job, we decided it was the right thing to do. We decided to maintain the façade of me being a divorcee…more flexibility, I guess, until I needed his help. That's when he took the job at the Y, and I was able to touch him in public again." She grinned at her husband, still clutching his hand across the table.

"Why did you need his help?" Ty asked.

"What?" Talia asked.

"You said you kept him hidden until you needed his help…with what?"

Her smile grew, and Lars was radiating back at her, and I knew.

Talia was pregnant.

Suddenly, I was in a panic. "Tal, your concussion! Trevor hit you so hard, and you flew across—"

She cut me off. "Everything is fine, Freya. She's just fine."

"She?" I asked, elated that my best friend was going to be a mommy, and forgetting that I had sat down to accuse her of being a foreign spy not five minutes earlier.

"What's going on?" Ty asked. Men.

Just as I opened my mouth to spell it out for the testosterone-challenged in the room, there was a loud noise from the kitchen... and then the front door. It sounded like someone was trying to break down both doors simultaneously. The four of us, all government-trained killers, leapt out of our chairs and sprinted out of the room. Lars and I were closest to the kitchen, and the other two headed to the front door. The Swede and I were just hitting the entryway, as several men in suits came busting through my back door, all armed, and not a one of them looking like Ed McMahon there to tell me I'd just won the Publisher's Clearinghouse Sweepstakes.

Lars managed to disarm the first few who tried to shove a gun barrel in his face, but there were just too many. I stood there, frozen, hands in the air, surrounded by nameless suits all aiming their weapons at my head. I wasn't sure who these minions were, but all I could think of was my three sleeping angels upstairs.

Then a familiar face came through the door, and my heart sank.

He was impeccably dressed, more so than I'd ever seen him, and raised a handheld two-way radio to his mouth. "We've got'em," was all he said to whoever was listening on the other end. Then he looked at me and smiled, and I felt like I was going to be sick.

"Hello, Freya," he said, and it almost sounded genuine, but I knew better. I would never trust this man again as long as I lived. I stood there and glared at him with all my might, willing his head to explode, but nothing happened. Except that he chuckled. Jackass.

"If looks could kill..." Another chuckle. "Come on, Freya, I'm the good guy. There is so much you don't know...and your friends are not who they say they are."

It was infantile, but I went with it anyway.

"Go to Hell, Trevor."

EPISODE 37
House Arrest

It was two in the morning. I'd been allowed to remain in my house, but only temporarily, I was told. The boys were still sleeping, thank God. Trevor was smart enough to tell his men to take us quietly.

I sat slumped in a chair in the breakfast atrium, all the ice in my almond chai melted, and my Nutella bagel cold. I don't know why I thought these two silly, material things would make me feel better. In a way, I didn't want to feel better. I was terrified, but I was reveling in it, trying to channel it to give me strength. I'd been praying for the past two hours for my children's safety, but I was having trouble receiving the warm sense of calm I usually got after I spoke with Him, because I was filled with rage.

I'd read somewhere that a study had been done to discern which of our human emotions was the strongest (our tax dollars at work), and the hands-down winner had been maternal love. As I sat in my dimly-lit atrium, trying to keep the nervous breakdown threatening the barriers of my sanity from succeeding, I knew the results of that study had been spot on. No emotion was more paralyzing than a mother's love for her children.

I glanced up at the "suit" Trevor had left to watch me, his robotic form unmoving as he stood in front of the back door...Talia's door, looking straight ahead.

I wonder where the "on" button is...I smirked at my little joke.

I decided to stare at him until the laser beams coming out of my eyes melted his brain. Ten minutes later, thirty seconds in reality, I sighed and looked at my chai. I decided to get a fresh one, and cause a little trouble. I clutched my glass, and then very suddenly stood, kicking my chair out behind me and cringing as it made that irritating screech noise on the porcelain tile. My "bodyguard" reacted, pulling his gun, and pointing it at me in one fluid motion. He was confident and steady, but I had seen something he didn't want me to see. Something in his eyes for the split second before he had retrieved his weapon. It was just a flash, but I was certain it had been fear.

Fabulous. It was the two teenage boys in the food shack all over again. Whatever Trevor had told his henchmen about me, this one was afraid I was going to hurt him.

I had to laugh. I walked over to the sink, dumped out my room-temperature drink, and then proceeded to wash the cup out quick, before heading to the fridge door for some ice. The whole time, and with every motion, the goon's gun followed me. He was a big guy, rippling muscles bigger than even Lars possessed, and I imagined taking him down would be like trying to tackle an SUV. Trevor wasn't taking any chances when he left this behemoth with me.

"You want some coffee?" I asked, as if he was a close family friend. I looked at him calmly, waiting for an answer.

He was frozen, both arms outstretched to keep the pistol steady and the barrel pointing right between my eyes.

I finished making my chai, and then stepped over to the coffee pot. "Take me five minutes…? Yes? No?" I stood there, shaking the empty coffee pot in the air at him. "Come on, Body…can I call you 'Body'? If you plan to stay awake all night making sure I don't transform into a weapon of mass destruction, you're going to need some caffeine…?" I raised my eyebrows in question, waiting for any kind of response. An eye twitch, even a blink would do. But I got nothing.

I set the pot down…and proceeded to make the coffee anyway. It helped me think, doing mindless tasks to keep my hands busy. I thought of Ty.

Trevor had taken him. Where, I didn't know, but there were a hundred awful guesses chasing each other in my mind. The winner at the moment was a star port in space, where my man was being encased in carbonite by the evil Darth Trevor.

I had no idea where Lars and Talia were.

I needed sleep.

By the time I'd started the coffee percolating, Body had relaxed his gun arm, but still clutched the revolver, and was back to playing statue...but his sea green eyes were boring holes through my head. I was going to walk past him and sit back down, my fresh chai in my hands, but before I had thought it through, I walked right up to him, nose to nose. I hadn't anticipated him being about a foot taller than me, and it ended up more like nose to sternum.

I looked up at his eyes, but they were now staring straight ahead, as if he was afraid to make direct eye contact with me. A bead of sweat rolled down his forehead, and I instantly regretted my wayward instinct to flirt with him. He started to raise the gun, his hand shaking slightly. There were few things more dangerous than a scared person with a loaded weapon.

For some reason, I couldn't move...couldn't back down so he would reconsider shooting me. I felt my fight or flight kick in, and something clicked in my head. Suddenly, there was a ringing in my ears. I stared at my would-be killer, and his eyes widened. He said something, but the ringing was so loud, I couldn't hear him, but I was able to read his lips.

He mouthed, "Your eyes..."

It was like a dream. A dream on fast forward. In two seconds, I had disarmed him and had wrenched his arm around behind him and pinned him against the wall. He had to weigh upwards of two-hundred-and-fifty pounds, and I was successfully restraining him against his will. Then the ringing stopped, and all I could hear was someone breathing heavily.

It was me.

I released him, horrified at what I had just done. Even though he may have decided to pull the trigger, I had definitely been antagonizing him, when he already believed me to be some sort of homicidal robot. Why had I done that?

I backed away, and was stopped by the edge of the atrium table behind me. The large man remained face to the wall. He glanced back at me, and then closed his eyes tight, obviously still afraid for his life.

"I'm not going to hurt you," I muttered.

He looked back again, but not at my face. He was focused on my right hand. I looked down and realized I was holding his gun. I immediately clicked on the safety and removed the clip. I scanned the room and then hurled the now useless pistol into the air over my prisoner's head. It landed with a thud on the ledge above the kitchen cabinets. I set the clip down on the counter, and stood there, waiting for him to relax.

Instead, he whirled around, pulling a small gun out of the back of his pants, and trained it at my head. I didn't flinch. I didn't move. I knew he had another gun. I was pretty sure he was going to pull it at some point. I was glad he had done it sooner than later.

"...and you're not going to hurt *me*," I said quietly.

Just then, Rowan wandered into the kitchen, rubbing his eyes and whimpering.

"Mommy…"

I gave my captor a pleading look, hoping…praying he wouldn't do anything stupid. I didn't want to hurt him, but if anything happened to Rowan, I wouldn't hesitate to give in to my killer instincts.

He looked even more afraid, looking frantically from me to Rowan, and back to me. I motioned for him to lower his gun, and after a few seconds, he did, but did not loosen his grip on it. I turned and went to my baby.

"What's wrong, honey?" I sat down in my chair at the atrium table and pulled him into my arms.

"I had a bad dream, and you weren't in your bed…"

"I'm sorry, sweetie."

Rowan seemed to become more alert and noticed that we had company.

"Who are you?" he asked the man directly, who had managed to conceal the gun behind his back just before Rowan turned to him.

I released a near-silent exhale of relief. "Rowan, this is a friend of Daddy's."

"What's your name?"

The man looked at me questioningly, and I cocked my head at him, pursing my lips and raising my eyebrows.

Tell him your name, stupid, I ordered him with my mind.

He opened his mouth, but no sound came at first. Then he managed a squeaky, "Cole."

He cleared his throat and said it again, this time in his real, Vin Diesel-esque throaty rumble.

Rowan smiled at him, then looked back at me and yawned. Then he asked, "Is it morning, Mommy?"

I grinned. "Look outside."

He looked past me out the atrium windows.

"It's still dark."

"It's still dark," I repeated. "And you should be in bed."

"I want to sleep with you," he whined.

"Alright. I was just coming up. Let's go."

I stood and guided my four-year-old toward the living room, pushing him in front of me. I turned to my new friend.

"Good night, Cole," I said.

"Good night, Cole," Rowan mimicked.

I made eye contact with the stranger in my kitchen, and his expression softened a little. Right before I lost sight of him, I saw him return his gun to the back of his waistband...and I swear he gave me a slight nod.

I was surprised when I fell almost immediately to sleep, Rowan breathing softly next to me. I awoke with a start at a loud crash from downstairs. I rolled over and checked the clock. 8:17 a.m.

The boys. They had to be up by now. It was Saturday, and they had Tae Kwon Do practice at nine...if Cole let us leave the house, that is. I leapt out of bed, and noticed Rowan was gone.

I ran down the stairs so fast, I barely touched a step. As I rounded the corner from the living room into the kitchen, I saw the boys. All three of them were dressed for Tae Kwon Do, and they were standing over something on the kitchen floor.

"Levi..." I started, and they turned and looked at me. Levi's eyes were alive with adrenaline, and Blaise looked like he'd just found out we were going to Disneyworld. They were both in defensive Tae Kwon Do positions. Rowan ran over to me.

"Mommy, Daddy's friend had a gun, and I don't think it was a toy gun, like mine!"

I looked up at Levi. "What happened?"

"Mom," he huffed, "who is this man?"

254 - **JUST KILL ME**

I walked over to them, and saw Cole sprawled out on the floor at their feet, unconscious.

"Levi, what happened?!" I asked, more insistently.

"We came into the kitchen to get some breakfast, and he was sitting at the atrium table, sleeping, with a gun in his hand!"

"So, you knocked him out? While he was asleep?" I tried to sound angry, but I was just so…proud.

"No! Rowan went up to him and shook his shoulder to wake him up, and the guy jumped up and pointed the gun at him!"

Blaise cut in, "Yeah! And then Levi yelled, 'Attack!' just like our teacher does, and we both kicked him!"

"Kicked him?" I had to hear the details. This was going to be the best Saturday ever.

"Levi did this awesome roundhouse kick right in the guy's chest, and then I got him right in his chicken nuggets!" Blaise was clearly having as good a Saturday as I was so far.

"If I promise to tell you everything, will you trust me and do whatever I say?" I asked.

They all three nodded silently.

"Good. Now, we need to tie him up. Levi, do you remember your knots from Boy Scouts?"

He grinned at me excitedly. "I'll go get my rope."

I looked down at the unconscious, muscle-bound trained killer on my floor who had been taken down by two boys with eighteen months of Tae Kwon Do experience, and smiled.

EPISODE 38
Jabba Babysits

I got in the van with the boys, and just started driving. I wasn't sure where I was going. I headed for the Tae Kwon Do academy out of habit, but felt like following our normal routine was the wrong thing to do. Ten minutes later, I happened to be sitting at a red light at a downtown intersection, and I glanced to my left. The old bookstore. I'd been in there a few times, but not since Ty had told me what really goes on in there.

It hit me like a lightning bolt. When the light turned green, I swerved into the left turn lane and gunned it. Ignoring the honks from the cars behind me, I made another sharp left into the store's employee parking lot, and stopped the van where it would be the least visible from the busy road.

"Mom, aren't we going to Tae Kwon Do?" Blaise chimed from the back seat.

I put the van in park, unbuckled my seatbelt, and turned toward the boys behind me.

"I'm sorry, guys. We can't go to Tae Kwon Do today."

How much do I tell them?

"I need to do something very important, and I can't tell you everything, because—"

Rowan cut in, "Is it top secret, Mommy?"

I smiled. My sweet little boy had given me an idea, but before I could continue, Levi asked, "Does it have something to do with why you brought your gun?"

I froze, shocked for a second. "How did you know I had my gun?"

"I saw you put it in your purse before we left."

"Mom, is someone trying to kill us?" Blaise asked, looking very worried.

"What? No, honey…why would you ask that?"

"Well, that man at the house…who was he?"

"That's what I'm going to tell you, if you'll let me."

"Sorry."

"Don't be sorry, be quiet," I said, setting them up for one of our favorite games…movie quotes, to try to lighten the mood. The last thing I wanted was for them to think they, or I, might be in danger. They did not disappoint. All three, including the four-year-old, responded loudly.

"Sorry!"

We all laughed. There just wasn't an unquotable line in *Spaceballs*.

"Okay, serious time. The man at the house is an agent. He's a friend of Uncle Rip's. We're doing sort of a fun exercise today, and you three get to be part of it."

"What do we get to do? Can I have a gun?" Blaise asked quickly.

"No, dummy, we get rocket launchers!" Levi mocked his brother.

Blaise looked at me with a pout. "No gun?"

I simply cocked my head, and gave him a "not even if you were the son of Rambo" look. He slumped back in his seat and folded his arms across his chest.

"Are we going to get in trouble because we knocked out Uncle Rip's friend?" Levi asked.

"Heck no!" I replied, grinning from ear to ear. "Serves him right… just means we're winning."

They clearly liked the sound of that.

"What do you need us to do, Mom?" Levi asked, always eager to make me happy, God love him. I took a deep breath, and prepared to lie through my teeth.

"The FBI wants to test me, and part of it involves…hiding you guys."

Six eyes filled with confusion stared at me.

"Hiding…us?" Blaise was perking up with interest again.

"Yes. They want to see if I can hide a witness so the bad guys don't find them. You've seen that on TV, haven't you?"

"Yeah…" Levi trailed off. They were waiting for more details.

"So, to make it fun, I said I'd hide you guys, and Uncle Ty—Rip... is going to try to find you...but he'll never find you here." I grinned at them, as if I was keeping a monumental secret, which of course, I was.

They all three peered out the window at the bookstore.

"We have to hide in an old bookstore?" Blaise asked.

"Yes, just for a few hours—"

"Hours!?" Blaise exploded. Levi reached across the seat to smack him in the back of the head.

"Levi!" I chastised, but secretly loved it when he did that. He mumbled an insincere apology to his brother, who was now rubbing the back of his head and whimpering, as if it had actually hurt.

"Don't worry. This is more than just a bookstore. Today, it's a criminal's hideout...and you three are the criminals."

Rowan started to clap and chant, "We are criminals! We are criminals! We are criminals!"

"Okay, okay, so here are the rules of this game."

Rowan stopped chanting and clapping and they all leaned forward in unison, determined not to miss a word.

Awesome. Now to make up some rules.

"Rule number one: Do not leave the building. Repeat."

"Do not leave the building," they responded together...more or less.

"Rule number two: Levi is in charge. Repeat."

They repeated.

"Rule number three: If you need me, text, don't call. Repeat."

Rowan repeated it verbatim, which I should have expected, and Blaise nudged him hard with his shoulder.

"Ow! What did I do? I repeated!"

"Blaise! Apologize!" I insisted. He gave Rowan his best fake sincere sorry, and I took a deep breath.

"Rule number four: Be smart, be nice, and be rewarded. Repeat."

This rule was alliteration I'd pounded into their heads since they were born. Whenever I left them with a sitter, I'd make them repeat it to me three times.

"Alright. Let's go through them one more time."

I repeated each rule, waiting for them to regurgitate it each time after me.

I couldn't help but think Trevor had discovered Cole at the house by now, and was looking for us. I needed to get the boys inside.

I told them to stay in the van for a moment while I disguised the gray Odyssey…part of the test, I said. Luckily, it was easily the most popular family vehicle in town, if not the state, and the country, right down to the medium gray hue, and that could only help.

Ty had taught me to remove any window stickers, or things inside the van visible from the windows that would give away that the vehicle was mine. Then, I put new window stickers on the back window that no one would ever associate with me and my family. I had bought the family stickers that were little stick figures of every member of the family, and as I put the Daddy, the Mommy, and then two little girls in pigtails, plus two dogs and a cat, I grinned. The final step was to cover the license plate. The FBI had a shop that made these license plate covers with random numbers, or vanity messages. They weren't real license plates, but basically photographs that, from a distance, were indiscernible from the real thing, and they snapped securely onto the actual plate. I had asked for a vanity message that said, "FAT N FAB."

The whole process took me about ninety seconds. Then, I had the boys grab their Tae Kwon Do bags, and we headed for the back door. They were excited to be part of this fictional test, and I knew I had no choice but to go through with it. I had to keep them safe while I searched for Ty. I just hoped Jabba didn't turn me away.

I approached the door, and knew what I had to do. I tried the knob and it was locked. Good. Then I knocked loudly, a specific pattern that Ty had made me memorize, in case I ever needed Jabba's help. After a few minutes, I repeated the pattern of knocks. Instantly, the door opened, and a lovely young woman was standing there, smiling at us warmly. She motioned for us to enter, and we followed her down a long, narrow hallway, and then upstairs. At the top of the stairs, she put her hand in the air for us to wait. She opened the door in front of us, and we heard a booming voice.

"Sister Lila, please escort our friends into the throne room!"

Lila smiled at us, and moved aside for us to enter Jabba's throne room. It was like a state-of-the-art teen center, except for the ornate red throne on one wall, and the gargantuan man sitting in it. He spread his arms wide.

"Friends! Welcome! Agent Douglas, you and your children are welcome here!"

I opened my mouth to ask how the hell he knew who I was, but he was one step ahead.

"You are the only one Agent Ripley shared the secret knock with…and he said you might need Jabba's help when he called me this morning."

"You spoke with him this morning? Did he say where he was? Is he okay?" The questions fell out of my mouth so quickly, I couldn't catch them.

"Peace, Agent Douglas." Jabba raised his hands in a meditative position and closed his eyes. After a few seconds, and deep breaths, he opened them again. "Let us make your children comfortable, then we can talk."

I nodded. I turned to address the boys, but they were no longer standing behind me. I panicked for a second, frantically searching the room, and immediately located all three plopped on bean bag chairs watching one of Jabba's young brothers play a video game I recognized. It was one of the Lego Star Wars games that all three boys had played at home until they had it memorized. They were currently zoned to the television screen as if they'd never seen it before.

Must be a boy thing.

"I'd say they're comfortable," I stated.

Jabba motioned for me to approach the throne. I walked up to him until I could see the stubble on his chin, and he smiled at me so big, I felt like I was being punked.

"Agent Ripley sounded…guarded and hurried on the phone this morning," Jabba said just above a whisper. "We spoke very briefly. I'm sorry, but I don't know if he's okay. I assume you are going to find out."

It hadn't escaped my attention that the third person speech had ceased. Ty had told me he suspected it was all an act, but I didn't think Jabba would let his guard down with me so soon. I merely nodded in response to his words.

"Do you need weapons? Backup? My resources are your resources, Agent Douglas."

I didn't know what to say. It was so much more than I had hoped for, I felt like Cinderella finding out she was going to the ball after all.

After a moment of thought, I responded, "All I need is to know my boys will be safe."

Jabba gave me such an intense look, I could focus on nothing else. "We will protect your children with our lives, if need be."

I prayed it wouldn't come to that.

EPISODE 39
I Invest in Platinum

As I headed toward FBI Headquarters, driving a small Civic that Jabba gave me, I couldn't help but think I'd been leaving my kids with some questionable characters lately. The funny thing was I trusted the sketchy sitters more than my own husband… understandably.

I was making a right turn when suddenly a scrawny man with shoulder-length hair jumped out in front of the car. I screeched to a halt, and the man rolled up onto the hood, slamming into the windshield. I thrust the gearshift into park and leapt out of the driver's door just as the man was sliding off the hood onto the ground. He moaned, but seemed unhurt.

I grabbed his arm and helped him to his feet. "Are you alright?"

He giggled as he steadied himself, and I wondered if he was just a little drunk…or high…or crazy. "Rip said you were intense, but I didn't think you'd run me over!"

I let go of his arm, and put my hands on my hips. "*You* ran in front of *me*, and you—" I stopped scolding him as something occurred to me. "Rip? You know Rip?"

"Of course I know Rip!" He was brushing himself off now, as if I'd sent him hurtling into a sandbox or something. He was a little rough around the edges, but his clothes were clean and he smelled like Irish Spring. He looked like one of those men you see volunteering to help troubled youth after turning their own lives around. I hoped he was like one of those men.

"Who are you?"

He looked up at me, surprise filling his hazel eyes. "I'm Leon. Rip's never mentioned me?" I think even if Ty hadn't mentioned him, I might have lied, just to make him feel better.

"Leon? Of course he mentioned you, I just didn't expect…well, you look different than how he described you…no offense."

He beamed at me, not offended in the least. "Thanks to Jabba. He took me in, gave me a family again. I'm a new man!"

He *was* like one of those men…except that he was living with petty thieves, albeit petty thieves with an admirable moral code. I guess it was all about baby steps, and who the hell was I to judge? I'd actually killed people, after all. According to Ty, the worst thing this poor guy had ever done was eat the food people left on their plates at the outdoor café downtown.

Suddenly, a loud honk behind me made us both jump. I turned my head and realized the Civic was still blocking the road.

"Get in, Leon, we're going to save Rip."

He didn't hesitate, and hopped around to the passenger door. "Woohoo! An assignment!"

We soon sped away, but I was still drawing a blank on formulating a plan when we parked a block from Headquarters. Leon had been chatting excitedly the whole drive, and I was really starting to like him. He was such an upbeat guy, it was hard not to. He really loved his new life as one of Jabba's brothers, and had been put in charge of the kitchen at the "palace."

Rip had never mentioned that Leon used to be a chef…or Leon was exaggerating. But I just wasn't getting that vibe from him. He was skinny, and I was always leery of cooks who didn't appear to eat, but then again, many of the famous ones were true "foodies," and they were always thin. As he described the chicken piccata he'd made the other night, I was convinced he was telling the truth.

But I was also trying to focus on how I was going to get in to Headquarters without being seen. Leon had stopped talking and we sat in the car in silence for a moment. Then, I sighed heavily, and mumbled, "I really wish I had a Platinum Card."

"You need a Platinum Card?"

"It would make things easier, but…" I sighed again, sure he had no idea what I was talking about. "I don't know what to do."

I gave Leon the highlights. Dating Ty, brain implants, evil Trevor, flashbacks, dear old Dad helping Trevor escape, and why we were now sitting a safe distance from the place I believed Trevor was holding Ty, and Lars and Talia. If I could spring them all, great, but my priority was Ty.

I finished, out of breath, and sighed a third time. "Any ideas?"

"Well, Rip never actually let me help him with a mission before, but…" He scratched his chin, and then ran his fingers through his sandy brown hair, letting it fall down to frame his fabulous cheekbones. If he was a lot less friendly, and worked out just a little, he could have easily been a male model. "You know, I could get in there…pretend I was looking for Rip. I could tell them I saw you leaving town or something."

That sounded like the beginning of a plan. I tried to expand it. "That's a good idea…but I still can't get in without my name being run through the system the second they scan my ID card…that is if security at the entrance aren't already looking for me. At the very least, I'm sure Trevor made Ainsley flag my name. He'll know the second I try to get in."

"Ainsley…" he said dreamily. "I met her once when Director Pixley tried to kill me with caffeine…"

What?

"She is hauntingly beautiful…" he finished.

"I said the same thing to Ty—I mean, Rip." I paused for a minute, letting myself get distracted by the possible romance between Leon and Ainsley. "You should ask her out."

"Nah, she can do a lot better than me…" Before I could argue, he pulled out a beat up leather wallet…it reminded me of Ty's old wallet, before I'd gotten him one of those flexible stainless steel ones for his birthday after he'd had his identity stolen a few years ago. Leon pulled out a shimmery credit card and held it out to me.

"Platinum Card," was all he said.

I just stared at it. "Oh, Leon, that's sweet, but the card I was talking about is a special, Top Secret—"

"G-I-C," he cut in. I just squinted at him in question. "Government Invisibility Card," he explained.

I widened my eyes as far as they would go, and my mouth fell open. I took the card, and scrutinized it. It just said "Platinum Card" on the front, and had an intricate barcode on the back. No name, no card number, no bank information...nothing. Could it be? I turned to Leon.

"This is really a...?"

He nodded and smiled at me.

"How on earth...?"

"I have to keep *some* secrets."

"Ty never mentioned that you had one of these," I said, raising one eyebrow at him.

He just grinned mysteriously and shrugged. "He never asked."

We ironed out the details of our plan, and then left the car, heading for the Headquarters building but then separating to reach the front entrance from different sides. I let Leon go in first and start the distraction as I worked on disguising myself. I had Leon's Army Surplus jacket, and a baseball hat I'd found in the car. I threw my hair up in a ponytail and put the hat on, hoping it didn't look too out of place on the head of a forty-something woman...it was a black "Call of Duty 4" cap they gave away with the video game. I knew that because Levi had the same one. He'd get a good laugh out of his old mom wearing one, I was sure.

Levi.

My boys.

I had to focus. If I screwed this up, they could be in danger for the rest of their lives. I took a deep breath, and headed for the entrance. I could hear shouting, and Leon trying to convince the security mandroids that he really *did* know Agent Ripley. I walked through the door, and got in line behind three other people who were mumbling with annoyance that it was taking so long. Then, Leon glanced back and looked at me. I gave him a miniscule nod, and he turned back to the guard and said he had some information for Agent Douglas about his wife.

That got the goon's attention. He was silent for a moment, contemplating what he should do. Then he took out a Blackberry and sent a quick text. A near-instantaneous response caused him to inhale deeply. He put the phone away, and looked back at Leon, then at a young guard manning the wall like a newbie.

"Take this low-life to see Agent Douglas."

Leon feigned offense. "Nice. You don't know me, Dude. You don't know me!" he yelled as the other guard pulled him toward the elevator by one arm. He caught my eye and winked, and I had to fight the grin trying to surface.

The three people in front of me moved slowly but steadily through the security checkpoint, and then it was my turn. The guard barely looked at me as I ran the magic card Leon had given me through the scanner. He glanced up at me, and I gave him a knowing smile. I had no idea what I was supposed to know, but luckily, neither did he.

He waved me through without another look.

I kept my head down slightly, so the baseball cap would conceal my face from the cameras that were everywhere, and decided to take the stairs instead of the elevator. I was alone in the stairwell as I ascended to the fourth floor. I was heading for Director Pixley's office. I didn't know where else to go. I'd have to take my chances that he wasn't part of all this mess somehow.

I knew something was wrong when I got to the secure entrance, and it was unguarded. I stood there, staring at the military grade security lock on the door, technology that was way above my head, and wondered…

What if…?

I pulled out the Platinum Card and swiped it through the narrow slot on top of the lock mechanism. The door immediately buzzed and popped open a few inches. I hesitated, but there was no one in the second entry, so I stepped in, closing the door behind me, and swiped my new favorite thing again. Again, the door buzzed and popped open.

A million thoughts ran through my head. I'd watched way too many conspiracy theory movies. This was too easy. Was it a trap? Was Trevor letting me get this far for some reason? Wait…but he didn't know I had a Platinum Card, and I wouldn't have gotten through the doors any other way. Unless…Leon was in on it too. But he was Ty's informant, and from what Ty told me, Leon had never much cared for Trevor. He thought he was too perfect, like a metrosexual robot. I chuckled quietly to myself.

Leon had no idea how right he was.

I took a deep breath and proceeded through the second door, scanning the hallway for agents ready to taze me, but again, it was empty. I was starting to think there had been a nuclear war and no one told me.

Where the hell is everyone?

I slowly approached Pixley's door and stopped. The door was so thick, I couldn't hear if anyone was inside. I would just have to push the call button and take my—wait. There was a scanner slot on Pixley's lock too.

No way.

Yes way. The door buzzed immediately after I ran my Platinum Card through, and popped open. I couldn't help but smile. I was pretty awesome, if I did think so myself.

My elation was short-lived, however. As soon as the door opened, I heard raised voices. I peeked in like a curious child and located Pixley sitting at his desk. He didn't look happy. He was arguing with someone who stood across from him, leaning forward and pounding his fist on the desk. It was Trevor. After fifteen years, I would know the back of that head anywhere…and it sickened me.

Suddenly, Trevor pulled his gun and pointed it at Pixley's head. The director immediately stood up, raised his hands in the air, and moved away from his desk.

What the hell? Were they joking around, or was Trevor really threatening to shoot his boss. Pixley kept his hands up, trying to talk Trevor down. They slowly circled the desk, until Trevor was next to the high-backed, white leather chair and sat down like he owned the place. He looked more ridiculous than Jabba did in his movie prop throne.

"It's a bad idea, Douglas, that's all I'm saying! I'll have no part of it!" Pixley said.

"Then you won't mind Federal prison—"

Just then, Trevor looked around Pixley and smiled at me.

Crap.

"Come on in, Freya."

I was so wrapped up in what I was seeing and hearing, I'd forgotten I was supposed to be hiding. Rookie mistake. I pushed open the door and walked in confident and tall, and marched up to the desk, standing next to Pixley as I addressed Trevor.

"So, you and dear old Dad were working together all along?" I accused.

Trevor chuckled. "Freya, I told you. I'm the good guy."

"Where's my Dad? Where's Ty? And Talia? And Lars?"

"We'll get to the traitors in a minute. First, we have a problem, and we need your help."

"Excuse me? What the hell could you possibly want from me? You've already taken the past fifteen plus years of my life, and pretended to be the father of my children. What else do you want? My kidney?"

"Freya, Freya…so dramatic," he patronized. "Have a seat."

I didn't move, and continued to glare at him. He nodded when he realized I was in no mood to be toyed with.

"Okay, stand. We need your help…finding your boyfriend."

"What? He escaped?" I was ecstatic.

"He had help."

I studied his face for a second before it hit me. "Jerry?"

"And a few others who will be dealt with, but you don't need to worry about that."

"Why the hell would I help you?"

"Because your father is unstable, and Rip is in danger."

EPISODE 40
I Become a Daddy

I woke up and felt like the world was spinning a million miles an hour. As my eyes focused, I realized why. I was in the passenger seat of a car, and we were barreling down the freeway. It was dark, and there were only a few other cars on the road. I was queasy, and it intensified as I slowly turned my head toward the driver of the deathtrap. I closed my eyes tight, and reopened them. I didn't understand what I was seeing.

Freya's dad, Jerry, was clutching the wheel, staring straight ahead at the nearly deserted road.

Suddenly a sharp pain shot through my head. I made a noise and held my head in my hands. It must have gotten Jerry's attention, because he gave me a fatherly pat on the knee.

"The headache will pass."

I sat up and winced at him. "You gave me something."

I wasn't accusing him. I was simply stating what I knew to be the truth.

He glanced at me but said nothing.

"The last thing I remember was Trevor throwing me in the sub-cell...and then you brought me a Coke..."

He ignored me, glaring at the road in front of him.

"What did you give me?" I asked, but then realized that wasn't the important question at the moment. "And where the hell are we going?"

He didn't answer. I looked out the window and searched for signs or landmarks. When the freeway sign sped by, I instantly knew where we were headed.

"We're going to Garrity…" I turned to him as something odd occurred to me. "How did you get me in the car without someone noticing?"

He chuckled. "I had a little help…our muscle-bound friend, young Jasper, was very eager to assist me."

"Jasper? The newbie guard you knocked out with his own gun? Why would he want to help you?"

"Let's just say he's very impressionable, and I'm very… persuasive." He smiled and shook his head.

"Something funny?" I was irritated. All I could think of was getting back to Freya.

"He was so ready to believe that it was all an exercise, you and Freya getting locked up, Trevor and I escaping…and well, when I told him he had performed in an 'exemplary manner' and might just get some notice from D.C. for it, he was practically humping my leg."

"Nice," I said sarcastically, sneering at the unwanted mental picture I now had, and eager to change the subject. "So, why are we going to Garrity?"

"I left something there."

"Yeah, a pile of burning rubble," I remarked. I tried to stay calm. I wanted to scream at him to stop the Goddamn car and tell me what the hell was going on, but a part of me wanted to see what was in Garrity.

"Are you going to tell me why you drugged me and kidnapped me? I mean, if you want to go to the hole in the ground you created the other day, why drag me with you?"

Without looking at me, Jerry responded. "I need your help."

"With what?"

He sighed, and slowed down as we passed an eighteen wheeler on the side of the road with its hazard lights on. I didn't think he was going to give me an answer, until…

"I didn't destroy everything. I need your help…retrieving the proof we need to put a stop to all this."

"What are you talking about? What proof? And if you've had this…proof all along, why didn't you just bring it with you when Freya and I came to get you?"

"I needed to be sure that it was time…"

"Okay, if you don't stop talking in riddles, I'm going to jump out of the car."

Jerry looked at me for a second, and smirked. Either he didn't believe I would really do it, or he was impressed that I was considering it. We were going 95mph after all.

"I'll do it, Jerry. It wouldn't be the first time I've had to bail out of a speeding car."

"Hold your horses, Evel Knievel, I'll tell you what I can."

I waited. And waited. Five minutes ticked by, and I reached for the door handle. It had been twelve years since I'd jumped out of a moving vehicle, and it had been no fun then. I still had the scars from the road rash. I glanced out the window, and realized we were off the freeway. In fact, we were getting close to Garrity, and I was running out of time to evacuate the premises.

"I drugged you because I knew you'd never come with me after I helped Trevor escape."

"Ya think?! Why DID you help that scumbag?"

"I had to. I owed him."

I waited for more details, but none came, so I tried to keep the conversation going. "So, you aren't working for him?"

"For Trevor? Hell no! I'm trying to stop him."

"Stop him from doing what?"

Jerry pulled into his driveway, the dirt road that used to lead to a dilapidated shack he had called home for a decade. He put the car in park, and turned to me, his face more serious than I'd ever seen it.

"Trevor told Pixley he was given a Priority One assignment twenty years ago to watch Freya…"

"I know…the whole marriage was a sham," I reiterated.

"It's not true. He wasn't told to watch Freya. In fact, as far as Washington is concerned, the two sleeper assassins created back then are dead."

I was silent.

"RVW's been written off by Washington. So many administrations have come and gone, well…eventually, some genius decided that the RVW Project wasn't worth keeping tabs on anymore, and they declared it a non-issue. That's when I initially came out of hiding…to try to talk some sense into them. I went to FBI Headquarters and went through all the proper channels…bullshit, all of it, and eventually got in to see the Director—"

"Wait, what do you mean, 'talk some sense into them'? Why is it such a bad thing if they forget about us?"

"Those things they put in your heads," he said with urgency, while tapping his pointer finger to my temple a little too hard, "…*we* put in your heads…" he looked sad for a second, like he was thinking of a bad memory, then he looked back up at me, "they need to come out. And if the program was completely blacked out, I thought that would never happen. I had to get them to keep the program open, but when I was turned away…told their records said you were both dead…I didn't know what to do."

I wasn't completely following, but I was trying. "When was that?"

"Ten years ago…right before I went into hiding again…here." He gestured outside the car at the spot where his house once stood.

"Why did you go back into hiding?"

"When I went to D.C., it stirred up some trouble. There were still a few old codgers in the Senate who remembered me, and didn't want the mistakes that were made twenty years ago to resurface. I didn't realize my reappearance would cause renewed interest in…well, you two. I didn't want to put you both, and my grandsons, in danger, so I ran."

"Mistakes?"

"You already know that Trevor altered your memories, and when I found out about it twenty years ago, he convinced me to make a deal…but what he did…what I know now…"

"You made a deal with the Anti-Christ?"

"It was stupid, but at the time, I believed it was the only way to keep Freya safe."

"How, exactly, did Trevor keep Freya safe?" I asked, not believing what I was hearing. I would have thought Jerry was smarter than to trust Trevor, but then again, I had trusted him for twenty years…with my life.

"He promised he'd take care of her, keep her safe by hiding her… by…"

"...by turning her into June Cleaver?"

"Yeah, I guess...but she was determined to go into the Air Force before she would marry him, and no matter what he put in her head, he couldn't talk her out of it. He even threatened to leave her, and she called his bluff. I guess even a brain implant can't overcome free will all of the time... maybe a part of her was resisting a life with Trevor...but..." He paused.

"But...she got out of the Air Force after four years, when she could have had a very successful career. She could have been a general," I thought aloud.

Jerry sighed. "Yes, she could have, but I was relieved when she resigned her commission. She wasn't safe in such a high profile job, not just because she might run into someone who'd been part of RVW, but because we couldn't risk her activating spontaneously in such an environment..."

"So, *you* had something to do with her not continuing in the Air Force," I stated.

"Trevor promised to do everything to keep her safe, even risk his own life, and I promised to help him whenever he asked. After four years of her still in the Air Force, he asked, so I helped."

"How?"

"I helped him get Freya pregnant."

"WHAT?!"

"That didn't come out right...what I mean is, we both knew Freya wanted kids, so when the time was right, I provided the necessary ingredient for the cocktail, shall we say..."

I gave him an even more horrified look and he made to recant again. "Boy, talking to you is like talking to a twelve-year-old...I mean, I found appropriate sperm...it wasn't *mine*...you have a very disturbing mind, you know that?"

"You should know...you've been in there."

He peered over the top of his glasses at me before shrugging and sighing again. "Touché, my boy."

We sat in the dark car in the dark driveway in silence for about five minutes. I was trying to focus and decide what to ask next. I had no idea how long Jerry was going to feel like answering my questions, so I had to hurry.

"What did you mean when you said, 'what I know now'? What did he do, Jerry?" I asked, although I was pretty sure I wasn't going to like the answer. He stared at me, taking several deep breaths before he responded.

"He put a timer in the implants."

"A timer…"

"After a certain amount of time, the implants will…"

"What? The implants will what, Jerry? Deactivate? Melt?" I didn't want to say it out loud, but I couldn't help myself. "Explode?"

At that, his eyes widened, and his mouth fell open.

"You're shitting me, right? You're just messing with me…the implants aren't going to literally explode?"

"Not literally, like a bomb, no, but more like a predetermined self-destruct. The implants will disintegrate on the programmed day and time Trevor chose."

"And when is that?" I demanded.

"Well, you can't say Trevor doesn't have a sense of humor…"

"Jerry."

He sighed so deep, I found myself gasping for air. "April twenty-third."

"This year? Two months?! From now? Why would he do that? After twenty years? Why would he program…for…twenty years? Why would he…" I couldn't think. I couldn't breathe.

"It's twenty years to the day the implants were put in. He's crazy, Rip. He always has been…ever since we rescued him, I knew he had the potential—"

"Rescued him?" I asked.

He looked at me and smiled. "That's a conversation for another time, my boy."

Suddenly, he seemed to perk up. Of course, *he* hadn't just found out his brain was going to burn out in about two months…and Freya. I couldn't think about that. Not now.

He held his key ring up to his face, and searched for a certain one. "Ah! Here it is!" He beamed at me, and I felt nauseated. As he moved to exit the car, he looked at me, and seemed to notice I was having a hard time dealing with the news.

"Cheer up, my boy! I need your young legs to climb down into my bomb shelter. You'll be in and out of there in a matter of minutes! Come on!"

Still, I couldn't move. I couldn't stop the horrible thoughts of Freya's head exploding from playing over and over in my head. I couldn't bear the thought…

Jerry sat back down in the driver's seat, but remained quiet for a moment.

"How about a little good news?" he finally asked.

I slowly turned my head and gave him a confused look.

"When you first signed up for the RVW program, we tested you in every way possible. We performed dozens of medical tests to ensure you were perfectly healthy. We collected a lot of bodily fluids…" He glanced at me with raised eyebrows. I stared back blankly. He gave a frustrated sigh, before continuing. "The FBI has an unsettling habit of keeping these fluids, for whatever reason, for decades, some on ice for preservation purposes…" Again, he glanced at me, and again, I was drawing a blank. I couldn't concentrate on what he was saying.

He slapped me on the back, startling me so much, I thought my heart had stopped.

"I'm trying to tell you, you're the father of my grandsons, boy!"

I looked at him, waiting for my emotions to take over, but I just felt numb.

"Rip! Do you understand what I'm saying? You're a daddy!" He was elated.

I quickly unbuckled my seatbelt, opened the passenger door, and vomited on the ground.

EPISODE 41
A New Enemy

"I don't believe you," I fired back, the anger burning my eyes.

"It doesn't matter," Trevor said dryly. "You will help me, or you'll never see your boys again."

Ever since I'd discovered what Trevor really was, I'd felt more and more disconnected from him, but for the first time, and without my implant activating, all I could think of was how I was going to kill the bastard. Reason climbed its way to the top, however, and I decided a gentler tactic might be more effective.

"Why are you doing this?" I asked, injecting pain into my tone. "I loved you—"

He thought that was funny. "You loved me because I programmed you to love me," he laughed.

Screw gentle.

"Why? Why did you do that? Why couldn't you just leave me alone?" I was losing the compassion in my voice, but I didn't care. I barely noticed the hustle and bustle in the office anymore, as a dozen agents, some I didn't recognize, milled about, talking on cell phones, texting, and coordinating with each other on iPads. Coordinating what, I wasn't sure. I was so livid at the familiar stranger in front of me that I couldn't focus on anything else. The rest of the room started to blur as I glared at Trevor. He met my glare with an evil glint.

"Why?!" he bellowed, and for a second, the din of the room softened...but just for a second. "You and I could have had a *real* life together, if it hadn't been for Tyler Ripley! He never left your side, never let anyone else have a chance with you...you...Freya McKenna...the veritable Fifth Element..." He seemed to be lost in thought all of a sudden, as his voice trailed off, but the crazy never left his eyes.

Did Trevor just compare me to Milla Jovovich as the supreme being?

It would have been flattering coming from anyone else. If I had ever thought he loved me, it was now becoming apparent that his obsession with me was borderline psychotic…minus the borderline. Suddenly, he swiped everything off Pixley's desk in one quick arm motion.

I glanced at the director, who was sighing heavily, but didn't seem overly upset that Trevor had just thrown all his belongings onto the floor.

"So, what's your story?" I asked him, not employee-to-employer, but more like parole officer-to-parolee.

He looked at me and shrugged. "I don't condone his current methods, but it seems your husband—"

I cringed.

"—is trying to clean up his own mess."

"What does he have on you?" I inquired, but Trevor broke in before he could answer.

"Director Pixley, could you please give us a moment?" Trevor asked.

Pixley threw his hands up and shook his head, but walked to the door and left, closing it all the way behind him.

Almost immediately, Trevor's demeanor changed. The anger in his eyes subsided while he smoothed his suit jacket and sat in the white leather chair. He took a deep breath and looked up at me, smiling like he used to…before I woke up.

Arrogant bastard.

"Sit down, Freya," he said sweetly. "Please."

I'm not sure why, but I sat.

He just looked at me for a moment, as if he was trying to read my thoughts. I stared into his eyes, searching for the real Trevor, whoever he may be, but all I found was deceit.

"I meant it when I said I'm the good guy."

I continued to burn him with my fiery gaze.

"So, I'm just part of your 'mess' now, am I?" I asked, and I felt vulnerable, still not believing my life had come to this.

"Freya, I'm going to tell you everything, but I need you to stop trying to bore holes through my skull."

I blinked a few times, and softened my eyes. I was interested to hear what lies would spew from his lips this time. I relaxed slightly in the chair, and squinted at him with skepticism.

He sighed again before he spoke, but it wasn't a frustrated sigh. It was like he was dreading what he was about to say. "Twenty years ago," he began, and I suddenly wished I'd stopped at the restroom on the way in, "I met you and Rip, and my life changed forever."

He shook his head as if trying to shake a memory loose, and chuckled. "I promise you, I didn't intend for this to get so out of hand. When we agreed to wipe your memories, I—"

"*We?* Who's we?"

"The three of us…me, you and Rip."

"What the hell are you talking about? Ty and I never agreed to anything." I tried to remain calm, but my voice was unsteady.

"I'm sorry," he said, which surprised me. "I need to start at the beginning. I came into the RVW program just a week before you and Rip were recruited. I was fresh out of college, and very young…I felt like I hadn't seen the sun in years. I was a bit of an introvert, thanks to finishing a bachelor's and master's degree in three years in a very intensive field, and—"

I cut him off. "What, exactly, did you study?" I asked, deciding to save the whole "Are you Russian?" thing for the zinger later.

"Neuroscience and Computer Technology."

I simply pursed my lips together and nodded for him to continue.

"I met you two, and you were so full of life, and so…in love." He said this like a good friend who was envious, not jealous, of what Ty and I had. I wondered what the hell he was playing at.

"You forced me to come out of my shell. You two showed me how to live, and I was so grateful. We were inseparable, the three of us." He smiled as if the memories were nothing but pleasant. Then, his expression changed. "When the word came down that the program was being terminated, and you two along with it, we…the three of

278 - **JUST KILL ME**

us…decided the only way to save you was to erase your memories, and hide you…erase everything about RVW…"

"And everything about Ty and me…why would we agree to that?"

"That was an unfortunate side effect."

I cocked my head and glared at him.

He threw his hands in the air. "I swear, Freya. I never intended to erase so much, but it wasn't an exact science back then. So much of it was a guessing game…I did the best I could. You both knew the risks. It was either that or be fugitives from the government for the rest of your lives…which probably wouldn't have been very long."

I still had no idea what to say. He was so sincere, I had to keep reminding myself that he was a lying son of a bitch.

"Freya, we were just kids. It may not have been the perfect plan, but it was something."

"Do you have any proof?" I asked, to which he responded with stunned silence. "I mean, if you knew we wouldn't remember agreeing to it in the first place, you would have had us sign something…or made a Houser to Quaid video or something…?" I waited for a response.

"We didn't…um…you weren't supposed to ever remember anything…we didn't think we needed…" he stammered.

I was silent for a moment, studying his face. He was sincerely struggling with his answer. I decided to entertain the remote possibility that he was telling the truth for the first time in his life. "If that's true, then why the charade? Why the Broadway performance to make everyone believe you're some mad scientist gone awry?"

"If Dunwaddle gets wind of what we did, he'll have us all killed so fast…he's already suspicious. I'm just trying to keep the focus on me. If he realizes you and Rip—"

"Dunwaddle? Who the hell is Dunwaddle?"

Trevor sighed and folded his hands in front of him. I leaned back a little and crossed my legs…something I only did when I was extremely agitated, because my legs had a tendency to get antsy when that happened.

"Dunwaddle is an ancient Senator, one of those old coots who refuses to die. He was the head of a committee twenty years ago that doesn't exist anymore. The committee that oversaw the RVW Project."

I was getting more and more confused. "Okay…why does he want us dead?"

Trevor looked worried now. "He was the one who ordered the program to be shut down completely. If anyone found out that you and Rip were still alive, with your implants still intact, well, he'd lose his job, and all his power. And he'd kill us in a heartbeat to save his own ass."

"But…my dad said the higher ups were okay with leaving us alone, as long as they thought you removed our implants."

"That's what he was told. They knew he'd fight it, since you're his daughter, but the order came directly to me. I was supposed to get you on the table under the premise of updates to the implants, and…" I could tell he had no desire to finish that sentence.

"You pulled off pretending to kill us…all by yourself?"

"No," his eyes grew wide, and so did his smile. "Freya, *we* pulled it off. The three of us did it together."

EPISODE 42
The Players Change...Again

"So..." I was trying to put it all together in my head. "If you were trying to hide us from this...Dinwiddle—"

"Dunwaddle," Trevor corrected me calmly.

"Dunwaddle," I repeated. "Why not just change our names, or put us in the witness relocation program or something?"

"It was too risky. We believed the implants would stay dormant as long as your memory loss was permanent...which obviously didn't happen, and I'm really sorry about that. Plus, Dunwaddle never knew your names. He only saw reports that referred to you as 'Subject 1' and 'Subject 2'."

"And they just took you on your word that we were dead?"

"Changing dental records and switching toe tags in the morgue was a lot easier back then," he replied mischievously, but I got the gist.

"And how did you overthrow Pixley, Supreme Chancellor?"

He laughed. A laugh so real, it reminded me of all the times we laughed together as husband and wife. I shook my head and blinked several times to get rid of the emotion welling up in me. I was suddenly being overwhelmed by the realization of the twenty years I'd spent living someone else's life. I didn't know how much more I could handle. I swallowed hard and sat up straighter, as if that would help me cope. Trevor seemed to notice I was losing it, and stopped laughing. He cleared his throat before he answered my question.

"Pixley was working at Headquarters in DC when he was given the menial task of transferring all the remaining paper files to digital about sixteen years ago. He came across the RVW files and there was one form, a form Dunwaddle never saw, that had your names on it."

I narrowed my eyes in question, but said nothing. He continued.

"It so happens, he'd also heard about a stellar Air Force Captain at the time named Freya Tamar McKenna, who had recently appeared on the 'Future Female Leaders' list that the Bureau puts together for the White House. Young women the FBI checks out and thinks should be groomed for high-level government jobs projected for the next twenty years or so. It's nothing that makes the papers, but Pixley had been on the task force to put the list together, and he recognized your name right away. It's not exactly a common one."

"They checked me out? And they didn't find anything suspicious?"

"We had done a pretty good job of filling in the blanks. Remember, you'd already had a security clearance done for the Air Force."

"I don't remember being on any list," I stated, nervously crossing my legs the other way.

"You wouldn't. They don't make it public knowledge. It's just an 'Eyes Only' memo for the POTUS and his immediate staff."

"So...Pixley's in cahoots with you now, or...?" I asked, still waiting for the punch line.

"Long story short, he made Assistant Director at the Minneapolis office ten years later. Then, when he took over here last year, and found out my wife's name was Freya...well, he started to ask questions. He called me into his office about six months ago. I thought he was going to rat me out to Dunwaddle, but instead..." He stopped to chuckle lightly, remembering the encounter. "Instead, he said he wanted to be part of it."

"Part of it...in what way?" I asked.

"He said ever since he'd read the RVW file, he'd wanted to meet 'The Bionic Woman and The Six-Million-Dollar Man,' as he put it. He was as giddy as a school girl when I told him (I felt I had no choice at the time) about what we'd done twenty years ago...erasing your memories and hiding you in Suburbia. He's been helping me ever since. We just...disagree on how to proceed from here."

"What do you mean?"

"It was his idea that I act like I was coming unhinged. He doesn't want me to tell you the truth. He thinks it's too risky, but I just can't keep up the crazy façade. I mean, I admit, I panicked at first, when I walked in on you three in the kitchen, and some of the things I said…well, I knew. I knew my picture-perfect life was over…and I didn't want it to be.

"You threatened to take my boys not thirty seconds ago," I said flatly.

"I know. That was over the line. I guess I'm still trying to save…us. I'm sorry."

"You would have been if you'd tried." I had never been more serious in my life.

"Oh, I know."

We sat in silence for a moment, regarding each other. Then, he sighed.

"Freya, I don't know what to do. Dunwaddle contacted me personally yesterday. He said he'd received an automatic message that someone had accessed your old FBI file, and I was the only person who was involved in the project who's still on the radar. I assured him the two sleepers were long dead, that I'd done my job, but…he's on to me…us. I think he knows you're alive."

He sighed and leaned back in the chair, and I immediately thought of the movie *The Godfather*. The whole scenario was surreal, to say the least. Then, he leaned forward again.

"Plus, your father refuses to believe a word I say. He believes he has proof to bring me down, but the truth is…I have no idea what he has. He's taken Rip to his old house in Garrity to retrieve it, and… we're letting him."

"So, Ty's not in any danger?"

"I don't think so, no."

"And you have been pretending to be my husband for fifteen years…why? Why didn't I just marry Ty if we were relatively safe hiding out in small-town America?"

He looked sad, and that made me angry for some reason. He had no right to be sad. Even if what he was saying was true, any of it, he had been given the luxury of choice these past two decades. Something that had been taken away from Ty and me.

"Ty asked me to keep you safe, whatever the cost. He didn't think you would be safe being with him, that the two of you together was too risky, so he asked me to…take care of you."

I couldn't believe the bullshit he was trying to hand me. "Ty wanted me to marry you?" I asked with utter shock.

"No...Freya, of course he didn't *want* you to marry someone else, but he didn't see any other way. He loved you—loves you more than anything. He just wanted you to be safe. We both wanted you to be safe."

"Why would you do something like that? Give up your own life to marry someone you didn't love? Even for a friend—"

"I never said I didn't love you."

I was speechless. He smiled at me and my heart skipped...like it used to when he looked at me like that.

"I'm not saying I jumped at the chance," he continued. "But...it was an honor...to be your husband. Even if I wasn't your first choice."

My head was spinning. I didn't know what to believe anymore. My life was unrecognizable from the one I had known just a few short weeks ago, and even that one had been all fake...orchestrated by Trevor, and apparently, a very young Ty. Or was it? My head started to pound, and my vision blurred. I looked up at Trevor, and he seemed taken aback.

"Freya, calm down. I'm telling you the truth. Try to calm down." His words were becoming slurred, and I knew it was because my implant was trying to activate, my defense mechanism trying to rescue me from all the emotion flooding my brain. I couldn't stop it, until...

"Beetlejuice, Beetlejuice, Beetlejuice," I heard Trevor say, muffled and hazy. My heart rate steadied, and my vision returned, but my head was still pounding.

"How did you do that?" I mumbled, feeling a little hung over.

"Just a little magic spell I programmed to override your implant. You okay?"

I nodded. "Beetlejuice?" I had to laugh, but winced as my throbbing head responded.

He grinned. "We saw that movie together, the three of us."

I lowered my head, but that just made the pounding worse. I looked back at Trevor. "What am I supposed to do here, Trevor?" I asked evenly, closing my eyes until the pain had reduced to a dull ache.

"I know this is a lot to take in, and you've been through so much the past few days, but I've been flying by the seat of my pants here. In our arrogance, we never made a contingency plan. We were so sure everything would be hunky dory forever, that we never thought...well, we never thought your implants would start to short circuit, for one."

"But..." I was remembering something Ty had told me the other day. One of his flashbacks. "Ty remembered my implant spazzing out back then too...?"

"Really?" He was genuinely surprised. "What did he say, exactly?"

"That my eyes would freak out and it was hard to get me to snap out of it."

He tilted his head back and his mouth fell open. "Oh, that."

I puckered my lips tightly and raised my eyebrows at him.

"That was an upgrade we tried, but had to remove. It was defective."

"Remove? How did you remove it?"

"It was a simple procedure, and before you ask," I had opened my mouth to ask, "yes, I can remove the implants, but..."

Why is there always a 'but'?

"...it's not going to be easy. Brain's been working on it for a year, but she's pretty sure she can do it."

"Ainsley? Is that what she's been doing? The rumor about Optimus Prime...?"

He chuckled. "Well, I think she might be building a giant Transformer too, but yes, she lives in a warehouse and knows more about security and computers than anyone on the planet. She was the perfect person to build the machines we need, and she was very happy to do it...as long as I paid for all of it, of course. Technology is not cheap."

All of a sudden, my back jeans pocket vibrated. I had been so into my conversation with Trevor, it took me a second to realize it was my phone. I pulled it out and saw a text from Blaise. My heart stopped, but immediately steadied. He was complaining about Levi not letting him have a second turn playing some video game. I turned it off and put it back in my pocket, mentally planning a little lecture for my middle child on what is and is not considered urgent.

"The boys?" Trevor asked, and I looked up at him and swallowed hard. Before I could respond, he said, "I know they're at Jabba's. They're safe, I promise."

"That's not what I—" I started, not surprised at all at this point that he knew where they were, but he cut me off.

"I love those boys, Freya. But I'm not their father. You already know that would be impossible." He didn't seem saddened by this. Sterility was just a fact of his life.

"Who...?"

"It was the least I could do for him, considering I got the girl." He smiled at me, so real, that I remembered what I'd loved about him for all those years, programmed or not.

"Ty?"

His smile grew. Just then, his phone rang. It startled both of us, but I literally leapt out of my chair. Trevor raised a hand to calm me as he answered.

"Yes?"

Pause.

"Yes, I just told her."

Pause.

"Give me five seconds..."

He hung up and set the phone on the desk, then walked over to the heavy security door and punched in a code on the panel. The door buzzed and popped open, and a tall, thin man entered, smiling at me.

It was Leon.

EPISODE 43
The Vault

I had expected resistance when I insisted on driving Jerry back to town, but he eagerly handed over the keys. He looked tired, and much older in the early morning light, and I almost felt sorry for him. Sorry that his life had been decades of hiding and avoiding the people he loved.

But then it passed, and I just wanted to get the hell out of there. I had spent the night in Jerry's storm shelter (nuclear bomb shelter, more like), and I was dirty and hungry. I still had no idea what I had retrieved, exactly. Only that it was a manila envelope marked "FREYA" that had taken me nearly four hours to locate in the dark chaos of the underground bunker, and that it couldn't possibly hold more than a few sheets of paper. It was so light, I had immediately started unwinding the string to verify its contents when Jerry snatched it from my hands. He assured me that what was in the envelope would shed light on the whole mystery. Why Trevor had reprogrammed Freya and me, and why he was still manipulating us twenty years later. But he refused to open it.

"In due time, my boy. Let's head back…we'll stop and get some breakfast at a little place I know, and then storm Headquarters with our greatest weapon." He was grinning from ear to ear and shaking the envelope at me as he said it. He walked around to get in the passenger side of the car, and I headed for the driver's door.

"Weapon?" I inquired, wondering what the devil I had just helped the crazy old guy do.

He stopped at the door, and waved the envelope again. "The truth, Agent Ripley!" he exclaimed across the top of the car. "We are now armed with the truth!" He hopped in the car like a kid going to get ice cream.

I took a deep breath and closed my eyes. I needed to see Freya. I pictured her face in my mind and took another calming breath. All I'd had to reassure me of her safety was Trevor's word right before he threw me in the sub-cell.

Jackass.

He'd had the balls to feign concern as he tried to convince me that his intentions were good. He just kept saying, "I'm the good guy, Rip. You have to trust me."

I didn't trust anyone but Freya, and I had to get back to her, but my Technicolor yawn the night before had left me feeling light-headed, dehydrated, and famished...and pulling an all-nighter with my would-be father-in-law wasn't helping either. I needed caffeine and food first. I would have to indulge Jerry a bit longer, but once we were back at Headquarters, I was taking charge.

I got in behind the wheel and sped out of Garrity almost as fast as I'd done the first time when there had been an inferno behind me.

We ate at a trucker dive in the middle of nowhere that served the best veggie omelet I'd ever had, and then I took a quick shower in the truck stop, buying a toothbrush and deodorant so I would feel human again. Then we hit the road. Jerry dozed off about an hour later, after we had emerged from the other side of the city, and we were sitting in a long line of cars waiting for a train to pass. I put the car in park when the train slowed to a near stop and I still couldn't see the end. I sat back against the seat and took a deep breath, blowing it out my mouth with frustration. It seemed the universe was against me getting back to Freya.

I glanced over at Jerry and he was fast asleep, clutching the envelope to his chest. I reached over slowly and grasped the edge of the envelope and tugged gently. Jerry suddenly stirred and readjusted, forgetting the envelope in his dream state, and released it. I pulled it free quickly and smoothly and stared at it for a moment.

I checked the train. It had stopped completely and several cars were giving up their spot in line in the hopes of finding a way around. I pulled up as those of us committed to waiting it out filled in the empty spaces. I put the car in park again, and returned my attention to the envelope that Jerry swore would solve all my problems.

I scoffed at the thought.

I unwound the string, and opened the flap, peering in. There was a single, solitary piece of paper inside. I glanced at Jerry, and then slid the paper out as quietly as I could. Although there was a noisy train, and cars honking continuously, I was sure Jerry would hear the paper as if it were gunfire over the din outside.

I freed the paper, and lay the envelope on my lap. I stared at the document in my hand until the information printed on it began to blur. I had no idea what I was looking at.

The paper was blank, save a handwritten notation on the top left corner that said, "3502." I turned the paper over to stare at the stark white blankness, then turned it back and scrutinized the paper itself. There were no watermarks, no impressions from important notes being written on neighboring papers, nothing. Nothing but the four-digit number.

3502.

A loud honk sounded from behind me and I shot a look in the rear view mirror. The driver behind me was throwing his arms in the air. I looked ahead and the train was gone. The cars that had just been in front of me were now blocks ahead. I threw the car in drive and slowly accelerated, still holding the disappointing paper. The first chance I got, I pulled over and put it back in the envelope, placing it between Jerry and I on the center console just as he snorted and woke himself up. He sat forward abruptly and blinked his eyes several times, trying to remember where he was. I had pulled back onto the road and was doing my best to pretend I'd never even thought of opening the envelope by the time he had gained his bearings. He suddenly looked around frantically, I assumed looking for his precious weapon of truth, and gave a huge sigh of relief when he found it next to him on the console.

He picked up the envelope and slid it into the pocket of his door, out of my reach. Then, he rubbed his eyes a few times and looked out the front windshield as if searching for something.

"Where are we?" he asked.

"About twenty minutes from Headquarters."

He relaxed a little, so I dared ask, "What, exactly, do you think is in that envelope that will help us?"

He gave me a sideways glance and smiled. "It's the answers to all your questions, young man," he assured me, clearly believing what he was saying.

"You don't have any idea what's in there, do you?" I guessed. He was way too confident, almost cocky.

"No, but you do...or you did," he grinned at me mysteriously, raising his eyebrows.

"What are you talking about old man?" I asked, frustrated with the whole situation.

I shook my head and turned back to the road. We didn't speak for the remainder of the drive.

We both expected to be detained as we entered Headquarters, but found no resistance. Jerry produced his Platinum Card, but before he could swipe it, the guard waved us through.

"Agent Douglas is waiting for you in the Director's office, gentlemen."

Of course he was.

When we got to Pixley's office, after finding the two entry points unmanned and wide open, the door was ajar. I slowly opened it enough for Jerry and I to fit through, and I was confused at what I saw.

Leon was sitting next to Freya, facing Pixley's desk, and Pixley was sitting in his white leather chair, grinning like a school boy picking out a puppy. Trevor was behind the chair, leaning back on the built-in cabinet and crossing his arms. The second I saw him, I was filled with rage. I thought about crossing the room right to him and taking him out, but Freya was my first priority. She turned and saw us, and immediately jumped up and ran to me.

My rage disappeared when she was in my arms, and I didn't want to let her go. After a minute, we released each other and I gave her a quick kiss, and a wink to let her know there would be time for more of that later. She smiled at me, radiating beauty, and I wished we could just walk out of there together and never look back. But as long as we were walking targets for the government, we would never be safe, our boys…

Our boys.

I hadn't let myself think about what Jerry had told me the night before until that moment. It had been too overwhelming. Now, I let it sink in. I was a father. The boys I knew and loved as my precious godsons were so much more, and I felt as if I'd always known.

"The boys…" I started.

"They're safe. They're at Jabba's."

"No, that's not…I mean, that's good. Good. I knew you'd think of it. I told Jabba you—"

"I know."

"But that's not what I was going to—"

"I know."

I stopped stammering and gazed into her eyes. She knew. I kissed her again, longer and sweeter this time, and suddenly felt like everything was going to be okay.

I glanced up at Trevor, and he was smiling at me like he used to when we were friends. Then I remembered it had all been a charade. I scowled at him and stepped in front of Freya protectively.

"You won't get away with this, Trevor."

Trevor stood upright and started to speak, but Pixley held up his hand to stop him. I turned my attention to the director, feeling my breath quicken.

"Agent Ripley, we have a lot to discuss," he said calmly. "Have a seat."

I hesitated, but then sat where Freya had been sitting when I entered, next to Leon. I gave him a disappointed stare. "You too?"

"Dude, I'm really sorry…but it's not what you think."

"I'm sure it's not," I replied sarcastically. Before he could say anything else, I turned back to Pixley, who was now looking at Jerry. I'd forgotten Jerry was still there. I spun in my seat and Jerry was still standing back by the door, clutching the manila envelope like a security blanket. He regarded Pixley warily.

"Mr. McKenna. The envelope please." Pixley's tone was gentle, but authoritative.

Jerry didn't move.

"I assure you, Mr. McKenna, we're all working toward the same goal here," Pixley coaxed. "We all want to keep Agent Ripley and your daughter safe." He was so sincere, I was having trouble not believing him myself.

"Jerry," I pleaded. "Go ahead. We don't have much of a choice."

Jerry glanced at me, and then stepped forward. Slowly, he approached Pixley's desk. I half-expected Trevor to tackle him to the ground, but no one else moved. The whole room seemed to be in slow motion. An eternity later, Jerry stopped at the desk and held out the envelope. Pixley squinted at him and then carefully took the packet from him. Jerry backed away, his eyes wide, until he ran into one of the chairs lining the side wall. He slumped down in the nearest one, defeated.

Pixley opened the flap and slid the single piece of paper out. We all watched in anticipation, until I remembered I already knew what was on it.

"It's just a number..." I started, but trailed off, not knowing what else to say.

Pixley raised the paper above his head, and Trevor took it. He stared at it for a second, then his eyes grew wide. He nodded and headed for the door, but then stopped and looked at me.

"Rip," he said. "Come with me."

"I don't think so," I replied, not having any intention of leaving Freya again.

"Freya can come too," he said, as if reading my thoughts. I liked those odds. Two against one if he tried anything. I cocked my head at Freya, and she shrugged, then stood.

I guess we were going with to...wait, where the hell were we going?

"Where are we going?"

"To the basement. To the personal vaults." He held up the paper for me to see. "Vault number 3502."

"How do you know it's a vault number?" I asked.

"Because you told me that's what it was," Jerry piped in from the wall.

We all turned to him. "What?" I demanded.

He chuckled, running his fingers through his dirty gray hair. He looked exhausted and old now. "You told me it was a vault number twenty years ago…right after you wrote it, and told me to keep it safe."

EPISODE 44
I Remember

One thing the movies don't exaggerate (much) is that FBI agents are always targets for bad guys. And, in the event of said "bad guys" succeeding in exacting their revenge, and to avoid grieving families having to search for important paperwork—such as life insurance policies and investment portfolios—the FBI began providing a Top Secret room of safety deposit boxes. The existence of the room was number five on the list of things agents were never allowed to talk about with civilians. Ever.

I'd been down to the vaults once before. About six years ago. An agent had died and I had been given the task of retrieving the contents of his vault and to personally deliver them to the pregnant wife he'd left behind. It was cathartic for me to ease some of the burden off this young grieving widow, and she actually smiled when she realized the stack of papers included a letter her husband had written to their unborn child.

I'd never had a vault of my own, or at least I didn't think I did.

It seemed I'd had a vault for twenty years. Number 3502. When I asked Trevor why my vault was here at this Headquarters when I hadn't started my career here, he explained that the vaults move with the agents, the numbers staying the same. According to Trevor, I had left explicit instructions that I never be personally contacted about my vault but that it still follow me wherever I go.

Right.

"Why the hell would I do that?"

Trevor looked at me suspiciously, and shrugged. "I'm hoping the contents of the vault will explain everything."

I was getting really tired of everyone's vague answers to my questions. I took Freya's hand as we followed Trevor down to the super-secret room.

Touching her made me feel better.

We reached the room, and it was so concealed, I felt like we were going into a crypt. When we were finally standing in the vault room, I started toward the wall to look for number 3502, but an alarm sounded when I crossed from the carpet to the bare tile in front of the vaults. A computer panel appeared out of the wall to my left, and when I stepped back onto the carpet, the alarm ceased.

I'd forgotten. A password was required to approach the vaults. I looked at Trevor, waiting for him to go to the panel and type in the password, but he just looked back at me.

"What are you waiting for?" I asked, not trying to hide my irritation.

He grinned, and I wanted to punch him in the face. "I don't know your password, Rip."

My mouth dropped open. "What? How the hell am I supposed to know it when I don't even remember getting the damn box?"

He was so calm. So eerily, frustratingly calm. "Let's just take a minute and think. Obviously, you would have used something that you would be able to guess right away, even without your memory."

I just stared at him. Was he serious?

"Wait. I thought you said we hadn't made a contingency plan of any kind?" Freya fired at Trevor.

"*We* hadn't," he answered, and settled his gaze on me.

Freya turned and looked at me, and I could see the wheels turning through her eyes.

"What?" I defended. "So, I got a vault without the two of you knowing…"

They continued to scrutinize me, and it was making me very nervous.

"You can't be mad at me…hell, I don't even remember doing it… whatever I did…can we move on, please!?" I burst out at the end of my rant, and they both snapped out of their trances. Freya put her hands on my shoulders, forcing me to face her.

"Honey, we're not mad...just try to think. If you were asked to make a password right now, what would you choose?"

Great. It suddenly felt like old times. Trevor and Freya standing together, and me...all alone. I closed my eyes and tried to clear my head.

If I had to create a password right now...? But I'm not the same person I was then.

I nodded at Freya and forced a smile. She dropped her hands and I turned and slowly approached the password terminal. I closed my eyes and delved deep into my memories. Since movies had always been a big part of my life, those were the first things that came flooding back. I remembered I was a huge Arnold Schwarzenegger fan, and *Total Recall* was my favorite movie back then, along with just about everything else that involved futuristic gun battles.

Who am I kidding? I still love a good sci-fi shootout.

As I tried to pull up a memory of that time, however, I realized that was all I remembered. Specifics of that whole year were still eluding me...hidden somewhere in my brain because of the implant. My head began to spin. I looked down at the floor and then closed my eyes again, tighter.

Nothing.

I decided to follow Freya's lead. What password would I choose today? Everything that came to mind I quickly dismissed because they were things I wouldn't have known about twenty years ago.

I kept going back to my buddy Arnold.

I was certain I would have chosen something that would make me laugh. That's just the kind of guy I am. Something from a movie. My mission was to discern what one word would have been funny to me then, and something the twenty-three-year-old me knew the future me would be able to figure out.

No problem. I sighed deeply with frustration.

"You only get three tries, and then the system locks you out for twenty-four hours, so..." Trevor suddenly piped in, and I opened my eyes, but didn't turn toward him.

"That's useful information, thank you," I responded sarcastically at the keyboard in front of me.

"Sorry. I just remembered."

The apologetic new Trevor was unsettling. I took a few cleansing breaths and stood up straight, positioning my fingers above the keys. I typed.

H-O-U-S-E-R.

A buzzing sound and the words "ACCESS DENIED" in red let me know my first guess was wrong.

Okay, then it had to be…

Q-U-A-I-D.

Buzzing and red words fill my senses.

Damn. One guess left.

There was only one word I could think of, but it seemed too easy. Too common a word to be a mysterious password that had kept… something…safe for twenty years. But I had nothing else. Either I'm right, or we wait twenty-four hours and try again.

I cracked my knuckles, and then typed.

R-E-M-E-M-B-E-R.

The mutant, Kuato's mumblings to one Douglas Quaid had been the second-most quote-worthy line of the epic movie, and I definitely did "remember" repeating it over and over, much to Freya's annoyance. We must have seen the movie together…before Trevor…before RVW…before they both ruined our lives.

A green light and then the panel slid from beneath my fingers, disappearing into the wall again. I turned and mentally prepared myself for what I would find in vault number 3502.

I stepped onto the tile floor, and paused. No alarm. I walked to the middle of the room and scanned the wall of boxes.

3500, 3501…3502.

It was too high to reach, even for Trevor's 6'5" stature. I searched the small cave and finally found an almost-invisible cupboard that housed a compact step stool. Even on the top step, I had to stretch my arm to its limit to reach the fingerprint scanner. I pressed my thumb against the small panel and, after a few seconds, the vault slowly came out of the wall. I pulled it free and climbed down, sitting on the floor like a child with his first Christmas present.

Freya sat next to me, but Trevor remained standing, although his expression gave away that he was just as anxious and excited as Freya and I were. I opened the box, and we all peered in at the contents. There was only one item inside.

A VHS tape with the title, "Remember," in black marker. It was my handwriting.

Now all we had to do was find a VCR.

EPISODE 45
We Meet Again

    We found it in a closet in the back of a small conference room, after searching what felt like a hundred offices and conference rooms. Apparently, the one and only VCR left on the planet. It was on top of a small plastic bin marked "ESK." Emergency Situation Kit. Every room in the headquarters building was required to have certain… things that would allow survival in various scenarios, from loss of power to terrorist attack. The bin was on the floor, pushed under the bottom shelf, and the VCR was shoved all the way back to the wall on top of that. It was a miracle we found it at all.

    I was understandably concerned that the damn thing wouldn't work. Ty carried it out of the closet and set it on the conference table in the middle of the room. Trevor grabbed the end of the cord and plugged it in, while I found the proper connections on the flat screen TV hanging on the wall and turned it on. Then, Ty pushed the power button on the VCR.

    Nothing.

    Something occurred to me. I walked over to the door and flipped every light switch to the on position. All the lights came on and a green light appeared on the front of the machine, and it began to whir. Ty tried to push the tape from his secret vault into the slot, but it wouldn't go. He cocked his head and then pushed the eject button. An old FBI training tape popped out. He quickly pulled it out and set it on the table. He slid his tape in and the machine swallowed it.

    The TV came to life, and a familiar countdown appeared on the screen.

    5. 4. 3. 2. 1.

Ah, the old days when the VCR was the pinnacle of technology. Then, static.

All of a sudden, we were looking at Ty. A young, smiling Ty. He was so beautiful. I looked over at my forty-five-year-old Ty and grinned. He was zoned to the would-be looking glass. He was still beautiful, and more so with every gray hair and deeper line on his face.

Holy shit. Ty *did* make a Houser to Quaid tape. I had to smile. It was so…him.

Trevor was sitting on the table, staring at the screen too. I had assumed he knew what was on the tape, but his face told me otherwise.

I looked back at the TV and the young Ty began to talk.

"Hello."

He looked apprehensive…and sad, but he forced a smile at the camera.

"My name is Tyler Ripley. This message is for Freya McKenna." He paused, trying to sort out what to say next. The three of us didn't move.

The young Ty cleared his throat. "I'm making this tape for you, Freya," he said sadly, and I swear, he looked right at me through the television screen…through time and space. It gave me goose bumps.

Ty noticed when I wrapped my arms around myself to shake off the chill and walked over to put his arm around me. I looked up at him and smiled. He tried to give me a comforting look, but I could tell he was worried. About everything.

"If you're watching, Frey…" the young Ty continued, "I know we agreed not to do this, not to leave any trace of what we are about to do, but…" He looked down at his feet and ran his hands through his hair. When he looked up again, he had a strained look on his face. "I guess you won't remember any of that, if everything goes the way it's supposed to…and you won't remember me, if Trevor keeps his word…and I know he will, but…I had to tell you why I'm doing this. If you're watching this, then you've discovered something about your past, and…well, I needed you to know why we couldn't be together."

He was silent for a moment, just looking at the camera. I could hear Ty breathing next to me. It had to be strange, watching yourself from the past saying things you don't remember saying. My head swam just thinking about it.

"Trevor."

Trevor stood suddenly at the sound of his name, and opened his mouth like he was going to answer, but no sound came.

"Trevor, if you're there, and if everything has gone according to plan, I can't...I can't tell you how much I appreciate what you're going to do...or what you've already done, I guess, from your point of view." He chuckled nervously. "At least, I hope everything has worked out the way we planned. Freya, if Trevor hasn't told you anything, and I know how you hate that, then he's kept his promise to me. He's a good friend...to both of us, and I guess...your husband, if everything is in place."

He cleared his throat again, and then took a deep breath.

"Okay, here it is. Freya. We were going to get married," he said suddenly, forcefully.

Ty and I looked at each other and raised our eyebrows. Clearly, neither of us remembered that important piece of information.

"We, you and I," he continued, "signed up for a government project called Rip Van Winkle. It was an experiment to see if a computer enhancement could improve normal human reaction time, decrease the time it took to learn a skill from months or years to...milliseconds. It was a program to see if they could turn already sharp human beings into...killing machines. They wanted sleepers that they could turn on and off and control. They recruited you, and I...well, I still think they only took me because you told them you wouldn't do it if they didn't..."

He grinned at us, and it was so surreal, I found myself grinning back.

"Anyway, that was almost exactly a year ago. Your dad was an agent on the project, some sort of shrink who was given the job of evaluating candidates to make sure our brains could handle it. When he found out you were on the list, he tried to talk you out of it, but you convinced him to let you do it. You always did have him wrapped around your little finger..."

Young Ty looked down for a second, then back up at the camera, a very serious look on his face.

"They put things...implants in our heads, Freya, to turn us into assassins. We killed people for the government. Our government. I promise you, they all deserved it, but that discussion would take up the entire tape, so...um...Trevor was our programmer. He invented the implants, and he was...*is* our best friend."

He stopped, staring into the camera, staring out at us from the past, and I glanced at Trevor. He had locked on to Young Ty's gaze, and his eyes were glistening. For the first time I could remember, he was producing real tears, though he fought to keep them from running down his face.

"Anyway, we were really good at our job. Apparently, someone in Washington thought we were too good. The senator who backed RVW, some jackass named Dunwaddler or something..."

Trevor snorted, and I glanced at him. He smiled. "You never could get his name right, man," he said to Ty, and then chuckled, which loosed a tear from his right eye. He quickly wiped it away, making eye contact with me for a split second before turning back to the screen.

Young Ty continued. "...well, he'd secretly funded the project with money he was supposed to spend on equipment for the war in Iraq. Someone on the Armed Services Committee got wind of it, and threatened to ruin him. Dun...Din...Dimwit had to get rid of us quick, so the word came down to terminate the whole operation. We were just fine with that...until Trevor got the order to terminate...us."

I closed my eyes and sighed, and Ty moved his arm from my shoulder to his side and he took my hand in his, squeezing it tightly.

The young Ty wasn't finished. "He knew better than to try to refuse the senator. This guy's a real piece of work; I really hope he's dead by the time you see this."

I rolled my eyes at that. If only.

"He's into all sorts of bad stuff, including getting our own guys killed in Iraq to serve his agenda. No one's ever been able to prove anything, though. Anyway, the three of us came up with the plan to fake our deaths and run...for the rest of our lives. The only way to ensure your—our—safety is to have Trevor erase all memory of the RVW program, and he's sure he can do it. After that, all it will take is a few bodies from the morgue, and a car 'accident' complete with blazing inferno to convince the prick senator. Luckily, our names have been kept confidential, so we figure if we go deep enough, we won't have to change those."

Young Ty took a few deep breaths before he continued. He looked so tired. It was easy to forget that this Ty, although his memories of making the tape were gone, was safe and sound in the year 2013, and was standing right next to me.

"What you don't know, Freya...or, at least the Freya here and now... *my* Freya..." I got a tingle. "Is that Trevor and I have made additional plans for your future...for all our futures. To make sure you are safe, I have decided that...it isn't a good idea for us to...stay together."

Although it was obviously very difficult for Young Ty to say, I suddenly didn't care.

How dare he make a decision of this magnitude without consulting me!

I didn't need anyone to take care of me. I never had. Who did this stupid kid think he was? And then he had the nerve to act so distraught over it? Really?

Without realizing it, I let go of Ty's hand and stepped forward, closer to the screen. I wanted to reach through the television and strangle the guy, but like a typical man, he still thought he was in charge of the moment and kept talking.

"So, I asked Trevor to...take care of you. I asked and then I gave him every reason in the book why he should say no, but he didn't. He's a great guy, Freya, and I know he'll be a good husband. I hope you can forgive me. I don't see any other way to keep you safe from Dun-what's-his-name. So, I wanted to say goodbye. I've asked Trevor to erase all our memories of us, so we don't try to find each other after... um... I'm going to miss you...well, I guess I won't if Trevor does his job. And you won't miss me either."

All of a sudden, Young Ty blinked several times, his arm abruptly stretching across the screen toward the camera, and then he was gone.

Static.

I was so angry, I couldn't move.

Then, I felt a hand on my shoulder. I turned slowly, and Ty was there, his eyes full of compassion. He held his arms out to embrace me, and I stepped forward.

And punched him in the face.

EPISODE 46
Trevor Tells All

"YOU SON OF A BITCH!" I screamed at Ty, as he lay on the floor, reeling from my right hook. His eye was already swelling.

"Freya! What the hell's wrong with you?!" Trevor asked, pulling my shoulders back so I couldn't attack Ty again.

"What's wrong with *me*?!" I yelled at him, wriggling to get out of his grasp.

Ty slowly got up, holding his puffy eye. I was surprised that he didn't look angry.

"Freya…" he tried to speak, but it seemed to make his head throb.

"Shut up! You don't get to talk!" I shouted. Trevor was still grasping my arms tightly. I forced myself to calm down, taking several deep breaths. When the fury began to pass, I turned back to my captor with pleading eyes. He scrutinized me for a moment, and then nodded and carefully released me. I stood there for a moment, taking more deep breaths to calm my heart rate, but it wasn't working.

Ty was now sitting at the table, and was just…looking at me. Then he lowered his head. I suddenly walked briskly to the closet we'd found the VCR in. I pulled out the ESK and popped it open. I rummaged through the contents until I found the first aid kit. Inside that was a reusable "ice" pack that I activated and gently put on Ty's eye. He took a deep breath of relief when the pack hit his swollen skin, and he smiled up at me so sweetly, I knew I would never love any man more than I loved him.

"You okay?" I asked softly, but not quite ready to sound completely apologetic.

He raised his head and met my eyes. His right eye was fat and shiny, and nearly swollen shut. He tried to smile at me but winced from the pain.

"What the hell were you thinking? Both of you?" I glanced at Trevor.

I suddenly felt exhausted. I closed my eyes and sat down on the floor at Ty's feet. I felt his hand on my shoulder.

"Frey...I'm so sorry. We were stupid kids..."

"Stupid is an understatement," I sighed. "You realize what this means."

Ty gave me a blank stare, and Trevor's mouth was hanging open as if the mere action would spontaneously produce words.

"It means you chose this." I leaned in closer to Ty, feeling myself get worked up again. "You chose to spend the last twenty years watching me and Trevor..." I trailed off, not feeling evil enough to finish my sentence, but Ty knew what I was saying, and he looked so sad, so vulnerable, I just couldn't blame him anymore. The Ty in front of me right here, right now, would never have done what the young Ty had.

"Why would I want to hang around all these years, torturing myself? If I trusted you so much." Ty looked up at Trevor questioningly, who continued to stare, mouth agape. "If I trusted you to keep her safe, why would I want to be the third wheel for the rest of my life?"

We both stared at Trevor until he recovered, his mouth snapping shut. He swallowed a few times before answering. "I'm sorry. I just couldn't stand to lose my best friend."

Ty and I must have looked like we weren't getting it.

"It was my idea to keep you in our lives," he said to Ty. "You didn't want to be anywhere near us, but..." He hesitated, seeming to get his thoughts in order before continuing. "You were the first real friends I'd ever had, both of you. The three of us were so good together...and what you did...it was so heroic and selfless, I guess I thought I was doing something nice for you. I programmed your implant with a strong desire to stay near us—me specifically. I didn't think that it might—"

Ty cut him off. "That it might be worse for me than anything even Fat Murphy could have done to us?"

I raised an eyebrow at him.

"South African crime lord...tell you later," he said to appease me.

"Trevor," I said, looking up at my once-husband. "Just tell us everything you know, everything you remember...please."

Trevor stood over me, a conflicted look on his face. "Freya, I don't know—"

"Too many secrets, Trevor," I shot at him, quoting one of our favorite movies.

He paused. Then, he was smiling, a faraway look in his eyes. "September 9, 1992."

I stared up at him. "What?"

"That's the day *Sneakers* came out. The three of us went and saw it at the theater."

"How could you remember that?"

Ty raised his head and answered before Trevor. "That's the day you both got your first assignments for the Air Force...and the day..."

"The day we officially became a couple," Trevor finished, but it was no longer a happy memory. His face was full of regret.

"You two are like Rainman," I commented.

"You don't easily forget the day the woman of your dreams becomes yours." Trevor smiled.

"Or the day the woman of your dreams becomes someone else's," Ty said quietly.

My heart became heavy, although I hadn't done anything wrong. I turned to Trevor. "Enough reminiscing, Trevor. Start talking."

Trevor had a deep wrinkle between his eyes as I pulled a chair from the conference table and set it next to Ty, plopping down in it and staring at him, waiting. He took a deep breath and held it for a moment, stopping time within the room. When the clock started ticking again, he started talking.

"There's so much...I never thought I'd be doing this, telling you both things we lived through together. I'll try to remember, but..."

"How about you start with the timers you put on our implants." Ty was starting to perk up again, and he set the ice pack down on the table.

"What?" I asked.

Ty looked at me. "Your dad told me...our implants are ticking time bombs."

We both turned to Trevor, who was wide-eyed.

"That's not true. I didn't do it. That was in the original orders, but I couldn't...I never did it. I just told them I did."

"Why would they order a timer on the implants?" I asked. "They wanted to kill us from the very beginning?"

"Of course they did. Our government isn't known for wanting to keep their assassins alive when it's done with them." Ty said this devoid of emotion, then looked up at Trevor. "Why should we believe you?"

"Because I'm telling the truth. I would never...could never...you were my best friends, I—"

"Save it, Trevor." Ty was becoming agitated now. "Timer or no timer, we want these things out of our heads. Can you do it or not?"

Trevor's hesitation to answer was far from encouraging.

"Trevor," I goaded.

"I hope so."

"You hope so." Ty was less than impressed.

"Ainsley has been working on it, Ty," I offered.

"Ainsley?" Ty directed at me, before looking to Trevor again. "She's been working for you this whole time?"

"For about a year now. She's close. But there's no hurry, I promise you, there are no timers—"

"A year?" Ty burst out. "Why would you ask her to start working on it a year ago? We just started having the flashbacks a few months ago."

His expression screamed that what we already knew was just the tip of the iceberg. I took a deep breath while we waited for Trevor to respond, silently praying he was telling the truth.

"You've been having flashbacks for three years, Freya. Rip, I don't know for sure when yours started."

We were quiet for a minute. I didn't know how to react. Three years? Was he serious?

"Why don't I remember?" I asked, half to myself.

"I'm not sure, but the first time was late at night, and I would have thought you were just dreaming, but..."

"But what?" I asked.

"But...we were...having sex at the time."

I felt Ty stiffen next to me, and he reached for the ice pack again. I gave Trevor the stink eye, and he shrugged innocently.

"Sorry…"

"How do you know I had a flashback? What did I say?" I wasn't sure I wanted a recounting of one of our sexual escapades in front of Ty, but I had to know.

Now it was Trevor's turn to stiffen and he suddenly seemed uncomfortable with the topic, although he'd brought it up.

"Trevor. What did I say?" I insisted. He wasn't getting out of this one.

"You…you said Rip's name…"

"During?" I asked.

"During…afterwards…about six times."

I glanced at Ty and he was now grinning like a school boy, triumphant and giddy.

"Anyway," Trevor continued, eager to move on. "When I realized your implant might be failing, I confided in Ainsley, and she was eager to help."

"Well, that explains why she helped me," Ty mumbled.

"What do you mean?" I asked, and Trevor looked confused as well.

"When I was searching for information about your past," he said to me, "before I realized I was wrapped up in this whole thing too…I had hit a brick wall, and Ainsley…guided me in the right direction, shall we say. She even referred to Freya as my 'girlfriend' and that was before…well, before you *were* my girlfriend."

Trevor chuckled. "That doesn't surprise me. She was all about it when I told her we were 'fighting for true love'."

"Really?" I had to laugh with him. "You used *Princess Bride* to convince her to help you? And she didn't catch on?"

"You'd be surprised how few classic movies she's seen."

"Clearly." I nodded, and we both laughed again.

Ty cleared his throat, and I couldn't help but think he was trying to prevent any intimate connection between Trevor and me. I put my hand on his knee and squeezed gently to reassure him he had nothing to worry about.

I wanted to get back to Trevor's detailed confession, but I was still confused. "So, why does my dad think you *did* put the countdown on our implants?"

"And why is he so convinced that you're the bad guy?" Ty added.

"I'm not sure, but I suspect Dunwaddle's been feeding him faulty information."

"Who's this Dunwatter guy?"

That's right, Ty wasn't in that conversation. I patted his knee.

"Crazy senator who ordered Trevor to kill us twenty years ago… more later," I said quickly.

He opened his mouth, but I beat him to the punch.

"Wait. He's been in touch with Dunwaddle all these years?" I turned back to Trevor.

"No," Trevor replied. "I think the senator had tabs on him, though, and Dunwaddle definitely owned the first guy your dad hired to keep you safe…the guy he told you got a better offer?"

I nodded. "Don't tell me…" I didn't like where this was going.

"I'm not sure. But the evidence I have so far points to Talia. I think Dunwaddle got to her right after your dad hired her…and she made a deal. He wouldn't have Lars deported back to Russia if she reported everything she learned back to him."

"But Lars is Swedish…?"

"When he joined the KGB, he gave up his citizenship. Technically speaking…he's a Russian."

"Like you?" Ty asked. I'd forgotten about that.

"What?" Trevor smiled so big, it was almost cartoonish. Then he laughed.

"I'm not kidding."

Trevor's laugh dimmed to a chuckle, then it stopped altogether when he saw Ty's face. "Wha—what are you talking about?" Trevor asked, genuinely shocked at the accusation.

Just then, the door to the conference room swung open, and we all jumped. I turned and saw my dad enter the room, a small pistol in his hand. I stood and approached him.

"Dad, what are you—"

He cut me off. "I'm not going to let him hurt you anymore, Freya. I should have done this twenty years ago, but I thought I could make him remove those goddam implants. Now I know that's impossible."

He raised the gun and pointed it at Trevor's head.

"Dad, it's alright—"
Before I could finish, he pulled the trigger.

EPISODE 47
Finally...Some Answers

I disarmed my dad in a split second, but it was too late. Trevor was on the ground, motionless. Ty had dropped his ice pack on the floor as he reacted and leapt to Trevor's aid. He was kneeling over him, tearing off his suit jacket as quickly but gently as he could. I had my dad pinned against the wall, but he wasn't struggling.

"Ty!" I yelled, hoping for some good news.

"I can't find it!"

"What?"

"There's no blood! I can't find any—" He stopped abruptly, mid-word.

"What's wrong?!"

Suddenly, Ty was laughing.

I slowly released my dad after checking him over for any other weapons, and went to Ty. I put my hand on his shoulder.

"Ty?" I said softly. He looked up at me with a smile. That's when I glanced down at Trevor, who was stirring. Ty had ripped Trevor's shirt open, trying to find the entry wound, and had revealed something neither of us expected. He was wearing a bullet-proof vest.

And the bullet was lodged in the thick fibers, right over his heart.

I took a deep breath, dropped down to my knees next to Ty, and started to laugh. Ty soon joined me. Just then, Trevor opened his eyes slowly, and mumbled something. We both stopped giggling and leaned forward.

"What, Trevor?" Ty asked softly.

"I said, what the hell is so funny?"

"Your uncanny ability to survive," Ty replied, knocking softly on Trevor's vest.

Trevor raised his eyebrows and exhaled. "I had a feeling it was going to be an...*interesting* day."

"Yeah, well, your feelings have always been pretty accurate," Ty said, and for a split second, I had a feeling of my own...a familiar feeling of the three of us, laughing together. And it wasn't a recent memory from when I was Trevor's Stepford Wife. It was much older.

I smiled, but didn't share my first genuine near-memory with the two men. I hadn't forgotten that my father had just tried to kill Trevor and he was still in the room. I turned to him, and noticed he was a wreck. His hair was a mess, his clothes rumpled from being worn for two days, and his face was a mix of confusion and horror.

"Dad?"

He looked at me, and I tried hard to feel sorry for him, but I just couldn't muster it.

"What the HELL were you thinking?"

The confusion took over. "I...I thought you wanted—"

"You thought I WANTED you to kill Trevor?"

"Yes...I...Freya, he's been lying to you...the things he's done...I just wanted it to be...over."

"Dad, killing Trevor isn't the answer. He's not the bad guy. He was just playing his part...and keeping his word to Ty." I glanced back and Ty was helping Trevor to his feet. He was a little pale, but was recovering quickly. He sat down at the conference table and took a few deep breaths, his shirt still open to the protective vest, while Ty came to my side.

"Jerry, Trevor confessed to all the lies, but what we found in my vault was even more enlightening," Ty said to my dad, who was starting to look less like a zombie as what we were saying began to sink in. "And it proves Trevor was just trying to keep Freya and me safe all these years."

"We're not done talking about what's on that tape," I said to my dad, though clearly directing it at Ty. "But Ty's right...it proves all Trevor is really guilty of is being a loyal friend...a loyal, stupid, testosterone-filled, pig-headed friend...crazy as it sounds."

"So…I…" my dad stammered, sewing the pieces of the puzzle together slowly.

"You shot a man while he was confessing, yes." Ty's lack of tact made me grin, but I was still fuming about what he and Trevor had done. I just wished there was a damn thing I could do about it.

Suddenly, Ty turned back to Trevor, as if remembering something. "Are you Russian or not, Trev?"

"Russian?! No…of course I'm not Russian."

"Why the devil would you think that?" my dad chimed in. "I thought he was a psychopath trying to manipulate my daughter, but he's no Rusky."

I turned to him, surprised at his reaction. He looked shell-shocked, but he was trying to participate in the conversation, still leaning against the wall I'd had him pinned against. I was really confused. If Trevor *was* Russian, Jerry would have known twenty years ago. At least, I assumed he would have known.

"I had a flashback…you were talking to some guy about giving me false memories to fix the 'blank space' the implant had made… and you were speaking in a Russian accent…?"

Trevor lowered his head for a moment, accessing the scene Ty had just described. When he raised his head, he said, "I remember the conversation, but I don't have a clue why you think I had an accent."

We were all silent for a moment, until Ty asked, "Okay…then who were you talking to, and what the hell did you mean by 'blank space'?"

"We have blank space in our implants?" I asked.

"No," Ty answered, "blank space in our memories."

"Well…isn't that already a given, since we don't remember what really happened?"

"We have false memories to replace the real ones," Ty reminded me. "That's different from blank space. Trevor made it sound like it could cause serious brain damage and trauma."

Trevor raised his hands in the air at us. "Hold on. There's no blank space in anyone's memories. I thought that's what it was…back then, but the technology has advanced so much in twenty years, you have no idea—"

"*Trevor*," I interrupted. "Just tell us."

He took a deep breath to keep himself calm. "Okay," he said. "When I said those things, I truly believed that's what was causing your implants to short circuit, but—"

"You said our implants didn't short circuit," I broke in. "That it was some upgrade you—"

This time, Trevor cut *me* off. "I'm getting to that." He took another deep breath, and I conceded with a small nod. "Rip, the conversation you heard (and I can't believe you heard it because you were under anesthesia at the time) was just after we tried an upgrade to your implants, strictly programming, no slicing and dicing necessary. It was causing more harm than good, and I didn't think I could fix it... until I got in there—"

"In where? You just said you didn't cut us open for the upgrade," Ty said.

"Relax...in the programming," Trevor replied. "Once I got in there, I was able to take out the upgrade, and it fixed what I thought was this void in your memories. But I was prepared to give you fake memories to try to fill in the blanks...I was relieved I didn't have to, but—"

"But what? You *did* give us false memories," I said, even though most of what Trevor was saying was starting to make sense...sort of.

"Yes, but not until later. The whole ordeal with the upgrade actually gave me the idea of how to rewrite your memories for real, when we needed a Plan B to save your lives."

"Oh yes, because that idea was pure genius," I stated in my best sarcastic tone.

I turned to my dad, who was looking a little more human as he listened to our conversation.

"Dad, how much of this did you know?"

"Everything...except for the part about Rip actually asking Trevor to write him out of your life. I was all for erasing your memory of RVW if it would keep you both safe, but when I realized what Trevor was doing, I lost it. I didn't believe him when he tried to tell me that he was doing what Rip wanted." Jerry looked up at Trevor now, guilt in his eyes. "He had no proof, and it just didn't make sense to me...but I was too late. Your memories had already been altered, so I threatened to tell Dunwaddle, which was just piling more stupid on top of the pile..."

I nodded in agreement as he continued.

"That's when Trevor and I came to an arrangement of sorts. He promised he would be good to you, and keep you safe. Since my only thought was your safety," he gave me a fatherly look that was vaguely familiar, "I didn't seem to have any other options…"

"But I never told him he had to stay away from you, Freya." Trevor offered this, and I couldn't help but give him a sad look.

My dad stepped closer to me, putting a gentle hand on my shoulder. "No, that was my decision." He smirked and then sighed. "It seems all the men in your life are complete idiots."

I looked at each of them, and they all seemed to agree, for the first time probably ever. At least since they had decided they were qualified to make life-changing decisions on my behalf. I'd never felt so loved, and so betrayed at the same time.

"But Trevor, I know I heard you speaking with a Russian accent." Ty wasn't about to let his flashback go, and I wanted answers just as much as he did.

Just then, Trevor's face lit up. He had remembered something. "The other guy!"

Ty raised an eyebrow at him.

"The guy I was talking to. You remember him, Jerry! The Russian dude!"

Jerry maintained a blank stare.

"The diplomat or royalty, whatever he was, with all the money!"

Jerry suddenly came to life, clearly catching up to Trevor's memory. "The fatcat! He was a Czar or something!"

"Yes!" Trevor rejoiced.

"Jesus, I'd forgotten about him…" Jerry mumbled, trailing off into his thoughts of twenty years ago.

Ty and I waited for them to remember we were in the room. After a few seconds, Trevor turned back to us.

"He was a big wig in Moscow, but he knew the war was coming to an end, and he knew Russia wasn't going to win. He promised Dunwaddle his money for the RVW program, and other stuff I'm sure, if the senator would arrange a very quiet and smooth defection for the guy when we won."

"The guy you were talking to…telling him all about our implants… he was some Russian millionaire?" Ty asked, not believing a word of it.

"I was ordered to tell him everything," Trevor shrugged.

"Still," Ty said thoughtfully, "why would I remember you with the accent and the other guy without one? It doesn't make sense."

Trevor shrugged…again. "In the simplest terms, we were messing with your head, and the implants have proved to be nothing if… unpredictable. You just *think* you remember us with the wrong accents. The brain is a very complicated thing."

"That's your answer? The brain is a very complicated thing?" I couldn't believe that was the defense he was going with, though I guess it did make more sense than a lot of other things about this mess.

Trevor suddenly cocked his head, raising one ear to the ceiling like he was listening for something.

"Trevor?" I inquired.

"I just realized…why didn't the alarm sound when Jerry shot me?"

"I turned it off before I came down here."

We all glared at him.

"Premeditated, Jerry. That won't bode well in court," Trevor said, and I wasn't sure if he was kidding or not, until he broke the awkward silence with a boisterous laugh.

And, as if convicting himself to life in prison, Jerry added, "And I waited until after five…building's practically empty."

"Dad…" I started, but just didn't know what to say. Nothing could take back the fact that he had walked into the room with the intent to kill Trevor, and would have succeeded if Trevor hadn't had the premonition to wear a bullet-proof vest. And, although I'd wanted to kill the guy myself several times over the past few days, I felt like I was starting to see my life in a brighter light…and it was finally making some sense. *Crazy* sense, but sense.

Trevor still wasn't telling us everything, of that I was certain, but I was starting to see him less and less as a real threat. The one thing I did believe was that he wanted to help Ty and me get the old senator off our trail for good, and that was all I cared about at the moment.

Then what my dad had just said registered with my mommy brain.

"Wait, it's after five? I need to go get the boys!"

"I'll go with you," Ty said.

I immediately headed for the door, Ty on my heels, when Trevor said, "Freya."

I stopped in my tracks and turned.

"I won't come home tonight if you want to tell the kids I'm still out of town."

I took a deep breath and tried to sort through the million things I wanted to say to him, and settled on, "I think it's time to tell them what's going on...that you won't be home...ever." I watched him and gauged his reaction. He surprised me with a smile.

"Do you want me to talk to them?"

"No...not yet. I want to talk to them first...with Ty."

Ty reached into his pants pocket and pulled out his keys, taking one in particular off the ring and holding it out to Trevor. "Stay at my place," he said.

Trevor froze for a second, then smirked as he reached out and snagged the key. "Thanks, man."

Ty nodded, and I couldn't help but feel good about the fact that there would be no fight to the death for my hand...although I had spent an inordinate amount of time fantasizing about it.

We were almost out the door when Trevor stopped us again.

"You're leaving me here alone with him?" he asked, an odd joking tone in his voice.

I turned back and realized that my dad had this lost look on his face again. I couldn't leave him there, unarmed, and with the guy he'd just tried to kill...who happened to still have his weapon. I didn't really think Trevor would hurt Jerry, but...

"Dad, come with us."

He happily trotted after us, probably glad for some escape from everything that had happened.

Ty drove, since my van was still at Jabba's, and he paid little attention to traffic regulations, which was fine with me. My dad was strangely quiet in the backseat. I wanted to talk to Ty about Trevor's accommodating behavior and his support for the two of us being together now that everything was out in the open. Even if everything he had told us was true, which seemed to be the case, was it really so easy for him to give me up? I didn't want to mention any of this while my dad was in the car though, since I still wasn't sure how much he was keeping from us. He and Trevor seemed to share their own vault of secrets, and I was too tired to open that door again today.

I texted Levi, and he texted right back, assuring me they were fine and having a great time, but I was still very anxious to get to them.

We pulled into the parking lot of the old book store and my heart skipped a beat. I wasn't ready to face this obstacle yet either, but it seemed I wasn't being given a choice. There was one other car in the lot.

It was Talia's.

EPISODE 48
Surprise Guests

I closed my eyes tightly for a few seconds…ten to be precise, counting slowly and deliberately, as if that would ensure the outcome I desired. It worked. I opened my eyes and he was still there, sitting on my couch.

And smiling at me like I was Aphrodite and he was under my spell.

What a day we'd had.

We'd gone to pick up the boys at Jabba's bookstore, and had unexpectedly run into Talia and Lars, who claimed they had been out to lunch and saw my van in the parking lot. I had disguised the Odyssey to look like anyone's but mine, so when I raised an eyebrow at Talia, she immediately reminded me that the dent on the back fender had been her doing, and it had caught her attention.

I pretended to be convinced. Ty and I had agreed in the car that confronting Lars and Talia would be a mistake at this point. Trevor was still waiting for confirmation that Talia was working for Dunwaddle, and he assured us that he would have the answer in the next twenty-four hours. So, though I was sure it would drive me insane, we decided to wait. I just wanted to get my boys home…all five of them. My father was strangely quiet as I quickly introduced him to his grandsons in the bookstore parking lot.

Not the atmosphere I had envisioned for this momentous occasion, but it would have to do. The boys didn't seem to mind, and were positively giddy, immediately vying for their grandfather's attention. Jerry looked a little overwhelmed, but shot me a smile as the boys pulled him into the van, all chattering at once.

We'd said goodbye to Lars and Talia at Jabba's, after making casual dinner plans for the day after next, and spent the fifteen-minute drive listening to all three boys excitedly tell us about their day simultaneously.

Once we were home, Ty had gone in first to make sure Trevor's henchman was gone. Not only had Cole been freed, but there was no evidence whatsoever that he'd ever been there. Once Ty was sure the house was secure, we all went in. Ty had then whipped up some chicken oven nachos and we'd all devoured every bite in near silence. It was nice to have the usually boring logistics of daily life distract me from the big stuff for a while.

Before we knew it, it was time to get the kids bathed and in bed.

Ty and I had also discussed when and how we would talk to the boys about the drastic changes our lives had been and would soon be going through, and had agreed to take a night off from making life-changing decisions. I was so relieved we were on the same page, I'd almost cried. I just couldn't handle any more drama today.

I tucked the boys into their beds, and I was glad none of them asked where their father was. I felt like Scarlett O'Hara. I just kept thinking to myself, *Tomorrow is another day.*

Back downstairs, I got my dad settled into the guest room and he went right to bed. I was giving him the night off too, but he was in for quite a Q & A tomorrow. I returned to the living room, and Ty was watching the evening news, but turned the TV off when he saw me, grinning awkwardly. I'd forgotten we had one more decision to make before the day was over.

Where was Ty sleeping?

I knew where I *wanted* him to sleep.

I also knew I had three very impressionable young men upstairs who wouldn't understand and possibly would never forgive me for what they would see as a definite betrayal of the man they knew as their father. We had to be careful until we told them the truth, especially if Ty ended up in my bed tonight.

I sat down on the couch and closed my eyes. When I opened them, trying to convince myself I wasn't dreaming, my smile was thwarted by his shiner. His eye looked better, but still a little puffy. Our perfect evening had softened my anger about young Ty's and Trevor's unrivaled stupidity. When I really thought about it, my wisdom level twenty years ago would have been equal to that of a jar of peanut butter, so who was I to judge them so harshly?

I frowned, and he leaned forward and took my hand.

"I deserved it," he said quietly, seeming to know what I was thinking.

"No. That young guy in the video deserved it."

"I was an idiot."

I leaned toward him. "I love you."

"I *don't* deserve you."

I leapt across the couch and landed in his arms, planting my lips on his. His shock passed quickly and he began kissing me back. We somehow found our way to my bedroom after all, and quickly made sure we locked the door, allowing ourselves to forget about the goings on of the day and just exist for each other for a few hours.

It was pure, unadulterated bliss.

The sun shone bright through the bedroom window the next morning, piercing through my eyelids and forcing me to get up. I reluctantly sat up, and rubbed my legs to get the blood flowing. A sound from the bed startled me, and I stood and turned, ready to take down the intruder when I remembered I'd invited him in. I relaxed and exhaled, smiling at a still-sleeping Ty.

I could get used to this.

Suddenly, there was a knock at the bedroom door. Then a small voice said, "Mommy?"

It was Rowan.

"Yes, honey?"

Ty began to stir.

"Mommy, I can't reach the cereal."

"I'll be right there, sweetie."

I heard little footsteps pattering down the stairs.

My morning was so...normal, I'd almost forgotten that my life was damn near unrecognizable from six months ago. The suburban housewife was long gone, and I was okay with that. What concerned me was how everything that had happened was going to affect my children.

I knew I was getting way too comfortable in my warm, cozy blanket of denial as I poured Rowan a bowl of Alpha-bits, but I just wanted to stay wrapped up in the happy little bubble Ty and I had made. The thought of talking to the boys about everything made me sick to my stomach, so I pushed it down. Way down. And I poured the milk.

As if on cue, there was a knock on the back door. I was surprised to see a fully-dressed Ty smiling at me from the small porch. Blaise let him in, and I nearly let the bowl overflow as I stared at him. He walked over to me and I whispered in his direction.

"How the hell did you—?"

"Climbed down from the bedroom window," he whispered back.

My eyes widened, and a grin spread across my face that I couldn't have stopped if I'd wanted to. The Amazing Ty still had a few magic tricks up his sleeve, it would seem, and I was so glad he was all mine.

"We don't have a lot of time," he said then, mysteriously.

"What are you talking about?"

"Trevor's car just pulled up."

Crap.

I was glad I'd thrown on my running clothes before I'd come downstairs. Trevor was no longer entitled to see me in my nightie. I took a few deep breaths and put the cereal box away just as another knock sounded at the back door.

Ty and I were both in for a surprise, however, when we turned and saw an unexpected face…actually faces, through the small window.

It wasn't Trevor at all.

It was Leon and Ainsley.

Although I'd drilled it into their skulls to never open the door for a stranger, Blaise flung the door open before Ty or I could stop him. I'd have to discuss that with my middle child later. The two hesitated crossing the threshold into my kitchen, until I nodded for them to come in. I couldn't speak. I had no idea what to say. Ty walked over and closed the door behind them. Leon was smiling at me, and Ainsley was looking at Rowan, who was sitting at the breakfast counter scarfing his cereal, as though he was a rare and beautiful bird. I wondered if she'd ever been so close to a small child before.

"What can we do for you two?" Ty asked, appearing back at my side.

"We, uh, have some information for you. Trevor sent us," Leon said.

I immediately put Levi in charge of the other two, and the four adults went into the dining room. Ty sat next to me, and Leon pulled the chair on the other side of me out for Ainsley to sit. Then he sat next to her. Leon cleared his throat.

"Trevor didn't want to come himself, for...obvious reasons," he began.

"Why couldn't he just call me?" I asked.

"He's been trying all morning. Both of you. Kept getting voicemail."

Ty and I looked at each other as we remembered the events of the previous night. My phone was dead, and I'd never thought to plug it in. It was currently sitting on my bedside table upstairs, completely useless.

I squinted at Ty, who responded, "I think I left my phone in the van last night."

I turned back to Leon and shrugged.

He chuckled before continuing. "Anyway, he sent us to tell you that Lars and Talia are gone."

I couldn't breathe.

"Gone?" Ty asked for both of us.

"Yeah, we lost track of them this morning. We think they skipped town."

"But we're supposed to have dinner tomorrow night..." I blurted out, then blushed with embarrassment. Alright, so the meticulous homemaker in me wasn't completely dead. And apparently, I was still about as smart as a tub of Jif. I decided to let Ty handle the rest of the conversation.

"What do you mean, you lost track of them?" Ty asked, sensing that I needed him to take the lead.

"Well, the bugs we placed in Talia's house all suddenly malfunctioned at about 7am. Same with Lars's apartment."

"So, they're just gone," Ty stated with disbelief.

"Seems that way, but there's more we need to tell you." Lars gestured to Ainsley, and she looked up at us nervously. Her first attempt at making a sound was a failure, so she closed her mouth and swallowed hard before trying again.

"Your implants...I can't..." she started, but a voice from the doorway cut her off.

"You can't remove them," Jerry announced, and I suddenly remembered he'd said something about that right before he shot Trevor. He looked well-rested, and had showered and dressed in jeans and a long-sleeved golf shirt.

We were all quiet as he entered the room, but he didn't sit. He hovered at the foot of the table. "Tell them the truth, Ainsley. Tell them what you told me yesterday."

Ainsley swallowed again and managed to squeak out, "You didn't let me finish yesterday. I was trying to tell you I couldn't remove the implants, because—"

"You can't remove our implants?" Ty interrupted. My heart sank, and I took a deep breath and closed my eyes. For a split second, I thought to myself, *Wake up, Freya! You're dreaming!*

Ty opened his mouth to say more, but I put my hand on his arm. "Let her finish, Ty." He glanced at me and was silent, nodding at Ainsley to continue.

Ainsley looked up at Leon, who urged her on with his own head nod, and then turned back to me and Ty. "I can't remove your implants...because there isn't anything to remove."

EPISODE 49
The 24

"Nothing to remove?" I blurted out. "What are you talking about?"

Ainsley shrank back at my tone, and I took a breath and smiled at her gently. The last thing I wanted to do was keep her from talking.

"Please, Ainsley," Ty asked sweetly. "Tell us what you mean."

Leon put his arm around her, and she looked up at him. His presence seemed to give her confidence. I wondered how long that romance had been going on. I sighed quietly as I added it to the mental list of lies I'd been told.

Ainsley turned and stared at the table for a second. "The implants were installed *so* long ago…" she began but trailed off. Her choice of words gave away her lack of experience with humans, speaking as if Ty and I were machines, plus the insinuation that my man and I were old. So long ago indeed.

I cleared my throat loudly. She gave me a nervous glance, but relaxed slightly when she saw that I wasn't angry.

"…the material used wasn't meant to last this long…*decades*…"

I cleared my throat again.

Ainsley swallowed before continuing, but didn't look my way. "…I believe the actual physical implants have long ago disintegrated, with the moisture—"

Ty snickered and I gave him a stern glare. The word "moist" or any derivative thereof always made him giggle. Men.

"…the moisture inside the brain, plus the various juices—"

Snicker. Ainsley and I both shot him an annoyed glare before she continued.

"...the juices of the brain, the materials most certainly are no longer intact."

"So, what are you saying?" Ty asked, regaining his composure. "The implants are just...gone...?"

I was hopeful, waiting for her answer, but my hope soon disappeared.

"Not exactly," she replied. "The information is still there."

I took a deep breath, trying to be patient with this eccentric young woman who welcomed the nickname, "Brain." I knew she knew her stuff, but she was going to have to start expounding on her answers or my own brain was going to implode from frustration.

"Ainsley, please explain what you think *is* still in our heads," I asked nicely.

"The digital information is still there, stored in your subconscious somewhere...most likely the long-term memory, since it was so long—"

I cleared my throat a third time, and raised my eyebrows as high as they would go.

"I didn't mean that...I..." she stammered.

I reached across and touched her hand. She jerked but didn't pull away.

"It's alright," I said softly, chuckling. "I'm just teasing you."

She smiled at me and mumbled, "You're amazing."

"What?" I asked, unsure of what I'd heard. I certainly didn't feel amazing.

"In the past few weeks, you've discovered your husband isn't who you thought he was, and that he put a computer chip in your brain to turn you into the Terminator...and you still have a sense of humor...I just think that's...amazing."

Wow. That was a long sentence for her.

I patted her hand. "Well, if I didn't, I would have stepped in front of a bus by now."

She smiled at me, showing her perfectly symmetrical teeth. She really was lovely. I considered bringing up the fact that she had known who I really was for a year, but I just couldn't put that on her. She had been a pawn in the game...just like I had.

"Seriously, though," I added. "Lay off the 'so long ago' and the 'decades' stuff, or I'll

run you over with my walker."

She stared at me for a second, and I got the feeling she was wishing people were as easy to read as computers. I let her off the hook, before she popped a blood vessel or something, and broke into a giggle. She sighed with relief and gave me an awkward smile.

"So, if the information is still there, coursing through our brains, there's no way to remove it," Ty thought aloud.

"That's right," Ainsley confirmed.

My dad, who'd been standing like a statue at the foot of the table all this time, finally chimed in. "What's going to happen to them?" he demanded of Ainsley.

"Um…happen to them?"

"If you can't get the information out of their heads, what's going to happen to them?"

"Dad…" I frowned at his tone, but he ignored me.

Ainsley was flustered. "I…don't know."

"Can you take an educated guess?" Ty urged. After all, if Brain said we were going to be okay, we would believe her.

"In my opinion," she started carefully, directing her response at me. "You should be just fine." Ty exhaled loudly, as if he'd been holding his breath. Ainsley continued. "Your brains have done a pretty good job of integrating the external information all these year—" she stopped herself, glancing up at me. I smiled coyly. "…so far," she finished instead.

"Well, I don't know if I agree with that," I argued. "What about the flashbacks, and the…eye…thing?" I asked, gesturing to my face like I was having a seizure.

"The flashbacks are actually why I believe the implants have been absorbed by your body. I think they're a positive sign that you're going to be just fine. And the ocular reaction is simply the result of adrenaline and other hormones—"

"What do you mean?" Ty asked.

I could tell dumbing all this down was taking a lot of brain power. Ainsley sighed. "Your brains are letting the information through to your conscious minds, which means whatever safeguards were put in the implants to prevent that are gone. It may take a while yet for the integration to solidify, but...I'd say it's happening, and it should happen without you really noticing." She was so convincing, I instantly felt better.

"So, are we going to be able to remember everything from the year that was erased?" Ty asked.

Ainsley thought about this for a moment. "There's just no way to know for sure. It's very difficult to completely erase something from a virtually healthy brain. It's like hitting the delete key on a computer. The information is almost always still in there... somewhere."

"I just want to hear that the...*information* isn't going to hurt them," my dad said, eyeing sweet Ainsley as if she was a weather forecaster and he was blaming her for the weather.

Leon, who'd been so quiet, we'd all nearly forgotten he was there, suddenly joined the conversation. "I think what Ainsley is saying, Jerry," he started, saying it with such authority, it didn't sound like Leon at all, "is that it's a bit like asking if they'll get hit by a bus tomorrow. Nothing but a crystal ball could give us the answer."

We were all quiet, staring at Leon.

"Who *are* you?" Ty broke the silence after a few seconds.

Leon grinned. "Man, I'm really sorry about all the deception."

"Thanks, Leon, or whoever you are. That makes it all okay." Sarcasm was an understatement.

"My name *is* Leon...well, my middle name anyway. I'm just a worker bee, like you, Rip. Got paired up with your boy Trevor about ten years ago for a fun little vacation to Russia."

"Russia? Trevor was in Russia ten years ago?" I asked. Leon opened his mouth, but I stopped him. "Never mind. I don't want to know." I ran my fingers through my hair and looked at Ty with frustration. He put his hand on my back reassuringly.

"So, what's your deal, Leon? You bureau?" Ty asked, gently massaging my back.

"Nah, man, nobody holds my leash. I'm my own dog. Worked NCIS after I graduated from Stanford." My eyes tried to leap out of my skull. "Got out when I realized I could keep doing what I was doing for a lot more money, if I didn't mind the dangerous stuff... which I didn't...until now." He gave Ainsley a shy look, and she caught it, blushing.

"What did you go to Stanford for?" I had to know. This guy was a true enigma.

"Criminal Justice and Psychology."

"Did Trevor say anything about Talia and Lars?" The question had been weighing on me ever since Leon and Ainsley had shown up at my door.

"We don't know where they went," Leon replied, repeating what he'd already told us earlier. "But it looks like they weren't working for Dunwaddle, or at least, if they were, it was all a ruse. We traced an encrypted email we were able to intercept on its way to Talia, and Trevor believes it originated from The 24."

We all stared at Leon, waiting for him to explain what the hell "The 24" was, but it appeared he thought we knew. Alright, I'll take the bullet, I thought.

"What's 'The 24'?"

If it wasn't bad enough that he'd gone to Stanford, he made us feel like chimps compared to him just by his expression.

"You're kidding, right?" He looked with disbelief from Ty to me.

"There's no such thing. It's a myth." So, Dad had heard of it.

Leon looked up at Jerry, who was still standing. "No, sir, it's real."

"Bullshit," Jerry said, but with waning conviction.

"What is it?" Ty asked, getting frustrated.

Ainsley answered. "It's a Top Secret group of Senators. Twenty-four of them, to be exact. When you're asked to be one of 'The 24' you don't refuse, and you are one for life. And if anyone finds out you are one, well...let's just say, they clean up their messes."

"What's the purpose of the group?" I asked, thinking it sounded a little too fantastic to be true myself.

"Rumor has it they are the true driving force for any and all new policy, from how much money goes into the Welfare and Social Security Systems, to who sits in the other senate seats..." Leon paused here for effect, "...to who gets elected President."

Jerry scoffed, and decided to finally sit at the foot of the table, folding his arms across his chest like a petulant child. He definitely wasn't buying any of it.

"Is Dunwaddle one of The 24?" I asked, going along...for the moment.

"Trevor isn't sure, but Ainsley..." Leon nudged her shoulder gently, urging her to take over.

"I've seen things," Ainsley whispered. "I've seen the list...and Dunwaddle isn't on it."

"And you haven't told Trevor about this?" Ty asked, confused.

"He hasn't asked me." Ainsley shrugged.

"So, what are we saying here?" I was trying to sort it all out. "Is Dunwaddle on some hit list for The 24? I mean, I know *I* want him dead, and I barely know him, so I can't imagine they like the guy... or are they courting him? If they wanted him in their elite group, they would've asked him years ago. He's in his 80's, right?" No one responded, so I continued. "Maybe they hired Talia to get herself hired by Dunwaddle, and then hired by Jerry..." I motioned to my dad, who was crinkling his eyebrows at me. "But why? Just to keep tabs on us?"

"There are only two things The 24 is ravenous for," Leon said, speaking as though he'd been waiting a hundred years to show his true, smart self to the world. "Power and Information. And you can't have one without the other. They want to know everything, and we can only assume they knew about RVW, and the nefarious dealings Dunwaddle was involved in."

Ravenous? Nefarious dealings? I smiled.

"Yeah, but isn't that par for the course? A crooked politician?" Ty asked.

"Only if it's sanctioned by The 24."

Enough with the big words, I thought. I was starting to crave bananas.

"So, The 24 is after us?" I voiced.

"If The 24 wanted you dead," Ainsley quietly replied, "you would be."

"Then what?"

"This is ridiculous!" Jerry pounded his fist on the table. "The 24 is a fairy tale!"

"Dad, you do not—"

Leon touched my arm. "It's all right. We'll go." He stood and pulled Ainsley's chair out for her, and she stood too. He gently guided her with a hand on her back to the kitchen. Ty and I followed, and at the backdoor, Leon turned to us.

"We'll keep in touch. As soon as we know anything else, we'll call...uh, charge your phones." He grinned at us.

We both nodded, and I closed the door behind them. I walked back into the dining room, but my dad wasn't there. I sighed and rolled my eyes. Then I felt Ty's arms wrap around me, and I melted into them. I turned and buried my face in his chest.

"I'm so happy you're the father of my children," I said after I came up for air. He squeezed me tighter and, after all the confusion and added conspiracy, I couldn't think of anywhere I'd rather be.

"Mom?"

I turned and my eyes met Levi's.

Shit.

EPISODE **50**
My Nightmare Comes True

"Mom?"

I went to Levi, but he backed away.

"Mom, what's going on?"

"Honey, I—"

"You and Uncle Rip have something in your brains?"

I was stunned for a second. That was not the question I expected.

"Oh. Um. You don't...uh..." I didn't know how to respond, and I gestured awkwardly back to Ty, trying to form a coherent thought.

"Don't you want to know why your mom and I were hugging?" Ty blurted out. I gave him a surprised look of exasperation. He shrugged and forced a weak half-smile.

I turned back to my son. "Levi, we've been meaning to talk to you about...well, a lot of things, but—"

"Mom, it's okay. I already know you and Uncle Rip are boyfriend/girlfriend." He rolled his eyes, saying it like it was a small matter he wanted to get out of the way before we got to the real controversial topic of the implants.

"I'm sorry, honey." I stepped toward him and he let me touch his arm. "Were we that obvious?" My teenage boy was much more perceptive than I gave him credit for.

"Well, yeah, but I already knew. Dad told me years ago."

I snapped my head to meet Ty's eyes, and we both froze. Once I could feel the blood pumping through my body again, I took a deep breath. "What do you mean Dad told you years ago?"

"It was a long time ago, Mom...can you answer my question? About the things in your brains?"

332 - JUST KILL ME

"No," I said firmly. "Not until you answer me."

He rolled his eyes again before reluctantly responding, something I was starting to realize teenage boys did to their parents a lot.

"He said that you and Uncle Rip are supposed to be together… and that he was just taking care of us until you remembered."

"That son-of-a-bi—"

I shot Ty a look of daggers and he stopped just in time. "What else did he tell you?" I asked, looking back to Levi again.

"I don't know…nothing."

"He said that once, years ago, and you remember it?" He couldn't remember to close the door when he was in the bathroom "reading," but this he retained.

"Nah, he used to say it almost every night. When he was home, anyway…whenever he would tuck me in."

"Why would he tell you that?" I asked him, and then a thought occurred to me. "Did he tell your brothers?"

"I don't think so. He said it was my job as the oldest to help them understand it someday." He really was taking this all in stride.

"Why are you not freaking out about this?" I demanded, trying not to freak out myself.

"I told you, I've known for years. Since Dad seemed okay with it, I guess it just…made sense." He took a deep breath and cleared his throat loudly. "Now, back to *my* question…"

"Yeah, yeah, brain implants, yes, we've got 'em, now why did you never mention this?!"

"It never came up—YOU HAVE BRAIN IMPLANTS!?"

I shushed him and made him sit down at the foot of the dining room table. I sat down in the adjacent chair, and Ty came to stand behind me. I leaned toward Levi and said in a hushed tone, "I don't think your brothers need to know about that… not until they're older anyway…much older." I closed my eyes and breathed in deep, then exhaled, opening them again when I realized something. "Where are your brothers, anyway? You're supposed to be watching them."

"They're fine. I put in a movie."

Ty walked around me to the doorway and peeked around the corner. He turned back and nodded, signaling that the two youngest were in fact watching a movie in the living room.

"What kind of brain implants?" Levi asked excitedly, but quietly.

"Seriously?" I was still in shock. "You've known that Ty and I were going to end up together for years, and the implants never came up?"

"Mom, you need to move past that. And tell me about the implants." He said it so calmly and matter-of-fact, he sounded like an adult. I craned my neck to give Ty a puzzled look, and got a chuckle and a shrug in response. I shook my head back and forth, looking down at the floor for some clarity.

Ty sat next to me, and sighed. "Levi," he began, "your mom and I volunteered for a government project twenty years ago. They put computer chips in our heads to make us into…well, killers… assassins, like in your video games."

Levi was silent, frozen for a few seconds. Then his face broke into a huge smile. "COOL!" he burst out.

Ty and I both shushed him at once, and I stood to check the status in the living room, but the other two were enthralled in *Howl's Moving Castle*. I sat back down and looked at Levi intently.

"All you need to know is that we're not assassins…anymore. And that we're fine. We just want our lives to go back to normal…" I trailed off.

"You mean like before you became an agent?"

That surprised me. I had avoided thinking about whether I was going to stay with the FBI or not after this mess was all over. In fact, I'd begun to think the mess would never be over. I was currently on administrative leave in light of everything that had happened, and Pixley was waiting to file anything until…until we could figure out what the hell to do about Dunwaddle.

My mind was the poster child for adult ADD, tuned to about a hundred different channels, and changing at random. I tried to focus.

"Would you like that? To go back to when I was home with you guys?"

"I don't know. You were different back then. You seemed happier when you started training. Like you were finally a real person."

"What do you mean a 'real person'? I was a real person when I was just your mom."

"I know, I know. I just mean that before, you were my mom, and you were awesome, but maybe becoming an agent…completed you or something. I don't know. That sounds stupid, but—"

"That doesn't sound stupid at all," Ty replied. "I think your mom knows exactly what you mean." Ty put his arm around me, and I smiled at him.

"Okay, if you two are gonna get mushy, I'm leaving." Levi was rolling his eyes again.

I turned back to my teenager and gave him a gentle smack on the arm. "Don't worry. We'll try to refrain from being mushy in front of you." Levi gave an exaggerated sigh of relief. "And you're really okay with…us?" I gestured to Ty and myself.

"Yeah," Levi said. "You and dad together…it was kinda weird, you know?"

"Yeah," I sighed. "I know."

As Levi trotted out to the living room to join his brothers, he turned suddenly in the doorway. "You want me to talk to the kids about all this?"

I did my best not to snort, but…

"Not yet, big man. We'll let you know," Ty said, very seriously.

Levi nodded and resumed his course to the couch.

I made it to my bedroom before I let myself have a laugh. My oldest son was handling it all so well. It was just what I needed to keep me going. A little bit of something good. I walked around the bed to my nightstand and plugged my phone in to charge. Immediately, I saw four missed calls from Trevor from earlier.

Oops.

Ty had gone out to the van to retrieve his phone, and within minutes, he joined me in the bedroom. I kissed him passionately, and then headed for the shower to get ready for the day. If the past weeks had been any indication, I probably wanted to be dressed for whatever today would bring.

I had no idea how right I was.

After Ty showered, we headed downstairs to spend some time with the boys, who were just finishing up their movie. When everyone was dressed and fed, we decided to go out to the backyard. I set out cleaning up the neglected landscaping while Ty played some catch with the boys. I heard my phone ring from the bedroom window a few minutes later, but chose to ignore it. Then it rang again. I ignored it again. Not two minutes later, it rang a third time. I told Ty I'd be right back, and ran inside and up the stairs to answer the damn thing. It had better be Trevor with some good news.

I took the stairs two at a time, and navigated around my bed to the nightstand. I picked up the phone, and hit the answer key.

The next thing I knew, I was standing in the backyard again, staring at Ty and the boys throwing the baseball around.

What the hell...

"Who was on the phone, babe?" Ty had run awkwardly over to me, with Rowan wrapped around one of his legs, giggling. If I had been in my right mind, I might have given Ty a tense look at him calling me "babe" in front of the boys, but I was most definitely not in my right mind. I had no idea who'd been on the phone.

And I had no idea how I'd gotten back outside.

"I don't know."

Ty reached for my hand, and I didn't understand what he was doing until I realized I was clutching the phone. He took it from me, and looked at the screen.

"It says the last call was from 'Unknown'," he said, doing a poor job of pretending not to be concerned. Then Ty hit the 'Call' button to dial the number back. He waited with the phone at his ear for a few moments, but then shook his head. No one had picked up.

"Are you okay, Mommy?" Blaise had come over to join the party, and he *did* look concerned. I had to make him feel better. Ty and I would figure out what had just happened to me later, when we could be alone.

I took a deep breath. "I'm fine, baby." I ran my fingers through his thick red hair, and he smiled.

Ty looked at me, and although I was afraid, I relished in the worried, protective look he was giving me. For the most part, I was a strong, independent woman, but sometimes, I loved knowing I had a strong man to take care of me when I needed it.

Blaise ran back to Levi, and Rowan unwrapped himself from Ty's leg to join them. They were getting out the horseshoes to play a tournament.

"Are you okay?" Ty was close to me now, and I could see he was waiting for me to lie and say yes. So I decided to be honest.

"No."

He put his hand on my elbow. "What happened?"

"I ran up to answer the phone. Then, I was back here. I don't remember anything in between."

Ty thought for a moment. I could tell he had nothing, but he wasn't about to say it aloud.

"It's okay. It's probably just the implant screwing with your head. Or I guess, the information, since the implants are most likely gone, according to Brain." He forced a smile. "Let's enjoy the day, and we'll talk about it after the boys are in bed, okay?"

I was good with that. I felt just fine. As a matter of fact, I felt great.

The rest of the day went without a hiccup. Blaise had won the horseshoe tournament and got to pick what we had for supper. No one complained when he chose burgers on the grill. That evening, after putting the boys to bed, we quickly realized there was really nothing to talk about. Neither of us had an explanation except for the usual strategy of blaming the implant. It was all we could come up with. And it made sense. I tried to let it go.

We kissed and said goodnight, after Ty made me promise to wake him if I had any other strange memory lapses. As I rolled over, I knew I wouldn't be able to sleep. I watched the clock on the nightstand click slowly from 10:32pm to midnight…to 1am…to 2am…at 2:15, my phone quietly vibrated. I glanced down and saw a voicemail notification.

I picked up the phone and played the voicemail, slowly bringing the phone to my ear. I closed my eyes and heard a strangely familiar voice…

I opened my eyes, and I wasn't in bed anymore. In fact, I wasn't in my bedroom anymore. I looked around frantically, taking in the tiny, bland, empty apartment I was standing in.

I was alone. I took a few deep breaths and tried to clear my mind.

Something felt heavy in my arms. I looked down and saw a large assault rifle. Instinctively, I knew it was an AK-74. The question of how I knew that dissolved as quickly it had formed.

An alarm sounded, and I raised my hand. I was wearing a large watch and the timer was going off. I silenced it, and walked to the window in front of me. It was eleven in the morning, and my target was almost in position.

I placed the rifle on the stand already set up in front of the window, and checked the sight on my weapon. Sixty seconds, and my mission would be complete. I carefully placed my finger to rest on the trigger and waited.

EPISODE 51
Just Kill...Dunwaddle

There he is. The fat bastard.

I peered through the sight and hugged the trigger. Just then, someone tackled me to the ground. Someone big. The gun fell to the floor. I pushed up with my legs and sprang to a standing position, taking mental note of how agile I still was, even after all these years. The sight of my attacker now standing across from me wiped the cocky smile off my face.

It was Lars.

"What the hell are you doing here?" I demanded.

"Stopping you from making a huge mistake." Either Lars had learned to throw his voice, and make it sound female, and American, or there was a third person in the room.

Talia stepped out of the shadows of the apartment's narrow hallway.

"What's going on? Why are you preventing me from completing my mission?" I asked.

"Freya, this isn't your mission," Talia said, and there was a hint of pity in her voice, like she was talking to a crazy person. Like I was crazy. That infuriated me.

"What are you talking about? I got the call."

"I know," she replied. "But that was a mistake." Talia sighed deeply, as if this whole ordeal was exhausting for her, and began to close the distance between us. I bent down and picked up my rifle.

"Freya, I'm your friend." She stopped walking and held up her hand in entreaty.

I kept the rifle pointed at the floor. "Friend," I repeated in a whisper. "You lied to me. Our entire friendship was fake. And then you disappeared…with your…husband…?" My anger faded as I started to remember who I really was. My eyes gravitated to Talia's stomach, still flat and tight, but I knew it wouldn't be for long.

It was so surreal. When I'd opened my eyes in the apartment a moment before, I *knew* I was a forty-year-old mother of three boys from suburbia, and I *knew* that mere hours before, I'd been with my boys, and Tyler Ripley…the love of my life. But until I had started talking to Lars and Talia, I hadn't actually *remembered* any of it.

Now it was all flooding back, and I was suddenly dizzy. I backed up until I felt the wall supporting me, and lowered my head.

"Freya!" Talia ran to me. I handed her the weapon, and she hesitated a second before taking it and setting it on the floor. She looked at Lars. "Get her some water."

Lars hopped to his woman's request, and returned quickly with a cold bottle of H2O. He opened it and gave it to Talia, who made me drink half the contents before letting me speak.

"Talia," I squeaked. "I don't know how I got here."

"Yeah, well I do. Red-eye out of LaGuardia."

"How did you know I was here?"

"I put a trace in your purse."

I looked around the empty living room space, but saw no bright yellow handbag.

"Don't worry, it's in the kitchen. You must have set it there when you got here."

"But…why the purse?"

"Are you kidding?" Talia said, genuinely shocked that I had to ask. "Ever since you bought that damn thing, you haven't gone anywhere without it…except the day Pixley had you kidnapped, of course, but… short of injecting a tracking device into your body, which would have been difficult to do without you noticing, I knew the purse was my best bet. Thank God your alter ego loves it as much as you do."

Realization of what I had been about to do was still dawning. I looked into Talia's eyes, my own conveying shock and horror. "I was going to kill Dunwaddle!"

"Yes, you were."

"Why didn't you let me?!"

"Excuse me?" She wasn't as shocked as I was at my response. The common sense part of my brain was clearly not in control, but I didn't fight it.

"All our problems would have been solved if that jackass...urg! I had him in my sight! Just one second later, and he'd be dead! Why did you stop me?!"

"Freya, you're not thinking clearly. You have a family. I couldn't let you go down for the murder of a senator."

I couldn't sort out all the information zooming around in my head. I thrashed free of Talia's grasp. "Let me go!" I yelled. I tried to stand upright, but my ass had other ideas. It hit the ratty carpeted floor with a thud, and I let my head fall back hitting the wall. My breathing was erratic, and my vision blurry. I closed my eyes and tried to slow my heart rate. I heard Talia talking to Lars, but their voices were faint and their words jumbled. Then I saw Talia's face hovering over me. She was smiling, but worried.

"Come on, Frey. Let's get you home."

"But...Dunwaddle...he's going to kill us...Ty..."

"Shhh...it's alright. Lars and I took care of that. Ty and the boys are fine. Don't worry..." Her words faded as I lost consciousness.

◦ ◦ ◦

I woke up on a military transport, strapped into a jumpseat next to Talia. When she saw I was awake, she smiled and winked at me, patting my leg reassuringly.

I remembered what had happened at the abandoned apartment, but I felt more like myself now. My whole body ached, so I stretched every muscle I could while remaining in my seat, and tried to deal with the fact that my brain was a mess. I thought about what Ainsley had said. The information from the implant was definitely mixing with the rest of my thought processes, and it was proving to be a challenge, to say the least. I couldn't very well hop on a 2am flight and try to assassinate a government official whenever I felt the whim.

But it hadn't been just a whim...

I turned to Talia. "WHO ACTIVATED ME?!" The sound of the aircraft made it necessary to shout. I tried to forget about the fact that a stranger had somehow turned me into a killer with a simple phone call. I would have been able to distract myself with the novelty of being on a C-130 for the first time, but now that my lost memories were returning, I knew I'd done this before, several times. It was all so familiar, right down to the thick canvas of the harness.

"SOMEONE WORKING FOR DUNWADDLE! DON'T WORRY ABOUT ALL THAT! LARS IS HANDLING IT AS WE SPEAK!" Talia replied.

"BUT ONLY TREVOR'S VOICE CAN ACTIVATE THE IMPLANT!"

"WE THINK HE HAD AN OLD RECORDING OF TREVOR! IT'S NOT IMPORTANT NOW! IT'S OVER!"

"SHOULDN'T WE HELP LARS?!"

"NO!" she replied, gently touching her belly, where a new little life now grew. "DON'T WORRY! HE HAS HELP!" She patted my thigh again.

I'd almost forgotten. Talia was pregnant. I smiled, and thanked God she was still my friend. I needed other women in my life. Something I'd come to realize being an agent and being surrounded predominantly by ego-maniacal men—and a soon to be ex-husband, new boyfriend, and three little boys. I took a deep breath as the plane lurched forward, turning onto the runway, I assumed.

Talia pulled a magazine out of her travel bag at her feet and opened it, pretending to be very interested in its contents.

"WHO'S HELPING HIM?!"

She raised her eyebrows but didn't look away from the article she was pretending to read about Brad Pitt and Angelina Jolie, as if I believed for a second that she hadn't heard my question.

I grabbed her arm, and when she gave me an annoyed look, I returned it with my best pleading eyes.

Talia let out a breath like a horse after a good whinny, and mouthed, "Trevor."

"Trevor," I repeated, not loud enough for anyone but me to hear. Of course, Trevor. Why should that surprise me? Why should *anything* surprise me anymore?

"SO, YOU DON'T WORK FOR DUNWADDLE?" I chanced. The direct approach was always my favorite interrogation style.

She turned away from the magazine and looked directly into my eyes. "DUNWADDLE THINKS WE DO!" she replied with conviction.

I believed her. "TREVOR THOUGHT THAT—"

"I KNOW! HE CAUGHT UP WITH US LAST NIGHT, AND WE HAD TO TELL HIM EVERYTHING! THEN WE CAME UP WITH THE PLAN!"

"PLAN TO DO WHAT?!" I yelled.

Talia closed the magazine in her lap abruptly, and turned to me as if I were a disruptive child. "REALLY?!" she yelled above the engine. "YOU WANT TO HAVE THIS CONVERSATION HERE?! CAN WE GET HOME FIRST?!"

"TELL ME!"

She hesitated.

"YOU KNOW, I REMEMBER EVERYTHING NOW!" I shouted, which was sort of true. "INCLUDING HOW TO INCAPACITATE AN ENEMY IN A PUBLIC PLACE IN THREE SECONDS WITHOUT ANYONE NOTICING!"

She shot me a questioning look, and I quoted Po from *Kung Fu Panda*, making the hand gesture while I said, "SKIDOOSH!" I gave her my crazy eyes, and she smiled.

Disney sometimes had its moments, but Jack Black was always a genius.

Talia squinted at me and yelled back, "I'M NOT YOUR ENEMY!"

I cocked my head, crinkling my forehead at her. A moment later, she rolled her eyes.

I won.

"FINE! I'LL TELL YOU, BUT IF WE'RE COMPROMISED, I'M BLAMING YOU!"

I looked around the cargo bay, and it was empty besides the two of us. I nodded my assent.

We put our heads together, and Talia began in as hushed a tone as possible. "Lars has a contact on Dunwaddle's staff, but we hadn't heard from him in months, until two days ago, when he called with some very interesting information. Dunwaddle is dying. Fast. He hadn't told anyone, but he suddenly started doing strange things, like liquidating all his assets, stocks, life insurance, everything."

"Why on earth would he cash in his life insurance if he's dying?" I asked.

"Because he doesn't want anyone else to get his money. He's got this crazy idea that he can live forever. He's heavily invested in some mysterious cryogenics project that claims, on paper, to be conducting research on how to freeze and store organic food to make it last longer without losing any nutritional value."

I furrowed my brows. "But really…?"

"But really," she picked up, "there's a rumor that their real research is in human cryogenics." She stopped for effect, watching my jaw drop with satisfaction.

"He wants to freeze himself?"

Talia nodded. "And now that the end is coming soon for him, he needs a lot of money to set up his luxury cryo-pad, and apparently paying rent upfront for eternity is expensive," she joked.

"And this contact, he's reliable?" I asked.

"Very. He handles all the big guy's finances, and Dunwaddle told him to transfer all his personal assets, which for him means his money, his taxpayers money, his illegal immigrant housekeeper's savings, you name it, right to this cryogenics company."

"He really thinks he can be frozen and just woken up sometime in the future?"

"Sure! Plus, it's been on the cover of the *Star* like seven times. They're rarely wrong, you know."

True.

"So, what are Lars and Trevor doing?" I asked, still trying to get the answer to that question.

Just then, the pilot came over the intercom to tell us we were about to take off. Talia and I both instinctively knew to tighten our harnesses and lay our heads back against the wall. Once we were airborne and had leveled off, Talia leaned toward me again.

"Trevor's going to tell Dunwaddle where you and Rip are, and then he—"

"WHAT!?!"

"Don't worry," she assured me. "Lars is number one on the good senator's assassin list."

I was quiet for a minute. I stared at Talia, but she didn't elaborate or continue. It had never been this hard to get details out of her when she'd gone on a date with a new guy. Of course, those stories were probably all made up, I realized. I thought if I talked it out aloud, that might help. I was starving and needed a shower, and those two things always made it hard for me to think.

"So, Trevor gives me and Ty up…and then Dunwaddle orders a hit on us…but he doesn't do it himself, because the real bad guys never get their hands dirty, so his lackey makes the call, and…we hope he calls Lars…"

"He will." Talia was so confident, but it didn't calm my nerves. I needed to keep talking through it.

"Then Lars reports back that the job is done, but really, we're not dead…we hope."

"You won't be." That confidence again. I wanted to be as sure as she was, but it wasn't *her* life that was in danger. I was convinced she wasn't telling me everything. Then it hit me.

"What about Trevor?"

She opened her magazine again before answering. "What *about* Trevor?"

"Dunwaddle's not going to just let him waltz out of his office, free and clear…is he?"

Talia shrugged, pretending to be enthralled by the pictures of Brad and Angie in a small village in Africa.

"Tal?"

She closed the magazine again, and looked at me, and the confidence was gone. "I don't know." When I responded by staring at the floor, my mouth agape, she put her hand on my shoulder. "Frey, he knew the risks. He wanted to do this. For you. For both of you."

I was quiet the rest of the flight, glad for the engine noise to give me an excuse for it, although I knew Talia could see my wheels turning. Try as I might, however, I couldn't think of any way to help Trevor. I couldn't put Talia in harm's way even if I wanted to, for fear of giant Lars seeking revenge on me, plus…*I didn't want to.* She had her secrets, just like we all did. She was my friend, and I knew I could trust her. You just have to do everything you can to keep those few and far between kind of people in your life for as long as possible.

We landed at a private airfield, I would discover later, just north of LaGuardia proper, and one of the crew came back to help us remove the harnesses, though we didn't need it. He was barely old enough to be an adult, and it made me think of Levi.

"Alright, agents, the transportation you requested to get you to your destination is parked right outside. Thank you for flying Air America. Don't tell your friends about us."

He smiled and helped us step down and out of the aircraft before disappearing to do his real job, whatever that may be. We walked around the front of the plane, and on the other side was parked a shiny, classic-model, black Impala. I scanned the area for any other modes of transportation, wondering where our vehicle was, when I saw Talia climb in the driver's side of the old muscle car.

I walked over to the passenger side, and got in, grinning from ear to ear. "So, I'm Sam, and you're Dean?"

She grinned back. "Well, you *are* taller than me, and much more mysterious."

"And you are the cute one with the surly attitude," I replied.

She winked at me. "Not true. You're much cuter than me." She reached under her seat and pulled out the keys. Giggling, she started the old girl up, and we were on our way.

"How in the world did you secure military transport, plus this gem?"

"Well, believe it or not, this baby belongs to Lars. Best thing he ever bought. As for the flyboys and their bus, well…I know some people…" she said, maneuvering us out of the airfield and onto the highway.

"Right." I just looked at her, willing her thoughts to enter my brain, until I remembered I wasn't psychic.

She gave me a sideways glance, and then seemed to decide something.

"Favors are easy to come by when you work for The 24."

EPISODE 52
Trevor the Hero

The 24 exists.

Talia and Lars had been working for them since the beginning. She had lied to me again, but I suppose, if I thought about things rationally, it would have been dangerous for me to know. Dangerous for everyone. It sounded so cliché when she'd first said it, that she didn't tell me to keep us all safe, but I believed her.

The best news yet, though, had been Dunwaddle boarding the bullet train to Purgatory. I had a pang of remorse, not for him, but for the fact that I couldn't muster any compassion for him at all. Then the pang was gone.

Talia and I arrived home in the Impala, and I received a very warm homecoming from the boys and Ty, after he managed to stop drooling over the car. I had a feeling Lars was going to be his new BFF.

Even my dad wandered out of his room to make sure I was alright.

As soon as I had a minute alone (and by alone, I mean me and Ty, since he refused to let me out of his sight after what happened last night), I tried to call Trevor. He didn't answer, so I left a vague, but urgent voicemail to call me immediately. Ty tried to reassure me that Trevor could take care of himself, and I pretended that his words made me feel a little better. Talia said Lars was ready to pull Trevor out if it got hairy, even at the expense of blowing his cover, but I couldn't relax. Not until I knew he was safe. And I could tell Ty was worried too.

Talia feigned confidence that everything would go to plan, but when she offered to go pick up Thai food for supper, I knew she was stressing. She always ate Thai food when she was nervous.

Ty allowed me *some* space, and let me tell him everything that had transpired at my own pace, and when little ears weren't listening. I couldn't tell if he was agitated because he had been so worried about me, or if he was getting intensely aroused from the thought of his woman wielding an AK-74. I decided either one was okay with me.

The fact that my episode had been instigated by an outside force, the bastard who thought it was a good idea to activate me with an old recording of Trevor saying the magic words, was slightly comforting. At least it wasn't just a short circuit.

Once the boys were tucked safely in their beds, we had a chance to sit down and talk to Talia, all of us attempting to take our minds off the lack of communication from Lars and Trevor. Our phones were lined up on the coffee table, charged and ready to receive a call or text. My dad insisted on waiting up with us but had already begun to snore in the recliner. We didn't wake him.

"So, why would one of Dunwaddle's men program me to kill his own boss?" I asked Talia as I leaned into Ty sitting next to me on the couch. Talia was on the floor, lying back against Rowan's bean bag chair and gently rubbing her tummy. She smiled as she shared her thoughts.

"We're still trying to figure that out," she started. "There are three possibilities, as I see it. Either the minion was an idiot..."

Shaky.

"...or he wanted Dunwaddle dead, and totally got the meaning of the term 'poetic justice' when he picked you to do his dirty work..."

More likely...and much more satisfying.

"...*or*," she emphasized, "...Dunwaddle ordered you activated to get you out in the open, and your brain came up with the target based on who you wanted to see dead..." she trailed off, thinking about the choices she'd just listed. "Okay, so there may be more than three options, because the third one sounded good in my head, but it doesn't explain how you knew where Dunwaddle would be this morning..." She sank deeper into the bean bag chair, thinking hard.

"Well, wait a minute," Ty said. "It was on the news last night, remember?" he turned to me.

"What was? Dunwaddle?"

"Not specifically the D-bag, no, but it was something about a high power breakfast meeting in New York City...a lot of senators in attendance. They were discussing something to do with the military budget, so I assume Dunwaddle was part of it."

I crinkled my brow, trying to remember. Nothing came to me, but I joked, "So, I could have had my pick of senators?"

Ty gave me that spine-tingling crooked smile and winked at me.

"Bummer," Talia sighed, and then laughed, looking up at Ty and me. "It would be awesome, though, wouldn't it?"

"What?" I asked.

"If Dunwaddle had you activated, thinking it would expose you when you tried, or God forbid, succeeded in killing someone and that someone ended up being him. Talk about poetic justice." She laughed again, rubbing her tummy some more. "I wonder if he could still be frozen with a bullet in his head...?" she mused, mostly to herself, as she reclined on the bean bag.

I snuggled into Ty, and he wrapped his arm around me, squeezing me tight. "So," he said, barely above a whisper. "Talia told me you were pretty upset that you didn't get to pull the trigger."

I looked back at him, mouth open to dispute his comment, but then just shrugged. "I don't really remember specifics. Just that I was really, really amped up, like I'd had three Monsters or something."

"Do you remember the initial phone call? If it was Trevor's voice?" Ty asked.

I closed my eyes and focused on that memory.

I ran up the stairs, rounded my bed to the nightstand, picked up the phone, sliding my finger across the touch screen to answer the call, and put the phone to my ear.

In real time, I raised my empty hand to my ear, trying to wake up my muscle memory.

Trevor's voice vibrated through the phone, but it sounded far away, like he was on a low-quality speaker phone. "Activate Freya 1, 2, 3, 4, 5...mission assigned...Operation Primary Threat...Senator Thurgood Dunwaddle...5, 4, 3, 2, 1."

I had said Trevor's words aloud, and Ty and Talia were both staring at me when I opened my eyes. I still had my hand to my ear, so I lowered it.

Ty leaned forward to make direct eye contact with me. "Trevor?" I nodded.

"So, that explains it. That was easy," Talia sighed, and laid her head back, closing her eyes. "Lars will be relieved…one less piece to the puzzle…"

"Were you—or we—sent to kill Dunwaddle back then?" Ty asked, confused.

"I don't know, babe. I don't remember," I replied.

"We must have if there was a recording of Trevor saying Dunwaddle's name…"

"Maybe it was the last order Trevor gave us. Before he was ordered to shut down the program…and us."

"But why—" he started, but I cut him off.

"Honey, clearly there was a recording, so he must have given us the mission."

Talia opened her eyes and sat up. "Well, then why is Dunwaddle still breathing? If you were given the order to kill him twenty years ago…"

Before either of us could respond, Ty's phone rang. We all jumped, and my throat seized as I tried to swallow. Ty grabbed the Android and answered.

"Trev?"

He let out a breath and patted me on the leg. It was Trevor. He was safe.

Just then, Talia's phone rang and she scrambled to answer. I focused on Ty's exchange with Trevor, assuming Lars was calling to tell Talia they were both okay and hopefully on their way home. Unfortunately, the half-conversation I was privy to from Ty consisted mainly of alternating "Yeah" and "Okay" several times. Ty hung up and turned to me. My assumptions had put a smile on my face, but Ty's expression immediately wiped it clean. He was worried.

No, he was scared.

"What?" I asked sharply.

He struggled a moment, then spit it out. "Their plan worked beautifully. They're about an hour away, but…"

"But…?" I urged him to continue.

"But…whoever Dunwaddle's goon called to make us disappear…"

Oh shit. "It wasn't Lars." I finished the sentence for him, calmly and evenly, though inside, I was having a meltdown.

He shook his head ever so slightly. "Not yet. Trevor said they might still call Lars, but we need to be prepared." He stood abruptly, saying with authority, "We need to run, Freya. Hide...I have a safe house about four hours from here. We need to wake up the boys and go. Now."

I stood and tried to remember how to breathe. Ty started for the stairs.

"Calm down, you two. No one's going anywhere." Talia had ended her call and was grinning like a Joker victim. Jack Nicholson, not Heath Ledger.

"Tal—" I began to argue, but she cut me off with a hand in the air.

"It's okay, I know who they called. You don't have anything to worry about."

"Who?" Ty demanded.

"Me." She waved her phone at us from her other hand.

Ty and I stood there, statues, until we realized what Talia was saying. I dropped to the couch like dead weight. Talia couldn't stop smiling. Then she began to laugh.

"Apparently, *I'm* number one on the D-bag's hitman list," she spurted between bouts of laughter. I couldn't help it. She had a contagious laugh. I soon joined her. Ty looked at us like we'd lost our minds for a minute, then sat down slowly next to me.

He was definitely more relieved than amused. I guess I should have been too, but laughing felt so good, I didn't want to stop. Then I remembered something Ty had said.

"You have a safe house?" I asked, more sharply than I intended. He turned and gave me a blank stare, and then shrugged. Add "Ty's Secret Safe House" to the list of things I didn't know about.

A loud knock on the back door was my killjoy. We all froze. The second round of knocking caused my dad to stir and he snored himself awake in the recliner. He opened his eyes and looked at us, confused.

Ty motioned for Tal and me to stay put as he crept to the kitchen entryway and peeked his head out. When he exhaled hard and looked up at the ceiling, I knew it was safe. I walked into the kitchen and was met by Leon and Ainsley's friendly faces peering through the glass door. I let them in. We resumed our comfortable spots in the living room and brought the couple with us.

An hour later, we were chatting away as if it was an impromptu gathering of old friends, and I decided to make brownies.

It was midnight.

The party moved to the kitchen, and that's when Trevor and Lars showed up, tired and hungry, but alive and well. They brought a third, unexpected party goer with them.

Director Pixley.

They were denied brownies until they told us what had happened with Dunwaddle.

Trevor whimpered but complied. "We went in. I gave an Oscar-worthy performance that he never would have bought had he not been preoccupied with the whole 'freeze me and put my pod next to Walt Disney' thing. I left. He didn't stop me. I met Lars in the parking garage, and we waited for about an hour for him to get the call. When he didn't, I called Rip."

We were all hanging on his every word. He looked around, nervous that he'd left something out.

Pixley came to his rescue. "They came to my office and filled me in, and I stumbled upon some information that I wanted to come and tell you myself." He paused for effect, reaching for the brownie plate, but I slapped his hand away.

The room got dead quiet, like I'd just slapped Mother Theresa in the face, but I glared at Pixley and he smiled.

"I had this whole mess documented from the beginning," he said. "The easier to cover up what outside eyes don't need to see. All I needed to do was send the final report to my boss. But I waited. I knew it wasn't over. Then, when I found out what these two clowns did today," he gestured toward Lars and Trevor, "I made a call to a buddy of mine in D.C. to check how bad the damage was. Turns out he was just going to call me because they had reason to believe an organization previously thought theoretical might actually be behind some of the recent chaos. A group called...The 24." He looked at Lars, and then at Talia, who were intently staring at each other, seemingly communicating telepathically. "He said two people believed to be involved with the group happened to live in my area, and when he told me the names…" He looked at Lars and Talia again, who were either contemplating running, or they both really had to go to the bathroom.

I was praying for the latter.

Pixley continued. "When he read the names to me, I assured him they both worked for me, undercover, and we'd hit a dead end with The 24. Clearly nothing worth wasting any more government resources on."

Pin dropping.

I broke the silence. "I think you earned a brownie," I said, a little too excitedly, and thrust the plate of warm chocolatey goodness under Pixley's nose. He smiled at me again, genuinely, and helped himself.

I glanced at Talia just in time to see her silent sigh of relief. Pixley wasn't looking to end his career by outing any black ops agents belonging to an elite group of government officials that may or may not exist. He just wanted a brownie.

The room slowly relaxed and returned to a medium din of casual conversation, thankfully not related to issues of national security. When the polite banter began to die down, however, the next important conversation took shape. Leon started us down the path when he asked a simple, innocent question.

"So, how do we clean this mess up?"

We'd all been thinking it. Pixley was right when he said it wasn't over. Not yet. The Rip Van Winkle Project may be long gone, but the information was still out there in one form or another, flowing through the now never-ending digital pathways, and someone, it didn't even matter who, might someday stumble upon the information and decide they could benefit from it. And I'll be damned if my children were going to have to live with that hanging over their heads. I turned to Ty, and he took my hand and squeezed.

"I think it's time Rip Van Winkle died," Ty said to me, and to everyone.

One suggestion after another, most of them constructive, ensued from the gathered group, and soon, we knew we had the makings of a pretty damn fine plan.

Ainsley went to work the next day just like she had for the past ten years, not talking or even making eye contact with anyone, briskly walking straight to the Brain Room. But today, she had a companion, her new beau, Leon. And today she had a mission. Today would be different from any other day since Ainsley had first signed her young life away to work for the FBI.

Just over an hour after she sat down at her computer, Leon sitting next to her, all the computer screens flickered. Just for a second. And not just the computers in the Brain Room, but the whole building. And not just their building, but every computer in the world tied in any way to the FBI database computer. Experts would later say it was a freak power glitch. No information was lost, according to all reports. What no one would ever realize was that all information on the RVW Project had been summarily deleted in that millisecond that the system was down.

Ainsley smiled. Leon gently placed his hand on her shoulder, and beamed at her.

Mission accomplished.

Ainsley then logged into her email and drafted a short letter of resignation, sending it to Pixley when she finished.

He was expecting it.

Then Leon and Ainsley left the building.

Lars contacted his man on Dunwaddle's staff, who told him the senator was scheduled for a lengthy "doctor's appointment" the next day, and had cleared his calendar after that…indefinitely. He also mentioned that there may or may not have been a small fire in the office that may or may not have destroyed any and all paper evidence that anyone named Freya or Ty were ever part of anything called Rip Van Winkle. Lars then convinced the young man to copy all of Dunwaddle's back door financial dealings to a portable flash drive and mail it directly to the Director of the FBI in D.C.

My dad returned to Garrity and, with the help of Lars and Director Pixley, destroyed everything he had stored before the explosion. Writing the newspapers had been cathartic, but his memories were nothing more than that. All those involved in any wrongdoing twenty years ago were either dead or no longer in the public eye, so the information was useless. (I found out years later, when my father passed, that he'd made copies of everything and placed them in his own secret vault at our FBI Headquarters. I immediately ran them through an industrial shredder, then burned them and used the remains as mulch in my garden.)

Trevor had gone to his office to get rid of any information he had about RVW, which he said wouldn't take long. He hadn't documented much. He hadn't needed to. He'd been there, and his memories were intact.

He had asked Pixley to give him an immediate transfer, something far away. Ty and I both insisted that not only was that not necessary, but we really didn't want him to disappear from our lives, strange as it may sound. He just smiled and said it was what he wanted. Who were we to stand in his way? He promised to say a proper goodbye to the boys, and offered to pick them up from school and take them out for ice cream to do just that.

The boys. I worried about them, and smiled as I thought of their sweet little faces. They would have to make the biggest adjustment of any of us.

Ty and I waited. I hadn't felt that helpless since Rowan choked on the quarter. With Trevor picking up the boys, we had even more time to pace around the big house, trying to keep busy. We talked a little about how, when, and where to tell the boys that Ty was their real father, but we just couldn't come up with a plan that felt right. It was going to be difficult, and we weren't looking forward to it.

I was rifling through the silverware drawer for a straw, because it was definitely time for a glass of almond chai, and came across something I hadn't expected. It was a small picture. A black and white of a lovely woman holding a small boy. It was the picture I'd taken from my dad's place. It seemed like an eternity ago when we had found him in Garrity and brought him home. I smiled at the picture, having no idea who the woman was. I flipped the picture over and someone had written in ancient handwriting, "Jerry and Aunt Lizzy, 1952."

Jerry.

It was my dad when he was a toddler, and his Aunt Lizzy. Lizzy...

Then it hit me. She resembled a young Elizabeth Taylor, but that's not what made my heart stop. She was the woman—much younger in the picture, but definitely the same woman—I'd met in the restaurant bathroom that fateful night when I'd realized I wanted to be an FBI agent. But it couldn't be. She must have passed away years ago. My mom had never mentioned an Aunt Lizzy, and I hadn't seen my father in so long...

I put the picture back in the drawer, needing to push it to the back of my mind for the time being. I made a mental note to ask my father about it later.

Leon and Ainsley stopped by just after lunch to check in. Having Ainsley in our corner was definitely a plus, and I gave her a gentle, but heartfelt hug before they left. She hesitated, and then hugged me back just a little. I asked them both to please keep in touch. They were leaving town, and didn't even know themselves where they would go yet. I was a little envious. They could go wherever they wanted. Anywhere in the world.

They left and the house was eerily quiet again. Ty and I sat at the atrium table with our respective beverages (almond chai for me, and an ice cold Guinness for him). I sighed and took a sip of my milky heaven, suddenly noticing he was staring at me. Those gray eyes. Thank you, God, for giving my man the most amazing eyes. I smiled and he reached across the table and took my hand. I felt a tingle, and I knew that even fifty years from now, his touch would have the same effect.

If it was just me and Ty, I would want to go to Rome. We would live in a tiny apartment like they show on "House Hunters International," and walk everywhere, holding hands while we practiced our Italian together.

But it wasn't just the two of us, I was shocked into remembering as my three all-boy boys tumbled through the kitchen door in the middle of my selfish daydream.

They all three carried what was left of their ice cream of choice, and Rowan's face and shirt were covered with the sticky dairy product. Trevor never washed them up properly. I stood to scold him when I realized he hadn't come through the door yet. In fact, he wasn't anywhere in sight.

"Where's your father?" I asked Levi, using the term out of habit.

"He dropped us off. He said he had to go to work," Blaise replied.

Before I could question Trevor's odd behavior, Rowan noticed Ty and ran to him, hugging his legs tightly. Ty looked up at me, confused, and I shrugged. We both smiled.

"Daddy! Daddy! Daddy!" Rowan said.

My eyes went wide and I snapped my head in Levi's direction. He walked over to me and patted my shoulder.

"It's okay, Mom. Dad—I mean, 'Uncle Trevor,' had a good talk with the kids. They get it."

I looked at Blaise, who was looking at me expectantly. "Are you okay, honey?" I asked him. He took a second to think about it before responding.

"Yeah. It's kinda cool. I mean, if Dad can't be our Dad, then my second choice would be Uncle Rip, so…"

I glanced up at Ty. "Second choice?" I repeated, gauging his reaction.

"I'll take it," he said, grinning from ear to ear, still with Rowan attached to his legs.

He was right. It was a start.

Just then, Rowan showed his chocolate-covered face and said, "Isn't it great, Mommy? We have a daddy who's our uncle, and an uncle who's our daddy!"

"Great?" I replied, prying him from Ty's legs and hoisting him up into my arms. "It's awesome!"

"I just don't know what to tell my friends," Blaise commented, looking worried.

Ty stepped to him and put a strong arm around him. "You don't have to tell them anything, if you don't want to. It's up to you, dude."

Blaise gave Ty a sideways glance. "Maybe…is it okay if I don't call you 'Dad' right away?"

"You just keep calling me 'Uncle Rip,' okay?"

Blaise nodded and smiled.

Levi approached Ty and held out his hand. Ty looked at it for a second before giving it a firm shake.

"So, I guess this means you'll be moving in here now?" Levi asked him, very adult-like.

"If that's alright with you, buddy."

"You plan on marrying my mom?"

Ty suddenly choked on an invisible quarter. When he regained his composure, he laughed, looking at me for an answer. I cocked my head at him. He was on his own on this one.

"I—" he cleared his throat, "of course, that's my plan, if that's what your mom wants, I mean—"

Levi interrupted him. "You mean, you haven't even asked her yet?" He was literally shocked and it was hilarious. I just stood back, holding Rowan and kissing his sweet, soft cheek. Blaise decided he needed to contribute, so he stood next to Levi, arms folded across his chest just like his older brother. They were a human blockade, and Ty was so flustered, I was afraid he was going to run out the door screaming, "NEVER MIND!"

He gave me a look like he was a deer and I'd just hit him with my van, and I smiled. I knew he wasn't going anywhere. His face softened, and he looked around the boys at me and said, "Freya. Marry me."

The boys both turned to me, arms still folded, waiting for my answer. Geez, now I knew how Ty felt. "Well, I think there might be some paperwork involved before I'm officially available, but…" I said coyly.

"Mom, you're ruining the moment," Blaise cut in dryly, as if he had any idea what the moment should feel like.

I stifled a laugh, and said, very seriously, "I'm sorry, baby." I turned to Rowan in my arms, and asked him, "What do you think? Should I marry him?"

"Can he spend the night?"

"Will you let me marry him if I let him have a sleepover?"

"Yes!"

"Then he can stay."

"Yay!" my little man yelled, and squirmed to get down. He ran over to Ty and grabbed his hand, pulling him toward the living room yelling, "Mario Kart!" Ty gave me a pretend pleading look as he disappeared into the next room with the boys.

I had resigned myself to the fact that I was now on my own making *Ty's* famous pizza, so I turned the oven on and went about mixing up the crust. Just then, my cell phone rang.

It was Trevor.

I thought about ignoring it, but something told me it might be a while before he called again, and I had some very important things to talk to him about.

I picked it up and slid my finger across the screen.

"Hello?"

"Sorry I didn't stay. I had some things to do."

"Uh huh," I replied.

"Did the boys tell you I talked to them?"

"Uh huh." I wanted him to hear the annoyance in my tone.

"Are you mad?" he asked, knowing the answer.

"Uh huh," I said again. Seriously, screaming "annoyed" here!

"Freya, I know I should have talked to you and Ty first, but—"

"Yes, you should have," I cut him off.

"I created this mess, I just wanted to clean it up…without your help."

I paused for a second. He was telling the truth, and I didn't know how to respond at first. "Trevor, why…no, *how* did you do it? How did you keep up the charade so long?"

"What do you mean?"

"I mean, didn't you ever want your own life…with someone who loved you for real?"

"I loved our life, Freya. It was real to me."

"And that makes it so much worse. I was your holographic wife that you could come to when you needed something, but that you didn't owe any real commitment to…"

"Freya, I never cheated on you."

"That's my point! Why didn't you?"

Now it was his turn to pause. I heard him take a deep breath.

"I guess I talked myself into believing you really loved me. I never wanted anyone else, because I had the only woman I'd ever loved."

"Trevor, I—"

"It's okay, Freya. I know you and Rip are meant to be together. I've always known. I started to tell Levi, I think, to keep myself in check. The last thing I wanted to do was betray my best friend, but I had started to believe it was all real, and I was so happy. I knew I had to confide in someone. Someone who wouldn't judge me for it."

"So you confided in a child?"

"He's an old soul, Freya, you know that. I knew I could trust him not to tell you or his brothers, and I knew he'd remind me every so often that I was just a fill-in."

"He *is* pretty amazing."

"Were you really so unhappy all these years?" he had the nerve to ask.

"Of course not! Thanks to you, I was programmed to be blissfully, naively happy!"

"Now just a minute, I only put the idea in your head that you loved me. I never programmed you to be happy...I hoped that would come naturally."

"What are you talking about? You didn't hardwire fake happiness into my brain?"

"Of course not. That would be impossible. It was a miracle that what I did put in there worked at all. I mean, your brain could have rejected the idea of loving me based on the memories I left you of Rip, but..."

"But it didn't," I finished for him.

"I guess not."

"Why not?" I wondered aloud.

"Maybe you really do love me instead of Rip?" he teased.

"Well, if the young Ty was telling the truth, then I must have loved you on some level, at least as a good friend."

His silence told me he was hoping for a different answer, so I changed the subject.

"Ainsley told us the implants are probably gone...dissolved into our brains."

"Yeah," he replied sadly.

"I think it's a good thing."

"You do?"

"I figure it's been a part of me longer than it wasn't, so…why not embrace it?"

"I like that," he said softly.

"The boys are taking all this very well," I changed the subject again.

"No thanks to me."

"You were a good dad…when you were around."

"I'm going to miss our life."

"No you won't," I said.

"I will…and you."

"Maybe someday I can forgive you two boneheads for all this."

"I don't expect you to."

"I appreciate that. It takes some of the pressure off," I said sarcastically.

"You deserved better," he said.

"Than you? I know," I said, only half teasing.

"Than all of this…" he remarked.

"I know that too."

"Can I keep in touch with the boys?"

"I'd have you castrated if you didn't," I said matter-of-factly.

"Too late," he said lightly.

"You'd better. For their sakes. And don't forget about Ty."

"Ah, he's better off without me," he admitted, and I silently agreed.

"Well, the boys. Don't forget their birthdays, and Christmas, and—" I started.

"I won't. I promise."

"Oh, don't do that. It just gets you into trouble."

"Goodbye, Freya."

"Oh, and Trevor?"

"Yeah?"

"I know that was no recording that activated me."

Silence.

EPISODE 54
My Moment

"What the hell were you thinking, Trevor? Why did you activate me?"

"It was a stupid thing to do, I know. I just…I wanted to see you in action one more time. You were so incredible back then, Freya. I wish you could remember. Angelina Jolie doesn't even come close. You were—"

"I could have been caught…or killed," I interrupted dryly.

"Nah, we were watching you the whole time. And just think how satisfying it would have been to kill Dunwaddle with your own two hands. I wanted to give you that…before I left."

"We?" I asked, ignoring the part about Trevor assuming I was hunky dory with being a cold-blooded killer.

"I'm so sorry, Frey. I promise I won't use my power for evil ever again. Scouts honor," he pleaded, trying to avoid my question. I imagined him holding two fingers up, making the scout promise.

"Pixley," I stated.

"If it's any consolation, he thought it was a bad idea too."

"Well, then, I might let him live."

"You are a wise and generous queen."

"So, you don't take orders from anyone now?" I accused.

"I said he thought it was a bad idea. Not that he told me not to do it."

Sigh. Was I the only one not seeing the appeal of my own personal Mr. Hyde? "Trevor, I have a very busy kingdom to run," I said, hinting that I wanted to end our conversation.

"I know."

We were both quiet for a moment. It was harder than I imagined it would be. He found the words before I could.

"Goodbye, Freya."

I hesitated. "Goodbye, Trevor."

I'd said those words millions of times over the past two decades, but this time, it really was goodbye.

◼ ◼ ◼

The next day, the news reported that Senator Dunwaddle had mysteriously vanished without a trace. Only the tabloids ran outlandish stories of alien abduction, moving in with Elvis, and entering a cryogenic stasis at an undisclosed experimental site in Canada. I was starting to realize that if the truth was too crazy to believe, the rags almost always had it right. Whether or not the cryogenic pod he'd paid a fortune for had been successful was anybody's guess. Maybe our grandchildren would have to contend with him in the distant future, but I was certain they would be able to handle it. In the here and now, we couldn't care less. I chose to believe he was dead, though I was glad it had not been by my hand, and slept like a baby every night.

And just like that, it was over.

It never ceases to amaze me how one moment in time, one split-second decision, or inevitable occurrence can alter the course of your entire life.

Ainsley's moment had been when she decided to take on the challenge Trevor had given her of removing our implants. He had pulled her out of her comfort zone, and shown her that although technology is everywhere, people still control the world, and that the oldest, cheesiest saying is eternally true.

Love conquers all.

She and Leon decided to move to Wyoming, where she started her own software company. She focuses on educational programs for kids. They also started a self-sustaining farm, where they live, and Leon home-schools their six brilliant children. All of them inherited Leon's strange resistance to the adverse effects of alcohol and drugs. It's essentially a commune for superheroes. We visit them as often as we can.

Leon's moment, of course, was when he took my advice, mustered up his courage, and asked Ainsley out. And yes, I plan to take credit for that forever.

Talia's moment had been when she made her family and friends her top priority over her job. The 24 never contacted her again, at least not that she mentioned, and six months later, she gave birth to beautiful little Freya Magdalene (nicknamed "Lelu"). She and Lars still live next door. Together they opened a firing range just outside of town. I teach a beginner's class for them called "Mama's Packin'" for bored housewives.

Lars is an open book. He told me once that his moment was the first time he laid eyes on Talia, and I believe him. Seriously. I'm not stupid enough to accuse Arnold Schwarzenegger of lying.

Jerry's moment came to him when Ty and I nearly killed him on that dark road. He missed his family and discovered that a lot can be forgiven when you're willing to change. He became the second-most influential man in my children's lives, and even got back in touch with his own son, my brother Loch. He then decided to play catch-up on the psychology of the 21st century, and went back to school. He eventually got a license to practice, something he'd never actually done before, and volunteered his professional counseling services at the local community center, where he could atone somewhat for checking out of society for twenty years. He moved into Ty's old apartment, and has dinner with us almost every night.

Jerry can afford to work for free, because three days before he was to sign the closing paperwork to sell his land in Garrity, an oil reserve was discovered below his fallout shelter. A year later, he paid for a fairytale wedding for Loch and his lovely fiancée in Rome, and flew the whole family to Europe to be there.

I eventually asked him about the picture I'd taken from his house of him as a small boy and his Aunt Lizzie. He smiled and told me she had been a very influential woman in his life. She had also been one of the first female "spies" for the American government. She was a trained killer, just like me, and her resemblance to the world-famous movie star hadn't hurt one bit either. I didn't tell him I'd met her, over thirty years after her death, for fear he would want to "analyze" me. I didn't need anyone else to know. Maybe I would tell Ty one day, but for now, she and I had our secret, and I liked it that way. I knew she was watching over me, and it made me feel safe...well, safer.

Trevor's moment came, in my opinion, after my first flashback, which he claims was three years before the profound one I experienced with Ty near that deserted bridge. It was the moment he knew I could never really be his.

Trevor eagerly took a transfer to the FBI contingent in Moscow, where he may or may not have grown up as a Russian-born lad. I may never know the truth about the enigma that is my ex-husband, and I don't care to. He sends the boys birthday and Christmas presents every year, but rarely visits. The boys miss him, but have several ways in this techno-age to stay in touch with him, and they all do. They eventually took to calling him "Uncle Trevor."

And I'm not allowed to answer the phone if the Caller ID says "Trevor" or "Unknown." Just in case.

Ty claims his moment was actually a series of moments, occurring here and there over the last twenty years, anytime he felt a pang of nervousness when he caught my eyes, or brushed against me accidentally. He couldn't recall the very first time it happened, but he said it gave him hope. He just didn't know for what at the time.

He decided to retire from the FBI and write a series of books, fiction of course, based on our life. It's an action/adventure series, each story featuring a heroine named "Isis." He's home a lot thanks to his newfound career, and the boys call him "Dad," because that's who he is.

It seemed like an eternity, but when I really thought about it, it had only been about four months since the day I decided to become an FBI agent...again. One day, I was June Cleaver raising the Beav and his brothers, and thinking my marriage was made in heaven, and the next, I was finding out the books on my bookshelf were all blank. Because I lived in a dreamworld. Even my relationship with Ty, the programmed plutonic haziness, had been all wrong. The only reality, the only constant was my boys.

As the information from the implant fully integrated into my brain, some of the enhanced reflexes and skills we had been programmed with came back to me. Although Ty claimed he didn't have the same experience, I knew better. He just wasn't interested in being a killing machine anymore. He lovingly refers to me as his "Bionic Wife," and the sex blows Edward and Bella (post-becoming a vampire) right out of the water.

My moment had been the wake-up call to beat all wake-up calls, so jarring because I had been asleep a long time. Thanks to my son's vivid imagination that a quarter was chewing gum, an act that had nearly cost him his life, the veil keeping me in my foggy dreamworld had been shattered. I realize now that being an FBI agent really was what I wanted, so much so, that I turned down a promotion to Assistant Regional Director to stay in the field a little while longer. I eventually took the position, but not until I'd had my fill of adventure, yanking Ty out of retirement every now and then when my undercover work required a love interest. I know my boys worried about me whenever work took me away from home, but mostly they just thought it was pretty cool to have a "Spy Mom." Ty blamed his ever graying hair on his constant concern for my safety, but he never made me think I had to quit just to ease his mind. Plus, his gray hair is sexy.

The journey toward becoming whole again had been violently thrust upon me, and I grabbed hold with both hands. I was scared, but the thought of ever being that numb Fembot housewife again was terrifying. Resistance was indeed futile. And I'd discovered that once, long ago, I'd been wide awake. Somehow, during my years with Trevor, I'd forgotten how it felt to be truly happy, or truly sad. Everything had been muted. Color. Sound. Emotion. I couldn't blame Ty or Trevor, or my dad. I couldn't even blame the government implant...not really. It had been my decision from the beginning.

I had no one to blame but myself.

And that realization freed me. Whatever I got myself into, implant or no implant, I was fully capable of getting myself out of. I owned it. Every mistake I'd ever made. Every wrong turn I'd ever taken. And all the mistakes and wrong turns waiting for me. It was all mine.

And I could finally start living.

THE END

Wendy Herman

Wendy Herman is a wife and mother, classically trained singer, lifelong writer, avid reader, crocheter, scrapbooker (don't hate), and closet Trekkie. Married to a sexy fighter pilot, she has lived everywhere from Cheyenne, WY, to South Korea, to Niersbach, Germany. Putting her dreams of being a rock star and writer on hold to raise a family while her hubby defended the freedoms of every American, she is only now beginning to realize her potential as a bona fide adult. She currently lives in Enid, OK (AKA Tornado Alley) and pretends to be a normal soccer mom. She chauffeurs her four boys to all their activities, she cooks, she cleans, she takes meals to neighbors when they have babies, but only her family knows the truth. She's a phoenix about to emerge from the flames. Careful. You might get burned.

THE ESERIES NETWORK

BigWorldNetwork.com is a new form of entertainment, with written and audio eSeries episodes, updated weekly.

Like television...in book form.

Visit us at
www.bigworldnetwork.com

Made in the USA
Lexington, KY
01 September 2014